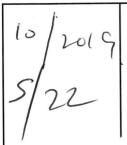

THE
SWEETEST
SOUND

YVONNE
BRISSETT

First published in Great Britain by Hansib Publications in 2019

Hansib Publications Limited
P.O. Box 226, Hertford, SG14 3WY, UK

info@hansibpublications.com
www.hansibpublications.com

ISBN 978-1-910553-06-0

A CIP catalogue record for this book
is available from the British Library

Design & Production by Hansib Publications Ltd
Printed in Great Britain

Supported using public funding by
ARTS COUNCIL ENGLAND
LOTTERY FUNDED

Dedication

To Mommy and Daddy, Rydel and Albertha Brissett.
Thank you for your incredible love, support and
passing on the creative gene. Words cannot express
how much I love and adore you.

Acknowledgements

First and foremost I would like to thank God for blessing me with this moment.

I would like to thank my family for their love and support. A special thanks to my amazing parents whose love and kindness knows no boundaries. Big shout out to my brothers and sisters, cousins, nephews and nieces. I'd like to give a special thank you to the following members; my sister Marvet, for all the love, my brother Desmond, for introducing me to hip hop and keeping it real, my sister Elaine, for the great sense of humour and my brother Lloyd, for the encouraging words. Tamar and Janna, thanks for your enthusiasm, giggles and harassing me to get to the end of this book. Judah, thanks for the love and banter. Sebastian and Olivia, thank you for the warm hugs and your 'moving mountains' mentality. To Vivene, Pierre and Yanique, thanks for the love and the positive feedback. Big love goes out to Reuben, Micah, Nehemiah, Rodney, Marina and Mimi. To my 'cuzzy' Julian, thanks for the vibes and all the positive energy. I'd like to thank my cousins Samantha, Kalise and Lymelle for the support. Big shout out to Uncle Tindayle, Uncle Eric, Aunty Melia and the rest of my cousins in the UK, America and Jamaica; Chun, Antonio, Ibby, Keteis, Dwayne, Arlene, Kim, Neil, Lisa, Pinks, Jenise, Rocky, Matthew, Ingrid, Richie, Latoya, Dejah, Cavel, Nathaniel, Sitota, Mickayla, Asheeba … and many more. Thanks for the love! I'd like to thank my gorgeous god-daughter Ashlee, for the love and hugs and extend a special thank you to all the little ones. A very special thank you goes out to Calvin Jones, for all the love, support and patience. Love you bad!

I'd like to thank my friends for the laughter, love, support, patience and encouragement. A massive thank you goes out to Donna Rowe, Yvonne Dawkins, Linda Cunningham, Joanne Asphall, Debra Mitchell, Fitzroy and Marianne Coward, Denise Alleyne, Mandi Kuller, Lalean Pryce, Marverine Cole, Liz Munro, Sandra Miller, Monica Brown, Naylah Ahmed, Norman Samuda-Smith, Ameena Cott, Sue, Dorothy and Marcia Hutchinson, Anisha Divecha, June of the Blackwood family, Marc Ryder, Nigel Weir, Patrick Headley, Nathan Stewart and Chubba.

I would like to thank the following colleagues for their support, advice and encouragement; Michele Paduano, Raj Ford, Abigail Uden, Lindsay Doyle, Mel Parmar-Harper, Dave Hart, Kat Affeldt, Audrey Dias, Sarah Falkland, Andy Knowles, Giles Latcham, Daniel Pallett, Bob Hockenhull, Sarah Foley, Richie Roberts, Jaspal Bilkhu, Harvinder Singh, Basil Haylett, Stephanie Haponski, Rosemarie Jeffrey and Carol Davis.

A big thank you goes out to Julie Andrew, Nicky Pretty, Tamara Cook and the rest of the team at Nationwide Building Society, Bennett's Hill, Birmingham, for continuous support.

I would like to thank Arts Council England for supporting me on this journey. To Alan Mahar and the delegates of Tindal Street Master Class 2012, I would like to say thanks for reading and for your significant feedback. I'd like to thank Naomi Jones and the members of the Nubian Readers' Book Club. A big thank you goes out to Glen Yearwood, launch director of BET (Black Entertainment Television Networks) UK.

I would like to thank my publisher, Hansib Publications Ltd, for helping me to make this dream a reality.

I'd like to say a huge thank you to you, the reader, for picking up this book. I hope you enjoy reading *The Sweetest Sound* as much as I loved writing it.

Love & Blessings
Yvonne Brissett

Chapter One

The truth is I like bad men.

You know the type. Tall, dark and handsome, with no fixed address or identifiable occupation. The sort that attracts you like a magnet, usually when you're feeling a little vulnerable and ends up leaving you more wounded than when he found you. Normally it starts with intense eye contact, often at a club or a bar, then a smile. He always has slick words. A compliment that makes you blush, giggle.

Then he makes it quite clear that he wants you in the worst way, but you try and convince yourself he's interested in your mind, captivated by your witty, intelligent conversation. Your mind's telling you no. Your body's telling you yes. A loud inner voice is screaming 'run' but you can't seem to respond. You are literally paralysed in that moment.

The small talk doesn't last long and before you know what, you've lost your mind! You're running around at his beck and call, always available when he wants to see you, constantly checking your phone to make sure you're not missing any of his calls, cancelling important appointments and taking sick days off work to be with him. You're spending time, money and energy investing in this guy, making him a priority, when the reality is, for him, you're just an option.

I realised my addiction was becoming a serious problem after flying halfway around the world from London to New York. I'd gone to visit a music producer who I'd met a few months before, whilst he was here in the UK working with an artist, only to find myself stood up at JFK airport. Yep, that's right. His ass was nowhere to be seen. He didn't turn up to greet me, meet me or even ring with an explanation. I headed straight back to England on the next flight home and I've had no contact with him since.

That was two weeks ago and one of the reasons why my best friend Camara was dragging me out clubbing tonight. Said she was fed up of seeing me moping around the house depressed. Argued she was tired of me dating 'thugs'. Wanted to help me find a nice guy, 'Mr Right for Me', 'The One'.

The thing is, believe me I wanna meet him. I'm ready to do the whole settling down, marriage and baby thing, if I could just get past this 'bad man' stage. But you gotta agree, bad boys are usually the finest, sexiest men with the most confidence and swagger and what can I say? I like sexy guys! However, I promised Camara that tonight I would keep an open mind. Maybe pay a little attention to the shy guy, the ugly guy, the one who blends in with the wall who you could probably take home to meet your parents.

With that attitude I stepped out, dressed to impress.

I knew I was the hottest chick in the club as soon as I walked in. I could feel all eyes on me as I strutted around in my little white Dior dress and Jimmy Choo stilettos. Moving smoothly between the hot sweaty bodies, bumping and grinding up against each other to the pumping, hip hop bass line, I glanced over my shoulder to check if Camara was still behind me. Hot on my heels in a sexy black flimsy DKNY number, she sashayed and shimmied along. I chuckled. See, I got the breasts, she got the booty, so I figure if I walk in front and she trails closely behind, I pull the men in with my cleavage and she keeps them glued with her ass.

Between us, there's enough eye candy for everyone. Right? Wrong!

We'd been in the club for over an hour now and not one single man had approached us, asked us to dance or even offered us a glass of water.

"This is a joke," Camara grumbled, propping herself seductively against the bar, her dress skimming her thighs, showing off long, silky, milk chocolate legs and strappy gold Louboutin stilettos.

I opened my mouth to agree with her, but quickly changed my tune as I spotted McKenzie strolling into the club. "Oh my God! Look who's here," I said, nudging her attention towards the direction of the door.

"McKenzie Jackson," Camara murmured, as I deftly slid around her, strategically positioning myself against the bar, so that I would be directly in his line of vision as he came towards us. His entourage flanked him on either side as he moved through the crowd.

"He's coming," I said, pinching Camara's arm without even looking at her, whilst licking my lips and smoothing my hair in preparation for his arrival.

"Ow, that hurt," she complained, nursing her new injury.

"He's in the Premier League. Did you know that?" I asked, beaming at Camara.

A footballer's wife! My ultimate dream.

"Yeah, I heard he's just signed with a top team."

"How beautiful is that man?" I studied his piercing dark eyes, chiselled features, flawless ebony complexion, slim, athletic 6ft 4 physique and sharp Armani suit. Flashing a smile, I thrust my already protruding boobs forward, so they jutted out as far as possible. I quickly yanked at the hem of my short, tight, white dress, so that more cleavage would be on display. This was my big moment.

"McKenzie!" Out of nowhere, a high-pitched voice, then a red blur, completely blocking our vision of each other. *He was only inches away!*

I scowled at the tall girl, clad in two strips of red material, looking like she'd just strolled off the set of an MTV hip hop video shoot. The flimsy silk barely covering her perky breasts, only just about skimmed her ass cheeks! *Hoe!* As McKenzie slid his arm around her back in a warm embrace, a close up of his large diamond encrusted Rolex was all I got. Yes, that's how near they were, standing right in front of me, but between her and his entourage I

9

disappeared into the crowd, as though I'd never been there in the first place.

The bitch was messing up my game. Worst thing about it, was that on closer inspection she had nothing on me. She was painfully thin with bad skin and matted hair extensions, whereas I'm petite, with a clear, caramel complexion, pretty eyes, a cute smile and curves in all the right places, at least that's what all the men tell me, not to mention, glossy long black hair, which yes, is all my own!

Damn Cheek! Not one to be outdone, I knew it was time for plan B. "Excuse me," I said, tapping red blob on the back of her shoulder. The bitch spun her head around and glanced down at me like I was a speck of dust. "Oh." I kept a straight face. "I thought you were someone else," I said, followed by one of my award-winning smiles, directed straight at McKenzie. He grinned at me, as his eyes travelled from my head to my toes. I could see that he was impressed. Entourage then moved in, steering him through the crowd, but that was fine. That was all I needed. To at least make sure he'd noticed me. By the end of the night, he'd be *begging* for my attention!

"Hey?"

Thirsty, I swung around to see who owned that deep, velvet voice. It had been at least an hour since my little 'exchange' with McKenzie and since then no one else had approached me. Well, apart from a few sleazy characters who I didn't actually regard as men so they didn't count. But this guy? He was fine! *Damn!*

Breaking out into one of my seductive, yet hostile, glares, I gave him the once-over. He looked a bit like the gorgeous model Tyson Beckford, who was good friends with the equally beautiful rapper Nas, who had the classic hip hop track 'Just a Moment'. The lyrics called for a moment of silence, which is exactly how I felt right then, as I stared up at this magnificent creation. 6ft 3, smooth golden-brown complexion, rippling biceps, diamond ear stud, platinum chain dangling around his neck. I mean *damn,* he was delicious.

"And you are?" I asked casually, as I'm not one to stroke any man's ego, unless I suspect there might be plenty of money or good sex involved. I held my stance.

"Jabari," he said, extending his hand. "But everyone calls me Money."

Now we're talking!

"And why would that be?" I asked, slipping my slender hand into his.

"From a young age people always said I carried myself like I was wealthy, so I guess I just lived up to the dream," he said, shrugging.

Swagger! I love it and confident too, I thought, whilst softly caressing the centre of his palm with my generous acrylic nails.

"Um, aren't you going to introduce me to your new friend?" Camara asked, nudging me whilst beaming from her resting place at the bar.

"Jabari, this is my friend Camara. Camara, Jabari," I murmured half-heartedly. Never really been one for other girls crowding my space, even if it was my home girl, so I shot her 'that look'. Y'know, the one that all best friends share. The 'go away, you're messing up my game' look. Taking the hint, Camara wasted no time.

"Oh, there's my cousin over there," she cooed. Bit dramatic I thought, but still a good enough reason to leave us alone. "Back in a bit," Camara added, disappearing into the mass of bodies, writhing erotically on the dance floor.

"So, can I get you a drink?" Money asked smiling, revealing a single deep dimple in his left cheek. *Cute.*

"That would be lovely thank you." Well, as he was treating me like a lady, I guess I may as well act like one, I reasoned.

"Personally I'm in a champagne mood myself," he said yawning, reaching into the back pocket of his True Religion jeans, retrieving a healthy wad of cash. "You indulge?"

Do I indulge? Champagne? This was the life I was born for. After standing around all night with a dry throat, do I indulge? Hell yeah!

"Depends," I coolly stated.

He raised an eyebrow.

"Well I'm only accustomed to the best," I said.

"A girl with standards. I like it," he said chuckling, ordering three bottles of Ace of Spades Rosé.

Damn! My luck was definitely in!

"It's always good to celebrate in new places with new faces," he added, as the bartender handed him the bubbly.

I took the bait. "Where are you from? Can't quite place your accent," I said in my most blasé voice. Wasn't about to show this beauty that I thought he was the shit!

"Miami." He skilfully balanced four glasses and the champagne bucket in his hand, leading me to a more secluded corner of the club.

Miami? One of my favourite places.

"I was there last year," I responded.

"Yeah? Whereabouts?"

"South Beach, for Memorial Day Weekend. I'm thinking about going again this year," I replied, smiling at the memory of thousands of good-looking men, ripped and glistening in the sun, showcasing their sexy physiques for what has to be the world's largest gathering of fine men.

"Ok," Money said, laughing. "So I guess you were one of those hot girls runnin' around half naked on Collins Avenue in your thong bikini, killin' all the men out there?"

I winked seductively. Wasn't about to agree or deny. Let him keep wondering.

Between the pimped-out cars, blazing sunshine, hip hop music blasting all day and night, fun-loving vibe, bikers, pool parties and the clubs, Black Beach Week was a yearly destination for me. I hadn't missed it in five years. "I had a wild time. I love it," I said reminiscing, before quickly catching myself and returning to my cool stance.

"I can see that," he replied chuckling, handing me a glass. "Ok." He raised his drink. "Let's toast to the hottest girl up in this joint who likes to get wild." We clinked glasses, although I wasn't altogether sure I was giving off the right impression here.

"So what brings you to the UK?" I asked, deciding to tone it down.

"Basketball." He sipped his drink.

A baller?

"Who do you play for?" I questioned, trying to sound knowledgeable.

"Newcastle Vultures."

Who the hell are they? I mean, was there any real money in basketball unless you were in the NBA? Although the way he was downing the champagne, looked like he had a lot of money to burn.

"So what are you doing here in Birmingham?" I probed, admiring this beautiful brotha'. I'd always pictured myself with a fine African-American boyfriend. His accent was so sexy.

"We out of season right now," he started, before taking another gulp of the expensive liquor, "so I'm just here kickin' it for a minute with my fam, before I go back to the States. Y'know, spendin' a lot of time in the gym, tryin' to maintain. What about you? Which lucky profession gets to enjoy you all day?"

How could I not smile? He was silly, but I liked it.

"I'm a television producer and presenter," I announced casually.

"For real?" he asked, genuinely impressed. He sipped more champagne.

"Yeah, for a station like BET, you know the black entertainment television channel, but on a much smaller scale. We cover fashion, music, films and that kinda stuff. Our channel's called 'Bling & Ting'."

"Oh wow. So not just a pretty face then?"

"Thanks," I said, lapping up the compliment.

"But no offence," he quickly added, "you look a bit young to be doing all that. How old are you?"

"It's rude to ask a woman her age," I scolded.

"Please! Save that for the next fool and just let a brotha' know."

I laughed, finding myself easily giving in to him. "I'm thirty-two."

"Just a year older than me," he realised, smiling. "Damn! You look about twenty-five. Life must be treatin' you good. You gotta be doin' somethin' right to stay lookin' so young. You in here lookin' like a supermodel with them sexy oriental eyes," he praised, admiring my slanted, almond shaped eyes. "You got Chinese relatives?" he quizzed.

I'd been wondering the same about him, as we had a similar look. "Nah. Both my parents are from Jamaica," I told him.

"*Sheeiitt!* I better watch what I say then," Money exclaimed, grinning. "I've seen how you Jamaican chicks like to get down. I need to stay on your good side!" he joked.

"I was born and raised right here in the UK," I corrected him, laughing.

"I don't give a damn where you was born. You Jamaican," he maintained, before taking a long swig from his glass. "But that's what I'm talkin' about! We gon' have some fun. It's all good." He smiled as a tall, fine brotha' approached us, with Camara beaming, in tow. "Oh, I see your girl and my cousin have become acquainted," Money observed, touching fists with the guy. "This is my cousin Danté," he began, "and this is... damn." He glanced down at me. "I'm so caught up in your beauty, I ain't even got your name?"

Very slick.

"Sahai."

"Exotic. Suits you," he said approvingly, whilst continuing the introductions and filling the two remaining champagne glasses for Camara and Danté.

The second Money and Danté started talking between themselves, Camara slid closer to me. "McKenzie's over there... on his own," she whispered urgently.

"Where?" I asked, swivelling my head around. With all of the hype and commotion surrounding Money, I'd completely forgotten about the main attraction. *Keep your eyes on the prize*, I told myself, as I made my excuses, reassuring Money that I'd be back soon.

Head high, shoulders back, I glided with one foot directly in front of the other, but this time added an extra bounce, a new tip I'd picked up from a recent episode of America's Next Top Model.

Chapter Two

Just like Camara said, McKenzie was bizarrely on his own, by the bar, so I slid into a far too tight space next to him, naturally brushing up against him breasts first, as I made myself comfortable. Easing away slightly, he looked down at me. "You trying to knock me over or something?" he asked.

"Or something," I quipped, whilst reaching for my Chanel purse, which had the sum total of about three pounds in there. "Either way, you look like a man who can handle himself," I teased, flirting. Like I said before, I only stroked a man's ego if I thought there might be a pay cheque or guaranteed good sex involved.

Glancing at my purse, he waved his hand across the bar. "Please, let me get it," he insisted. "What are you drinking?"

Hmm. Let's try a different technique.

"You choose," I purred. My mum had always taught me that it's best to make the man feel like he was in control.

"Give me a Mojito and my usual," he ordered. The bartender instantly scurried away, no hesitation, then promptly returned with our drinks.

I had never experienced such speedy service in this nightclub. The bartender even smiled, which was a first. They were normally all stressed out on busy nights like tonight. Without handing over a penny, McKenzie picked up his Hennessy and passed me my drink. *Celebrities! No wonder they're so rich.* All the money in the world, but they never have to pay for anything. Didn't make any sense to me at all, but hey, who was I to question it, if they were willing to share their blessings with me?

"Thanks," I said, sipping the delicious cocktail. Couldn't remember the last time I'd had one of these. I'd forgotten how nice they tasted, I thought, greedily taking a huge gulp. This was more like it. Finally the night was picking up, with the right men paying me the kind of attention I deserved. Feeling a little buzzed off the champagne I had already drank courtesy of Money, I tossed back my flowing dark curls and relaxed against the bar.

"I noticed you earlier," McKenzie began, "you're very beautiful. A stunner. I wanted to speak to you but saw that you were wrapped up with your little boyfriend over there." He nodded towards Money's direction.

I glanced across to see Money, Camara and Danté talking and laughing. "Oh him?" I frowned and laughed. "That's not my boyfriend. That's my cousin. He's over from the States, Miami, so I thought I'd take him out, show him the nightlife."

"I see," he said, relaxing. "So what about your man? Left him at home? Sexy girl like you, I know you must have a man tucked away somewhere."

"Actually I'm single," I replied, as the loud, familiar beat of Chris Brown's club banger 'Loyal', flooded the room. "I love this track," I told him, rocking back and forth.

"Then dance for me," he ordered.

Whoa. I wasn't expecting that.

"Excuse me?" I asked, smiling nervously.

"Dance."

I hesitated.

"You said you like this song, so dance. For me," he told me, straight-faced.

How arrogant? I was about to protest then I remembered my place, as the struggling television producer, working for an equally struggling station, rapidly losing viewers, unless we came up with 'the next big thing' soon. And I remembered his place, as the talented Premiership football player, who had just signed with one of the biggest and richest teams in the world!

So shaking what my mama gave me, I did my best Beyoncé 'Crazy In Love' routine in slow motion, which culminated in me hitched up on his leg for dramatic effect. Don't worry, I kept it sexy, seductive and smooth, not the over the top chaotic mess you see girls doing in nightclubs when they try to re-enact Beyoncé.

Think it worked, as McKenzie smiled appreciatively, steadying me.

"Damn! Where did you get those moves?" he asked. He looked so serious.

I laughed. "Y'know, just a lil' something I cobbled together," I said, brushing it off. "And if you liked it that much, then where is the love? Didn't see any notes floating my way," I added cheekily.

"I can do better than that," he offered, still clearly stunned by the show I'd put on for him. "Let me take you out for a meal."

Oh my God. I'm in there. "That would be nice." I smiled. "When were you thinking of?"

"Well, I'm a little busy this week, with training and sponsorship meetings and whatnot, so maybe sometime next week?"

"Training? Sponsorship meetings?" I questioned confused. "What do *you* do for a living?"

He looked at me bemused, with an *'are you kidding me? You don't know who I am?'* expression.

Another tip from my mum. Whenever you meet a rising star, act like you don't know who they are, so they'll always think you genuinely liked them for their personality initially, not for the fat cheque you're anticipating later.

"You don't watch football?" McKenzie asked, retrieving a business card, placing it in my hand. Just then I noticed a group of excited young girls edging towards us, probably trying to get his autograph and some photos. Before they even had a chance to get too close, his entourage swooped in and whisked him away. "Call me," he mouthed, as he disappeared into the crowd. I smiled, looking down at the business card with his mobile telephone number on.

Within seconds Camara was by my side, gushing. "Oh my God. What happened? What did he say? You two looked like you really hit it off! I think Money was even getting a little jealous when you started dancing. What the hell was that all about? You looked like you were dancing for your life." We giggled.

"I *was* dancing for my life," I confessed, still feeling a little breathless. Resting against the bar, I made a quick mental note to get to the gym. "I can't believe I was lucky enough to get any of his time at all on my own, without his entourage!"

"Well, I read in a magazine that he doesn't like the whole idea of having bodyguards," Camara informed me. "Apparently he sees it as an intrusion of his privacy. So when he's out, he often asks them to leave his side for about fifteen minutes and mind him from a distance, so that he can have a little space and do his own thing. As soon as that time's up, or if they see anything happening, then they always move back in."

"So that's what that was all about," I realised. "Well I didn't let on that I knew who he was, but looks like I'm going to have to take more of an interest in football," I told her. "Can't be turning up for our date acting totally ignorant."

"Date?" Camara practically jumped and screamed, glancing towards McKenzie's retreating entourage. I shot her the 'calm down, we're hot girls remember' look, which means maintaining an air of cool in public at all times.

"As you can see I've been busy too." She grinned, flashing her mobile phone showing off Danté's number saved in her contacts as 'Mandingo'. "He's gone outside. Said he'll call me tomorrow."

"Nice one," I said smiling, as I strutted back towards Money, who was now stood by himself. Well, he might be useful as backup. No point in burning any bridges.

"Hey shorty," Money drawled lazily, as I slid next to him. "I see you in here havin' fun, with ya boy over there."

"My boy?" I asked, confused.

"Yeah, that slick lookin' playa' who you was dancin' with or should I say dancin' for?"

"Oh him? That was my cousin." I giggled. "He's really competitive, challenged me to dance, but then backed down once I started moving as he knew there was no real competition."

"I could see that," Money said, chuckling.

"Been like that since we were kids. That's how we roll," I added. "Anyway, what's good over here?" I swiftly changed the subject.

"You... with that sexy-ass British accent. What else?"

Smooth. I smiled, running my tongue over my glossy lips. Money was looking sexier by the second, mesmerising me with his soft full lips and hypnotic eyes.

"Listen, I'm about to bounce," he said. "You comin'?"

"Coming where?"

"Back to my cousin's crib. You and your girl?" He glanced at Camara, who had now joined us, but was busy scrolling through her phone. "We can hang out? Have a lil' fun." He swigged the remaining drops of his Rosé.

"Sorry, I don't get down like that."

"No?" He looked surprised. "You ain't tryin' to have some fun? Be happy?"

"I'm already very happy thanks," I said huffing.

"But you know what the great thing about happiness is?" he responded, twirling the stem of his empty champagne glass between his fingers. "There's no limit to it."

I smiled. That was polished. But I wasn't budging. Realising this, he placed the empty glass on the counter and leaned into me.

Wow. What aftershave is this? Smells beautiful.

"On a real I'd love to see you again," he murmured.

So clean and fresh, I thought, losing myself in his fragrance, recognising the scent as Armani, Code. Between that, the heat coming from his body and the loud thumping beat of Ciara's sexy slow jam 'Body Party,' throbbing around us, I began to feel weak.

"So let me get your number baby girl," he continued, whispering into my ear, sending a tickling sensation along my spine.

Hell nah. I'm not making it that easy. He'd barely earned it.

"Sorry. I don't give out my number to strangers."

"What?" he asked, frowning at me as if to say, *'Oh, I'm a stranger now? You weren't saying that when you was drinking my champagne'*.

"Yeah, you know, just a habit."

"Baby, I don't do habits. I do fresh. It's a new day, so come on, hit me with the digits," he said, retrieving his iPhone from his pocket.

"Camara, please tell him," I insisted, feigning determination.

"She never gives out her number," Camara stated like a robot.

Money glanced between the two of us, incredulous. "Baby, it's time to change your ways, but trust me, I ain't gon' be the one to change you, so keep doin' you and it was nice meetin' you," he said smiling and walked off.

That didn't go down right. I was only playing hard to get. Damn, he was fine as well! I glanced at Camara, panicking. She shrugged. "Don't look at me," she said. "Your game. Your rules. Your move."

It was alright for her, she'd already got her Mandingo's number, so she was sorted.

There was no way I was running after Money. That was just not my style.

Not gonna cry about it, I decided, as I scanned the club to see what other talent had arrived, whilst I'd been distracted.

Chapter Three

No matter how early I got up, I was always late for work and this morning was no exception. As usual things were not going to plan. There was some form of drama every day. If my hair didn't delay me, it was my make-up. When my front door keys weren't hiding, my car keys were. Today I'd planned to breeze into work bright and early, with Starbucks coffee and Krispy Kreme Doughnuts for everyone. Instead I arrived harassed, late, empty-handed and in trouble.

"This is why our people can't get nowhere." A voice, coming from somewhere up above, as I slid quietly into the chair at my desk. I sheepishly glanced up. Bailey McKnight. Tall, dark and sexy thirty-something. I admired his smooth ebony scalp glistening under the artificial office lighting. "All I ask of you is to get here on time," he continued, placing the palm of his hand flat against the surface of my desk, "and do a good job," he added, as he leaned down towards me. Mmm, he smelled so good, wearing his signature Hugo Boss aftershave.

"Well…" I began to protest weakly.

"Sahai," he calmly stated, cutting me off, whilst raising his right hand in the air. Huge hands... hmm... and his fingernails, neat, clean, I noted, feeling a little excited. "When I set up this business," he continued, "everyone warned me, don't employ your own people. They're gonna take liberties and be late every day. But no," he went on, gesturing with both arms outstretched as he stood upright. "I said, you know what? It's time we started owning more and supporting our own. My parents always complained that as African-

Caribbeans we don't own enough and when we do, we don't develop our community, so what did I do?" Bailey waved his arms around the small empty office. "I employed all my own people… and where the hell are they?"

The higher the decibel, the deeper the voice. I liked that. I made a mental note to get him to raise his voice more often. "It's 9.50 am, Monday morning, you're the only one here and even you're almost an hour late," he ranted, kissing his teeth.

On cue, Darren strolled into the office, head nodding to music from his phone, looking as relaxed as though it was Sunday afternoon in the park.

"Darren," Bailey muttered with a low chuckle, as he shook his head and drew himself up to his full 6ft 2 height. Stylish white tailored shirt, blue stone-washed jeans. Nice.

Glancing in our direction, Darren casually flicked out his earphones.

Bailey spoke again. "Darren, what time is it?" he asked calmly.

"Nah the car, giving me bare trouble. Mad ting!" Darren explained, as he removed the strap of his Gucci bag from across his chest, slinging it down on to his desk.

"You know what?" Bailey leaned back, surveying the two of us as he crossed his arms stiffly across his chest. I admired his muscular, toned, frame. "When everyone else arrives, I want you all in my office," he announced, as he started striding towards it. "I'm gonna fire somebody today," he bellowed, slamming the door shut behind him as he entered his domain.

"What am I paying you for?" Bailey scanned the room. I loved the way his eyes narrowed as he made direct eye contact with each of us. It was now 10.15am and the remaining three staff members who made up the full team, had just finished trickling in. "To turn up when you feel like and chill out like you're at next door's barbecue? Is that it?" he asked, his gaze landing on Marcus.

I was relieved 'cos I really wasn't ready for this onslaught. I was still nursing a slight hangover from last night. Didn't get in from the club till four o'clock in the morning and I was knackered! If anyone could handle this, Marcus could. After all, he was one of the most experienced producers here. *Need to stop partying on Sunday nights,* I made a mental note, as I tried to focus.

Bailey squinted, dark eyes glinting, as he studied Marcus for a few seconds before speaking. "When was the last time you came up with a good idea?"

Marcus smiled confidently, his handsome features and sexy dimples in full effect. "B, you know 'I dream of Hip Hop' was sick. Look how many viewers we got. We're still getting loads of tweets now."

"Marcus." Bailey closed his eyes and reopened them slowly. "Yes, 'I dream of Hip Hop' was a huge success when it aired to launch the opening of this station four years ago in 2010. We are now in 2014 in case you haven't realised, and my question is... when was the *last* time you came up with a good idea?" he repeated coolly.

Marcus, ever confident, grinned. "I got su-um for you still, but I can't even talk about it too tough right now. I just need to make a few calls first. Trust me though, it's butters!" Marcus raised his right hand in what appeared to be a gun salute, then balled up his fist and tapped it twice against his chest in a black power signal. He looked like he was doing the latest dance straight out of Jamaica.

"Monique?" Bailey sighed, rolling his eyes away from Marcus, disappointment etched all over his handsome face. "What you got for me?"

Monique, with her pretty, bright eyes sparkling, piped up. She looked much younger than her twenty-six years and was always so bubbly. "Well, I've been thinking a lot about a kind of down and dirty with the stars celebrity spot. Y'know a sort of behind the scenes backstage look at their life. Following them around at home, on tour. That kind of thing."

"Monique." Bailey shook his head sadly. "I don't know if you've ever heard of a television channel called MTV Base, even though they're our main rivals and only probably the longest running, biggest urban music channel in the country. Maybe you should try watching them sometime. They've been doing that for years."

"BET's been doing it too," Kimar added. "They got the one with Keyshia Cole, and a next one with Monica. Trey Songz has got his own show on there as well, and some others."

Bailey stared at Kimar, his youngest employee. At just eighteen and one of the newest at Bling & Ting, Kimar was hungry to prove himself. Always had fresh, exciting ideas.

"Ok, seems you got so much to say Kimar, how about sharing your latest thoughts?" Bailey probed.

"Well, I was thinking about the X Factor the other day and thought wouldn't it be crazy if instead of singing chart hits or big band themes or having Michael Jackson or Elton John week or whatever it is they do, contestants get to sing songs that viewers have requested, instead of their mentors choosing the songs?"

"Good idea," Bailey agreed. "But I'm sure they did something like that last year and anyway, how exactly does that affect *our* station Kimar?" Bailey asked.

"R&B Supastar! Simples," Kimar said smiling. "We do our own thing. Could be like the X Factor with a lil' urban twist… we get the audience to direct it. The whole series! To be honest, if you think about it, we been doing talent shows for years in our community. Only difference with X Factor is that Simon Cowell took it to the world stage."

"And as a consequence of that, where do you see our place for this in the current market Kimar?" Bailey quizzed, annoyed.

"I see a market for it," Marcus cut in. "I mean, look how successful P. Diddy was when he did his thing with 'Making The Band' in the States, but on a real, what have we got coming out of the UK to showcase African-Caribbean talent?"

"On Fleek Awards?" Darren offered.

"Please!" Marcus rolled his eyes. "Maybe when they first started they celebrated Original Nubian Fearless Lyrical Excellence, but how many awards even go to Black British artists anymore?"

"Quite a few actually," Monique stated.

"True," Bailey murmured. "They've stepped up their game, they seem to be doing their thing and we have to give them props for starting the event in the first place. It's good to see Black British artists finally getting the recognition they deserve."

"But look how long it's taken and we could be doing more," I said, putting my two cents in. "I'm feeling the whole UK scene right now and proud of how we're repping... but there's so much more talent out there, outside of London as well... right here in Birmingham... Manchester... Bristol... other cities. What about those artists? So... if we created our own platform to start launching people, we could really be on to something."

"Exactly!" Kimar said smiling, pleased that we were getting it.

"Well, it's good that at least one of you is thinking about how we can increase ratings." Bailey stroked his goatee. "This station needs an extra edge. Kimar, I like your idea," Bailey concluded. "You and Marcus brainstorm it and see if you can develop some more angles. Sahai, I'm disappointed I haven't heard anything from you this morning."

I shifted in my chair as Bailey's gaze fell on me. *Now why did he have to put me in the spotlight?* Especially when I'd just made an effort to engage in the discussion whilst nursing a thumping headache. "I have got a few ideas Bailey," I lied. "But I didn't wanna say anything until I've developed them a bit more, y'know, thought them through properly. I've been working on the treatments and thinking about what it would involve as these ideas are big." *How stupid did I just sound?*

"Hmm," Bailey muttered, looking at me with irritation. "As I said earlier, I think it's time I downsized this company. Someone needs to get fired and you're looking like a real good candidate right now. I mean, Sahai, you haven't approached me with a decent idea for weeks, months even, so why are you still on my team?"

"Oh come-on Bailey," I said, slipping into the familiar light-hearted tone that reflected the cordial employee/employer relationship that we shared, whilst laughing nervously. He often liked to pick on someone as the sacrificial lamb in these meetings and today clearly it was my turn. We never took him seriously 'cos he was a softie really, more like a big brother than a manager, although he did seem to have a particularly dangerous glint in his eye today. "Bailey, look how many good ideas I've brought to this station over the years?" I reminded him. "You know I'll come up with something soon."

"Tomorrow," he ordered.

"Tomorrow what?" I squinted. *Damn, this headache.*

"Tomorrow is when you'll come up with something. I want the full idea on my desk in writing in the morning."

"Well it might not..."

"Sahai." He glared at me, cutting me off. "We're a specialist market," he stressed. "So we always need to be thinking about the next level. My parents told me that I'd have to work twice as hard to get half as far as anyone else. That may be the case, but more than that, I have to work smart. I need to be focused. Quality *and* quantity. That's my recipe for success and the mind-set I started this station with and that's what I expect from you lot."

"I hear all that Bailey but my idea's not ready yet..." I began to protest.

"That's the problem. What's the solution?"

"I need a few more weeks," I requested.

"If I don't see your idea on my desk by 3pm tomorrow afternoon, you're fired. Darren, how you getting on with tracking down the archive footage I asked you for last week?"

How rude? Just like that, Bailey switched the subject and turned his attention away from me. Ok, so I guess he was tired of everyone always being late for work and probably stressed about the ratings, but there was no need for such drastic action. He didn't have to take it out on me. I mean, for the first time in four years I actually believed that Bailey would carry out his threat. He said it with far too much conviction, instead of the way we would usually banter.

Rubbing my temples, I looked down and closed my eyes tightly. My head was thumping. I felt like it was in a vice, a clamp. Why did Bailey have to pull this one on me today of all days? I had no ideas at all. Lately I'd been feeling totally demotivated. I was still upset about what had happened when I went to see that guy in New York.

I'd really liked him, and not even one phone call. I just couldn't focus. The last thing on my mind was making good, entertaining programmes, I was barely managing to get out of bed every morning. I'd completely lost my mojo.

I guess the only new exciting thing was getting McKenzie Jackson's phone number last night. I smiled as I remembered the look in his eyes when I finished dancing for him, how mesmerised he'd been, but it was still too early to know what was gonna happen with him yet, so no reason to get my spirits up.

It was definitely time for me to settle down. Meet 'The One'. I was tired of the whole dating scene. I hadn't expected to be single and still searching at the age of thirty-two. How ridiculous was that? I should've been married with at least one or two kids by now. It was embarrassing being in this situation, when most people I knew my age were locked down. I was truly fed up with it all.

As I heard Bailey's voice droning on and on, interrupting my thoughts, my head started pounding even harder. This was one of the disadvantages of working in telly, the bit I didn't love; the fact that no matter what was happening, the show must go on.

Chapter Four

Later that night, curled up alone in bed, bored and single, I was trying to remember why.

Why I'm still single. Reaching underneath the bed for my treasured photo album of ex-boyfriends, I began to lazily flick through the pages, scanning the images, reminiscing about the good times and some of the bad. Might not be a bad idea to try and figure out why some of these relationships went wrong before calling McKenzie I thought, as I definitely wanted things to go right with him.

I decided I would give it a few days before I rang him. Didn't wanna come across as desperate. I was also racking my brains trying to come up with a good programme idea for the station. It was no surprise our ratings had dropped so badly in the last few months. With so much competition from channels like E! Entertainment, MTV and BET and websites like YouTube, it felt as though no one was watching us anymore.

Bailey had been warning us for months that things were looking dire, that we might lose the station, clearly with my job being the first to go after the way he'd handled me earlier. I flicked through the pages, studying the photographs of my exes, my mind working overtime.

What we needed was some kind of hot reality show that everyone could relate to. Maybe it should be about relationships I thought, as I scanned the pages, landing on a picture of my first love 'Finesse'. I smiled. He was so sexy. We'd met at a Jodeci concert, back in 1996. I must have been about fourteen at the time. I was so happy

I'd managed to persuade my mum to let me go because Jodeci were the shit! Anyone who was anyone was gonna be at the NEC in Birmingham. Tickets were like gold dust, especially as rumours were flying around that this would be their final UK sell-out tour before the group broke up.

Jodeci, four fine guys from the States, had me losing sleep with their damn album 'Diary of a Mad Band'. I spent many a night listening to it on repeat, fantasizing about my dream man. I treasured all of their albums, because as far I was concerned, Jodeci still held the title as one of the best male R&B groups of all time, along with Boyz II Men.

The concert was off the chain!

Amongst the herd of screaming fans, I'd spotted Finesse in the crowd. Couldn't miss him really I guess, as although only sixteen, he easily stood about 6ft 3, towering above everyone else. Standing there rocking, he looked so cool, calm and collect when all around him was chaos.

I watched Finesse as one of the lead singers K-Ci Hailey tore off his shirt and began flexing his body. I continued watching Finesse as the beautiful DeVante Swing reached out into the audience and touched a female fan's hand, who promptly passed out. I stared harder as Mr Dalvin got busy rapping on stage in between JoJo's sweet crooning, before throwing his sweaty flannel into the crowd. Even harder as a small scuffle broke out behind me... apparently between girls weeping and wailing, grappling for a piece of the used hand towel.

Unfortunately I didn't see any of this 'cos like I said, at that point I only had eyes for Finesse. But I had a good laugh when Camara filled me in later that night about the mayhem, but not before I'd tracked down Finesse, hanging out with his crew in the foyer.

Feeling sexy and confident in my tight black leather mini skirt and matching halter neck belly top, I made sure Finesse noticed me as I passed him on my way out, by bumping into him accidentally on purpose. My petite frame was no match to his, so naturally I stumbled, dropping my purse at the same time. He apologetically bent down to pick it up. As he handed it back to me, a small scrap of paper fell out. He swiftly caught it and held it out to me. Maintaining eye contact I pushed his hand back. "Keep it, it's yours," I purred and strutted off leaving him with written details of my name, phone number and lyrics that I'd borrowed from one of my favourite Jodeci songs, 'I'm Still Waiting'. In red pen, I'd scrawled a few simple words, *'another day might be too long'*. I know, I know. Corny and yes, I did always carry these pieces of paper around with me. A born flirt and professional opportunist, it was an essential handbag item throughout my teenage years. A 'must not leave home without'. I cringe when I think about it now, but believe me, it was a winning formula during those days. That bait reeled a lot of 'em in. I mean, I'm under no doubt it was those words that inspired Finesse to ring me later that same night.

I slid out of bed laughing, remembering how I had a relevant piece of paper for every occasion. For example, if I was going into town on a Saturday afternoon I knew I'd probably spot someone I fancied on the ramp in front of McDonald's, leading into the Pallasades shopping centre. I was convinced that all the finest guys hung out there, modelling their assets. Whilst many of them would be handing out flyers promoting the latest club night, I'd be slipping my advert to some of them in return. At the time I was going through a bit of an identity crisis. Kinda borderline good girl stroke gangsta' bitch. My standard inscription read *'No jeans. No trainers. No hats. Just hoods...'* No word of a lie.

Now and then, on a Sunday, my Aunt Sylvia would drag me to her Pentecostal church. Men in suits! Bliss! Well, for those occasions, you know I had to do something a little extra special. On the piece of paper I'd slide along the pew to my admirer would be written a bible verse, something profound like, *'know the truth and the truth will set you free, John 8 verse 32'*. That always both surprised and impressed these church boys. The knowledge that I was so upfront and knew my bible, even though I wasn't a regular visitor, made them wanna share a few more scriptures with me, away from the confines of the church, if you know what I mean.

I guess we all have something a bit disturbing in our closet that we used to do when we were younger that we thought was so cool at the time. I laughed, as I approached my CD rack, reaching for Jodeci's debut album. As the classic track 'Forever My Lady,' soothed the air, I climbed back into bed, lay my head on my pillow, closed my eyes and continued reminiscing about Finesse.

Shortly after the night we'd first met, we began dating and had a lot of fun doing all the usual things like cinema, bowling, roller-skating, playing computer games on PlayStation, hanging out in town, window shopping, chilling with friends on the street and all that good stuff. Finesse made me feel so special, he loved holding my hands in public and showing me off proudly. I could talk to him about anything and we soon became really close. He was so damn sexy and fine, had mad swag and was really popular.

Plus he bought me things with the money he earned from his part-time job at Burger King. Stuff like chocolates, flowers and sometimes the odd item of clothing or jewellery, which was a big deal to me 'cos growing up I had nothing. I mean, my mum did her best raising me as a single parent, working three jobs to make ends meet, but the fact is we were poor and we struggled. I'd had to beg Camara to lend me the money for my Jodeci concert outfit.

Mum hated men, especially my dad, who I'd never met. He was a womaniser according to her, who'd cheated on her repeatedly throughout their five year relationship. It seems that when she was seven months pregnant with me, she'd caught him in bed with another woman. Devastated, she'd split up with him and left London where she'd been living since emigrating from Jamaica when she was eight years old.

Moving to Birmingham, she'd refused all contact from my dad and vowed never to get involved with another man again. This suited her fine, as a few years later her younger sister, my Aunt Sylvia, followed her to Birmingham to be closer to us, so we always had company. My aunt had a little boy the same age as me and they're who we ended up pretty much spending a lot of our time with.

But all I could see was that all my friends who had a dad, always had new things and fun days out. Take Camara for example, her family had moved in next door to us a few months before Aunt Sylvia came. Camara was always rocking the latest fashion, enjoying family day trips, eating out at restaurants and going to the cinema, gymnastics, swimming and other activities after school that my mum couldn't afford. Camara's dad had a well-paid job at a car factory, whilst her mum worked part-time as a receptionist at a solicitors.

Mum didn't like Camara's dad, said she thought he was too full of himself, but as she got on so well with Camara's mum, we still ended up getting close to their family. As we grew older, Camara and I became best friends, but needless to say, mum still detested her dad.

One thing for sure, was that I never wanted to end up lonely and bitter like my mum. The only thing I knew about my dad was that like her he'd been born in Jamaica, raised in England and that they were both the same age, just 21, when they split up.

She always said men would be attracted to me because I'd inherited my dad's good looks and her pretty features. Then she'd add a bunch of negative comments like, it would probably only be for one thing though, so best for me to use men to my advantage, make sure I get something out of them. That wasn't really my intention when I first met Finesse, but if a man wanted to buy me things then hell yeah, why not? I almost died when he bought me a pair of Reebok Classics for my birthday! Oh my days! It felt good to have nice things and it felt good to be Finesse's girl, but not long after we started dating, it all began to go downhill.

It only took me a couple of months to realise that Finesse was totally obsessed with one thing! Music! In particular, slow jams. I'm talking hundreds of TDK tape cassettes that he listened to constantly. As a result, I quickly fell into line as number two, behind his first true love. Music.

All and I mean all Finesse listened to was R&B love songs, artists like Jodeci, Keith Sweat, Silk, H-Town, Usher, Aaliyah, the lot. Now you'd think that it would be a good thing for your man to love all that soft, sexy, romantic music, with deep, pulsating beats, but it didn't really benefit me at all. As I chuckled remembering how crazy this guy was about his music, I started analysing the way he used to behave.

Back then, still pretty much innocent, we'd spend hours in the evenings and during weekends lying on Finesse's bed, holding each other, looking out into the night sky. His beauty mesmerised me. He was so fine. Finer than a thread of hair. He had beautiful dark eyes and a kind of rich golden-brown, bronzed complexion, like the sun was always shining into his face. Soft, juicy lips that he kept wet by licking repeatedly just like hip hop star, LL Cool J, made them so kissable and he had the whitest, flawless teeth and the sexiest grin.

But whilst my pulse raced to the sounds of Silk whispering about licking me up and down, or R&B girl group, Changing Faces, asking if he'd mind if I stroked him up, Finesse would look into my eyes and sing of how the love we shared made life so sweet or don't be afraid as he'd never hurt me.

Like really? Now and then he'd go even deeper, creating a sexy mood with the smooth sounds of Marvin Gaye's 'Let's get it on' or 'Sexual Healing,' followed closely by the rumbling baritone of the love daddy himself, Barry White. So you can imagine all the sexual energy flowing like water when we would hook up. Only problem was, whilst The Isley Brothers suggested we go 'Between the Sheets', Finesse would be too busy roaming around in his dad's vinyl collection for more timeless soul classics. Which of course led to Teddy Pendergrass telling us to turn out the lights, but not before Luther promised miracles if this world were mine.

Finesse was *obsessed* with this music. For him it was all about love! Except making it that is. And this bored me. I mean, this went on and on and on and we'd been together now for three years, yes... that's what I said! *Three years!!* The romancing, soft kisses and warm embraces he showered me with were simply not enough. What I *really* needed at the time was a good seeing to. Action. Pleasure. Simple as that. I hadn't gone all the way yet with any guy and I needed to know how it felt. All my friends at college were experiencing it one by one and according to them, I was missing out big time.

The day after hearing the full details on how my class mate Shania had 'climbed the walls', it got to the stage where I started seducing Finesse with raunchy lingerie in a desperate attempt to take our physical activities to the next level. I mean, yes we'd agreed to wait at the beginning because I was too young, but I was seventeen now and he was nineteen! But Finesse wasn't having any of it. For me, he had nothing but a love he could only express through holding, staring and reciting his favourite song lyrics. Which of course were the romantic, sweet, loving, kind and caring ones.

To be honest, I think the only reason I stayed with him for so long was 'cos he was a genuinely nice guy and we got on so well together. But come on, three years with *no real* action? Thinking about it now, he was never really into the raunchy, hot, wet and wild lyrics that I favoured and fantasized to. Bottom line is I got rid of him. There was only so much time wasting I could take.

Three months later, and by this time desperate to experience some real loving, I met my first lover, Levi, a talented DJ. It was the night when Camara had persuaded me to go to a popular nightclub, Juicy Fruit, where they'd be playing mostly reggae dancehall music. As a hip hop chick, I'd never been into the whole ragga/bashment scene, unless it was a Stone Love dance, but as it was her 18th birthday, I decided I'd go. As soon as I'd walked in, I'd noticed Levi. He was on the decks mashing up the place with Bounty Killer's latest tune, 'Anytime'. I was captivated by Levi's vibe and the way he kept the party jamming.

Lying in bed, closely studying the photograph in the album of Levi posing and smirking confidently, like he held the master key to every woman's desire, something started becoming clear to me.

Swiftly flicking back and forth through the pages of the photo album, I began making an interesting connection between my exes, a little bizarre maybe, but fascinating all the same. Shifting in bed, an idea for a television programme began forming in my mind as I scrutinized Levi. I can't lie. He was beautiful, with his long dreadlocks, swishing around, skimming his smooth caramel coloured complexion. Dimples so deep you could drink champagne out of, added to his sex appeal.

As soon as I'd first seen him, I could tell that Levi was a few years older than me, and instantly I knew he was gonna be the one to rock my world. But, if I'd paid more attention to the music he pumped in his pimped-out black BMW, complete with tinted black windows, I'd have caught on a lot earlier that he was actually rocking several worlds. As we cruised the streets of Handsworth many evenings listening to pirate radio stations, his favourite reggae DJs and artists boasted about having girls in every corner of the globe and how it was only fair to share their many different styles of loving around, due to the ongoing man shortage.

Needless to say, Levi broke my heart. We didn't last long. A true player, his thing was all about loving as many girls as he could get away with at the same time, then leaving them, if they got... difficult. In other words, found out about each other and like me, weren't willing to share. He insisted that as a true Rasta he was entitled to have as many women as he wanted. It was his duty. Levi brought a whole new meaning to the world-famous slogan pushed by Bob Marley, 'One Love', with Levi, of course, being the main attraction. I mean, anytime I accused him of cheating he would look to the skies and chant, *"Prophesy!"* as though he'd been put on earth to carry out some kind of spiritual sex-fest under the guidance of The Almighty.

To this day I still have no idea what the hell he was talking about! Hell! Half the time I don't even think *he* knew what he was talking about. That might've had something to do with the fact that he was always high, or as he liked to say, 'lean'. Levi smoked ganja hard, all day, *every* day. The scent of the potent high-grade weed used to really get on my nerves as we drove around. Pulling on his spliff, he didn't seem to care that I couldn't stop coughing as the strong fumes burned the back of my throat, and he always complained when I tried to wind down the window, mumbling something incoherent about 'Babylon' and 'The System'.

The final straw came when he started borrowing money from me, just until he got paid. First it was ten pounds, then twenty, then more. The problem was he just never seemed to give me the money back, even though, unlike me, *he* was the one with a full time job! Hell to the no if I was gonna be using the little bit of money I made braiding hair now and again to support his drug habit! Damn! *He* was supposed to be the one giving *me* money! I chuckled, wondering how he even managed to hold down a job, the way he used to smoke, as I admired his beautiful complexion again. The more I looked at these pictures of my ex-boyfriends, the clearer the idea for a reality TV show became in my head. Crystal clear.

Just to make sure I was thinking straight, I slowly went through the pages again, examining all the images, until the intimidating, piercing glare of my ex Jerome forced me to slam shut the photo album. Switching off the bedside lamp, I snuggled down under the warmth of the quilt and felt myself falling into a content, peaceful slumber, knowing I'd just created a genius idea for a fresh, original, hot new reality show.

I couldn't wait to run it by Bailey tomorrow.

Chapter Five

"*Sex Me Down On Ya Headphones*?" Camara laughed, one eyebrow raised. "Are you crazy? Who's gonna watch that?" she asked, as we enjoyed lunch at Nando's.

"Everyone! Come on think about it?" I said, challenging her, between sips of Coke. "Everybody loves music. Most people would do anything to get on TV. We all wanna be in a happy relationship. I really think it can work," I said, snatching my pages of scribbled, messy, handwritten notes out of her hand. Despite my efforts, I'd been unable to fall asleep last night and had ended up staying up most of the night formulating my idea on paper.

"Look." I pointed at some of the key words on the page. "All I need is some desperate single women and some sexy guys." I flicked over the page as I pushed my glass to one side. "Alright, here it is, fit guy walking down the street listening to music on his iPod, bring on available girls, they have to guess what music he's listening to, you know, reggae, jazz, hip hop, R&B, the list goes on, the one who guesses right gets a hot date with him. If she…"

"Hello?" Camara rolled her eyes. "Who says this innocent guy walking down the street isn't married or something? He might not even want a date."

"Simple. We just try someone else."

"Plus are you *really* trying to tell me that depending on what music he's listening to, you reckon you can tell what sort of a man he is and as a result, who his ideal girl would be?" Camara was incredulous.

"Camara," I said, smiling confidently. "It's taken me a long time to realise this, but the truth is yes, you can definitely tell a lot about a man's personality by his preference in music… trust me, I'm serious," I rambled on, tucking into the succulent chicken burger the waitress had placed in front of me two seconds before. "Honestly, you can learn loads about a man by listening to his favourite music," I insisted. "And what better way than on a reality TV show? Look at the success of programmes like *Big Brother, The Only Way is Essex, Keeping Up with the Kardashians.* People love that kind of stuff."

"Yeah maybe, but *Sex Me Down on Ya Headphones*?" Camara asked, frowning.

"Trust me," I said, grinning, "it's gonna be the next big thing." I nibbled on a piece of stray lettuce.

"Are you for real?" Camara sighed, shaking her head and staring at me, whilst spooning sweet potato mash into her mouth.

I was beginning to wonder if running the idea by her for moral support, before presenting it to Bailey this afternoon, was such a good thing, by the way she kept frowning at me. I could think of a hundred better ways to spend my lunch break. Obviously the concept seemed ludicrous to her. The whole notion of being able to tell what a man was like, by the music he listened to. She just couldn't see it.

"Who died?" my cousin Dijon asked, sensing the tension, as he strolled into the restaurant and flopped down into the empty chair beside Camara.

"No one died. It's cool," I said, smiling. "I ordered your favourite," I began, as the waitress appeared simultaneously with some spicy chicken wings and peri peri chips, placing them in front of him.

"Now that's what I'm talking about." He grinned, winking at the blushing waitress. "It's all love!" He chuckled as she scurried off.

Good-looking and funny, Dijon was a hit with everyone, especially the ladies. We'd grown up more like brother and sister than cousins, we were so close. I loved him to bits. I knew *he* would at least have my back and give me his full support.

He glanced at Camara as he tore a shred of chicken flesh straight off the bone with his teeth in one swift move. "What's going on with you two? It feels a little hot in here," he said, chewing and eyeing us, back and forth.

"Oh just another one of Sahai's ridiculous ideas," Camara grumbled, through a mouthful of chips smothered in perinaise sauce. "In fact, actually you're the best person to ask about this," she realised, suddenly perking up. "Considering that you're a man, a DJ *and* you work in a record shop, you should know."

I had no idea why she was hating so much. It's like she wanted to see me flop. I loved Camara. She was my best friend, but sometimes I wondered if the feeling was mutual.

"I should know what?" Dijon stuffed a handful of chips dripping in tomato ketchup into his already full mouth.

"Well, Sahai's latest brainwave is she reckons you can tell a lot about a man by the music he listens to. What do you think?"

Dijon's face broke out into a wide smile as he looked across at me. He whipped another chicken wing off his plate and laid into it. If you ask me, he looked a bit guilty, like he'd been caught doing something naughty. Right then, I knew I was on to something.

"The thing is," Camara continued, without waiting for Dijon's response, "you know I love you Sahai, but your theory's a joke," she reasoned.

I looked to Dijon for support, but he was focused on his plate. He wasn't about to let even one chip escape, as he dipped a batch of them into a smidgen of dark yellowy brown mustard and stuffed them into his mouth. *Disgusting! Who likes mustard?*

Apparently his mum, my Aunt Sylvia, had developed a real thing for the stuff, whilst she was pregnant with him. She craved it. Directly after he popped out, she kept calling for Dijonnaise mustard. They say that's how he got his name. Now, in his true namesake, it seemed he too was addicted to the stuff I realised, as he licked a bit of the stray sauce off his lips. He even walked with a bottle I noticed, as I watched him carefully tighten the lid on the small jar of mustard he'd produced from his inside jacket pocket, before slipping it back in.

"I mean, talk about stereotyping," Camara nagged. "For example, are you saying every guy who listens to hip hop is a gangsta'?" she grilled, bringing me back to the moment.

"No." I knew she was gonna go there. "That's what *you're* saying. A lot of the hip hop *I* listen to is political," I reminded her. "Y'know, conscious hip hop."

To prove my point I reached for my iPhone and scrolled through my extensive playlist, picking one of my favourite albums. I switched my phone on to loudspeaker and selected track 14. A hypnotic beat filtered around our table, creating the dark landscape for 'What Goes Around' on Nas's album, 'Stillmatic'.

"Big tune," Dijon said, in between sucking on chicken bones.

For a few minutes the three of us nodded our heads silently in unison with the beat as the lyrics set the scene. We listened to Nas rapping passionately about drugs being poison and schools teaching kids lies, until I noticed a few customers at other tables glancing our way, no doubt irritated by our music.

"So," I asserted, switching off the loudspeaker, "people who love this kind of hip hop, addressing issues like drug abuse in our communities or institutionalised racism within the education system probably fall into the conscious, raise awareness, personality type."

"You mean like your ex, Jerome?" Camara scoffed, rolling her eyes.

Just hearing his name made me wince. I didn't know why she was even bringing him up as he'd been a bit of a sore point between us.

"He was a joke," Dijon said, before swigging his juice. "A propa *eedyiat*," he sneered.

"No he wasn't," I argued, defending Jerome. These two were seriously pissing me off. Not only weren't they supporting my idea but why were they now talking about my ex? "Jerome was militant. A bit intense maybe? But he stood for what he believed in," I mumbled, deflated by their lack of energy and enthusiasm.

Maybe my idea wasn't so good? I was starting to lose confidence at the prospect of presenting it to Bailey this afternoon. I wondered if there was some way I could get out of it. Perhaps I could ring Bailey and say I'd fallen ill during my lunch break and just not go back to work? I'd expected a better response from at least Dijon, but it seemed he was now stuck down memory lane.

"Jerome was a dickhead!" Dijon stated. "The guy was a fake, just face it Sahai," he added. "With all his theatrics," he said laughing, as dark memories of Jerome began clouding my thoughts.

Ok, so Jerome was a little over the top maybe, certainly a bit of a character, but not fake, I thought, remembering how music had totally influenced him. The Public Enemy album, 'Fear of a Black Planet', was without a shadow of a doubt, the soundtrack for his life. It was the late nineties when we'd met, a progressive time for people of colour, according to Jerome. Songs like Public Enemy's 'Fight the Power', which had been released almost a decade before, provided him with 'excellent' themes for the lectures he gave at local community centres and universities.

He was often invited to talk at African-Caribbean Student Society meetings. Sometimes I think our relationship only lasted so long, two years in total, because I was in awe of him. Both mesmerised and intimidated. Might have had something to do with the fact that I was still only eighteen, quite young when I think back, compared to Jerome who was in his mid-twenties at the time.

Personally I think he should've gone out with Camara. He was definitely more her type. They had similar interests, like history, culture and 1001 ways to promote positive role models for young kids and keep them off the streets. If it wasn't for her we'd have never met. As a part-time netball coach at our local community centre, Camara was always encouraging me to sign up. I had no interest in sport, but after reluctantly getting involved in one of her netball games one evening, I got suckered into sticking around to listen to Jerome giving a talk on Malcolm X, in the adjacent hall.

Camara promoted Jerome as some guy who was really clued up. Said I needed to know about the major contribution Malcolm X had played in fighting for basic human rights for African-Americans, in the racist America of the 1960s. I had to remind her that a few years before, she'd forced me to read Malcolm X's autobiography, so I did in fact already know, but said I'd snooze in the back row anyway, whilst waiting for her to give me a lift home. She'd managed to pass her driving test earlier that year, two weeks after her 18th birthday, which was proving to be very convenient indeed.

Back then she'd complained that I only ever seemed to read Jackie Collins novels and that I needed to read other stuff. What she didn't realise, was that the author's sexy, seductive heroine, Lucky Santangelo, in my favourite book, Chances, had taught me more about being a confident, independent, ambitious woman than anyone I'd ever met. I'd aspired to be just like Lucky. Powerful, influential and admired in a male-dominated world.

Anyway, I did enjoy reading Malcolm X's autobiography. It was compelling, but when I tried to talk to people about him no one seemed that interested. Now, years later the same people couldn't stop raving about him. Trying to tell *me* who Malcolm X was. All of a sudden everyone at college was becoming militant and talking about fighting for 'the cause' and to be honest I just found it hypocritical, tired, pretentious and boring. So I folded my coat into a cushion, made myself comfortable in the back row and nestled down into the seat to snooze… that was until I saw Jerome.

I was bowled over by his striking dark features, powerful presence and the passion and sincerity with which he delivered a sermon on the educational, social and economic struggles we faced as young African-Caribbean people growing up in Britain. He made several references to Malcolm X's work as a freedom fighter, focusing on its global significance and the late activist's legacy. Midway through, he paused to play us a track about police brutality from the hip hop group N.W.A's debut album, 'Straight Outta Compton', then followed this up with some old black and white scratchy footage of Malcolm X's visit to Britain in the 1960s.

Watching Malcolm X walking the streets of Smethwick, less than a mile away from where we were right now, demanding equal rights for *all* UK citizens, only seemed to fuel Jerome's passion, as he hovered around the screen mesmerised by Malcolm X.

Jerome looked so earnest, pleading with 'our people' to wake up and pay attention to the politics that were holding us down. I woke up and paid attention all right, to scribbling one of my special notes personally for him, and what better lyrics than, '*by any means necessary... we must link up.*'

But by the end of the session I realised how immature and silly my note would look to someone of his stature. So instead I approached him with nothing but praises about his inspirational delivery and was a bit thrown to see his eager eyes scanning my body and his level of conversation reduced to how he could get with a 'fit sistah' like me. And you know I wasn't about to say no. So, one thing led to another and well, I had a bit of explaining to do when Camara remarked on how ironic it was that we became an item. Secretly, I think she was jealous. With my obvious disinterest in politics during those days and Jerome's clear goal of educating the masses, she couldn't figure us out.

Chapter Six

As Camara and Dijon continued dissing Jerome, I sat there quietly, picking at my food, remembering how he used to drag me along to some of his talks at universities for moral support. I enjoyed tagging along. I liked going because since finishing my A levels I'd been drifting, trying to decide what I wanted to do with my life. Just being on campus sometimes gave me a progressive feeling. I remember one of his lectures getting so heated though. It was entitled 'How Mythology is Created.'

Jerome started off by talking about the history of black people in Britain. He corrected a mainstream belief that people of colour had only been in the UK in large numbers since 1948, with the arrival of the Empire Windrush. He explained how the first black Queen of England, Queen Philippa of Hainault, wife of King Edward III, had reigned centuries before in 1327. He clarified that since the 16th Century, we'd held a significant presence here.

"In fact," he said, "the first historical record of an African living in Britain was in 210AD. But," he added hastily, wagging his finger at top speed, "for some strange reason, these facts have been erased from our history books and instead the first reference to African-Caribbean people in the UK is of transatlantic slavery, with that degrading image." He dropped his head, his tone solemn. "That image of the slave ship with rows of men and women shackled together like animals, packed together like a tin of sardines, enduring inhumane conditions, lying in their own excrement." He paused, for dramatic effect, before continuing.

"The truth is," he informed, "that by 1596 there were so many dark-skinned people living in England that Queen Elizabeth I issued an edict ordering the 'blackamoors' to be deported. She wanted us all out of the country. Her attempts were unsuccessful and the community grew. All this before the British Triangular Slave Trade had even begun to flourish. So why then," Jerome questioned, "were these important stories and images, omitted from His-story books?" he asked, emphasizing and separating the two words 'His' 'Story'.

Students, who didn't quite realise this was actually a rhetorical question gingerly stuck up their hands, only to be ignored and overshadowed by Jerome's raised tempo as he began pacing the room, frantic, passionate, throwing random names, dates and bullet points into the air.

"Ignatius Sancho, 1729, actor, writer and composer, first African bestselling author to be published in England. Phyllis Wheatley, 1753, a poet, described conditions of life for black Britons. Olaudah Equiano, 1745, a free man by the age of 21, did extensive abolitionist work in Britain to free other men and women from slavery. 1st of August 1834, slavery officially abolished in the British Empire, although the system made sure they kept us in chains as most slaves were still held captive as *Apprentices.*" He shook his head sorrowfully... and continued ranting, spit flying from his mouth, sweat trickling down his forehead.

I could see students were getting a bit fidgety, like they wanted to say something, or pop out of the lecture theatre for a smoke or to use the bathroom, but were too scared to interrupt Jerome as they didn't want to seem rude or God forbid, *disrespectful* or *uninterested.* I mean, don't get me wrong, Jerome was cool, but when he got on a roll about this subject so close to his heart, I don't know if he even realised how intimidating he came across to some people, especially in these group situations.

When someone finally did get a chance to speak, much to Jerome's obvious dismay, it was the one and only European girl in the room, girlfriend of the African-Caribbean Student Society President.

"What's the point of going on and on about the past?" she asked. "Wouldn't it be better to forget about that and concentrate on building better race relations for now and the future?"

Well... who told her to say that? Jerome went berserk. He launched into an out and out attack on her saying that she was speaking from a point of privilege, supremacy, power and a sense of always being included and knowing where she came from, who her ancestors were and the good things *as well as* the bad things about her people. It was this exact attitude of 'forgetting about the past' that had erased the 'real' story of African-Caribbean people from the history books and the same mentality that continued to create negative images, he concluded.

"We need to wake up people, take control of our lives!" Jerome admonished.

"Don't you think we've come a long way now though?" squeaked a bony dark-skinned male student sat at the front, wearing a traditional African Kente-Cloth Kaftan and hat to match.

Jerome threw his head back and laughed like a Hyena, his narrow nostrils flaring uncontrollably. "Come a long way from where and to where?" he yelled. "You sit there, clothed in the authentic royal, sacred robes of a king from the Ashanti Kingdom, yet you know nothing. Don't you know we were once kings, queens, rich in mind, body, spirit, soul *and* wealth before the missionaries exploited and pillaged our beautiful African homeland to divide and conquer us? *That's* how slavery started! We have a race and history to be proud of!" he blared at African hat. "If you don't know where you're coming from, you don't know where you're going, said the late great Marcus Garvey. Do you?" he practically shouted, a little bit too patronising even for my liking and *I* was there to support him.

"What's your point?" a pretty brown girl in the row in front of me asked, cutting in. I squirmed as Jerome marched through the aisle and bounded up the lecture theatre stairs like a kangaroo. The girl visibly retracted.

I was glad we were at the start of a new academic year so hardly anyone knew I was with him. I'm sure he could've adapted a slightly calmer approach. As she leaned back, the girl's long braided hair extensions caught between her back and the bench she sat on, causing her to jerk forward just in time to meet head on with Jerome. His dark ebony skin tone, cool complexion and handsome chiselled profile, complimented her soft light-brown features. Maybe *they* would make a nice couple?

"My point is," he hissed, nostrils flaring wildly again, "as a people we need to be recognised for the contributions we have made and continue to make in the world. Things need to change."

"How?" a tall skinny youth in the corner queried.

I admired Jerome's graceful posture for a second, as he silently jogged back down the steps, moving as sensual and elegant as a black panther, until he simply stopped dead in his tracks, swung around and took on the demeanour of a wild, caged animal. I mean, he was literally foaming at the mouth, snarling, glaring and lunging at students.

"How?" he roared. "By all of us standing up, making a noise and being counted. That's how. We need to fight harder for equal rights. Make it clear we are not happy being treated as second class citizens. Which is why I salute hip hop royalty Public Enemy, the Chuck Ds of the world, writing lyrics that address these issues."

With that said, Jerome spun around and launched into one of Chuck D's full raps.

What the...? I didn't know Jerome was an undercover rapper. Students started glancing around at their friends, smirking and holding back laughter, as Jerome pranced and lurched back and forth, animatedly bobbing his head and punctuating the air with an off-key version of 'Burn Hollywood Burn', complete with a hip hop dance routine that I'd never like to see again. He was worse than the amateur rappers I'd seen at talent shows. Giving it his all, he seemed oblivious to any ridicule. Once he'd exhausted himself with the story of how for decades African-American actors were traditionally cast in demoralising and degrading roles, he collapsed against a banister for support, scanning the room.

"Have any of you… listened to… Public Enemy's… awesome album, 'Fear of a Black Planet?'" he panted, out of breath, as sweat trickled down his forehead. I cringed.

"I've had enough of this," a pale boy in the corner exclaimed as he jumped up and stormed towards the door. "You coming?" he called to a short dark round girl. She shot up and scurried in his direction. Must have been his girlfriend.

"Yeah that's right," Jerome yelled after him. "Run away and take your 'exotic' little token with you."

I cringed again, as groans of disgust, nods of agreement and gasps of shock filled the room. Hands darted up, questions were fired at Jerome and comments hurled around the lecture theatre. Some of the students simply got up and walked out.

"Ummm…" the Society President said, standing up to speak. "People people!" He patted outstretched arms down into thin air, trying to assert himself and regain some kind of control and order in the room. "We're not here to insult each other or fight or incite racial hatred." He faced Jerome squarely. "Your attitude is totally uncalled for and I think this brings us to the end of this meeting. We've run out of time. This room's been booked for another session."

"How convenient," Jerome sneered, scowling.

"Excuse me?" the President asked, taken aback by Jerome's comment. Everyone could see the President was politely telling Jerome to piss off, but at the same time, trying to remain professional to set an example to the rest of the students. He huffed and puffed, embarrassed. "I think you should leave now. We invited you back as we enjoyed your last lecture so much, but you've evidently overstepped the mark."

"Overstepped the mark?" Jerome scoffed. "By whose definition?"

Along with the rest of the students I remained speechless. Like spectators at a tennis match we eyed the contenders back and forth. I knew that Jerome didn't respect the President because according to Jerome, the President was 'lost', disconnected from his African roots, 'sleepwalking'. Jerome believed the President had a serious identity crisis.

Luckily at that minute, a bunch of scruffy, long-haired, energetic students bustled into the room, some carrying musical instruments. "Sorry mate," one of them said, eyeing the President apologetically. "We booked this room ages ago. We've been waiting outside for twenty minutes. We need to start practice. Our band's playing tomorrow night," he informed, slinging his guitar across his shoulder.

"We were just leaving," the President clarified, as the African-Caribbean Student Society members began to gather up their papers and rucksacks to leave the room. Some of the students eyed Jerome like he had the plague as they filed out. I sank down into my seat deciding to join Jerome after everyone else had left. I wasn't exactly trying to promote the fact that we were together. A couple of students approached him just before we finally left the room.

"Yeah man! That was deep," the tall skinny youth who'd asked a question earlier said, pressing a piece of paper into Jerome's hand. "Respect. Here's my number. Let me know where you're speaking next." 'Cos frankly, we all knew it wouldn't be there!

Jerome and I didn't last much longer after that 'lecture.' In fact we had a huge argument a few weeks later when we were in my bedroom one evening, chilling. I tried to reason with him, explaining that attitude is everything and that whilst I understood his passion, respected his knowledge and actually agreed with some of what he taught, his approach was all wrong. In response he ignored me, turned the volume up full blast on the stereo and proceeded to mouth along to Flava Flav chanting something about, *'can't do nu-un for ya man.'* I think he was trying to tell me something 'cos minutes later he turned down the volume, accused me of being a 'sell-out' and left. I never saw him again.

Ironic that he'd labelled me a 'sell-out', implying I'd turned against my own race and culture, considering I was the one now working at Bling & Ting trying to promote the exact positive images he was always bleating about.

"So you're really gonna pitch this ridiculous idea to Bailey this afternoon then?" Camara said, pulling me back into the present, as she chomped on her final mouthful of sweet potato mash. She swivelled around to face Dijon who was busy doing something on his iPad.

Seeing that he was paying her no attention, she stared directly across at me whilst finishing her food. I noticed at this point that Dijon had not engaged in the debate at all. Clearly he'd decided to leave the two of us to battle it out between ourselves as he casually scooped up his last chicken wing and leaned back in his chair watching us, as though he was being entertained at the circus, amusement written all over his face.

I glanced around the restaurant taking in the burnt orange walls, colourful abstract art and sparkly, ornate lampshades hanging low over every table. I looked around at people laughing, eating and enjoying each other's company. The lively Afro-Cuban beats added to the vibrant atmosphere in Nando's. I smiled inwardly.

Regardless of what these two thought, they'd done me a huge favour bringing up my ex-boyfriend, forcing me to think back to what he was like. Reminiscing about Jerome had confirmed everything. It had sealed the deal. Music was his life. It ruled him. And he wasn't the only one. Finesse, Levi, other men I knew, even Dijon. It was the same thing. They were *all* about their music. Totally influenced by it. I noticed Camara staring at me, smug, taking my silence as defeat, not realising I was now fully energised and filled with fresh inspiration.

"Bailey's gonna love my idea," I finally told her. "It's about experimenting, taking risks. I know I'm on to a good thing. What do you reckon Dijon?" I asked, as his mobile phone started to ring. He licked the remnants of mustard off his fork before answering his phone.

"Yes Bless?" Dijon said, mobile clamped to his ear. He paused for a few seconds. "Nah star! That can't run. OK. I'm coming." He hung up. "Ladies, ladies…" he said, using his hands to stabilise himself against the table as he pushed his chair out and stood up to excuse himself. "I would love to stay and chat, but I got runnings. It's been a pleasure as always." He pulled out his wallet, removed a twenty-pound note and placed it down on the table.

"But Dijon, what do you think about Sahai's idea? You still haven't said," Camara grilled him, as he turned to walk away.

He smiled. That menacing smile again and then he was gone. His silence spoke volumes.

Chapter Seven

"Yes!" I was now trying to convince Bailey. "The single factor that destroyed all my relationships was the definite connection between the music and the man and my inability to identify this fatal flaw," I prattled on, pacing back and forth around his office as he reclined in his high-back leather chair, stroking his goatee, silently studying me.

It had been an hour now since I'd presented the idea to Bailey at 3pm on the dot in a very neat typed up draft and he'd finally called me into his office to discuss it. The suspense had been killing me but I knew, I just knew that he was feeling it.

"So, um, did you do your research Sahai? Find out if other women shared similar experiences? If men could relate to your theory perhaps?" Bailey quizzed.

"Nope. This is the beauty of my idea. We get to test it out and prove the point live on TV! How revolutionary is that?" I said, buzzing.

"So basically we are taking a gamble with no evidence?" Bailey sighed, annoyed.

"That's what you've always said about Bling & Ting isn't it?" I reminded him. "To break new ground, go where no one else has trod. Set trends," I quoted.

"Correct."

"Well this is what I'm doing. This programme could save a lot of women from heartache and heartbreak, 'cos if they can identify this whole man, music thing early on, it could help them make the right decision about who they want to get involved with."

Bailey looked at me like I was mad. "You really believe that?"

"Not only do I believe it, but I'm going to prove it." I was adamant. "I mean, we only have to look at the huge influence music has worldwide, for example, the phenomenal grieving that took place when Michael Jackson died? And others before him, Elvis Presley, Bob Marley. Look at how the music business dominates the entertainment world. It's a billion-dollar industry, so a perfect product to build our idea around. Come on Bailey, let's do it."

"Well, the idea is certainly original. It's fresh, innovative and different." Bailey stroked his goatee. "I've never seen anything like it anywhere before. What inspired you?" he asked.

"Men. Music. Relationships," I explained. "I was trying to figure out why some of my past relationships had failed and I found a common thread. Most of my exes were obsessed with one thing, apart from sex. Music. It ruled their lives. The music they liked definitely had an influence on their attitude, their expectations, the way they treated me in our relationship."

"I see," Bailey said, swivelling slowly back and forth in his chair. "I'm sure the way your ex-boyfriends treated you had nothing to do with their musical tastes, Sahai. And I'm sure the *last* thing a woman is concerned about when trying to choose a partner is what damn music he listens to." Bailey sighed, exasperated.

"Why you hating? This is the best idea I've had in ages."

"Hating?" Bailey asked, frowning. "Who are you talking to? I'm not one of your little friends in the club. I'm running a serious business here Sahai. When my staff come in here and present ideas, I don't hate. I listen. Carefully. This station is my life. My livelihood. I'm trying to keep a roof over my head, so I can't afford to entertain your theatrics. I'm not buying it."

"Give me one reason why?" I asked, irritated by his lack of vision.

"Because the idea's nuts. Simple as that. It's too risky," he replied, standing up. "I'm not commissioning it, so if there's nothing else, I suggest you go back to your desk and think of a concept that can actually work," he concluded, ushering me towards the door.   .

Sitting back down, he picked up a folder and began rifling through it, signalling that our meeting was over.

"Look, won't you at least just think about it?" I hovered by the door. I was not prepared to give up that easily.

He glanced up at me, then picked up some paperwork on his desk, flicking through it before handing it to me. "Look at these figures Sahai. We're so far down on the ratings ladder we practically don't exist anymore. No one's watching us. Right now this station needs something really hot. A programme guaranteed to pull the viewers in. We need big audiences and you come to me with a ridiculous idea you've done *no* research on?"

I approached his desk ignoring the notes outstretched in his hands. "Come on Bailey!" I objected. "It doesn't need research! Music is a universal language. All of us have an emotional connection to music. Like when you hear a song that you haven't heard for years and it takes you right back to a time and place. Or even just how music makes us feel, the mood it evokes, and what about the way certain songs remind us of someone. Our audience are gonna love it. My own personal experience with my exes is enough to go by, and you're always saying you want our station to stand out." I waved my arms around the room. "Bling & Ting, bringing you *the next big thing?*"

"Damn!" Bailey rubbed his head. "What is wrong with you? I'm not interested in your exes and music! I don't give a damn what music they listened to or how it made them feel or how they treated you! I couldn't care less. I hired you because you're a top producer and you're smart. Where is *that* Sahai?"

"Right here," I said quietly.

"Sahai." Bailey's voice softened as he leaned forward, sincerity written all over his face. "I employed you because I rate you, you've got your finger on the pulse. You know what the people want..."

"Then trust me," I said, cutting him off mid-sentence. "Let me do it Bailey."

"Are you trying to finish me off?" he asked. "Is that what this is about?"

"The opposite actually, if you'd give me a chance."

Bailey looked at me. Hard. Long. It seemed like forever before he spoke. "Alright, ok, I don't know if this is the best decision or the worst decision I'm making Sahai, but I think I'm gonna let you give it a shot," he said, finally relenting.

"That's what I'm talking about." I was elated.

"I mean, if nothing else it'll certainly make for entertaining telly. That's for sure," he conceded, scanning through my notes again. "I might lose all my viewers, my credibility and the station in the process but hey, at least it was a good watch."

"Thank you Bailey," I said, laughing. "Trust me. It's gonna go viral." I was jubilant.

"Just two things though," he said, eyebrows raised. Anxiety swept through me. I hoped he wasn't gonna try and change the format or anything. "I don't want to have to buy in any freelancers to work on this," he said. "We're barely managing as it is. You're gonna have to find a way to make it work with the team we have here. Do you think you can do that?" he asked.

"Definitely. I'll rope everyone in," I promised. "All hands on deck."

"Good."

I swallowed, nervously anticipating what was coming next.

"The other thing," he continued, "is that we might have to seriously look at changing the name. I mean, *Sex Me Down on Ya Headphones?* Really?"

I laughed out loud, relieved that was the only change he wanted to make. He started laughing too. "Let's just shorten it to *Sex Me Down* for now as a working title. We can think about a new title later," he suggested, sifting through a few more notes. "So how's this gonna play out then? We definitely need a celebrity angle to pull the viewers in."

Relief flooded me as I could see that he was finally buying into it. "I've already thought about that." I opened my note pad and flicked through some pages. "What about if once we select our contributors and establish their favourite artists, we approach some of the stars and find out if they'll do a little jingle, about what inspires them, the messages, the meaning behind some of their lyrics, so that viewers feel they are getting an insight into the artist?"

"Nice thought, but not convinced the budget will stretch that far."

"Bailey, you've got the most contacts, people owe you favours worldwide, we must be able to pull some kind of celebrity angle off?"

"I guess. I'll look into it. So when do you wanna start this and who would you like to work with you on this project?"

"I can probably start it in the next few weeks, as don't forget I need to finish filming and editing my concert series first. With *Sex Me Down* I'd like to change things up a little."

"A little how?"

"Well, I was thinking of bringing my cousin Dijon in."

"Your cousin?" Bailey asked, perplexed.

"Well yeah, you know he's a DJ, he knows a lot of people, a lot about music and has loads of contacts. He could be useful on this project."

"I'd rather you worked with someone from the office Sahai. This station ain't a free for all y'know," he grumbled. "Like I said, I'm running a serious business here and you're telling me about your cousin! How about you collaborate with your *colleague* Kimar?" he suggested. "As I've already just said I ain't got money to be paying outsiders."

"Well... Kimar can work on it too, but I just thought Dijon could bring a lil' extra flavour. I'm sure he'll be willing to do it for free. Let me speak to him and get back to you."

"I'll start thinking about the celebrity angle," Bailey said, completely ignoring my suggestion, as he jotted down some words on a pad. I decided not to pursue it for now, choosing instead to simply enjoy the fact that Bailey had actually said yes to my idea. *Result!*

"Ok cool. Thanks Bailey. You won't regret this." I left his office on a high.

Marcus and Darren were all but propped up on the other side of the door, waiting to see how I'd got on. They didn't know the details of my idea, but understood the gravity of the situation when Bailey had given me the harsh deadline. I smiled. A huge smile.

"So you ain't leaving us just yet then?" Marcus said laughing, as Darren touched fists with me.

Monique rushed over and gave me a hug. "Congrats." Excitement was written all over her face. "Can't wait to start working on it, whatever it is," she added, full of her usual positive energy.

I felt my mobile phone vibrating in my pocket, as Kimar approached me. Thrilled at the news Bailey had singled him out to work on the idea with me, Kimar gave me a massive bear hug, as I felt my phone going off again. Excusing myself, I made my way over to the water cooler. All the begging I'd gone through with Bailey had left me with a dry throat, so I helped myself to a tall cold glass.

Relaxing in the chair back at my desk with a new-found sense of achievement, I retrieved my phone to see that I'd received the longest text message from Camara, with about a 100 emojis attached. It started off with her gushing about the guy she'd met at the club the other night, Danté, before she finally got to the bit that caught my attention, causing me to bolt upright in my seat, spilling water all over my computer keyboard. *Shit. I hate when this happens,* I cursed, hastily mopping up the fluid with some tissues from a box I always kept in the corner. The text said I'd been invited to go on a double date. With her, Danté and his cousin, *Money!*

I checked to make sure the computer keyboard was still working properly and the keys weren't sticking, before looking at her message again, to make sure I'd read it correctly. *OMG! This evening?* Like where is the notice? For an event of this magnitude!!

I began to visualise Money, remembering how gorgeous he was with his silky smooth butterscotch complexion, fit body, juicy lips and sexy eyes. The man was in a league of his own! What was I gonna wear? What should I do with my hair? He'd already seen it naturally wavy, playful, so maybe I could straighten it, give myself a chic look? I'd have to buy some false eyelashes, get my nails done.

All these thoughts were racing around in my head when a single concern took over and hit the finishing line; how to convince Bailey to let me leave early! I still had almost two hours left at work, but I needed to start getting ready right now. I glanced across at Bailey's office, already concocting some crazy story in my head as I began to gather up all my things to leave.

Chapter Eight

Don't you just hate it when people give you barely any notice for big events? Just drop it on you at the last minute? Rummaging through my wardrobe looking for the perfect ghetto-fabulous, sophisticated, demure number, I silently cursed Camara whose text earlier had been so random. Luckily as I was in Bailey's good books for a change, he didn't put up a fuss when I'd lied that I had a headache and asked to leave work early. In fact he joked it must have been as a result of all the pressure I'd been under trying to pitch my idea to him. I was just happy he'd let me go, so I could race home and concentrate on the mission at hand.

Apparently Camara had really hit it off with Danté, talking on the phone and texting non-stop since they'd met. She said it was his suggestion that we all go out for a meal tonight. Even though I was still a bit annoyed with her from our lunch date earlier, *for a chance to see Money, Jabari or whatever his name was, you didn't have to ask me twice*. I'd already messed up my chance of getting closer to him once, by not exchanging numbers, and as much as I hated to admit it, that mistake had been playing on my mind, so I wasn't trying to go down that road again. Camara had already put a bit of a dampener on the evening, by telling me not to get too excited as she'd found out that Money was a bit of a player, but who cared? Right now, he was interested in me and I was gonna make the most of it.

After stepping out of a hot steamy shower, I lotioned my body from head to toe with Victoria's Secret 'Pure Seduction' moisturizing body cream. I'd already stopped off at my friend Brandy's beauty salon, *Brand New*, on my way home, to get my eyelashes and nails done, but I was still in a quandary about what to wear. Finally deciding on some True Religion skinny jeans, a Gucci tight t-shirt and my black suede Kurt Geiger ankle-length boots with the killer heels, I finished my outfit off with my sexy little D&G black cropped leather biker jacket. Swinging my hips to the sound of Drake's 'Hold On, We're Going Home', flowing from the stereo, I did a 360 in front of the mirror and winked at my reflection. I looked hot! But then, didn't I always?

Perfect timing, as two minutes later Camara beeped her car horn impatiently. Clearly she couldn't wait to see her 'Mandingo' again. Grabbing my bag I stepped outside and strutted towards her black Audi. Oblivious to my presence she carried on beeping.

"Calm down," I snapped, as soon as I slid into the passenger seat. "Remember, you're the commodity, not him," I reminded her, in full diva mode.

"He's so nice though," she said, giggling like a five year old. *Shit. This was gonna be interesting. She was already gone.*

"Damn. What's he been saying to you?" I quizzed, intrigued to know what had gotten her so goofy. "I mean, you only met him like two days ago."

"Just little things." She beamed as she made a left on to Broad Street, heading to Bank Restaurant. Classy. Danté's idea. Expensive choice I noted. The feeling must be mutual. How she managed to suppress all this excitement earlier today at lunch beat me, but then again I'd been busy gushing about *Sex Me Down* so it all kinda made sense.

"Credentials?" I barked.

"Well," she blurted, eager to keep him on the tip of her tongue, "he's 29, got no kids, originally from Miami but moved here when he was three years old…"

"Enough of that, where does he live and what car does he drive?" is what I wanted to know.

"Oh my God… see for yourself." She swerved, distracted, as she glanced across past me. Following her dreamy eyeline, I looked out of my passenger window at the beautiful black Range Rover sitting on chrome rims, cruising alongside us. Danté was behind the steering wheel with Money reclined back in the passenger seat. Kendrick Lamar's track 'Poetic Justice', pumped from the vehicle so loud, that I felt like I was in the club. Noticing me staring, Money winked as Danté smoothly pulled his ride into the car park, with us following closely behind, ending up a few parking spots away from them. As Danté strolled over minutes later, embracing Camara like they were newlyweds, Money swaggered towards me, giving me a quick once-over, nodding approvingly. I forgot how cocky he was. *Great! This was gonna be fun.*

"Hey baby girl," he drawled lazily, his sexy, heady, intoxicating, Armani cologne turning me on instantly.

"Hey yourself," I purred.

"Oh, so you're talkin' then?" he surmised, chuckling.

"Excuse me?"

"Well, I don't know about you, but my parents taught me never to speak to strangers. I mean, correct me if I'm wrong but *stranger* is the word you used to describe me the last time we saw each other, if my memory serves me right." He yawned, glancing at his Rolex, like he had somewhere better to be. This guy was just too 'nuff.

"Very funny," I said, snarling, admiring his outfit. He was rocking some navy blue and grey Timberlands, navy Armani jeans and a light grey Polo shirt, with rippling biceps on display. *Why did this idiot have to look so good?* As Danté manoeuvred through parked cars, beckoning for us to follow him, Camara shot me a glance, as she picked up on my attitude. I shrugged, letting her know that it wasn't my fault if Money was a dickhead. Maybe this date wasn't such a great idea after all.

As soon as we walked into the plush restaurant I soaked up the atmosphere and the stylish, modern décor. Classy, contemporary, chic, pretty much summed up the interior. Most of the tables were occupied and the vibe was lively as we were led past a sleek, long bar lined with elegant red stools, to a dimly-lit window table with a superb view overlooking the canal. Losing myself in the moment, my joy was short-lived as before I could even stop him, Money slid in closely beside me at the table as soon as I sat down. I'd been hoping to sit next to Camara so there would be no physical contact between me and Money. I wanted to distance myself from him. As if reading my mind, his hand skimmed mine under the table and damn, if that wasn't a spark of electricity I felt. *Shit.*

"So, what would you like to drink baby girl?" he asked, picking up the wine menu, flashing his billion-dollar smile.

"I'm saying we go all out with some champagne for these beautiful ladies," Danté insisted, locking eyes with Camara, who beamed, blushing like a 15 year old schoolgirl.

"Sounds like a plan," Money agreed, hailing a waiter. "Let me get two bottles of Cristal?" he ordered, as the waiter approached.

Impressive gesture, but waste of finances if you asked me 'cos I wasn't planning on drinking any, although Camara was a lost cause and would probably drink the whole bottle in one go if Danté told her to. Danté seemed like he was on the same page as her and as for Money, well, he had the swagger of a king, priest and prophet all rolled into one, so at least one of us had to keep our wits about us.

We began looking through the menu. Only took me a minute to decide what I fancied, so I sent Dijon a message on WhatsApp whilst waiting for the rest of them to choose. Thought I might as well let him know where we were in case the date took a turn for the worse. Don't know why, but I was feeling so uptight, edgy and defensive. Money just seemed to be having that effect on me. I glanced at him chuckling at something on his iPhone. He seemed totally self-absorbed as the waiter returned with our drinks and took our food order.

"Hey Sahai," Camara piped up as soon as the waiter had walked off, "be interesting to see what these two think about your idea?" she said, as she nudged her chair closer to Danté's. *Hell nah,* I thought. I wasn't really ready to test it out on anyone just yet, but too late, Money was intrigued. "What idea?" he probed.

"It's nothing, just a little something I came up with for a new television programme."

"Lil'?" Money laughed quietly. "I know you out here doin' big things baby. I'm sure there's nothin' lil' about it."

"So what is it? I'm guessing music or fashion maybe, because you work for Bling & Ting right?" Danté said, joining in.

Clearly Camara was talking about me and telling him my business, because I hadn't told him jack. I didn't even know the guy! I'd never even had a conversation with him before. I cut my eye at her letting her know that I wasn't happy about it. She squirmed ever so slightly in her seat. "Yeah," I confirmed. "I do work at Bling & Ting. I'm a producer and presenter there, but I'd love to run my own entertainment company someday. My idea is for a new music programme."

Seeming relieved that I appeared open to discussing the idea, Camara blurted, "Sahai reckons you can tell a lot about a man's personality by his preference in music. She wants to make a programme about that."

"That's dope," Money said smiling, as he poured champagne into my glass. "You right on the money with that one."

"You think?" I was surprised, as it was the first positive response I'd had since mentioning it to anyone. Maybe it wasn't such a bad thing sharing the idea with people after all.

"Oh fo' sho'. I mean, music has definitely opened my eyes, given me some of my finest ideas. What you sayin' D?" he addressed his cousin. "Put us anywhere on God's green earth and we'll quadruple our worth, ain't that right?" The two of them clinked glasses, as Money put his own spin on Jay Z's lyrics.

"I think you could have a lot of fun with that idea," Danté considered. "How is it gonna work?"

"She's gonna quiz a man about his favourite music," Camara said, smirking.

"And then what?" Money asked, curious.

"Match him up with his ideal woman," Camara retorted, rolling her eyes. "It's called *Sex Me Down On Ya Headphones.*" She giggled.

"Not anymore," I hissed, as she mocked me.

"Damn! That's… hot," Money said nodding, as a slow smile crept up one side of his full, soft lips whilst he glanced at me from the corner of his eyes, without looking directly at me. *How sexy?*

"So, um, this err… theory, I guess it works both ways. What's your favourite music?" Danté asked Camara. "Let's see if we're a good match babe," he said, gently taking her hands in his and losing himself in her eyes.

Was the man glowing? They were making me wanna heave, acting like lovestruck puppies. They'd only known each other for two minutes. I could see by Camara's sudden change in body language that she was less than impressed he was taking my idea seriously.

"Are you for real?" she asked him. "You believe it?" she pressed.

I made a mental note to speak to her later about her attitude. She might not agree with my idea but no need to be out here spouting my business and criticising me so openly in front of guys she'd just met and didn't know from Adam. What happened to loyalty? I wasn't feeling her behaviour at all. Smitten or not.

"Who knows? Sahai might be on to something," Danté reasoned, smiling. "You look like you're probably into some of the same stuff as me, Sade, Jill Scott, maybe a little Alicia Keys?"

"Oh wow," I said laughing, as Danté rolled off three of Camara's favourite artists, much to her annoyance. Any other time she would have been impressed, but as she was so busy hating on my idea, she just shut down and stared at the waiter approaching our table with a bread basket. I wasn't letting her get off that easy though. Once he'd gone I picked up right back where we'd left off.

"So you two both like the *same* music," I emphasized, beaming across at her and Danté, rubbing it in. "Maybe that's why you're getting on so well?" I teased. "Come on Camara, you must be able to see the gem in my idea now?" I pushed.

"Well… not really," she mumbled. "What did Bailey think?"

"Who's Bailey?" Money asked, as he chomped on some warm buttered bread rolls.

"My boss." I was now lightening up, enjoying the champagne that I hadn't been planning to drink. "He liked it. Wants me to develop it."

"That's what's up!" Money said, genuinely pleased.

"Brilliant. Great news," Camara murmured, surprised.

"I'll look forward to watching it. Let's toast," Danté proposed, raising his glass along with the rest of us. "To a successful production of the hottest programme to hit our screens this year."

I smiled. Sweet gesture. He seemed like a cool guy. The more I looked at him, the more he reminded me of the actor Morris Chestnut, exactly as he'd appeared in the film, 'The Best Man.' Very good-looking. I could see why Camara was so besotted, even though her behaviour was irritating me. We clinked glasses.

"Thanks. Anyway, enough about me, what do you do for a living Danté?" I asked.

"I'm a Personal Fitness Trainer and a Sports Injuries Physiotherapist."

"He works with celebrities, *footballers*," Camara divulged, beaming.

Was she trying to take a dig at me or something? The way she'd emphasized the word 'footballers' knowing full well that I was pissed off after trying to ring McKenzie Jackson earlier today. He hadn't answered. Yes, I know I'd been planning to wait a few more days before calling him as I didn't want to come across as desperate, but I just couldn't resist. I'd told her about the missed call at lunch before we'd got on to the subject of my programme idea. Now, watching her cooing and gushing, I decided to let her little attitude slide as she was clearly on a Danté high.

"Your job sounds interesting," I admitted, trying to remain positive. "Enjoy it?"

"Has its moments... especially when I'm working with hot, sexy clients," he teased, as Camara hung on to his every word.

"Yeah, I know how you feel," she shot back. "Working for a model agency, I get to travel, drool over fit guys and assist them as they get naked in between fittings."

"Yeah?" he said. "But do you get to touch them though? Massage their tired aching joints? I mean, I've got this one particular female client I'm working with at the moment, an international swimmer, minor injury but abs like you've never seen, so toned," he emphasized.

"Damn... these two are goin' *in*," Money observed, turning towards me as they bickered like a couple of kids. I found the whole thing stupid. I mean, what was this? *Their first lovers tiff? Really?* They needed to get a room.

"So how was your day today? What did you get up to?" Money asked, giving me his full attention.

"Just work and stuff, nothing major, yours?" I asked, with minimal interest, remembering how gorgeous McKenzie was. Why did Camara have to go and mention footballers? Now she had me here thinking about him. I was gutted he hadn't answered my call earlier. Money may have been good-looking, but I doubt he shared the same kind of bank account as McKenzie. Plus he didn't even live in this country, so what could he really offer me? I'd been so excited about meeting up with Money, but my excitement was fading. Camara's little football jab had me wishing it was McKenzie sitting next to me.

"My day was alright," Money answered. "Did the usual stuff... kickin' it with the fam, gym, but yo, I'm goin' back to Miami in a few weeks. You gon' come out there and see me?"

"Now why would I wanna do that? You're a stranger remember," I said, caught off guard by his random invite.

"That's history baby, we're getting more acquainted right now ain't we?" he asked.

"Starters!" A waiter announced, placing more delicious hot bread dripping in garlic butter on our table, along with king prawns, crispy duck spring rolls, chilli squid and chicken skewers. We all started hungrily tucking in.

Chapter Nine

Five minutes later, Camara and Danté were still entwined, feeding each other bits off their plates and giggling, so Money continued right where he'd left off. "Let's spend some time together over the next few weeks. Hang out. That way, when you come out to the States to see me, we'll no longer be *strangers*."

"Firstly," I replied, irritated by his ego, "I haven't agreed to visit you and secondly, I have a job. I can't just take off and leave the country at a moment's notice." I savoured the taste of the spices in my spring roll. "And most importantly," I added, "I barely know you. So no, I won't be coming."

"Oh you're gonna come." He chuckled. *So confident*. "You just don't know it yet, but believe me, you're coming," he said laughing. "Mark my words. In the meantime let me take you out this weekend. Friday," he persisted, not at all fazed by the frosty treatment I was giving him. In fact, he seemed to be enjoying the challenge.

"Can't do Friday, I'm working," I replied.

"In the evenin'?" he asked suspiciously.

"Yeah, Rihanna is in concert. I'm filming there."

"Word?"

"Just all in a day's work," I shrugged, trying to show him it wasn't all about him. I had my thing going on too.

"Oh, so you got it like that?" He smiled, dipping his prawn in *my* dip, on *my* plate. I shooed his hand away, moving my dip out of his reach as there was only a tiny bit left and he weren't letting up.

"Come on now, don't be selfish." He stretched across for it.

I slapped his hand lightly. "I'm not used to sharing … being single and all that," I said, finishing the sauce with my last bit of spring roll. "But I guess you wouldn't know about that."

He raised an eyebrow at me. "You should never assume."

"Ok. Are you single?" I asked.

"All day, every day, baby girl."

"Yeah right! You must have girls swinging around your ankles, chaining themselves to your rims, fine guy like you."

"I get my fair share of attention I guess, but it's not about who likes me, It's about who *I* like that matters," he said, looking me dead in the eye.

As much as I was fighting it, he was slowly but surely beginning to grow on me, especially as I had now downed two large glasses of Cristal. Our conversation was cut short as two waiters appeared, within minutes of each other, one to clear away our empty plates and the other with our main courses.

I'd opted for the spicy chicken breast with sweet potato, whilst Camara was trying the hickory smoked barbecue St Louis cut ribs. Money wasted no time tucking into his sirloin steak and Danté immediately started digging into his lobster. The food was so delicious, no one really spoke for the next five minutes. But Money was right back in there as soon as he'd got past those first few bites.

"Tell me something about yourself. What do you like to do for fun?" he asked.

"Travelling, partying, cinema and oh yeah, can't forget about my piano. I love playing. It relaxes me," I told him.

"Piano? I'm impressed."

"Don't be, you haven't heard me play yet," I joked.

"We can make that happen tonight though. At yours." He stared at me. My whole body tingled. "Let's just say we can treat it as the warm up, for what we gon' do on my white baby grand when you come to see me." *Could he get any cheesier?* The only thing that saved him was that he seemed to have the complete package, beauty, body, brains and possibly a bank balance to brag about, so I remained silent and let him carry on talking. "With your first class plane ticket and my luxury beachfront apartment, it doesn't get much better than that baby."

He wants to buy my ticket? Well, this puts a whole new spin on things.

"Blazin' sunshine, lazy, hazy days, just say the word," he said, tempting me as he put a large chunk of juicy steak in his mouth. "It's all yours if you want it."

That's when that all too familiar voice came into my head.

Bad boy! Run!

"Sounds good," I admitted. "But as I said before, I don't really know you."

"Here we go," he said, sighing. "You gon' start that back up? I'm a stranger again now? What? You think I ain't for real? I look like a joke?"

Run!!

"Money, let's face it. We've only known each other for what? 48 hours?" I reminded him. "Which means, you don't actually know me at all. So why would you even invite me?"

"Because I'm feelin' you shorty. Is that a crime? And we got a whole lotta' hours to get to know each other better, startin' from right now! You need to relax baby. Chill. It's all good. I don't know why you're makin' this so hard for me, but here's the deal. I'm gon' make it real easy for you. I'm gon' give you a taste of the five-star treatment you deserve, take you on a tour of Money's world, then maybe you'll begin to understand what's really good." I raised my eyebrows at him, curious to know exactly where he was going with all this. "Tomorrow, after you get off work, I'm takin' you on a shoppin' spree. I saw a couple of outfits in the Gucci store today that you would look fresh to death in." He stroked my thigh.

Damn! Let's get married, I thought, as his touch sent a single tingle through my entire body. He was now speaking my language. *Gucci.* I polished off my third glass of champagne. Camara, still stone cold sober shot me a glare. She didn't approve of me drinking heavily, said I got too wild, but hey we only live once and right now I was feeling very nice. It was only fitting for me to start showing a bit more interest in Money, seems he was offering me a free holiday *and* shopping spree.

"What do *you* like to do in your spare time?" I asked him.

"Spare time? Baby I ain't got no spare time! I'm out here *grindin'*. Gettin' that paper! Yo, I'm just tryin' a eat! I'm a businessman, a hustler, always workin'."

"Businessman?"

"Yeah, the ballin' doesn't really pay enough, so some years back I started investin'. Right now, back home I own a couple of nail salons, food outlets, a car wash, a dry cleanin' company and a bookstore."

Damn! "That's impressive. How old are you again?" Now I was practically polishing my wedding ring finger. It seemed like his bank account might actually be in line with McKenzie's after all. Maybe I'd been barking up the wrong tree?

"I'm thirty-one, but I started playin' basketball when I was young, about twelve... went pro by the age of seventeen, never made the NBA but played for a lot of top teams in Europe. My moms made me start savin' and investin' when I was about twenty, so by the time I was like twenty-five, I was able to start makin' power moves. You feel me?"

Hell yeah, I thought, swigging more champagne.

"I'm preparing to retire from basketball now," he continued, "so I need to make sure I'm set. Jabari Anderson is ready to do the damn thang," he chuckled, swigging more Cristal. It seemed he and I were the only ones drinking the champagne, which was probably a good thing, considering Camara and Danté were both driving.

Anderson. Anderson. Sahai Anderson! Has a nice ring to it! I smiled.

I glanced around and noticed the restaurant growing emptier.

"All finished?" The waiter queried, as he arrived to clear our dinner plates.

"Yes. It was lovely thanks. Please can we have a look at the dessert menus?" Camara requested.

I was surprised she was able to break away from her little love-fest long enough to say all that.

"Be right back," the waiter told us, scurrying away and returning quickly.

"So yep, that's my future laid out," Money carried on, as he scanned the dessert menu. "What's your financial plan?" he asked.

"Financial plan?" *To marry you?*

"I mean, do you wanna be a millionaire?" he wanted to know.

"Money isn't everything," Camara stated, jumping in. Seems she'd finally decided to come up for air for good.

"Isn't it?" Money questioned.

"Are you ready to order desserts?" The waiter interrupted, glancing at Money first.

"Yeah," Money said, looking at me and biting his bottom lip. "But I'm not sure you have what I need on this menu," he added seriously, looking up at the waiter, then glancing at me again and stroking my face. I was so embarrassed I could feel myself blushing. The waiter, uncomfortable, immediately directed his attention towards Danté.

"I'll go for the chocolate brownies with vanilla ice cream," Danté ordered.

"And I'll take the Tiramisu please," Camara added.

"I think I'm gonna try the crème brûlée with cinnamon and orange shortbread." I decided.

"Bring me a New York cheesecake," Money commanded. "Yeah and put some cream on it," he instructed. The waiter scuttled off.

"I think you really embarrassed him," Camara said, chuckling.

"He needs to get a sense of humour," Money drawled. "I mean, we in here spendin' damn near a thousand bucks… I mean… *sheeiitt.*" He swigged more of his Cristal.

A thousand pounds? I was now busy eyeing the drinks menu and realising his calculation wasn't that far off the mark because the two bottles of Louis Roederer Cristal we'd been drinking had come to nearly six hundred pounds alone. The food wasn't cheap and the night was still young, so there was a good chance another bottle of bubbly might be coming our way. *Sahai Anderson,* I thought gleefully. Things were looking up by the second. I noticed Camara and Danté were busy lost in each other again, so I gave Money's question some thought before answering him.

"I'd like to be wealthy, comfortable, you know, have nice things, but I'm not bothered about being a millionaire," I lied.

"Why not?"

"Because like Camara just said, Money isn't everything. Happiness is more important." *Preferably with a few cool million lying around courtesy of you,* I thought, but wasn't about to say it, as I wanted to come across as the sort of person who wasn't that interested in money, so he wouldn't think I was just after his cash, which of course, I was.

"Yo... peep this though, you need to understand the connection between money and happiness," he said, as the waiter returned with our desserts. Money immediately placed a large chunk of cheesecake in his mouth and continued talking. "Success, baby girl, isn't about having a flash car or a big house or designer clothes. Success is personal. It's about waking up in the morning and doing exactly what you want to do, what you need to do, whatever it is that fulfils you and gives you a sense of purpose and achievement in life. It's about marching to the beat of your own drum and baby *this*," he said, flashing a thick wad of cash from his pocket, "affords you the privilege to do that. You feel me? So answer me this. Do you want to be a millionaire?"

"Yes." I was definitive as I thought about where we could get married.

"Now that's what I'm talking about! It's all about thinking big. Having an action plan. Making that dream a reality." Money swigged the remaining drops of Cristal from his glass, as I pictured myself in the gorgeous Vera Wang wedding gown I'd seen online.

For the next hour the four of us drank coffee, talked and enjoyed the rest of the evening. I was beginning to sober up a little and was disappointed to see the night coming to an end as we finally left the restaurant and headed to our cars.

"Seriously you must have women stalking you," I said to Money, as we strolled through the car park.

"You got jokes. Never that baby girl," he told me, laughing. "I am as single as the day I was born."

"Why?" I refused to believe him. "You got the looks, the swag, charisma, ambition, sexy body, the whole nine."

"But everythin' means nothin', if I ain't got you," he sang, whilst clutching at his heart, grabbing my hand and scrunching up his face.

"Yeah right," I said, once I'd stopped laughing. "I bet you say that to all the girls," I assumed, as we walked towards Camara's Audi. She was now trailing behind with Danté. I was slightly in front of Money and I knew he was eyeing my bottom as I jiggled between cars, so I put an extra switch in my hips.

"Yo, what's poppin'? Where you rushin' to?" he asked, pulling me back. "Ain't you comin' with me or takin' me with you?"

"Um no. I got work in the morning. Remember?"

"So you're blowin' me out... again?"

"Money. Thank you for such a lovely evening, great company, delicious meal, but a girl needs her beauty sleep. I mean, it is late and I need to be sharp in the morning 'cos Bailey is gonna wanna discuss my idea with me."

"Forget Bailey! He got you there like some damn slave. You're rollin' with me tonight."

"Rolling with you where?"

"To the telly."

"The where?"

"The hotel. Hyatt? Marriott? Pick One. Your choice."

"Money, I would love to but..."

"Or is it that you want me all up in *your* place so I can bless the spot." He smirked.

It was my turn now to sing, so I gave him my best shot at Bobby Valentino's 'Slow Down'. "I just wanna get to know you," I sang softly.

He let out a low, warm, chuckle. "Let me take you to a hotel," he gently persisted, draping his arm around my shoulder. "We don't have to do nothin'," he slurred.

Yeah right! He must've thought he was speaking to a sixteen year old. I glanced at my watch. "Sweetie, when it's almost midnight and a man and woman check into a hotel room together, they are usually going there to do one thing and one thing only."

"I ain't tryin' a hear all that baby girl. Let's just see where the mood takes us."

"Give me your phone," I said, slipping it out of his hand, quickly entering my number and passing it back. "Call me tomorrow." I broke away from him, slid out of his reach and hot-footed it towards Camara's car. Her and Danté had somehow overtaken us and were now leaning up against it.

"Damn shorty, you killin a brotha'," Money called after me, as I nestled into the passenger seat. I leaned across tapping the inside of the driver's window for Camara to hurry up. Wasn't trying to mess up her night, but if she wasn't quick, any minute now I'd be changing my mind, jumping out of the car, running off with Money and heading straight to the gutter. Thank God she had my back, as literally seconds later she got behind the wheel.

"Drive!" I yelled at her like she was the getaway driver in a bank heist.

"Why are you shouting?" She screwed up her face, as I saw Money swaggering towards me.

"He wants to take me to a hotel."

"And the problem is?"

"I've only just met him, he is damn fine, so if I go with him, I can't be responsible for my actions. It's not part of the plan."

"You're so funny. What plan?" she asked, selecting first gear and pulling off without a backward glance.

"The plan to be Mrs Jabari Anderson! If I sleep with him tonight, he won't respect me in the morning as we barely know each other, and that's hardly gonna qualify me for a place in the long run as wifey, and I need to be wifey 'cos he's rich!!"

"Scandalous!" Camara laughed, as she sped up quickly and peeled out of the car park with me and my dignity still intact.

"Thanks bestie." That's what I loved about Camara, even though she annoyed me at times, she was always looking out for a sista'.

Chapter Ten

Surfing the internet at my desk, I felt my phone vibrate in my pocket for what felt like the hundredth time this morning. Reaching for it I smiled when I saw that it was Money. *Again.* He'd been ringing and texting me repeatedly since I'd got in last night.

"What's good sexy?" he asked in a text message.

"Apart from you, not a damn thing," I lied, stroking his ego as I reclined in the chair at my desk. I'd been having a great day at work so far actually, with Bailey talking about my genius idea and the rest of the team buying into it.

"Then let me b the one 2 change that baby. Give me a chance 2 brighten your world. Meet me 4 lunch, outside your workplace. D said he'll drop me off. I'll c u there at 1pm."

"I'm working through lunch today. I'll call you later," I text back, asserting myself. As much as I was beginning to like him, he was still way too arrogant and sure of himself for me. He'd have to wait until after I finished work to see me, like we'd already planned, for this shopping trip he'd insisted on. I scrolled through my emails and deleted a few.

"Nah babe. It ain't about Bailey working u 2 death. U gon eat and I'm gon b the one 2 feed u. C u at 1pm"

"Do you never give up?" I asked Money as we tucked into our cheeseburgers at Gourmet Burger Kitchen.

"Not when I see somethin' I really like and right now you're lookin' real good."

"Thanks. Just trying to keep up with you," I joked.

"A slick talker as well. You know how to keep a brotha' on his toes."

"I try."

"So how's it goin' so far with your idea?" he asked.

"Splendid thanks. Shame you won't be around to see it though. By the time it comes on TV you'll be back in Miami."

"TV? You *need* to be puttin' it all over the internet. Facebook, Twitter, Instagram, Snapchat, the whole nine! What did I tell you last night, about thinkin' big?" he drawled.

"I know, I am," I said, quickly reassuring him. "People will be able to watch it online once it's been aired on our channel. I just meant *you* won't be able to watch it with *me.*" I bit into my burger, then swiftly changed the subject before he launched into another one of his lectures. "How was your morning?"

"We might not be able to watch *that* together," he said, reverting back to the subject. "But we can watch somethin' else this evenin' though, after we go shoppin'. Maybe some new joint at the flicks?"

"I can't stay out late sorry, I've got to do some research, prepare for Rihanna's concert. I've managed to get some really good press tickets with all access back stage passes, the lot."

"Sheeiitt, I need to be rollin' with you," he said, chuckling.

"I have actually got a spare ticket."

"That's what I'm talkin' about."

"I didn't say anything about you coming though, did I? In fact, I was thinking of taking Camara."

"Baby, you know you wanna drag me along and show me off to ya lil' friends."

"Why are you so arrogant?" I asked, as I stirred my strawberry milkshake. "It's very unattractive. Why do you have to act like that?"

"Why not? I know what I'm workin' with."

"Can't you try to be humble? It might suit you."

"I am humble, but I look at it this way. Why represent like a sparrow, when I know I'm an eagle?"

"Ok, I can see there's no bringing you down a few notches, so I best get back to work," I told him, enjoying the final sips of my milkshake and easing out of my seat, as I indicated for the waitress to bring the bill.

"Listen, I really enjoy bein' around you," Money confessed, reaching for my hand. "So what's crackin'? Come to Miami. Let me book your flight. I got you."

So he's really serious about this trip! "I'll think about it," I said haughtily. Couldn't show him how excited I actually was at the prospect of going. *Mrs Jabari Anderson,* I beamed inwardly. I still hadn't managed to get hold of McKenzie yet, so right now Money was looking like my best bet. I mean, really if I was gonna choose between Money and McKenzie, it would be Premier League football every time as that's where the real money was, but considering I couldn't get hold of McKenzie, then I guess Money's bank account wouldn't come in too bad at second place.

"You'll *think* about it?" Money asked. "You know everythin' is paradise baby, so chill, you said you were thinkin' of goin' out there for Memorial Day Weekend anyway right? Look at it this way, you still get to go, but this time with the kid! In style! Times are changin' baby. You're movin' up."

I laughed at his arrogance as I put on my jacket. Still caught up in his own hype, he continued talking. "I'll give you a weekend you ain't gon' never forget. Trust me." He stood up, towering over me with his sexy self. I could feel my heartbeat racing. I was not liking the effect he was having on me at all. It was a dangerous feeling, one I knew all too well, that toxic combination of lust and disgust.

"We'll see," I muttered. He definitely had something about him, but at the same time he was just that little bit too cocksure. He acted like he was God's gift, which he kinda was, but to be honest, he was that arrogant, I probably wouldn't even have still been talking to him if it wasn't for the fact that he was *paid!* The boy was *rich!!* I observed, as he retrieved a hefty wad of notes from his pocket to pay the bill.

"So what time we goin' to Rihanna's concert?" he enquired.

"I haven't even said you can come yet," I reminded him.

"Baby girl, you and I both know you ain't goin' to that concert without me." He removed a few strands of stray hair from my face, allowing his finger to linger. I swallowed hard. *That touch!*

"Whatever," I mumbled.

"It's jumpin' off in here, didn't realise you guys get down like this," Money shouted, bopping through the crowd at the concert a few nights later. Naturally he'd managed to talk his way into coming to see Rihanna with me. After the shopping spree, how could I say no? I mean, he'd kept his word and gone all out. The man had bought me clothes, jewellery, bags, perfume, shoes, it was ridiculous.

"Yeah, Rihanna's due on in a minute, so everyone's hyped. This is how it always is," I told him, as Marcus, close behind me, held the camera high above his shoulder, hoisting it even higher. Bailey had pulled some strings so that we could film anywhere in the venue. I turned to face Marcus. "Let's get some shots of those guys over there." I pointed at a crew of dancers.

"Damn baby, you turnin' me on bein' all commandin' an' shit," Money teased.

"Just working sweetie."

"You need to bring that work ethic to the bedroom. Tonight." He squeezed my bottom. "Let's get this shit on and poppin'."

Bad guy. Run for the hills, I screamed inwardly.

"Stop that," I said, giggling. "We're working remember."

"Nah shorty, you're workin'. I'm just tryin' to keep you inspired an' shit."

"Alright, well inspire me when I get backstage to do the interview."

"Fo' Sho'." Money was in his element. "There are some fine girls up in this joint," he observed glancing around. "But none as fine as you," he quickly added, as Rihanna graced the stage. The venue erupted into deafening applause as we edged closer to the front.

Thirty minutes later, whilst she wowed the crowd with her smash hit 'Diamonds,' we made our way backstage to see what we could capture on camera. Marcus led the way, but Money was acting like my damn bodyguard, a sexy one at that as he chatted to people, sizing up who was who.

The way he worked backstage, collecting friends and making himself a total asset was impressive. I managed to film in a few areas that I thought were off limits, thanks to him working his charm. Money's whole swag was turning me the hell on. I think it was at that point I knew I'd definitely be going to Miami.

For the rest of his time in the UK, we hung out pretty much every spare minute. He complained that he'd travelled to a lot of cities playing basketball, but never actually got to see each place as he was literally just in and out, so I managed to get a few days off work and took him to some of my favourite places. Starting with the Cotswolds in Gloucestershire, he loved the beauty, peace and tranquillity of the quiet countryside. "This is the *sheeitt*," was all he kept saying, as we toured the endless lush, green pastures.

Then we headed for the coast, to a beautiful seaside resort in Devon. Once again he was in awe of the magnificent view, the rock pools, soft sand dunes and breathtaking coastline. Strolling along the edge of the shore, he gazed around in wonder at the stunning scenery. "I had no idea there were places like this in England," he confessed, admiring the spectacular stretch of golden sand and sparkling blue sea. "Didn't know you guys were living this good," he admitted, as I reminisced about the time Camara's family had first taken me there with them on one of their family holidays when I was about 10 years old. Ever since then I'd held fond memories of Woolacombe Beach and visited as often as I could.

Over the following days Money and I hung out a few times with Camara, Danté and Dijon, then finally I took him to London to show him Buckingham Palace, Big Ben, the River Thames and London Bridge, although he was more interested in seeing the 'hood' and insisted we go to Brixton in South London, as he'd heard it was the ghetto and wanted to compare it with parts of Miami.

I laughed at him as he sidled up to various shady looking characters hanging around outside Kentucky Fried Chicken on Cold

Harbour Lane. I think it was his way of trying to see what their hustle was and gain some understanding of street life over here.

He wasn't impressed with Brixton market though, grumbling non-stop about the pungent odour of raw meat as we passed through. So I quickly got him out of there to Brixton Tube Station and we jumped on the tube, heading for Oxford Circus.

It's a shame Z Bar had closed down some years back as that's a spot I knew he'd have enjoyed. We would've stayed overnight so he could get to experience a bit more of the South London vibe. He still managed to enjoy a taste of it outside Satay Bar, as we'd gone there to eat before the market. With it being a hot day everyone was out, styling and profiling, keeping the streets lively, much to his amusement.

He even took me shopping again. Gucci, Armani, Harvey Nichols, D&G and a few other designer shops. We ended up in Selfridges on Oxford Street, where he spent a fortune on me, before heading to Covent Garden on a red double-decker bus, just for the experience, for a quick look around, then Trafalgar Square for food.

As well as all the days out, after spending a few hot nights in together, I began to understand why he was so confident and cocky. He was definitely working with something impressive. I was in heaven.

Needless to say, I was disappointed when it was time for him to go home. But like with everything else he did, Money left in style, getting Danté to stop at a travel agents on our way to Heathrow Airport.

Whilst Danté and Camara waited in the car, Money dragged me into the shop and bought my flight to Miami across the counter there and then. The first thing I did when I glanced at the tickets was check the dates. I was due to fly out on Saturday May 24th. I looked up at him with the biggest grin.

"Memorial Day Weekend 2014 in style baby!" he yelled. "We doin' the damn thang!"

It was his final grand gesture before he left the UK, so it was set. I'd be heading off to Miami to see him in a few weeks.

Chapter Eleven

Naturally I was a bit apprehensive about going to Miami after what had happened when I went to see that music producer in New York, but Money hadn't stopped ringing me since he'd left and it wasn't like I'd be there for a long time. I was only gonna be there for five days, like a long weekend.

The nine hour flight from Heathrow Airport went pretty smoothly, if you excuse the brats that were sitting behind me. They were screaming like they were competing for a place in a toddlers' talent show, but the good thing is I was able to tune them out by watching one of Idris Elba's latest flicks on my iPad. Wacking up the volume on my headphones I completely lost myself in his whole aura. I mean, the man just oozed sex appeal. Before I knew it, we were preparing to land.

As soon as the plane touched down at Miami International Airport at about 9pm, I started having butterflies. I felt queasy and kept praying that Money would be there to meet me. I had told him to collect me at about 9.30 as I was adding extra time to go through airport security and customs. Took a little longer than I'd expected now that they'd started doing fingerprints and whatnot.

Finally at about 10pm I stepped outside on to the concourse, smiling at the familiar sight of palm trees swaying in the cool breeze as the warm night air enveloped me. Glancing around I watched various couples, families and friends greeting each other for a while. Mild anxiety started setting in as there was no sign of Money. I didn't even have any idea what he was driving. I think he said something about a black truck, SUV, Escalade maybe? But everyone seemed to be riding around in black jeeps and trucks. Pulling out my mobile phone I was relieved to see that international roaming had kicked in, so I had a network connection and signal. My palms were sweating as I anxiously dialled Camara's mobile. "Hey girl, I'm in Miami baby!" I yelled, as soon as she answered her phone.

"Yaay!" She shared my excitement "Glad you reached safely."

"Be even better if Money was here."

"You what? Where are you? Still at the airport?"

"Yep, but can't see him anywhere."

"You called him?" she asked.

"No, not yet."

"Well what are you waiting for? Call him and call me right back." She hung up. Nervously I dialled his mobile number. Straight to voicemail. *Shit*. I couldn't believe this was happening to me again. Looking around I glanced at my watch another time. It was now almost quarter to eleven. I hastily dialled back Camara.

"No answer," I informed her. I was kicking myself for travelling in killer heels and a sexy little black dress. The shoes were killing me and the dress was drawing unnecessary attention. I scowled and turned my back on an ugly guy wolf-whistling at me as he walked by.

"He must be on his way. Probably stuck in traffic," Camara reassured me. "Let me quickly call Danté and see if he can track him down and I'll ring you right back," she insisted, before hanging up. I wheeled my suitcase over to a bench, sat down and waited. Minutes later Camara called back. "Danté can't get hold of him either," she said.

Great!!

"Just keep trying. I'm sure he'll be there soon," she ventured, trying to sound optimistic.

"Thanks and I will."

"Ok cool. Keep me posted."

"Alright," I mumbled, ending the call.

I sat there for what seemed like an eternity watching people come and go. I tried Money's number numerous times with no success. I couldn't believe this shit was happening to me again. It was less than two months ago that I'd gone to New York to see that producer who hadn't turned up, but this was supposed to be different. I'd really enjoyed these last few weeks with Money. We'd had a lot of fun, he seemed so sincere. *Why me?* I thought, hunching over, burying my head in my hands.

"Damn baby girl, you look good!" The deep, sexy, familiar voice came from up above. Opening my eyes they rested on some size 12 Jordans that could only belong to one person. Looking up, I didn't know whether to laugh, smile, cry or get mad. He looked so fine in his fresh white T-shirt and dark blue jeans.

"Money, you're over two hours late," I snapped.

"Sorry baby girl." He yawned, reaching for my hand to pull me up. "I had some business to take care of, then traffic was a bitch. Why you ain't have your mobile on? I tried to call yo' ass."

"My mobile is on and I don't recall any missed calls from you."

"Yeah? That's 'cos I couldn't get through, but come here, give me a hug, you lookin' fine shorty."

I wasn't budging. He wasn't getting away that easy. Seeing that I wasn't gonna stand up, he sat down beside me and placed my hands in his. "On a real, I ain't mean to keep you out here waitin' like this. Real talk Sahai."

"What took you so long?" I barked. "It's practically midnight and I had all sorts of dodgy guys trying to talk to me."

"Why wouldn't they? Look how beautiful you are, wearin' the hell out of that dress! Come on let's go, let me make it up to you." I was beginning to melt, staring into his deep brown eyes. "Matter of fact you lookin' so dope," he said, "we goin' straight to the club. We about to hit South Beach right now."

"Money that sounds great but I need to freshen up first, take a shower. I've been travelling all day."

"I feel you, but peep this? As you already know, South Beach ain't that far away, but my penthouse in West Palm Beach is a couple of hours drive and my condo in Fort Lauderdale is a way out too, so we may as well hit the club first. I need to show you off, make all these mothafuckas out here jealous. My boys are already at the spot, so let's roll."

By now I was no longer protesting as I could see his mind was already made up so I followed him quietly to his car. *Oh My God,* I screamed inside, as we approached his diamond-black Bentley convertible, sitting on chrome rims.

"I left the truck at home as I figured my lady might wanna ride in style," he explained, as he saw my face light up.

"Nice ride," I complimented. He was well worth the wait. In fact, *what wait?* I thought as I sunk into the plush soft leather interior. Luxury at its best.

"So, where are we heading?" I asked. I could barely contain my excitement as he switched on the engine and cruised out of the airport, merging into traffic on the 1-95 highway. I felt like I was gliding through clouds, the ride was so smooth.

"I'm thinkin' a club on Washington Avenue or maybe 'Nikki Beach' on Ocean Drive," he said yawning, as my mobile started going off.

"Is he there yet?" Camara asked panicking, as I answered. "Danté can't get hold of him."

"Yeah, he's here now." I smiled.

"Well... thanks for letting a sista' know," she snapped. "I've only been sat here worrying for the last how long."

"Sorry," I said sheepishly, as I sank further into the luxurious seat.

"Well the main thing is, I'm glad you're alright, so have fun and keep me posted."

"Most definitely." I smiled, grinning at Money as he placed his hand on my thigh.

"Say hi to Money for me and make sure you call me tomorrow," Camara reminded me before abruptly hanging up. I knew she was pissed off about me not calling back, but right now I was in heaven, feeling high as a kite as the cool breeze blew through my hair and Money softly caressed my thigh. His other hand, on the steering wheel, easily navigated the Bentley through traffic. I felt like a superstar as other drivers admired our car. *Sahai Anderson.* It was sounding better by the minute.

"So how was the flight baby girl?" Money asked, as we cruised smoothly on the highway.

"Fine," I confirmed.

"You cool with me now… or you still in yo' feelings?" He chuckled, stroking my face. *Damn, if he keeps touching me like this…*

"I'm cool," I confirmed, as he switched on the car stereo. Rick Ross's rugged tones instantly filled the air, lifting my mood even higher. For some reason, listening to Rick Ross made me feel good. Free. He had a swag, a voice and a vibe that did it for me. As usual he was hollering something about being the boss. Money, nodding smoothly to the loud hip hop beat, smirked in my direction, like the song was written about him. Irritated by his smug expression I glanced in the opposite direction and admired the view as we glided past neon-lit buildings, flash cars and palm trees swaying in the cool night breeze.

I loved it out here. Everything always looked super shiny. I could feel growing excitement as Money continued to softly stroke my thigh, weaving in and out of traffic, bobbing his head to the track 'Magnificent', blasting from the speakers so loud, that I'm sure you could've heard us for miles. Rick Ross was in his element, yelling something about swimming in women, over a banging beat.

"That's right," Money said, squeezing my thigh, as his eyes roamed my body hungrily. At this moment I was more convinced than ever that my theory about men and music was real. My programme was gonna be a total success. Hands down, it was a no-brainer. Confident in this knowledge, I kicked back and enjoyed the view as we rode the rest of the journey with Rick Ross rapping about everything from being a baller to feeling super-high to partying till the sun comes up.

"That's exactly what we gon' do," Money agreed, laughing, as he eased the car on to Collins Avenue.

As usual, thousands of people drenched in bling, swarmed the sidewalk, spilling over into the road. Cars were bumper to bumper, with loud music pumping from every direction, including the various bars lining the street, as we cruised along. A large convoy of sexy male bikers coasted the strip. Clad mainly in wife-beaters and cargo shorts with no helmets, their tattooed muscles were on full display, gleaming, as they sat astride pimped-out motorbikes.

In strong competition were the convertible Cadillacs, Pontiacs, Chevy Impalas and other American vintage classic cars that had been restored and preened for the occasion, in a range of metallic colours from deep-purple to sky-blue, to hot-pink and mint-green.

One particular Cadillac caught my attention, a candy-apple-red drop-top. The roof, partially reclined, was suspended in the air revealing leopard print suede upholstery. Gold rims spinning briskly, sent golden daggers glinting in every direction, as the car bounced up and down on hydraulics, but what really got me were the passengers.

The driver, a creamy coffee-coloured slim black man, with one hand on the fluffy white steering wheel in a gangsta' lean, looked to be in his late thirties. Wearing a zebra print suit jacket, a red silk shirt, yellow tie and a zebra print Stetson hat with a long peacock feather sticking out, he crept along, bumping to the beat of 'Wu-Tang Clan's' track, 'C.R.E.A.M.', blasting from his vehicle. Thick auburn sideburns snaked down the side of his face, a fat Cuban cigar dangled from his lips and his eyes seemed no more than a slit.

Beside him, a beautiful Puerto Rican looking female, with long flowing honey-coloured hair, knelt up high in the passenger seat, clad in a flesh-coloured skimpy bikini top. Hands flung high above her head, she laughed playfully, writhing seductively to the music, occasionally swigging from a bottle of Moët. I had to blink twice to double check if she was naked. No mistaking the three topless girls in the back of the car though. Perched up high around the edges of the vehicle, the three blonde babes laughed, cavorted and caressed each other as their bottoms, displaying tiny thong strings, poured over the frames of the Cadillac.

"Crazy right?" Money said, following my stare. "Only in Miami," he added chuckling, before pressing a button which automatically speed-dialled someone's phone.

"'Sup cuz?" A guy answered on the third ring, his deep voice on loudspeaker, filling the car, drowning out the music.

"Yo, where you at dawg?" Money yelled.

"Wet Willies... but we about to hit 'Players' baby. You comin' thru'?"

I glanced at my watch to see that it was now almost 1.15 am.

"No doubt," Money replied. "I'll be there in a few. A'ight. One," he said, and disconnected the call. "With the flyest chick, lookin' all fine as hell," he added, grinning at me.

I was beginning to feel light headed, intoxicated with his sexy vibe. He had a mad yoyo effect on me. One minute he would be annoying the hell out of me and the next I was totally mesmerised by him. *Not good!* As the car crawled slowly along the humid street pulsing with activity, I studied the heaving masses, taking in revellers noisily gambling over dice and card games with piles of dollars stacked up on little wooden makeshift stools between them.

A group of fit, ripped men, looking like they'd just strolled off the beach, wearing nothing but shorts and towels slung over their shoulders, approached a gathering of hip hop honeys clad only in heavy makeup, glamorous fake hair, designer thong bikinis and killer heels.

A man staggering along stumbled and almost fell on to our bonnet, our headlights illuminating him, as he swigged from a bottle of sea blue liquor. Random people sat on the edge of the sidewalk rolling blunts, wanna-be rappers caught up in MC battles, freestyled in little cliques and clubbers formed huge queues outside nightclubs, contained by tall burly security guys who looked larger than life. Memorial Weekend was nuts.

I marvelled at the chaos of it all. It was insane. As I watched the bouncers working hard to control the queues, one particularly beefy bouncer with thick hair cainrowed down his back, simply picked up a weedy looking guy trying to push his way through and dropped him straight into the gutter. The victim got up and staggered off down an alleyway cursing expletives. I turned my attention back to the road. *Was that a famous rapper driving past?*

I pointed and looked at Money who smiled and nodded confirmation that it was.

"The club's just along here," he told me, as he pulled the car on to Washington Avenue. "But we ain't gon' have to queue tho'. I got it like that," he boasted.

Players was the spot! As soon as we walked in, I soaked up the ambience. The decor was on point. Queen sized beds, draped in flowing silk chiffon, were softly lit in a cerise pink and purple glow. A giant circular bed in the centre dominated the nightclub. Pole dancers were doing their thing, amidst hundreds of wild and reckless thrill-seekers, partying hard.

Hip hop music blasted and bounced off the walls, as skimpily clad cocktail waitresses shimmied around the place. Grabbing my hand, Money led me to a plush, extravagant VIP area, cordoned off with red velvet rope, where about ten of his friends, a mixture of male and female, were lounging around intimately on a huge bed, nestled in oversize pillows, enjoying steamy music videos on a large plasma screen whilst knocking back cocktails and from what I could see, obscene amounts of Ace of Spades champagne.

"Yo, Money in da house," one of his goons yelled as soon as he spotted us, reaching up to touch Money's fist.

"Damn, who dis?" another one asked, eyeballing me. "She fine as *hell* man! She a badass bitch!" he slurred, swigging from a bottle of Grey Goose, as a sea of faces looked up at me.

"Shut yo' ass up Dre!" Money barked. "Have some respect. This is my girl, Sahai."

"Hey, nice to meet you all." I flashed one of my award-winning smiles.

"*Sheeiitt!* Where *you* from?" Dre gasped. "Soundin' all proper an' shit. You be killin' me wit' dat accent yo!"

"I'm from England."

"That accent sexy as hell," Dre mumbled. "Say somethin' else."

"Showtime over," Money growled. "Where my drink at?"

"Right here playboy," said a good-looking guy in the middle, reaching for a fresh bottle of champagne, as he passed Money a couple of glasses. "Let's get this shit started son!" he bawled, as he popped the cork, fizz bubbling and liquor flowing everywhere.

Moving bottles and limbs, Money cleared a space for us to plop down on the bed.

Two hours later, I was feeling nice and tipsy, enjoying the crazy banter of his friends. I'd noticed that someone had been blowing up Money's phone all night, but he'd kept ignoring the calls. I wondered if it was some girl giving him a booty call because realistically who else was gonna be calling him after 3 in the morning, but decided against spoiling the night by acting all jealous and questioning him.

"You ready to go baby girl?" he whispered, leaning into me, nibbling lightly on my ear, sending tingles through my body.

"Yeah." I was horny. The soft kisses he was placing all over my neck had my pulse racing. I couldn't wait to get back to his place.

We said our goodbyes, exited the VIP cubicle and merged into the crowd, mingling with the glitterati. I was in my element. But no sooner than we'd stepped into the mix of clubbers, a beautiful, tall dark girl approached Money, threw her arms around his neck and literally started dancing on him. He glanced back at me and signalled me to wait a minute as he spoke to her. The next thing I knew the two of them were locked together grinding all over each other, with her thrusting up against him and him running his hands up and down her body enjoying it.

Oh hell no! I couldn't believe he was disrespecting me like this. *We* hadn't even danced together all night! Did he think I'd flown all these miles across the world to watch him dancing with some next chick? To make things worse, they were dancing to *my* song, 'How Many Drinks,' by Miguel. I loved the dark, provocative bass line on this track. Watching *them* slow grinding to it was killing me.

I had the urge to storm off, but storm off and go where? The bitch was all over him and he was lovin' it. My next desire was to step between them and beat them both down, but here I was, abroad, alone, with limited funds, on a ticket that he'd bought for me, so I wasn't really in a position to be creating enemies.

Livid, I stood there as the two of them laughed and danced together. Eventually he kinda prised her off him and joined me.

"Ready?" he asked. I was furious. No explanation or acknowledgement of my mood. "What? She's just a friend," he explained, finally picking up on my attitude.

"How could you be dancing with her like that when I'm right here?"

"It was just a dance baby. Come on, I know you ain't gon' let some lil' chickenhead ruin our night."

"I think you're doing a fine job of that on your own," I snapped, as he led me out of the club. At this point I didn't really wanna go anywhere with him. I felt so humiliated, but what choice did I have?

Chapter Twelve

As we approached the Bentley his whole demeanour changed as he spotted a beautiful, Hispanic looking girl, arms folded across her chest, leaning against the car. He looked like he saw a ghost as his entire body tensed up.

"You know her?" I stupidly asked.

"Um yeah," he mumbled.

Seeing us nearing the car, the girl gave me a vacant once-over, then shot him the darkest look.

"Let me talk to her a minute." He moved away from me.

I watched as they seemed to be in some kind of argument. Although I was in ear shot, I couldn't understand one word as they were both speaking fluent Spanish. She was angrily pointing at his phone, so I suspected that she'd probably been the one ringing him all night when he'd kept ignoring the phone calls. Money was turning out to be a man full of surprises to my dismay.

I just wanted this girl to hurry up and get lost so I could go back to his place and get some sleep. Pissed off to the max, I was now exhausted. Jet lag was kicking in. Minutes later he approached me and rested his hands on my shoulders, staring down at me, looking deep into my eyes.

"Um listen, that girl, that's Carlita. She... um... works for me. Remember I told you about all my businesses. She kinda manages them... like a personal assistant."

I began fuming as I noticed that the stunning girl had some kind of overnight bag that she seemed to be loading into the Bentley before climbing into the backseat. *Where the hell did she think she was going?*

"There's been a change of plan," he continued. "I got an emergency. I'll drive you back to the penthouse in West Palm Beach, then I gotta go take care of some business and I want you to stay there with Carlita till I get back."

"Are you crazy?" I yelled. "I'm not staying at some strange apartment with some girl I don't even know."

"I'll only be gone a couple of hours baby girl," he said, attempting to pacify me. "I'll make it up to you when I get back."

"I can't believe this." I was irate.

"Come on, let's go," he urged. "Carlita will take care of you till I get back. She's a good girl. She doesn't speak any English though. Only Spanish, but you'll be alright."

He dived into the driver's seat and fired up the ignition before I had a chance to protest again. A deathly silence followed as I slipped into the passenger seat and we began the journey to West Palm Beach. Money, totally tense, fiddled around with the car stereo, selecting Lil Wayne's album, 'I Am Not a Human Being,' and kept it blasting, whilst driving at turbo speed.

I couldn't believe this shit! Came all the way out here for this? Money was driving so crazy, like a mad man. As he swerved, randomly missing a collision with a Ferrari, Carlita started screaming and slapping his back until he pulled the car over, screeching to a halt. A heated argument followed between the two of them, but as it was in full Spanish, I couldn't understand one word but *what the fuck?* A lover's quarrel? This girl did not feel like no damn personal assistant to me.

Next thing, she jumped out of the car, he jumped out, she jumped in the front and he climbed in the back. I glanced back at him for some kind of explanation.

"She wants to drive." He shrugged his shoulders and then reclined in the seat, closing his eyes.

Pulling off, Carlita drove smoothly for the rest of the silent journey.

The penthouse was insane! A huge, white marble fountain in the foyer, showcasing a life-sized, pearl-black statue of a naked woman with an hour glass figure, greeted us as soon as we walked through the front door. The sound of the gushing water, cascading down her back, echoed all around us.

A beautiful white baby grand piano held court off to the right, underneath sparkling low hung chandeliers. The far left corner boasted an elegant black and chrome chaise lounge, near a tall glass bookcase, displaying what I assumed were Money's basketball trophies.

Wall to wall windows were complimented by a mirrored ceiling, leading into a lounge with a deep, white, plush carpet. Abstract black and white artwork added style and glamour to the expansive room. Luxurious white leather sofas enhanced the stylish glass coffee table with marble legs, serving as a centre-piece.

A fifty-two inch plasma screen graced the wall, above a state-of-the-art chrome and glass music entertainment centre. With a slight clap of his hands, Money's tall, slim, surround-sound speakers began oozing the sexy, edgy intro to Jhené Aiko's, 'The Worst'.

"Home sweet home baby girl," Money whispered in my ear as he wrapped his arms around me from behind.

"Don't baby girl me." I spun around. "I mean, what the fuck's going on?" I spat.

"Baby... I..." he attempted.

"Who's this Carlita chick?" I snarled, cutting him off, noticing that she was nowhere to be seen.

"Like I said, she's my personal assistant. I didn't know she was gon' try and meet up with me this weekend."

"Do you think I'm fucking dumb? She don't look *or* sound like no fucking assistant to me. Why is she hooking up with you in the middle of the night and why has she got to stay here?"

"Because she doesn't live in the area. She lives in Coral Springs, which is a way out from here."

"How convenient," I hissed.

"Carlita knows me and my boys roll at Players so that's why she came down there," he continued. "She was under the impression that we had some work to do."

"Really?" *Did he take me for a complete fool?*

"She'd been ringin' me all evenin' apparently to tell me she was gon' try and meet me. But listen, like I said, I need to bounce. I got a lil' business to take care of," he said, reaching for his mobile phone and car keys, and practically lunging towards the front door.

"I'm not staying here. Take me to a hotel." I crossed my arms. My eyes blazed into his.

"Baby, there are no hotels around here and seriously, even if there were, you ain't gon' find anywhere nicer than here to stay. There are five bedrooms up in here. She'll sleep in one, we'll sleep in another. Let her show you to our room, make yourself comfortable and I'll be back before you know it boo." He opened the door. I was livid. "Gotta rock baby girl," he cried, before scurrying out of the penthouse. All I could do was stand and stare at the empty spot he'd left behind.

"Hey Chica."

I glanced around to see that Carlita had the nerve to be swanning around the apartment like Queen Bitch, rocking the sexiest red and white lingerie I'd ever seen. No doubt an item that she'd brought in her overnight bag to stay with her *boss!* I could feel my temperature rising as my blood boiled. Bastard! *How fucking dare he?* I was about to go off on her when I realised that she was probably as much in the dark about me as I was about her and I could see that she was attempting to be friendly as she gestured at me in poor English.

"Your room, zeees way," she said, pointing along a hallway. "But first I give you tour."

I picked up my suitcase and reluctantly followed her. As she walked ahead of me, her glossy bronze curls bounced on her back, complimenting her silky, light golden-brown complexion. She was blessed with a gorgeous figure, tiny waist and generous behind. There was no way this *stunner* was his fucking *assistant!* At this point, I was so mad and so knackered, that I just wanted to sleep my way out of this nightmare.

Ten hours later I awoke from a sound sleep, but where the hell was Money? Stretching out in the ridiculously huge empty bed, I lazily buried myself in the soft, snow-white bedding, complete with oversize pillows, before stumbling out of bed, taking in the magnificent view. The penthouse overlooked the sparkling blue ocean and sun-drenched palm trees lining the streets. I couldn't wait to hit the beach.

I could smell the faint aroma of cooking, so assumed Money must've been in the kitchen, making us breakfast. Grabbing my towel and toiletry bag, I stepped into the white marble en-suite bathroom and enjoyed a steaming hot shower. After moisturizing all over with Dior's J'Adore perfumed body lotion, I sprayed on the same fragrance, slipped into a white vest and some cut-off jean shorts and headed for the lounge.

Carlita was in the spacious open-plan kitchen looking radiant in a cute little yellow sundress, with a pretty sunflower in her hair, whipping up what appeared to be some kind of Spanish omelette.

"Hola," she chirped, as she glanced across at me smiling, then walked over to the fridge and pulled out a carton. "Juices?" she offered.

What was this bitch's game?

"Oranges?" She shook the box.

We're not on the same team! I wanted to scream at her. Why was she being so friendly? Shit. Maybe she was trying to poison me so she could have Money all to herself?

"Where is Money?" I asked.

"Mo... neee?" she repeated slowly and frowned. I matched her expression and pointed to a glass framed photograph on the kitchen counter of Money, blinged out, beaming, sitting on the hood of a black jeep. "Oh." She tossed some red and green mixed peppers into the frying pan. "Jabari?"

"Yes." Couldn't believe I was spending my first morning in Miami on a fucking language course!

"He... phone?" she attempted, holding her thumb to her ear and baby finger to her mouth. "He say... back soon."

"Thanks," I snarled and marched back to my quarters. Grabbing my mobile I dialled his number. Voicemail. *Prick*! I slammed the phone into the bedding. I had to get out of here. Picking up the phone I dialled Camara.

"Full details so far?" she demanded excitedly, as soon as she heard my voice.

"You're not gonna believe this shit," I warned, before breaking down the whole story to her.

"You what? You're kidding right?" was all she could manage as soon as I finished talking.

"I wish," I said glumly.

"So... what you gonna do?"

"I was hoping you'd tell me that," I admitted.

"Well it sounds like he'll be back soon. So you might as well just wait it out," she suggested.

"Might be my only option," I realised. "I mean, I don't know where the hell I am. I got no money and I'm fucking screwing! I'm gonna kill him."

"You want me to speak to Danté? Get him to try and track him down?"

"Nah. Leave it. This is embarrassing enough as it is. I don't wanna make a big deal out of it." I felt humiliated.

"I hear you." Camara was sympathetic. "Ok then, well... just sit tight and keep me posted. I'm sure he'll be back soon."

"Let's hope so," I wished, hanging up.

Five hours later and ten failed attempts to contact Money, there was still no sign of him. With no idea of where I was, I'd sat outside on the balcony in the sizzling heat, reading a book, whilst Carlita flounced around the place, doing housework, humming and trying to speak to me. *What the fuck did she have to be so cheerful about? And when was she gonna disappear and do some of this damn office work that Money had mentioned?* I was beginning to lose it, so I joined her on the sofa when she finally sat down.

"Is there any other way we can contact him?" I asked.

She shook her head vacantly.

"Ja... ba... ri...?" I emphasized. "Fa... m... ily?" I questioned.

"Me no know," she offered.

Great. I stormed off to my room and decided to take a nap. He was gonna have to come back at some point, so maybe I could continue to sleep my way out of this misery until then.

I awoke disorientated. It was dark outside. I sat in the stillness for a few moments trying to get my bearings, before washing my face and leaving the room. My belly was rumbling. I needed to eat.

Carlita was curled up on the sofa laughing at a Spanish sitcom on the plasma screen. It was obvious she was very familiar with this apartment.

"Hey Chica." She glanced up at me.

"I fell asleep." Why I was explaining my absence to her I don't know, but seems she held a more supreme position than me in this kidnapping without a kidnapper, I may as well stay on her good side. I'd once read somewhere, that in any kidnapping situation the best thing to do was try and befriend the kidnapper.

"You... eat? I make... fajitas." She smiled. My mouth watered as I smelt the delicious aroma of onions, spices and sauces coming from the kitchen, but as I still wasn't sure of her position, I opted for some dry bread and mineral water.

"Look, this is ridiculous. It's almost midnight," I snapped, as I tried Money's phone again, only to get voicemail. My attempts to be friendly didn't last very long. I was hungry and mad as hell.

Switching off the television, she took on a serious demeanour and turned to fully face me. "I... worried," she muttered. "He never... do dis... before. Stay away... all day... all night… maybe... he have accident?"

For fuck's sake! This is all I need.

"He say... you... teleeveesion producer," she said, pointing at me. *What was this? A fucking bonding session?* "He say... he work with you," she carried on. "You film him."

"Oh did he now?" The lying bastard! "He said you're his personal assistant," I informed her.

"What ees… personal aseestant?" she asked.

"Secretary. Staff. Employee. Worker." I spoke very slowly, emphasizing each syllable.

"Oh no no no." She looked horrified. "I… girlfriend," she blurted, pointing at herself.

That's why the fucking snake wasn't coming back!

"How long you two been together? Dating?" I was fuming.

"To… get… her? Da… ting? One momento." She ran across to a bookshelf and came back with a fucking Spanish/English translation dictionary! This was getting better by the second. Flipping through some pages, she smiled, chuffed that she'd deciphered my question.

"Three years." She beamed.

"Three years!" I screamed.

"Yes… we try for baby," she said smiling, rubbing her stomach. I felt sick to mine. "What if… he hurt?" Her smile faded as she suddenly started crying. *Shit! Now what?*

"Well, why don't we ring some hospitals? Police? See if he's been involved in a car accident. If he's been admitted?" I suggested.

Her beautiful tanned, golden complexion became ghostly. "Hospeetal? Poleecia? Oh no. Cannot do dat."

"Why?" I asked.

"He have no… how you say… no driving license?" she uttered, getting more tearful. "And… he driving my car…" *The Bentley wasn't even his? It was hers. That explained why she wanted to drive last night after the reckless way he was driving! And how the fuck could she even afford a car like that anyway? Personal assistant, my ass!*

"And I am…" she tried to explain, flicking through the dictionary. "How you say? Deesqualified… illegal… banned from driving."

Fucking hell! So I'm in Miami, rolling with Bonnie & fucking Clyde?

At that point I couldn't give a shit if Money was dead, alive or incarcerated. I just needed to get on the first thing smoking out of town.

"Where is the nearest bus or train station or taxi rank?" I asked.

"Bus? Train?" She looked confused, then mortified. "Oh no, please... don't leave me," she pleaded, tears trickling down her face as she clutched on to me.

Unfuckingbelievable!

The next morning there was still no sign of Money. Clearly the little shit wasn't coming home to his girlfriend and lover holed up in the same apartment. He had literally skipped out on us. Weak ass Negro!

It had been too late for me to go anywhere last night, but dammit if I was staying around again for another day of this shit. I had to get to the airport. I'd spent the best part of last night counselling Carlita with the aid of the dictionary. He obviously thought we wouldn't be able to communicate because of the language barrier. Dickhead! He couldn't have been more wrong. I'd managed to inform her of his relationship with me and needless to say she was devastated. She seemed like a nice enough girl so I felt she had the right to know, but I made sure I'd slept with my bedroom door locked and one eye open.

As soon as I woke up, I reached for my iPad and googled the nearest train station. I'd managed to calm Carlita down long enough for her to tell me exactly where we were. I'd worked out that we were quite close to West Palm Beach train station on South Tamarind Avenue, south of First Street and Banyan Boulevard. The trains ran once an hour and would take almost two hours to get to Miami International Airport. I'd also found a few local taxi numbers, so I could see a clear route. It was gonna be a bit of a trek, but at least I could get there.

After showering and dressing, I brushed my teeth, put the remainder of my toiletries in my suitcase and left the room. Entering the lounge, I saw Carlita curled up on the sofa in the fetal position, still wearing the same clothes she had on yesterday, eyes all puffy and red. She looked like she hadn't slept a wink. A hot mess.

"Hear anything?" I asked.

She shook her head and burst out crying. Shit. I had to get out of there. Reaching for my phone, I made one last attempt to call Money. He answered on the first ring.

"Where the fuck are you?" I yelled, as Carlita perked up.

"I told you I had some business to take care of," he said evenly.

"You also told me you were coming back a few hours later." I matched his tone. "You fucking prick." I couldn't hold back. "How the hell you gonna have me and your woman holed up in the same apartment you little shit?"

"She's not my woman," he calmly stated. "I told you. She's my personal assistant."

"How the hell you gonna invite me all the way to Miami and leave me fucking stranded in an apartment for two fucking days Money?" I screamed at him.

Snatching the phone out of my hand, Carlita started doing her own screaming into it, her voice verging on hysteria. Snatching it back, rage consumed me. I couldn't believe this shit.

"Can you at least come and get me and take me to the airport?" I spat, as Carlita, riddled with angst, staggered around the room, clutching her head in her hands, hysterical.

"Why did you tell her about us?" he asked, ignoring my request. "And why the fuck you leavin'? Your flight's not for another two days. I said I had an emergency. It took a lil' longer than I'd expected, but I'm on my way back to the crib now. We can still have some fun," he said smoothly.

"Are you nuts? You really think I'm gonna stay here another day in this bullshit?" I screamed. *What part of the game was this?*

"Well... fuck you then!" he exploded. "I told you this weekend wasn't the best time to come, but you insisted." He totally switched on me.

"You what?" I shrieked, thinking about how much he'd begged me to come *and* chosen the dates *and* bought my ticket. It was at that point I realised he had mental health problems. I was dealing with a fucking psychopath! *Great!*

"All you bitches are the same," he raged. "All y'all wanna do is spend all my fuckin' money. I saw how you acted when we first met in the club. All up on that other baller', fuckin' lyin' that it was your cousin, fuckin' gold-diggin' bitch. Well if you wanna leave... fuck off." He hung up.

Oh no he never just spoke to me like that! I was livid! Carlita was frantic, pacing the room sobbing like she'd just found out her whole family had been murdered. Ignoring her, I bolted to my room and quickly scraped my things together. I needed to get the hell out of Dodge. Fast.

Chapter Thirteen

"So why did he invite me over if that was the way he really felt about me?" I was curled up on Camara's bed with wet eyes and a box of tissues trying to understand Money's motives. It was almost midnight.

"Well… apparently," she proceeded sensitively, "he told Danté that initially he did like you and that he enjoyed all the time you spent together, but he could see that you were only really interested in his bank account and it pissed him off."

"Hold on a minute. He was the one flashing the cash. I never begged him to." I was embarrassed that Money was talking about me like that to Danté, who I barely knew. Ok, so they were cousins and they were tight but that didn't lessen the blow. "Then why did he still encourage me to go to Miami to see him?" I asked, snivelling.

"He said you're hot and you were giving it up, so he took it. Sorry." I could see Camara genuinely felt bad for me.

"Bastard! He had me in that penthouse in Florida with his *girlfriend*! How humiliating? I didn't even see any of Miami. We weren't even anywhere *near* fucking South Beach in the end… holed up in that damn apartment!"

"He told Danté that she's not his girlfriend, just his on and off chick on the side. Nothing serious. Just a bit of skirt," she explained, trying to console me.

"Just a bit of skirt? His side chick? I don't think so. Camara, you didn't see her, the girl was stunning… and she went bananas when I told her that Money was cheating on her with me. She had a major meltdown, going on about how they've been together for years and trying for a baby. I had to counsel her for hours to calm her down, then sweet-talk her for ages to help me get a cab out of there before Money returned. I wasn't ready for a full on confrontation with those two psychos. At one point I could swear she was trying to slice her own wrist with the bread knife, weeping and wailing. Then I had to pay a hundred pound to get the airline to change my flight. The whole thing cost me a bomb."

"Well just thank God you got back safely," Camara said, sighing.

"I hate men," I fumed. "He insisted on lying to me that she was his personal assistant. Yet he had no problem admitting to Danté who she really was." *Jackass!*

"You know how men are. They're always gonna confide in each other and stick together. And once she'd turned up, it's not like there would have ever been an ideal time for Money to tell you the truth?"

"How about before he bought my plane ticket? Or maybe that first date, when he'd lied that he was single?"

"Obviously he wasn't expecting her to just show up like that."

"Whose side are you on? Why are you defending him?" I was frustrated with her growing lack of sympathy.

"I'm not. You asked me why he still invited you over and I'm just trying to see it from both sides," she reasoned.

"Whatever. Anyway that's it. I'm not going out with anyone else now. I'm staying single," I vowed, burying myself further into her pillows.

"Yeah right... and the sky's green." Camara laughed. "Please, you couldn't stay single if I paid you."

"Shut up," I griped, throwing a pillow at her.

"Look, you were too good for him anyway, it wasn't gonna work," she said, scooping the pillow up from off the floor. "You can do much better than that," she assured, comforting me. "And I did try and warn you. I told you that I'd heard he was a player before that first date. Either way, if a man's dumb enough to walk away from you, you need to be smart enough to let him go."

"But I really liked him. We had such a good time over here. We got on really well. Why did he have to do that?" I moaned, reaching for some fresh tissues. I knew I was repeating myself, going over the same ground, but I felt violated. "He could've handled the situation completely different. Considering *he* was the one who begged *me* to come, he could've told his *side chick* to jog on. He didn't have to deal with me like that."

Camara pondered over my question. "It's a difficult one. I mean, you've only known him for like, a month, so you don't really know him that well at all."

"But you've only known Danté for the same amount of time and look how close you two are."

"Yeah, but it's different with me and Danté."

"How do you mean?" I got on the defensive.

"Well, Danté's nothing like Money and we're taking it slow, still getting to know each other. No point rushing into anything, and, I love the way he makes me *feel,* like, really good about myself. Yes, we talk on the phone regular and see each other a couple of times a week, but I ain't trying to get intimate with him yet. It's about building a friendship first..."

"But it's not like I slept with Money on the first date!" I cut her off fuming.

"It's not like you waited until you knew him either…"

"And how can this happen to me twice in the space of two months?" I yelled, cutting her off again. "First New York and now Miami and I don't know which one was worse. The music producer who didn't even bother to show up to meet me at the airport or Money who shows up and then proceeds to diss me in the club dancing with some hoe and then have me over there practically kidnapped!"

"Calm down," Camara soothed. "You weren't kidnapped."

"Why is this happening to me?" I whined.

"Look Sahai, you gotta remember that people can only treat you how you let them. If you respect yourself, people will respect you, if you don't, they won't."

"Meaning?" I snapped.

"Well, you're not genuine. You never like men for who they are, you're only ever after what you can get out of them and you're not learning from your mistakes." Camara shifted on the bed. "With Money and the music producer and other guys you've checked, it's always the same pattern. You barely know them. You don't even really give a toss about them, you only like them 'cos they have money... and should you be flying around the world to see guys you barely know anyway?"

It was obviously a rhetorical question because Camara was on a roll.

"We all make mistakes in life, but the important thing is," she emphasized, "that as long as we learn from our mistakes and use the experience to help us grow, then things should only get better."

"He called me a gold-digger," I reflected, grimacing.

"And...?" Camara asked.

"Fucking cheek."

"Hold on a minute Sahai, not trying to be funny, but aren't you the one always preaching about only dating a guy who's loaded?"

"Well, yeah... but..."

"No buts, because this is the problem... can't you see it? You reap what you sow. The guy usually turns out to be a dickhead, a thug or a player. These guys ain't stupid. They can see right through you. Maybe if you were genuine, they'd treat you better, whether they have money or not," she scolded. "It shouldn't be all about the dosh, but that's all you seem to care about."

"So you're agreeing then, that I'm a gold-digger?"

"There's nothing wrong with wanting a man who is financially stable, someone who can take care of you, but you take it to a whole new level! You should be focused on taking care of yourself or even helping your man out financially if he ever needed support, but instead it's just all about what you can get," Camara nagged, getting on my nerves.

"If a man really wants to be with me then why should I have to keep paying my own way? Aren't men supposed to be the providers?" I was tired of going back and forth with her. "I've watched my mum struggle all her life, working three dead-end jobs, stressing herself out until she made herself ill trying to make ends meet, and I ain't going out like that. I want a man who can offer me more than just a good time, 'cos a good time don't pay the bills."

"And what are you offering him?" Camara asked bluntly. "It's about give and take. What are you bringing to the table?"

"Hello?" I rolled my eyes. "Look at me. It doesn't get much better than this."

"Yeah? And where did that get you with Money?" she asked.

"Um… when's the part where you start making me feel better?" I asked her. I'd heard of keeping it real, but Camara was taking the piss.

"I wouldn't be a true friend if I just said what you wanted to hear. All I'm trying to say Sahai is that you're in a good job making your own money. You shouldn't be constantly scheming on men. You should be happy you're independent and that you can support yourself."

"That's 'cos I have to. I would be happier if I didn't have to work at all," I grumbled. "I'd much rather be living in a mansion, driving hot whips, enjoying a ridiculous lifestyle full of spa breaks, shopping sprees and leisurely lunches, when I'm not busy travelling to exotic destinations," I said dreamily. "Who wouldn't want that? Who wants to be under the kind of stress I am, day in, day out, trying to come up with ideas for Bailey?"

Camara studied me shaking her head as she rose off the bed and walked across to the window. "I'm not trying to patronise you Sahai, you know you're my girl, but bwoy, you've got a lot of growing up to do. Relationships should be fifty-fifty. They're supposed to be a two-way street."

Two-Way Street? Hell nah, forget that, I cursed silently, as I made a mental note to try the footballer McKenzie's phone number again soon, as I knew he was definitely rolling in big bucks. Which Premier League player wasn't? *No point crying over spilt milk, I need to keep it moving,* I thought, as Camara's mobile started ringing.

Seconds later she was purring into the phone to Danté. I was glad for the intervention as I was sick of her judging me, even if she was only trying to help. Still feeling miserable, I reached for my phone to call Dijon. Maybe he could cheer me up? I also wanted to see if he was up for getting involved in my programme as we hadn't talked about it again, since Bailey had agreed to do it.

"You what?" Dijon was livid after I briefly explained why I wasn't still in Miami. "So when did you get back?" he yelled over the loud music in the background.

"Calm down. This evening." *Shit*. I shouldn't have told him about Money 'cos I knew he'd wanna get the next flight to Miami. He was so overprotective.

"Nah dread, I ain't calming down 'cos no one fucks with my family like that. What? So he thinks 'cos he's in the States, he's untouchable. Boy betta' know, I'll fucking silence him. For good," he threatened. "Man will lock off his lights! Trust me, anyhow I see dat yout' again, it's pure arms-house! I ain't ramping."

"Please Dijon... listen... let's just forget about it. That's not what I'm ringing you for." The last thing I needed was Dijon getting into any beef. "We need to get together to knock heads about my idea. Remember the one I was telling you about to do with men and music."

"You still on that?" He sounded distracted.

"Yep."

"Cuz, you just got fucked over by some wannabe baller, after flying over four thousand fucking miles to see him and you're ringing me on some jokes bizness? Nah bredrin, that's fuckry. The geezer needs to get dealt with. Immediately. I ain't interested in nu-un else right now rudeboy."

"Look, where are you?" I asked, as Camara plopped back down on the bed, edging me to move over a bit, so she could snuggle down into her pillow. The girl was practically snogging the phone.

"I'm in town at Candy Bar. I'm about to hit the decks. Got a sixty minute set. "

"Ok. I'll see you down there. I'm on my way."

"Later," he said and hung up. I hoped Dijon would have calmed down by the time I got to him. I didn't wanna think about Money or talk about him anymore tonight.

Grabbing my purse and car keys off the bed, I mouthed, "seeya later," to Camara who was still gushing and cooing into the phone, beaming.

The deep soulful house music was driving the crowd wild as I walked into Candy Bar. Listening to Dijon on the decks, smoothly mixing Disclosure's 'White Noise' into Skepta's, 'Too Many Man', I fought my way to the bar through the heaving mass of teenagers dancing as if they'd lost their minds.

I studied a few of the young men, wondering what kind of girls they liked. I hadn't really considered grime or soulful house music as an option for my show, but looking at the crazy atmosphere in Candy Bar as Kyla's hit, 'Do You Mind', lit up the dancefloor, I knew I'd find contestants who were into it.

"Can I have a Red Bull and a pineapple juice with lemonade please?" I asked the harassed looking bartender minutes later, whilst rocking to a tune I absolutely loved, 'Superman', by 'Black Coffee', before making my way through the pulsing crowd to the DJ booth.

Smiling down at me, Dijon reached for the Red Bull and took a quick swig as he continued taking us back in time, mixing Donaeo's club banger, 'Party Hard,' into Wiley's smasher, 'Wearing My Rolex'. The place was on fire, with teenagers marching, charging, and throwing themselves around.

As Dijon carried on playing a mixture of UK garage, grime, bassline, funky and soulful house, I sang along with the lyrics, wondering if maybe each week we should have a different music theme for my programme. Maybe hip hop one week, funky the next, reggae the week after and so on, I thought, impressed with the identical twins next to me cutting shapes. The sisters had the popular dance down to a T, as a little circle began to form around them admiring their technique.

The lively atmosphere was beginning to cheer me up after what I'd just gone through in Miami, so I found a little corner to bubble and got on a vibe as another one of my favourite tunes flooded the club. Dancing and singing along with the artist Egypt to 'In the Morning, Let Your Love Come in', I could feel some of the tension of the last few days releasing, whilst Dijon began winding down his set.

By the time he joined me, about twenty minutes later, I felt totally relaxed.

After greeting me, he tilted his head back to swig the remainder of his Red Bull. Stumbling, he immediately jerked forward, spluttering and choking, as drink flew out of his mouth. He spun around to see who'd pushed so hard into the back of him. A very pretty dark chocolate-coloured girl wearing barely anything, with black cherry lips, sleek hair extensions, blue contact lenses and a seductive glare, stared up at Dijon. Hands on curvaceous hips, her eyes were piercing as she broke into a sexy smile.

"I like the way you played," she said, nodding towards the DJ booth.

She couldn't have been any more than about fifteen years old, but she had the body of a fully grown woman.

Totally ignoring her remark, Dijon placed his can on the side, picked up his CD box, grabbed my hand and started leading me towards the exit.

"Jailbait," he cursed. "That's why I hate deejaying for kids," he complained, as we stepped outside of the club. "Trying to get man locked up an' shit," Dijon grumbled to himself.

"We can't leave yet. I need to talk to you. I didn't drive all the way here just to go back home without even discussing my idea." I smiled with puppy dog eyes.

"Nah dread, I ain't interested in that convo right now. Serious."

"Listen, I can't go back to work without a clear idea of what I'm doing. I need your help," I admitted.

It took about ten minutes, but thankfully I managed to finally persuade Dijon to go back inside. After ordering a few drinks, we found a comfy spot in the chill out zone, where we sat and talked for a good while.

Although I was still pissed off and jet-lagged, I was glad I'd gone to see him 'cos he had a way of always making me feel better. Once he'd got over his initial rage about what Money had done to me, we spent most of the time joking and laughing.

On our way back to the car, we bought some fish and chips and spent about another hour just chillin' and chatting shit. By the end of the night I'd stopped thinking about Money altogether and was looking forward to going back to work in a few days and getting my show on the road, literally.

Chapter Fourteen

"So you want to go out and start road testing it today?" Bailey asked, as I scooped up my paperwork from his desk.

"Yup. I'm ready."

"As I said before, take Kimar with you. He's got his finger on the pulse. Knows what going on out there."

"So what do you reckon? Are we just going from the angle of what music men are listening to, or women as well?" I wanted to know.

"Let's start with men for now and then we'll look at whether we want to expand it to women in Series Two."

"Series Two?" I beamed. It was good to know that Bailey was seeing a future for this project.

"Let's just see how this recce goes first shall we, and then we'll know what we're working with for sure," Bailey said, still clearly not a hundred percent sold on the idea or convinced it would work, but I was and couldn't wait to hit the streets. "And Sahai," he added, "no riff raff. I want decent people," he warned.

"Cool."

I left the office and located Kimar who was busy at his desk bopping to a low hip hop beat coming from his computer, whilst posting pictures on Instagram.

"Ready?" I grinned.

"I'm on it," he said, logging off right there and then. He'd loved the idea of S*ex Me Down* from the minute he'd heard the details, especially as his R&B Supastar idea hadn't taken off. In the end Bailey had decided searching for the next hot singer had already been done to death.

"Ok, fifteen minutes then and we're out." I breezed back to my desk as he reached for his camera kit to start assembling equipment and packing everything together. I noticed a few missed calls on my mobile, only to realise it was Money. Again! He'd been blowing up my phone since I got back from Miami, but I'd ignored every call. Can't believe he had the audacity to think I'd even wanna talk to him. *Dickhead!* Grabbing my stuff, I left the office with Kimar.

The first place we headed was New Street in the city centre, right outside McDonald's on the ramp. It was always busy at lunchtime, so a prime spot. No more than two seconds later, a tall, handsome young guy came swaggering towards us from the Pallasades Shopping Centre, carrying a Foot Locker bag and swigging from a can of Red Bull. His Dre Beats headphones accessorised his outfit as he nodded slightly to the music.

"Excuse me please?" I approached him.

He gave me a quick once-over, smiled and removed his headphones. *Great start. A flirt, just like myself. This was gonna be easy.*

"Sorry to bother you. Have you got a minute?" I asked.

"Bwoy, for you I'm sure I can offer more than a minute," he grinned, trying to sneak a peek at my butt.

I extended my hand. "Hi, I'm Sahai Martini and I work for Bling & Ting, the entertainment channel. This is my cameraman Kimar and we're putting together a music programme. I was wondering if I could ask you a couple of questions. What's your name?"

"I'm Javon." He shook my hand.

"Nice name. Do you mind if we film this? We won't be showing it to anyone, it's just for research," I explained, as Kimar raised his video camera.

"Yeah... you can film it," Javon said, nodding. *Damn. Easier than I thought.*

"Thanks," I replied, as Kimar gave me the signal that he'd pressed record. "Can I ask you what music you're listening to at the moment?"

"What I'm listening to?" Javon was puzzled.

"Yeah. It's for a new programme idea. We're trying to find out what people are listening to?"

"Ok... um... I'm listening to Drake," he said, glancing down at his phone.

"Drake... he's hot right now." I smiled. "Which song?"

"Started From The Bottom."

"Good taste. I like that song. Any reason why that particular track?" I prodded.

"Um... 'cos maybe I like it too?" Javon said, looking at me like I was crazy, then glancing into the camera.

"Sorry," I explained, trying to relax him. "It's just a routine question."

"Nah it's cool." He smiled. "So is that it now? Can I go?"

"Well... I was wondering if you'd be interested in maybe taking part in a reality show?"

"Reality Show?" He frowned. "Like Big Brother?"

"Well kinda, but sort of a bit different."

"Are *you* gonna be in it?" He grinned, trying to take another look at my ass. He *was* sexy. A bit young for me though.

"Nah, I'm producing it, but there *will* be a lot of hot girls in it. Are you single?"

"I can be," he said, winking. "What would I have to do?"

"Um... just listen to music and chat to girls."

"Sounds like my kinda programme still," he admitted, laughing. "I got skills... done a lil' acting, people know me on road innit," he said, bigging himself up.

"Nice nice," I encouraged him. "Well my colleague here can take your details then we'll get back in touch with you when we have more info." I signalled Kimar to stop filming.

"Yeah, that can work," Javon said, as Kimar dug into his rucksack, replaced the camera with an iPad and started entering Javon's details, as I moved on to the next potential contributor.

Three hours later and back at work we'd secured about twenty phone numbers of people who said they'd be interested in taking part in

Sex Me Down. Granted, they didn't really know what the hell the programme was about, but who cared? I was elated.

"I'm trying to work out whether it would be better for us to do it live or pre-recorded," I reasoned with Bailey. "'Cos the minute we asked them what they were listening to was definitely a Kodak moment. Pure gold! Captured on tape. We had so many different reactions. Look." I hit the play button and Bailey laughed as he watched person after person display a range of emotions from amused to confused, surprised to bewildered and excited to baffled. "This is the beauty of it. The idea is so original. People can't work out if we're crazy or serious," I said, noting down some points on a pad.

"True," said Bailey, stroking his goatee. "Although with the format, I'm not sure it really matters whether it is pre-recorded or live. We could actually use some of this footage once we get them all to sign release forms. Either way, I think we're ready to go into production. Sahai, I'm gonna leave it to you to select twelve contestants to start with. Let's keep it simple. Six girls and six guys. Lock down the best six of those guys and you can hit the streets again to secure the girls. I think we're all agreed that a good location for the filming is a nightclub or a wine bar, so Kimar, speak to the owners of Sugar Suite, Mirrors, Myyst and Candy Bar."

"Yep, I'll do that," Kimar said, ejecting the tape from the machine.

"And we need to brainstorm a new title," Bailey added. "We'll be a laughing stock with *Sex Me Down*."

"I was thinking about that when we were out filming earlier," Kimar piped up. "How about... *If music be the food of love...*"

"Nah, too Shakespearean... too common... we can go stronger than that," Bailey insisted, immediately rejecting Kimar's idea, although I quite liked it.

"What about something like *Time to Face the Music...*?" I suggested.

"Bore off Sahai." Kimar yawned. "That sounds like a game-show my Nan used to watch."

I laughed along with him. It did sound a bit dated. "Well what other ideas have you got then?" I asked.

"I think we need something current like S*weet Wicked Symphony* or S*weet Dark Serenade,* a title that draws you in," Kimar offered.

"You're right," Bailey concurred. "But not one that implies a sinister outcome."

"Alright then, how about *Lyrics, Love & Lust* or *Sweet Music, Crazy Love*?" I ventured, trying to think of something contemporary.

"Now you're talking about yourself," Bailey said chuckling. "And it's still too dark. Listen, we've got plenty of time to come up with a title. I just want you to at least be thinking about it. Right, let's meet again next week, see where we are with it all. Can you ask Marcus and Monique to come in here in about ten minutes," Bailey requested, picking up his phone to make a call, signalling the end of our meeting.

Later that evening I felt great. I'd selected six men from our filming earlier, contacted each one and they'd all agreed to take part. I knew I was working with gold dust. In good spirits, I poured myself a glass of the Prosecco I'd picked up from Tesco Express on my way home, relaxed in the sofa and decided to try ringing the footballer again. I was pleasantly surprised when McKenzie answered on the second ring.

"Hello," I purred, seductive and cool.

"Who's this?" He sounded busy.

"It's Sahai. We met briefly a few weeks ago at Bel Air."

"Bel Air?" he murmured, as though trying to recall. "Sorry, you'll have to jog my memory. It's been a busy few weeks."

"We spoke at the bar. You bought me a drink," I said.

"Oh yeah, I remember… the blonde with the sexy blue eyes and the hot pink dress."

"You're mixing me up with someone else," I quickly corrected. "I'm talking about Bel Air Nightclub, about a month ago?"

"Oh," he said. "It's coming back to me now. I recognise your voice. The solicitor. Cute smile, leggy, you'd just won that big case?"

Exactly how many girls had he bought a drink that night? Or was he getting confused with another night? Insulted, I almost hung up the phone, as lyrics from the Miguel song that I used to love playing in my car every day, until I'd had to endure the humiliation of watching Money dance to it with that girl in Miami, flooded my head. On the track, Miguel blatantly asks how many drinks it would take for a girl to leave with him.

"Actually," I said coolly, "I was wearing a white dress and my hair is long, black and wavy."

"Okaaayy." He started laughing. "I remember you now. Petite, pretty brown skin, cat's eyes. How could I forget you after the way you danced for me? I mean, damn... I'm still thinking about that now."

Clearly not, as he couldn't even recall me.

"So how you doing?" I asked, determined to try and stay positive, as I remembered the next bit of Miguel's song, about him having money, but not wanting to waste his time.

"I'm good thanks. Just busy training and stuff," McKenzie said. "How about you?"

"Fine thanks, the same, busy working and stuff."

"My offer still stands you know, to take you out for a meal. When can you fit me into your busy schedule?" he asked, flirting.

"Shouldn't I be asking you that question?" I shot back. "I'm in Manchester at the moment," he told me. "But I should be back in Birmingham by next weekend, so what are you up to?"

"No plans as yet," I admitted. "Friday evening would be good," I specified, a bit too quickly for my own liking, sounding desperate. *Great!*

"Friday it is then. We can grab something to eat somewhere quiet," he suggested.

"Yeah, that would be nice."

"Ok. Gimme' your phone number and I'll give you a shout nearer the time."

I fired off my digits and then hung up, instantly dialling Camara.

"OMG! I've got a date with the footballer!" I screamed into the phone.

"When?" she screamed back, matching my excitement.

"Next week Friday. Oh My God. I just spoke to him. What am I gonna wear? I need to find something sexy for my future baby daddy. We need to go shopping."

"Please, I hate that expression. Future baby daddy? How about future husband?"

"Camara… can I just have this moment?"

"Alright. Yes. I can go shopping with you. Just let me know when you're ready."

"Cool." I hung up and dialled Dijon.

"'Sup?" he answered casually.

"I need to know everything you know about football," I yelled. "Managers? Players? The Premier League? All of it. Right now."

"What are you talking about cuz? You know I only deal with my team," he snapped.

"Listen. The main point is you know more about football than me and I need you."

"Why, what's so important?"

"I got a date with a footballer," I shouted.

"Who? Better not be one of dem mans on some *eedyiat* ting. Hotel 'three in a bed' and all dese tings!" He kissed his teeth.

"Dijon." I rolled my eyes as though he could see me. "You can give me a bit more credit than that. It's McKenzie Jackson."

"You ain't going."

"You what?"

"Sahai, he's a wasteman. Trust me. You're talking about that geezer who used to play for Links United right?"

"The same one," I said gushing.

"Cuz, are you for real? He's on some different shit. I've heard some mad stories about him," he warned me.

"Stop hating Dijon. I'm gonna call you back later. Make sure you got the info," I said, briskly hanging up before he could say another word. I grabbed my laptop and logged on to ASOS, to see if I could get some ideas of the hottest new styles for inspiration on my shopping trip.

Chapter Fifteen

Friday night couldn't come quick enough. The past week had flown by in a blur. McKenzie had suggested I meet him at the canalside, by a popular stretch of upscale restaurants, designer shops, businesses and luxury apartments, known as The Mailbox. It felt a bit weird meeting him at the side of a canal, but he'd insisted, so who was I to argue with a man who earns £100,000 a week? He was now fifteen minutes late though and I was beginning to feel a little anxious. The only thing that kept me calm was the knowledge that if I played my cards right, I could soon or at least someday be a *footballer's* wife! A millionaire!

Just as I was about to glance at my watch for like the twentieth time, I saw him walking towards me, flanked by two of his beefy bodyguards. Oh my God, the man was fine! That smooth ebony complexion, goatee, rippling muscles. He was wearing jeans and a nice shirt. I could see diamonds glistening in one ear and on his wrist.

I was in love.

For the first time I was truly thankful for all the designer gear Money had bought me on our shopping sprees 'cos at least it made me *look* rich, although I didn't have a pot to piss in.

"Looking hot Beyoncé!" McKenzie joked, as he approached me.

Seems like maybe that dance really had done the trick, etching me into his mind permanently.

"Hey," I responded sweetly, as he leaned down and gave me a kiss on the cheek, before having a quiet word with his bodyguards who nodded and backed off a little.

"May I?" He was a true gentleman as he took my arm, escorting me to a small canal boat docked a few feet away. Leading me onto the deck, we descended the stairs into a restaurant. I was impressed with the plush 16th Century Elizabethan style décor. Swathes of crimson and gold, velvet and silk drapery hung in soft folds over elaborate tables, revealing beautiful, ornate carvings on burnished bronze legs. Huge murals of colourful ancient battles depicting swashbucklers brandishing swords and shields, covered the walls.

"McKenzie!" exclaimed a short round middle-aged man, dressed in flamboyant medieval finery. Resembling a cartoon caricature he flounced over in his white tunic with a high frilly neck and big loose ruffled sleeves. His flowing black velvet robe and floppy black and gold hat, toppled from side to side, as he greeted McKenzie jovially like old friends.

"How's things?" McKenzie accepted his vigorous handshake. "This is Sahai."

"Beautiful name for a beautiful lady," the man applauded, taking my hand and kissing it. Soft old English Elizabethan music floating around added to the ambience, as McKenzie spoke cordially with the man, then placed his hand at the small of my back, leading me past the few tables occupied by couples to a cosy little window table. I felt like I was being taken back into Tudor England. I almost expected King Henry VIII to make a brief appearance.

"This is... different... nice," I commented, peering out of the window into the shimmering canal. The reflection of the neon lights from the surrounding bars, in hues of red, yellow, blue and green, danced across the still water.

"Yeah, it's a perfect spot I discovered years ago, for when I feel like some quality food and drink, but don't wanna get harassed by fans. I can always have a nice time here in peace. The owner, as you just saw, is cool. He takes good care of me."

"Are we... moving?" I said dumbly, as I could feel a slight motion.

"Yeah. It's a three hour cruise. You'll get to see Birmingham by night from a fresh angle."

"Wow." I quickly shut up, trying not to sound too ignorant or too impressed. I wanted him to see me as a good catch, educated, cultured and talented, with something to offer. It wasn't all about him. *Or was it?* I thought, captivated by his good looks.

"It's nice to see you again," I admitted, mesmerised by his gorgeous, deep brown eyes.

"You too." He ordered our drinks, followed by an awkward silence as we sipped them, with me trying to think of something interesting to ask about football, but failing miserably. I was stuck for words. I couldn't remember a damn thing Dijon had told me. McKenzie was that fine.

"It's hard to believe you're single," he finally said, breaking the ice. "I mean, you're beautiful, talented and you've got a bangin' body. Most men must find you irresistible."

"Thank you." I blushed. "I get a lot of attention from guys, but I guess I just haven't met the right one yet," I confessed, sipping more of my delicious strawberry daiquiri.

"You know why that is, don't you?" McKenzie said, as he leaned forward taking my hand in his, staring deeply into my eyes.

"No. Why?"

"Because women are like apples on trees. The best ones are at the top of the tree. Most men don't want to reach for the good ones because they're afraid of falling and getting hurt. Instead, they sometimes take the apples from the ground that aren't as golden, but easy. The apples at the top think something is wrong with them, when in reality they're amazing. They just have to wait for the right man to come along, the one who is brave enough to climb all the way to the top of the tree."

"Wow." What more could I say? He was definitely a smooth talker. Wasn't sure what was intoxicating me more. His words, his presence, the alcohol or the intimate setting?

"Happy Birthday McKenzie!!" A bubbly blonde waitress, dressed in full black and white Elizabethan regalia, appeared at our table with two more huge cocktails. "For you, on the house," she gushed, placing the drinks in front of us. "I'll be back to take your orders in a sec," she sang, before skipping off.

"Your birthday? Today?" I was surprised, chuffed, flattered that he'd chosen to spend it with me. "Why didn't you tell me? I would have bought you a gift or something."

"That's ok. I'm not into making a big fuss on my birthday. Just quite happy to do something low-key, something special with someone special."

He was pouring it on real thick and I was loving every second of it. I couldn't help it.

"Maybe you'd like to give me a birthday treat, a little later on," he suggested, winking, as the waitress appeared again to take our orders.

Shit. He wants me to go back to his place. I didn't think I'd be able to turn down his offer if he mentioned it again. Yes, I know I'm not into sleeping with guys on the first date. It's not cool, but maybe I could bend the rules a little in this case. I mean, after all he *was* McKenzie Jackson and it *was* his birthday and he could be with any girl tonight but he chose to be with me, so God forbid I come across as *boring!!*

"Ladies first," he insisted, nodding towards the menu in my hands, breaking my silent reverie.

We both went for the sirloin steak dinner and enjoyed three hours of candle-lit cruising, interesting conversation and a lot of laughter. Turned out we had a lot in common, the same musical tastes, similar family backgrounds and we were both an only child, raised by a single mother, which we thought was rare as most of our friends had numerous brothers and sisters. Discovered both our mums had been so bitter about men, they'd never got with another guy, so we'd watched them suffer emotionally and struggle financially.

I told him about how my mum had finally given up on England and migrated back to Jamaica, after sickness had forced her to take early retirement a few years ago. She no longer wanted to stay here, especially as my Aunt Sylvia had packed up and moved back to London, after Dijon had left home and got his own place. McKenzie's story had ended differently. He was happy that he'd been successful enough to buy his mum an eight-bedroom mansion in the suburbs and that his mum had finally found a man who loved her and treated her like a queen.

An eight-bedroom mansion! Damn! I could see myself living like that.

I visualised him presenting a magnificent glass beach house to me in L.A., wrapped in a huge red silk bow, glistening in the sunshine, surrounded by miles of sparkling blue ocean.

"You ok beautiful?" he asked, as he'd noticed me drifting off daydreaming.

Am I ok? Am I ok? I've fucking died and gone to heaven!

"Yes, I'm having a lovely time thanks." I even managed to remember a few things about football once I'd relaxed more in his company. "Must feel good playing for a team who've had some of the best footballers of all time," I casually remarked, stroking his ego. He peered at me. *Was that a new level of interest I just saw on his face?* I continued to share all the knowledge Dijon had blessed me with a few hours earlier, until I ran out of facts.

"I didn't realise you were such a fan," he said, warming to me, impressed.

"I love football. I've been a supporter since I was little," I lied.

"Not just a pretty face then," he observed. "Feels good being able to talk football with a girl," he admitted. "We'll have to do this more often."

I could hardly contain my excitement, as we continued to share goals, dreams and aspirations for a while longer and it was with ease that he got the bill and paid for everything, without letting me put my hand in my purse. By the time the boat docked, I was feeling merry, light-headed and up for pretty much anything.

As we disembarked the boat, his two burly bouncers appeared from seemingly nowhere, flanking us again. The three of them engaged in a small exchange whilst I stood back, demure. They waited patiently as he approached me again.

"I've got a hotel booked tonight. It's literally two minutes away. Would you like to join me at the bar for a drink before we call it a night?" he offered.

Hell yeah! Right now I'd join him anywhere. "Well, it's a little late, so I should be heading home," I declined. Really didn't wanna come across as easy.

He glanced at his blinging watch, blinding me with diamonds. "It's not even midnight yet Cinderella," he protested.

"I know but I've got work in the morning."

"On a Saturday?" he asked, frowning. *Shit! I was tipsier than I realised.*

"Oh yeah. It is Saturday tomorrow," I weakly offered. Well, fast forward and you guessed right. He had me tangled up in some luxury, thousand thread-count Egyptian cotton sheets, in his hotel bed in some Presidential Suite, losing my mind.

I clutched the headboard as 6ft 4 of smooth, dark, chocolate, took me to a place I'd definitely never been before.

"Oh yeah, that's the spot," I purred, arching my back.

Eyeing his rippling biceps, I smiled as my eyes travelled further down. The man was like a damn sculpture! Glistening with sweat, his ebony six pack was toned to perfection and the way he was moving? Those thighs. Nothing beat footballer's legs. I felt weak as my eyes travelled back up to his face. Mesmerised, I just stared, stunned. How could God make one man so beautiful? Full, soft lips, chiselled cheekbones, dark twinkling eyes, framed by long silky lashes, sparkling white teeth. Not one flaw.

I screamed. I mean, I wasn't trying to scream, but between the way he was moving and the music, hot, throbbing beats, coming at me from all angles through the surround sound speakers and the moon, shining through the slit of the curtains illuminating him like some kind of Black Panther, I just couldn't contain myself.

Chuckling, he stared deep into my eyes, before leaning in for an intense, passionate kiss. All the time he didn't even break his stroke. I was in heaven, hell, somewhere. I matched his rhythm and did my thing! Well, that thing I saw someone do in one of those X-rated movies. Just a little move I'd picked up. It seemed to be working by the sheer ecstasy on McKenzie's face, every time I opened my eyes long enough to glance at him.

"Oh God," he moaned.

Hell nah, I don't think so. What could have possibly made him think that I'd ever want this moment to end? I fully relaxed my body and slid from underneath him, deciding it was time for his special birthday treat.

"What the?" He rolled on to his back laughing, excitement and anticipation all over his face, as I snaked my arm down the side of the bed and retrieved a couple of ice cubes from the champagne bucket he'd ordered up. Well, I'd also seen this in that movie and hell, now was as good a time as any to try it.

"Happy Birthday, birthday boy" I purred, dripping the icy water on to his chest as he squirmed and flinched, whilst it trickled slowly across his body. I'd heard that what I was about to do next was the ultimate in pleasure.

Chapter Sixteen

"So where the hell is he?" I asked Camara, as we left our Zumba class that evening.

It had been two weeks now since my date with McKenzie and I hadn't heard from him. We'd had no contact at all. I'd called him several times, but he kept ignoring my calls, sending them straight to voicemail. He hadn't responded to any of my text messages either. I was a bit upset as we'd had such a good time that night. I knew I'd blown him away in the bedroom. He couldn't stop raving about it afterwards, calling me a freak.

"He's probably just busy, working. I mean, after all he is a Premier League footballer, so his schedule must be crazy," Camara said, leaning against a wall in the car park to stretch her legs.

"He had no problems calling me to set up the date, so what's changed?"

"I don't know. Could be anything. I mean, did something happen to indicate that he might not wanna see you again?" she asked, stretching the other leg.

"No. He said he really enjoyed himself."

"Well look, it's only been two weeks. Give it a bit more time," she suggested, stretching her arms high above her head.

"Um, do you really need to be doing all that?" I was getting annoyed watching her. "Zumba finished like thirty minutes ago."

"Yeah but them salsa and reggae moves were crazy. My girl was going *in*," Camara emphasized, as she completed her cool down routine with a little hip wiggle. What that was I don't know, but she look like she'd finished. She was in a bright, breezy mood this evening 'cos earlier Danté had invited her to meet his parents for the first time this weekend coming. I was happy for her as it was clear their relationship was getting serious. She was pretty nervous about meeting his mum, especially as it was still early days, but he'd told Camara she was the only woman he'd even liked enough to take home in years, and reassured her his mum was gonna love her, so Camara was floating on cloud nine and full of positive energy.

"Stop worrying," she said, smiling at me. "I'm sure he'll call you."

"Yeah, you're probably right," I replied glumly. "I just got a feeling he won't though."

"I told you he was a wasteman, on some *eedyiat* ting," was Dijon's response when we joined him half an hour later at Nando's, which kinda defeated the object of going to Zumba in the first place, although Camara insisted it was alright if we just stuck to grilled chicken salad. "Forget about him cuz. 'Low it," Dijon added, as he tore into a chicken wing. "Bun' dat."

"Easier said than done," I grumbled, gutted at the thought of my rags to riches, diamonds and pearls lifestyle slipping away. I'd given it my all that night. Really tried to make an impression on him.

"Sahai. The geezer's a Premier League footballer," Dijon said. "You know dem man chirps bare gyal. Man an' man must have bare peng tings, and you know footballers like dating celebrities. No disrespect cuz, I know you're doing your thing, but you ain't got it like that."

"Thanks Dijon. You're making me feel a whole lot better," I snarled.

"Just keeping it real," he said belching. "It is what it is."

"But what if something's happened to him?" As soon as the words left my mouth I immediately regretted it as Dijon glanced at me like I was from another planet.

"Cuz," Dijon said smirking. "Are you nuts? When a man disappears on you, I can guarantee you he ain't lying in the gutter somewhere calling out *your* name. Trust."

"Look, he obviously likes you," Camara intervened, trying to comfort me as she noticed my mood sinking further, as Dijon's words hit hard, "or he wouldn't have gone out with you on a date in the first place. As long as you didn't sleep with him, which I know you didn't," Camara said, glaring at me, "then it's all good. Obviously if you'd slept with him on the first date, then as you already know, he probably wouldn't have any respect for you, plus there would be nothing more for him to look forward to as you gave it all up on the first night, but as you didn't do that, if he doesn't call, it's his problem, his loss."

A lump formed in my throat as I listened to Camara's words. I'd managed to keep that bit of information from both of them.

"That's bullshit," Dijon counteracted, chuckling. "If a man likes you, it doesn't matter whether you give it up on the first date or the tenth date, it's all the same. Trust me, if a man wants you, nothing can keep him away. If he's not genuine and he's gonna leave you, he's gonna leave anyway."

"I disagree," Camara objected. "If you give it up so easy, he's gonna think that you're like that with every guy, so nothing about you will be special to him. You won't be a challenge and we know how you guys like a challenge and he won't appreciate you because he didn't have to work for you or earn you. With you men, it's all about the chase."

"That's some ancient shit Mara," Dijon said laughing, using the nickname he'd given her. "It's 2014. The game's changed now baby. I expect a girl to give it up ASAP. I ain't got time to be wining and dining her for how many damn weeks before I can even get a piece of the goodness. A girl needs to bring her A game to my table immediately." He slapped the table for dramatic effect and we all laughed.

"Anyway, I need to be getting home," I said, using this as a perfect opportunity to get away before the spotlight came back to me.

"Why you going so soon? It's still early," Camara complained, glancing at her watch.

"I know, but it's my big filming day tomorrow remember?"

We'd now secured all our female contestants for *Sex Me Down*, by taking our male contestants to the streets. Strategically positioning each guy in a different part of the shopping centre, we'd approached random girls and asked if they could guess, from a distance, what music the guy was listening to on his iPod or phone. We took all the girls contact details but didn't let them know whether or not they'd guessed right. We just let them know that all would be revealed if they were successful in making it on to the show. Their answers weren't shared with the guys either. The information was kept strictly confidential. Everyone would find out in due course.

"You still got the shooting schedule for tomorrow right?" I asked Dijon. I'd managed to persuade him to speak to the owners at Candy Bar. As he was one of their resident DJs, he was able to negotiate a dirt-cheap price for us to use the venue as our filming location. He'd also agreed to DJ for us at the shoot.

He pulled the rumpled, stained script out of his back pocket. I snatched it off him and smoothed it out.

"Dijon, you can look after this a bit better. This is my masterpiece," I grumbled.

"Nah love… when you've made enough money for me to retire and I'm kickin' it on a beach in the Caribbean," he commented, taking the script out of my hands, crumpling it up and putting it back into his pocket, "then it's a masterpiece," he explained, as we all laughed.

I loved that vision, being in the tropics, relaxing. *There had to be a way for me to lock down a wealthy man through this programme,* I thought. That would have to be my main focus, if there was a second series. *Hell if I was gonna break my own back to live decent?*

The next morning I summoned Kimar first thing and the two of us pored over our files, going through the contestant's details.

"Right, break down who we got again," I said, so I could start picturing it in my mind. I closed my eyes.

"Ok. First up we got Reuben Thomas, 24, from Jamaica. He's been living in the UK for ten years and says he hates being referred to as a yardie. He loves bashment, works in a call centre and has no preference in girls as long as she's got a big booty, it says right here." Kimar laughed, pointing at his notes.

"What's his problem with being called a yardie?" I asked.

"He says 'yardie' is a negative label and he's not feeling it," Kimar elaborated. "He claims it's a derogatory term the police came up with, to identify criminals from Jamaica."

"That's not true." I'd been to Jamaica, spent time in Kingston. "The word comes from Jamaicans born and raised in tenement yards in Trenchtown, from back in the day. *They* called themselves yardies," I corrected him.

"Maybe so, but he says because people over here associate it with a negative stereotype of all Jamaicans who move to the UK, the meaning has changed. He insists that as he's neither a gangsta', gunman, hustler or drug dealer, he refuses to be identified that way. He'd rather just be called Jamaican."

"Ok. I hear that. Who we got next?" I was already building a mental picture of which girl Reuben would match with from our selection. Be interesting to see if I was right.

"Josiah Andrews. 26. Loves soulful house, works as a computer programmer. Wants an MTV Base girl, hot, sexy, a party girl who likes to have fun."

"Doesn't every man?" I laughed. "Next."

"Omar Ashere. Thinks he's the next Usher or Chris Brown, loves R&B, trying to make it as a singer, 25, unemployed, Then there's Javon Baker, remember the first guy we met, loves hip hop, fancied you, 27, sales assistant in a clothes shop, whilst doing his masters in Criminology."

"That's impressive," I smiled. "We should do a programme with him about criminology."

"Then there's Tyree Lewis, 28, got a thing for jazz music, works as a legal assistant, is looking for his queen, his soul mate and finally Kieran Andrews, 25, works as an accountant, real smooth on that neo-soul tip, said he wants a natural girl, someone who is not materialistic but who's in touch with her spiritual side."

"Ok," I assessed. "So to sum it up we have a lively mix of mainly professional guys all in their twenties. Remind me of the girls again?" I said, examining my notes.

"The girls are Tia, Dionne, Misha, Tasha, Cherelle and Jasmine."

"Lovely." I checked the names against my notes. "So our twelve contestants are Reuben and Tia, who love reggae, Omar and Cherelle, who like R&B, Josiah and Tasha, who are into soulful funky house, Javon and Dionne, hip hop lovers, Tyree and Jasmine, crazy about jazz and Kieran and Misha who are into neo-soul. Is that right?" I asked.

"Correct," Kimar clarified.

I smiled. I could see it all clearly in my head. Couldn't wait to prove my theory right.

"Trust me, this programme is gonna smash it! Totally change the game. We're ready to finally put Bling & Ting on the map for once and for all," I predicted.

"For real," Kimar agreed.

"Come on then, let's go," I said, glancing at my watch. "The others should already be there by now and the contestants are scheduled to arrive within the next half an hour."

"Cool," Kimar said, hopping up, gathering the paperwork together. "Any decisions yet on the titles that we brainstormed?" he wanted to know.

We'd come up with a shortlist of about six possible names for *Sex Me Down* and ran them by Bailey about a week ago.

"Yeah, didn't I tell you? Bailey got back to me a couple of days ago."

"Nah, you joker. What is it then? Which one we going with?"

"*The Sweetest Sound*." I smiled.

"*The Sweetest Sound*," Kimar repeated slowly. "I like that. Got a nice ring to it. Catchy."

Chapter Seventeen

"So, this is how it's gonna work," I began, an hour later as all the contestants gathered around me in Candy Bar. "For the next fifteen minutes, I'd like you to all lightly mingle and get acquainted with one another, share some of your hobbies, interests, dreams, passions. Please try and make sure you work the room and talk to everyone. I know there are quite a few of you, but if you all stick to the script and keep it moving, there should be enough time. We're gonna be walking around you filming, but please, try and ignore the cameras. Once you've all met, for the following thirty minutes, our lovely DJ, Dijon," I said, indicating towards my cousin, who was busy doing a sound check with his friend Kelloggs, who he'd insisted on bringing along, "will be on the decks, playing."

"My man's dope! Trust me," Kelloggs interjected, before I glared at him, reminding him this was my show.

"As I was saying," I continued, "he'll be switching the tempo on a regular basis, so we get to hear a range of music. Got that?" Everyone nodded. "The important thing is," I said, "to keep dancing and partying to all the music, even if it's not your particular taste, as we are trying to keep the vibe lively and upbeat. I know it may not feel like the most natural thing to do, but believe me, when you see how we edit it together, it will all make sense. Then after the partying we'll separate you into two groups and then I'll tell you what happens from there."

Everyone nodded again. "We know this is the first time you have all been in one room together, so the first time you are meeting each other properly," I went on. "Do any of you already know each other?"

The contestants looked around the room. After a few seconds they all shook their heads with a no.

"Ok. Good. Please remember the rules of this show are that under no circumstances are any of you to discuss music in general or your personal music tastes with another contestant. If you do, you will be instantly disqualified. Whilst mingling, you can talk about anything else, but if you talk music, game over. Is everyone absolutely clear?" I checked.

"Yes," they said in unison.

"The other rule is that when the music starts, you cannot stick to one dancing partner. You must move around the room and dance with each other, throughout the thirty minutes. Please don't just dance to the songs you like. Equal effort needs to be put into each song. Understood?" I asked.

"Yes," they all agreed.

"Thank you," I said. "Right, looks like we're ready to get started. If you could all move across to the bar where there will be a soft drink waiting for you, as soon as you've helped yourself to one, please start mingling and remember we are recording everything. As I said before, anyone who breaks the rules will be instantly disqualified," I warned, as I reached over to my bag behind the bar for my compact mirror, to double-check my hair and make-up. I was ready to go into presenting mode.

From the corner of my eye, I could see that my small team were on the ball and I was loving it. Bling & Ting were out in full effect. It was a great feeling. It had been a while since we all worked together like this on a shoot. Marcus and Kimar had their cameras rolling and ready to go. Darren was manning a locked off camera in the corner to get a wide shot of the whole room and all the action, whilst Monique was by the bar making sure everyone had a drink in their hand and knew what they were supposed to be doing.

As Marcus pointed the camera at me, I smiled professionally and started walking slowly towards him.

"We all know there's someone out there for everyone," I began. "Single men and women around the globe are on a continuous search for Mr or Mrs Right," I proclaimed, peering down the lens. "We've seen a rise in internet dating and Facebook love; it seems people are trying everything and anything to meet their ideal mate."

Was that Kelloggs I could see from the corner of my eye, trying to position himself alongside me? I ignored him and carried on. "Well today, we are going to look at one element of attraction that has never been explored," I explained. "Our journey has brought us to the heart of England, Birmingham, to the plush surroundings of Candy Bar where these single, young, hot, twenty-somethings may *look* like regular professionals, enjoying a quiet drink after work, but like many of you at home, they all have *one* thing in common." I paused, surveying the contestants. "They are *crazy* about music! And whether they realise it or not, the music they love is dictating their lives!" I assured. "Do you believe the music they love can influence who they choose as their potential soul mate? Their ideal partner?" I threw it out there. "Does it matter? Keep watching and let's find out," I invited.

Marcus swung the camera away from me and it landed squarely on Kelloggs, who beamed into the lens, then on Reuben, who was engaged in a very strained conversation with Tasha. Marcus went in for a close up as I hovered in the background, eavesdropping.

"Well, I don't see a problem with it," said Tasha, whilst tugging at a strand of her hair.

"Are you for real?" Reuben asked. "You've never been to a carnival? You're not interested? But you're from Trinidad. You guys *started* carnival! Bwoy, if you don't know about carnival, you're kinda... lost," he said, glancing around the room as though looking for someone else to talk to.

"That's a bit of a sweeping statement," Tasha protested. "And anyway, what do you know about it? You're a yardie."

Oh no she didn't go there. Things were about to kick off. I chuckled, as I signalled for Kimar to come across and finish capturing this golden moment on tape, as I noticed Marcus now had his camera pointing elsewhere.

Moving on swiftly, we bypassed Kelloggs who was happily bopping around, looking like he was desperately trying to be on camera again. *Wasn't he supposed to be helping with the music?* I thought, as we approached Javon who was in a very animated conversation with Dionne. They looked like they were thoroughly enjoying each other.

"Quick, over here." I beckoned Marcus to follow me as I spotted Omar nestled in a corner with Jasmine who looked very uncomfortable. Kelloggs was now floating around *them*.

As we neared Omar, he seemed to warm to the camera. His voice went up a few octaves as he talked about his desire to be a mega star and how the world wasn't ready yet for a singer-songwriter of his calibre. *Typical wannabe,* I laughed to myself, realising that he probably saw this programme as his claim to fame, his opportunity to get noticed.

I stayed there a little longer just to make sure he wasn't talking about his actual taste in music. When he paused to stare into the camera lens, Jasmine saw this as her opportunity to escape and practically flew into the arms of Tyree nearby. Two seconds later, she was smiling and laughing. We continued to film for fifteen minutes before calling a break ahead of the club scene.

"What do you think so far? Reckon it's working?" I approached Dijon with a drink at the DJ booth.

"Bare jokes cuz," he said, laughing. "Did you see when that guy over there?" He pointed to Josiah. "Was trying to make a move on her?" He nodded at Misha. "She proper cussed him off. I'm sure your boy Kimar caught it all on camera," he said, before swigging his Red Bull.

"Yeah, it was a good laugh," I said, reflectively. "Let's see how this clubbing scene goes now. Hopefully it will up the stakes a few levels. You ready?"

"You know me cuz. I was born ready." He reached for his CDs.

"Oh yeah and check your boy Kelloggs! Sort out your peeps," I advised. "Didn't you bring him here to help you with the music? I'm sure he's in every shot," I snapped, strutting off.

Back in presenter mode, I started talking again as Marcus trained the camera on me. "You've now seen how well these guys hit it off over a drink. Let's see how they fare on the dance floor."

On cue, the popular bashment tune, 'Love Dem,' by dancehall artist Vybz Kartel, drowned me out, encouraging half the contestants to run on to the dance floor showing off their skills and the other half to hold back a little. Reuben held court in the middle of the floor, doing the latest dance straight out of Jamaica, beaming into the camera, whilst Javon, stood next to him, coolly bopping. Monique scurried around trying to round up the other contestants to get them all on to the dance floor. Seeing that she was having no success, Darren joined in to help her, along with Kelloggs, who wasted no time placing himself in the mix and soon all contestants were having a lively time.

"Make sure you get that on camera," I ordered Kimar, as I noticed Reuben grinding up on Tia. The chemistry between them was insane. *I knew it. So obvious.* I smiled to myself. All those psychologists banging on about the laws of attraction. This was it right here. Music!

Within seconds of Dijon smoothly mixing Kartel's 'Dumpa Truck,' into Tinie Tempah's smash hit, 'Pass Out', Tasha and Josiah had locked limbs and were involved in some mad kind of regimental dance. First they marched like soldiers in the army, then they were shimmying and shaking all over each other. Kieran and Cherelle were bumping and grinding, *Kelloggs* was trying to dance with Misha, Tyree had a little two step going on with Jasmine and Omar held his own, popping and locking.

So it went on for the next twenty minutes, with Dijon on the decks playing everything from Beenie Man to Biggie Smalls. From my observation, it seemed that the contestants were innocently gravitating towards the person who preferred the same music as them. It was a no-brainer and pure entertainment.

When the time was up, everyone, including Kelloggs, collapsed into the sofas, so I called a short intermission.

"Ok," I said, as soon as the break ended. "I'd like all of you girls to go downstairs and I'll come down in a minute to instruct you further."

The girls smiled eyeing the guys one last time, before heading downstairs, leaving Monique to explain to the guys what they were gonna do next. I was proud of the contestants I'd selected as they were positive and upbeat. Each of them had something about them. I didn't think anyone would be disappointed. Marcus had his camera downstairs trained on the girls and Kimar had his camera upstairs focused on the guys. I ran downstairs to greet Darren spreading six big cards across the table. Each had a different number and a music genre written on it.

"Right," I said to the girls. "I want you to each think carefully about the man you were most attracted to, who you would like to go on a date with. Then I'd like you to pick the number with the music genre written on it that you believe best matches with that man." I knew Monique was upstairs having a similar conversation with the guys about the girls. "There is only one of each card, so think carefully, but don't spend too much time as it will be first come, first served."

After filming them choosing for a few minutes, I switched from producer to presenter, as Marcus focused the camera back on me. "You've seen them mingle, you've seen them party, who do you think is gonna pair up with who?" I approached Tasha and pushed the microphone in her face. "Who did you like?"

"Well, I thought Reuben was really good-looking, but me and Josiah seemed to have more of a connection," she said, giggling.

"Mmm. Who could miss the chemistry between you two?" I commented, before moving on to Jasmine, who confessed straight away that she liked Tyree.

"It seems we've come to the moment of truth. Time for some revelations." I faced the camera. "Which one of our handsome young men gets to date this beautiful lady?" I singled out Dionne, beckoning her and the rest of girls to follow me upstairs, where the men were lined up in a row. Dionne clutched on to my hand until we got to the top of the stairs, then let go to line up along with the other girls, facing the guys. I asked her to step forward out of the line, and hold up her number discreetly to the camera as

Kimar zoomed in for a close up. She was holding the number three marked Hip Hop. None of the other contestants could see the number. Only the viewers at home would be entitled to the sneak preview.

"Looks like the lady has chosen," I spoke into the camera. "Now Dionne, I'd like you to take your time and look carefully at the men. Who do you think shares your number?" Dionne scanned the guys, nibbling on her bottom lip. Marcus panned the guys with the camera several times to increase the suspense whilst she made her decision. "Dionne, I must tell you," I explained, "if you guess correctly, the two of you get to enjoy an extravagant date. If you guess wrong, then you go home with nothing." The contestants gasped. "Take your time," I warned her. "Think carefully."

After a few moments, she looked at me. "I've chosen someone," she said.

"Dionne." I gripped her hand. "Will you please reveal to us who you think shares your number?"

She pointed at Javon.

"Dionne, just so we are all clear," I emphasized, beaming into the camera. "Can you please say the name of the person who you believe has the same number as you."

"Javon," she stated confidently, smiling at him.

"Javon," I announced loudly, before looking at him. "Javon, will you please step forward and hold up your number, so everyone can see it."

Javon proudly stepped forward brandishing his card emblazoned with the number three.

"Dionne can you please hold up the number you have chosen, this time, so that everyone can see it." Dionne immediately raised her card with the number three on.

"We have a match!" I screamed, as the other contestants began whooping, hollering and clapping. The couple embraced each other happily, whilst we laughed and cheered, as Javon picked Dionne up slightly off the ground and swung her around a little, before giving her a big hug. He gripped her hand and held on to it firmly.

"Not so quick!" I jumped between them. "Your challenge is not over just yet. There's one clause," I announced, as everyone gasped and the happy couple looked surprised. I stared into the camera. "Earlier, before the contestants ever met each other we took to the streets and asked each woman to guess what each man's favourite music was. If and only if Dionne guessed Javon's favourite music before she'd ever actually met him, will she be eligible for a date with this handsome young man. If she guesses wrong, then I'm afraid it's gonna be a sad song. No date for these two. Run the VT," I commanded, as the anxious couple glanced towards a huge plasma screen on the wall behind the bar, lit up by blue and red fluorescent lighting.

As we played the original footage of Javon, strolling casually out of the Pallasades shopping centre, listening to music on his phone, thirty seconds of hushed anticipation and tension was met with audible relief and delight, when the video tape revealed Dionne guessing straightaway that Javon was listening to hip hop, both his and her favourite music.

The contestants screamed and clapped to the soulful sounds of artist D'Angelo crooning, 'You're my lady', as the new couple were led off screen by Monique.

An hour later, every single contestant had been paired with their predicted compatible mate and I was in my element as I wrapped up the show on camera.

"Well, it's safe to say," I concluded beaming, "there is definitely a connection between a man, his music and his woman. So to all you single ladies out there, the next time you meet a potential mate, if you like his music, celebrate. But if his music isn't to your taste, then you'd better think twice before going on that date!" I warned, pausing, for dramatic effect. "That's goodbye from me, Sahai Martini at Bling & Ting, bringing you the next big thing! *The Sweetest Sound!* Too hot to handle, too cold to hold. Remember, you saw it here first!"

Chapter Eighteen

"So now are you convinced?" I gloated at Camara as we walked around House of Fraser. She'd promised to buy me something if my theory proved right, so here we were and I was milking it.

"I still think the idea is nuts," she confessed. "The way you did it was practically a set up," she griped, as I spritzed on a sample of the new Marc Jacobs fragrance at the perfume counter.

"Nah man," Dijon said, as he led us out of the store. "Trust me, all them contestants came into that bar with no idea of what to expect, and the way they connected with the person who liked the same music as them was so random. Like a proper reality show."

"It *is* a proper reality show," I said, scowling at Dijon, wondering when he was ever gonna start taking Bling & Ting seriously as a bona fide entertainment channel. BET was still stealing too many of our viewers, and now the new weekend Jamaican channel, JAM TV, was taking a share of our audience too, but we were planning an all-out advertising campaign with *The Sweetest Sound*.

"You'll see it for yourself when you watch it Mara," Dijon continued, as we headed towards the Bullring Shopping Centre. "For real. It's the full one hundred! It isn't about looks or anything like it usually is when it comes to dating. It's all about the music. Believe. When's it coming on TV?"

"Well, we still have to film a few more episodes and all the dates over the next few weeks to see if any sparks fly between any of the couples. Then there's all the editing, plus after watching the footage, Bailey's now saying it's very likely there may be a second series, so we need to find and secure more contestants, so we're looking at our first transmission probably in maybe a month or two," I informed them. "Have to see what Bailey wants to do."

"I thought a reality show was supposed to take place in real time. Be happening as you watch it," said Dijon, as he led us into JD Sports and picked up a pair of red, white and black Jordans.

"That's one way," I said. "But the other way is the way I'm doing it, when it's pre-recorded but filmed as real events take place, so it's still reality, like how they film auditions for example, for talent shows, so you see regular people doing something on the spot in its raw format."

"Either way, sounds like big business rasta. We must be able to make some kind of a raise off this. On a regs. Can't you have a phone-in or something where viewers have to guess who's gonna choose who and ring one of them hotline numbers where the caller pays like five pounds a minute?"

"Who's gonna waste their time and money phoning in to do that?" Camara whinged. "It only works if it's benefiting the audience? Like on talent shows people ring in to vote for their favourite contestant, hoping that person will win, so that they can enjoy their album when it comes out."

"True," Dijon realised. "Well you need to do something cuz. Didn't you say you were gonna get celebrities involved? I gotta make some money man. I'm brassic," he grumbled, admiring the trainers from all angles. "Buy me these cuz. You make more than me." He gave me the puppy dog eyes. "I'm going outta town with the man dem this weekend. I *need* these."

"Why do you think *I'm* trying to hook up with a wealthy guy?" I reminded him, taking the footwear out of his hand and putting it back on the shelf. "'Cos I'm broke too. Damn!" We all laughed, heading towards Selfridges.

Dijon and Camara were mistakenly under the impression that I earned loads, but that wasn't the case at all. My salary barely covered my bills and basic expenses. Working for a small up and coming station meant constantly waiting for the business to take off before being able to earn decent money. Right now I was living pay cheque to pay cheque. I could easily look for another job, but Bailey had offered me this one at a time when I was getting rejections from everywhere else, so I felt loyal to him.

"I do need to try and find a way to make some money with this idea though," I admitted, agreeing with Dijon.

"For real," he mumbled, leading us to the floor where the men's designer clothes were.

I'm sure this shopping trip was supposed to be about me, I thought, as he held up a nice midnight blue, Barbour jacket. Just as I was about to usher him and Camara to the level where women's clothes were, Dijon began talking again. "You need people like him on the programme." He pointed towards a guy carrying several designer shopping bags. A Movado watch gleamed on the man's wrist.

"Forget the programme. I need *him* in *my* life."

"Yeah that's gonna be 'real' love isn't it?" Camara said, making little quotation marks with her fingers.

"Who's talking about real love? We're talking about cold hard cash." Dijon laughed. "I mean, on a real, think about *where* you're finding your contributors."

I stared at him as the penny dropped. *He was right*. Forget about going into the city centre to find the next batch of contestants, we needed to go where the movers and shakers were, the money makers, I realised. It was time to step up my A game and find that perfect spot. "Thanks for that little gem." I high fived Dijon, knowing that my future husband could possibly be at that same location.

That 'location' happened to be a Business Convention a few weeks later. I'd attended some of these conferences before, representing Bling & Ting and noticed these events seemed to attract a lot of young, single, successful entrepreneurs, many of whom could be found hanging around outside in between seminars. We were encouraged to network during breaks, but in my experience only a few of us tended to mingle. Most of the delegates seemed far too self-important to speak to anyone else, so didn't really circulate as they should. Either way, today it was working to my advantage.

A business angle on *The Sweetest Sound* could be interesting. Attract a wider audience. Maybe we could have entrepreneurs one week, students the next, athletes and so forth. I was still working on the idea, but right now the handsome guy I'd just spotted, suited, booted, shiny and sharp was looking real good, so I put on my winning smile and strutted towards him as he leant against a wall, listening to something on his mobile phone. Whatever it was had his full attention as he appeared to be in deep concentration.

"Excuse me," I said, hoping I wasn't interrupting an important conversation or even worse, a lucrative business deal. He gave me an appreciative once-over and gladly obliged, popping his earphones out. I'd put on a suit my damn self for the occasion, as I knew power dressing today would be a plus. It was a fitted black Karen Millen with an extremely tight skirt which I'd complimented with killer heels. I smiled confidently. "Hi, we're from the TV station Bling & Ting and we're here doing some research." I'd rehearsed my lines well.

"Yeah?" He seemed interested.

That's what I loved about business people. They were always looking for their next hustle.

"Sorry, I should introduce myself properly. I'm Sahai Martini, I'm a television producer and this is my colleague Kimar," I explained, extending my hand.

"Hi, I'm Sadiq." He shook my hand, holding on to it a little longer than he needed to.

"We just wanted to ask you a question? Do you mind if we film?"

"No go ahead." His eyes were glued to my breasts.

"Can I ask you what you were just listening to?" I pointed to his phone, with the attached earphones now dangling.

As usual, we captured his initial confused expression on tape, before he easily responded. "Music."

"Any particular genre?" I replied.

"Classical actually," he informed. "A symphony by Mozart. Been listening to him and Beethoven all day. Relaxes me." He obviously felt the need to explain himself.

"I like classical music too," I shared, which appeared to relax him even further.

"Why do you ask?" he probed.

"Because we're doing a programme about music, motivation and dating, due to be aired later this year. Are you single?"

"I am." He didn't hesitate.

"Well maybe you'd like to take part?" I suggested. "Could we get your details?"

"I'd like to know a bit more about it first. Do you mind switching that off now if we're only dealing with formalities?" he asked, nodding towards Kimar, who in turn hoisted the camera down off his shoulders and backed up a little, sensing that Sadiq wanted to talk to me in private.

As soon as Kimar was out of earshot, Sadiq wasted no time.

"What I would really like," he stated clearly, "is to take you out on a date."

I blushed at his direct approach.

"I mean, that's if you're single and you'd like to," he added. He had a look about him of the singer and actor, Tyrese. Striking.

"Yes, I am single and I would like to." *Shit. I'd turned into a damn parrot, repeating every word he was saying.* Perhaps that's because not only did he look good, but I'd just glimpsed the business card he'd placed in my hand and saw three letters. C.E.O.

Any Chief Executive Officer of anything had to be minted. Rolling in dough.

"Please excuse me if I seem a bit forward," he apologised. "But seriously, you're absolutely stunning. Beautiful. I couldn't let this opportunity to get to know you pass me by. I admire an ambitious woman and you seem to be doing your thing."

"Thank you," I said, accepting the compliment gracefully, as I glanced down again at his card. "So, you run your own... courier company? Based in London. Lucrative? Enjoy it?" I casually questioned, when all I really wanted to know was *how much money you got in the bank?*

"Yeah, that's just one of my ventures. I haven't got all my cards on me today. I also own a window cleaning service, we do a lot of the tall buildings, and a hip hop clothing store, selling mainly designer."

"A hip hop clothing store?" I was surprised.

"Don't be fooled by the suit and the classical music. I get down just like anyone else," Sadiq bragged winking, obviously trying to show me his rugged side. This brotha' was clearly a bit insecure and self-conscious, but right now who cared, as I pictured myself rocking a hot little Louis Vuitton freebie.

"I'm impressed. I'll have to pop into your store some time," I cooed, going into full ego stroking mode. Evidently he was worth it.

"Anytime," he said smoothly. "Listen, my seminar's about to start," he told me, glancing at his white gold and diamond Cartier watch. "I need to go back inside. Have you got a card or some way I can contact you?"

I practically thrust one of my business cards into his hand without hesitation and pointed out my personal mobile number, as he said his goodbyes and excused himself. *Well, it was definitely worth coming here today,* I thought, as I beckoned Kimar to rejoin me, before scanning my surroundings for my next target.

Chapter Nineteen

The next couple of weeks were hectic. Work kept me busy with *The Sweetest Sound*, but mostly I was disappointed that McKenzie had dropped off the face off the earth. Well, not quite... as naturally I'd kept track of him on his team's website and he was absolutely fine. The new football season would be starting soon, I'd even thought about maybe turning up at a game or two, but as much as I liked him, stalking wasn't really my thing, so I didn't push it.

Can't lie, I was pissed off though. He still hadn't returned any of my phone calls or text messages. Seems like I'd been played again and it was hurting. I mean, I'd really liked him. Who wouldn't? Tall, dark, handsome, charming, rich, fun-loving, sexy as hell, an athlete... the list was endless.

"I'm not sure what's getting to me more, the rejection or missing out on my dream," I complained to Camara over the phone, as I applied a little more lip gloss and admired my reflection in my bedroom mirror.

It was seven pm on a Thursday evening and I was getting ready for a date with Sadiq. We'd been speaking on the phone every day since I met him and although he was based in London, he was back in Birmingham for a couple of days on business.

"I hear that," Camara sympathized. "Rejection is always hard and I mean, we are talking about McKenzie Jackson," she consoled. "But look at it this way, everything happens for a reason. It just wasn't meant to be."

"Doesn't make me feel any better though." I slipped on my sexy Louboutin heels that Money had bought me. It set off my outfit perfectly.

"I know, but you gotta remember, every disappointment paves the way for something better to come along and whatever is meant for you won't pass you by."

What could be better than being Mrs McKenzie Jackson? I wondered, slipping on my jacket.

"The best is yet to come and you're gonna create it. I mean, come-on Sahai, you're the one always talking about being a 'hot girl,' the 'commodity,' so act like it, practice what you preach. If you don't believe in yourself, no one else will," she said softly. "And let's just say, for arguments sake, that you *were* McKenzie's woman. Like Dijon said, he's a footballer who has girls throwing themselves at him every day. You'd probably end up living in a luxury mansion, isolated and alone whilst he's out there, living the player's life having a ball. So think of it this way... every rejection is God's protection."

"I guess you're right," I mumbled sulking, as I grabbed my car keys.

"Stop stressing. You're too blessed to be stressed," she said warmly. "You've got so much going for you. Don't focus on what you haven't got, focus on what you have got," she advised, full of positive energy.

"Thank you." I smiled, feeling lucky at that moment to have her as a friend. For a change, her positive affirmations and little sayings weren't annoying me. She was actually making me feel better.

"It's his loss... and who knows what's gonna happen tonight?" she murmured. "I already like the sound of this Sadiq. He sounds like the kind of guy I'd introduce you to. A corporate, hardworking, sensible businessman. He might be the one."

"Well I'm not holding my breath," I grumbled, walking out the front door. "Not after everything I've been through with men these last few months."

Plus the way she'd described Sadiq bored the hell out of me. Even though I'd been initially attracted to him because of his good looks and prospects, truth be told, he did come across as a bit of a square and deep down I loved rough-necks. Yes, I liked my men rich, rugged and rough around the edges, although in Sadiq's defence, I had to admit he was definitely putting the work in. He face-timed me on a regular and seemed so interested in my life. He wanted to know what I was doing every minute of every day. He probably knew my schedule better than I did, could list what I ate for breakfast, my work hours, which gym I attended and when, my favourite food, you name it. He was that fascinated, paying me more genuine attention than any man had in a long time, I realised, as I got into my car.

He was constantly telling me how good it felt talking to me, how much he liked my vibe and how I seemed like the kind of woman he was looking for *to share his riches with, I hoped.* Sadiq had a way about him that I found very attractive. Warm, caring and complimentary, he always had something positive to say and to be honest, it was a nice feeling, so for now I guess I could overlook the fact that he was a bit square and just take it one day at a time.

"Anyway gotta go," Camara announced, pulling me out of my thoughts. "Danté's on the other line. Have a good time and make sure you text me to let me know how it's going," she said and swiftly hung up. She'd definitely lucked up with Danté and I was happy for her.

I smiled to myself thinking about them, as I drove towards the Jewellery Quarter where I'd arranged to meet Sadiq. Danté was turning out to be a true gentleman, kind, loving and affectionate. She said he phoned her every day, took her out often and worshipped the ground she walked on and they hadn't even slept together yet, she'd admitted. Maybe I should try that, I thought. No sex. That might be the key. Maybe I shouldn't have slept with McKenzie so soon? *Nah, forget that. I'm glad I did.* I grinned, remembering the dizzy heights he'd taken me to on that night. *He was too delicious to resist.* Gosh, some lucky bitch was gonna end up with him as her *husband.*

Getting depressed at the thought, I tried to refocus on Camara and Danté's romance to cheer myself up. They made a nice couple, and as a bonus his family had loved her from the moment he'd introduced her to them. Her family also adored him. Her dad in particular, who had now retired from his job at the car factory, was even allowing Danté to go in his shed at the bottom of their garden and *no one*, not even his wife, was permitted to go in that precious shed, I remembered, laughing.

When we were little, he used to go nuts when we tried to sneak in there. In the end he'd simply padlocked it. The fact that he now invited Danté in there sometimes, for a Guinness and a game of dominoes, said a lot and Camara was over the moon about it.

The only thing that disturbed me about their relationship was her refusal to accept expensive gifts and extravagant trips from Danté, instead opting for quiet nights in and small tokens. That was crazy. The guy was loaded! If that was my man, I'd soon help him enjoy the lavish lifestyle he wanted, but for now I was happy that she was happy and hoping that Sadiq wasn't expecting me to contribute to *our* meal, because I only had about four pounds on me, I realised, as I exited the car and walked towards the Italian restaurant he'd suggested.

Originally we'd planned to go to The Jam House, to take in a bit of live music whilst we ate, but he'd insisted on trying out the menu at this place, which looked alright actually, I thought, admiring the exterior. The place looked clean and authentic. As I was about to enter the building, my phone rang. I smiled when I saw the caller id.

"Hey Sadiq, sorry I'm late. I'm just walking in now," I told him.

"No. I'm the one who's sorry," he apologised.

"Excuse me?"

"I can't make it tonight," he said.

"And you're just telling me now?" I snapped, glancing at my watch. "I'm at the restaurant."

"I'm really sorry Sahai. Something came up last minute and I couldn't get out of it. I'm still in London."

Was he for real? After how much he'd insisted on taking me out tonight?

"So why didn't you ring me earlier?" I asked, thinking about the time, effort and petrol I'd wasted getting ready for this date.

"I wanted to, but I couldn't. I had a little… situation."

I'd heard enough. I didn't respond.

"I'll be back in Birmingham tomorrow though," he quickly added. "Maybe we can meet up then?"

This joker was having a laugh if he thought I'd be wasting another minute on him.

"Maybe," I said.

"Cool." He sounded relieved. "I'll call you tomorrow then."

"You do that," I replied, hanging up the phone knowing full well that I wouldn't be answering any more of his calls. How dare he stand me up or cancel at the last minute? Same difference if you asked me. *And on our first date?* This would be the first and the last chance he'd get to do that.

His lousy explanation made me know something wasn't quite right but I couldn't put my finger on it, so I decided to leave well alone.

Chapter Twenty

"It's hot," Bailey acknowledged, about a week later, after viewing the first cut of *The Sweetest Sound*. "I'm impressed." He stroked his goatee, as he finished watching the end of my masterpiece.

Marcus and I had spent days in the editing suite perfecting it and had only this afternoon proudly applied the finishing touches in preparation for Bailey to view it. Sadiq had been calling me non-stop throughout the process since his no show, but I'd ignored every single call.

"Just a few small changes to make," Bailey observed. "But our viewers are gonna love it! Take it back to the top so I can look at it again properly," he instructed Marcus and whipped out his pen and pad. "Ok, so I like the way it starts with the qualities contestants are looking for in a partner. The whole club scene really works, but *who* is that guy in the background? He seems to be popping up everywhere."

"Oh, that's Kelloggs." I sighed wearily. "Dijon's friend. He brought him along to help with the music."

"People!" Bailey shook his head. "This is why I try and get you to separate your little friends from your career Sahai. In the next edit, try and lose him from as many shots as possible, coming across like some damn cupid," Bailey said, laughing.

"Trust me," Marcus agreed. "I tried to edit him out of some scenes, but the man's practically everywhere."

"I'll take another look tomorrow and work on it," I mentioned, planning to have words with Dijon. He'd insisted on bringing Kelloggs to the shoot and against my better judgement I'd agreed. I

150

knew I should have said no because it had proved impossible to keep him away from the cameras. Either way I'd be having words.

Keen to quickly change the subject, I addressed Bailey. "How did you get on with the celebrity element?" I asked him.

"I've spoken to a couple of my contacts and looks like we're gonna have some input," he notified. "Some of the artists have agreed to give us a flash of inspiration about what was behind the lyrics we heard them singing in the club scene."

"Oh wow. That's brilliant." I was chuffed.

"It'll be an interesting angle that we can incorporate when we edit how the dates went," Bailey added. "The reveal at the end might need looking at as well, but other than that, nice one Sahai. Top work, excellent," he praised, as he left the editing suite.

"Looks like your job's definitely gonna be alright after all," Marcus remarked. "I don't think you'll be leaving us anytime soon."

"Thank God and thanks for all your help," I said, grabbing my coat. "Let's hope the audience love it as much as we do." I was tired, couldn't wait to get home and sink into a hot bubble bath.

"Enjoy your evening golden girl," he said, with a hint of sarcasm.

"Marcus, if I remember correctly, you've been here longer than me and you came up with the original idea that put this station on the map, so don't hate, congratulate and come up with something that Bailey will rate," I rhymed in a silly fashion, as I bounced out of the suite. Even though I was exhausted, nothing was gonna bring down my good spirits. I'd proved to myself, Camara, Bailey and the rest of the team that my theory had legs. Now I just needed the audience to run with it.

For the next few weeks Sadiq continued to bombard me with phone calls, but I completely ignored him.

"I can't have people polluting my comfort zone," I told Camara, as we sat in the sauna after a vigorous work out in the gym one evening. At least this was one good thing that had come out of meeting McKenzie. I'd kept my promise to myself to start getting fit after dancing for him in the club and was now in the best shape I'd been, in ages.

"He cancelled one date Sahai. That hardly qualifies. Give him a chance," she said.

"Why? First impressions always last. If he's like this now, who knows what lies ahead?"

"Oh stop being so dramatic," she said laughing, as she eased up off the bench. "He's the first decent guy you've met in ages, who's actually making a consistent effort to get to know you. Why don't you just speak to him? Hear him out?" she asked, as she picked up the scoop, threw some water on the rocks and climbed to the next level.

"Nah. Not interested," I said. "Anyway listen, I'm getting out, it's too hot in here." Really I was tired of our conversation because the truth was I did like Sadiq with his fine, sexy, corporate self, but I was fed up of being messed around. I knew Camara thought I was overreacting, but that wasn't the case at all. For the last few months it had been the same shit, different person. One after the other. I'd had enough. I got up and wrapped my towel around me. "See you in a bit," I mumbled, and left Camara in the sauna.

Moments later, I sank down into the Jacuzzi, enjoying the warm soapy water bubbling and fizzing around me, creating a heavenly sensation. There was no better feeling than the way the foamy lather caressed and soothed my tired, aching muscles. But the more the frothy liquid attempted to calm and relax me, the more heated I got, reflecting on all the bullshit I'd been through with men these last few months.

The more I tried to unwind, the harder it seemed to get Sadiq off my mind. He was funny, interesting and had started to grow on me, but like all the rest, he'd let me down. I mean, what 'situation' could possibly have prevented him from even just sending me a text to let me know he wasn't gonna make it that evening? Why did he leave it to the last second to cancel? That was beyond rude *and* inconsiderate. He knew how busy I was. That act alone didn't sit well with me at all.

In the changing room Camara was still trying to persuade me to meet up with him, but I managed to switch the conversation on to Danté, so by the time we left the gym about half an hour later, we walked outside laughing and joking.

As we began to make our way through the car park, I glimpsed someone who looked familiar. I thought my eyes were deceiving me, but a double-take confirmed they weren't. I couldn't believe it. Lurking in the shadows, leaning against a wall, just posted up there quite comfortably like part of the brickwork, the person was gazing straight at me. Noticing, Camara commented.

"Damn. You know that guy? Look at the way he's staring at you. He's fine."

"It's Sadiq."

"Sadiq?" she whispered loudly, beside herself. "*The* Sadiq? As in, who we were just talking about? How did he know where to find you?" she asked.

"Because thanks to you encouraging me to be more open, I've told him my whole frickin' life story," I hissed back, through gritted teeth. "He knows my schedule better than I do."

"Go speak to him," she urged.

She didn't have to urge for very long 'cos he was striding towards us.

"He's gorgeous," Camara murmured.

"Hello? Danté?" I chided her. "Remember him? Your boyfriend?"

"Just because I've had my dinner, doesn't mean I can't look at the menu," she quipped, as Sadiq approached us.

"Hi," he said, handing me a single red rose and a box of Cadbury's chocolates, followed by a warm smile.

"Hi," I replied, with an icy glare.

Clearly he wasn't prepared for such a frosty reception, but what did he expect? I'd told him how tired I was of men letting me down and he'd simply jumped to the front of the queue. So now I was supposed to be happy to see him? Hell no! He looked a bit embarrassed, before quickly finding his voice again and it seems a bit of confidence too.

"I remember you telling me you go to this gym, Wednesday evenings, circuit training," he said coolly. "Sahai, this is not my style. I do not chase after women. I've emailed you, text you, been to your office, I've sent you messages on Facebook, Twitter, Linked-In, posted images on WhatsApp, Instagram, Snapchat, you won't answer my calls, so this is my final attempt," he pointed out.

"So what do you want? An Award?"

Camara, unimpressed by my sarcasm, gave me a sharp jab in my back, but he deserved it. His little stalking fiasco wasn't really working for me at all, I thought, as Camara tugged at the back of my jacket.

"Sadiq, this is my friend Camara," I introduced. He took her hand in his, bent his head and kissed her hand ever so gently.

"My pleasure," he said, as she gawped at him, looking like she was about to pass out. Anyone would think she was single, instead of dating one of the hottest brothas' I'd ever seen.

"Well, gotta go," she shrilled, flustered. "I'll leave you two to it."

"But... you're driving?" I protested. We often took her car whenever we went anywhere together 'cos she liked to be in control.

"I'll take you anywhere you need to go," Sadiq intervened. "I'll drive you home. I'm parked right there." He pointed to a sexy pearl-white Lexus and right then, I knew I was going with him.

"Sorted. I'll call you when I get in," I told Camara, as she studied his car for a minute before hot-footing it towards her car. I knew she'd been making a mental note of his car registration plate number. We always looked out for each other like that.

"Why won't you just leave me alone?" I wanted to know, as I nestled into the heated passenger seat of his beautiful luxury Lexus, minutes later.

"I had a situation, my bad. I messed up our date. I want to make it up to you."

"Surely me ignoring your calls should let you know that I ain't got time for time wasters."

"Don't get it twisted. I'm far from that, which is why I'm here now. I'd like to reschedule. In the meantime, where are we going?" he asked, as he activated the start button and the vehicle began easing smoothly out of the car park.

"You tell me. You're driving," I huffed, folding my arms tightly across my chest.

I was tired and wanted to sleep. It had been a long day so I easily gave in when he insisted I let him drive me home.

"So are you going to invite me in for a coffee?" We were parked outside. "I'll be a gentleman," he said, smiling.

"A gentleman? Sadiq, you're practically stalking me. There's nothing gentleman-like about that."

"I'm really sorry I let you down that night." He looked sincere.

"What was so important that you couldn't text or ring earlier to cancel?" I asked.

He looked disturbed. "Like I said I had a situation." His mood darkened for a fraction of a second. "Let's put that behind us. Just one date. That's all I'm asking for. Let me make it up to you."

In fairness, he was looking sexier by the minute, with his athletic physique and dark brooding looks. "Ok," I said, remembering his status as CEO. "I'll think about it."

I suspected that like Camara, he probably thought I was overreacting, but he was in a long line of men who'd given me the whole speech about how amazing I was and all the great things they wanted with me, and then for one reason or another couldn't, wouldn't or didn't deliver. I was tired of the whole scene.

"Don't keep me waiting too long," he warned, as I got out of the car. Possibly had a good point there. I was surprised no one had snapped him up already with everything he had going for him.

As soon as I got indoors and rang Camara to let her know I was home safely, she couldn't stop gushing about how good-looking, charming and fit Sadiq was.

"Gosh, he even had *me* hot and bothered," she confessed. She was loving it, finally glad to see a corporate brotha' running me down. "Sahai and Sadiq," she kept repeating. "Got a nice ring to it."

Dijon, on the other hand, was not pleased about the situation at all, the constant attention and phone calls. He was concerned that Sadiq seemed a bit too eager. Overfamiliar. Plus he was a London man, Dijon complained, whatever the hell that was supposed to mean. Dijon was so attached to his Birmingham postcode I think he'd forgotten that he himself was actually born in London, even if he had been raised in this city. He didn't trust anyone who wasn't from the Birmingham streets where he grew and repped like a loyal soldier… his 'manor,' as he loved to call it.

Dijon grumbled that I didn't know anything about Sadiq's life or background, then proceeded to reel off some random story about previous altercations involving knives, samurai swords, motorbikes, baseball bats and hospitals. Said he would have to recreate those events if I went down to London to visit Sadiq and anything happened to me. Could he *get* more territorial?

I'd had to remind Dijon that I'd travelled all the way to Miami to see Money, a practical stranger who we knew even less about, and came back home quite safely, even if a little ruffled, at which point he'd reminded me that Danté, as Money's cousin, was insurance, at which point Camara had told us not to get Danté involved. In the end I had to reassure Dijon that I had no plans to visit Sadiq in London, but might date him the next time he was in Birmingham.

Secretly, I was still hoping the footballer McKenzie might miraculously resurface, but it seemed there was slim chance of that happening, so always useful to have a plan B!

"And you know Money still wants to talk to you," Camara said, bringing me back to the moment. "He keeps asking Danté how you are."

"I've got nothing to say to that man." You would've thought he'd have got the message by now since I hadn't responded to any of his texts or calls since I'd left Miami.

"I think he's really sorry about what happened. Seems to have genuine regret. Wants to see you."

"Seriously Camara, I ain't interested in Money. After what he did, he ain't hearing from me ever again! He's the dumbest man in the history of life if he thinks he could ever get another chance with me! He can kiss my ass."

"Alright. Calm down. Just letting you know he's still trying."

"Well too bad, he's missed the boat."

"I hear you. Anyway gotta go, early start."

"Yeah me too, I'm knackered."

"Let's catch up tomorrow then. Night."

"Goodnight." I hung up, irritable.

Why was it that these men always wanted you back after they'd messed you about, humiliated and hurt you? And always just when you had finally got over them? It irked me to know that Money was still trying after wasting the time we could've had together. But trust me, I wouldn't be losing any sleep over him tonight. That man was officially in the same category as the banana peel, rotten apple, half-eaten tuna sandwich, mouldy cheese and filthy rag I'd seen in the bin down the road, when I'd thrown away a tissue on my way to the shop earlier.

Chapter Twenty-One

I was nervous as hell. The big day had come. *The Sweetest Sound* was finally being aired for the first time this evening on Bling & Ting and I was anxious about how it was gonna go down. Would we get the viewers? The ratings? Would it be as popular as I'd hoped?

Granted, we'd had a big advertising campaign, been interviewed on all the local radio stations and had huge posters put up around the city. We'd placed flyers in takeaways, barbershops, hair salons, record shops, on bus stop shelters, lamp posts and in clothes shops, even handed them out around town and outside nightclubs. We needed a hot, young audience who would all be lining up to take part in a second, third and fourth series. We wanted the world to recognise music as one of the single biggest laws of attraction, as first seen explored on Bling & Ting. We were bringing ground-breaking, revolutionary concepts to ordinary folk. We were innovators, shot callers and we were excited.

Bailey had given it a prime time, mid-week, evening slot of 7.30 pm and my phone had been pinging and popping all day, mainly with Sadiq bless him, reassuring me that it was gonna be a hit. He'd also had a big bunch of flowers delivered to my workplace this morning, which was very sweet. I loved his support, even though I still hadn't made any more time for him.

Dijon and Kelloggs had come down to the studios of Bling & Ting, so they could watch it go out with 'the rest of the crew and production team'. Kelloggs' idea! Camara had also come into work to give me some moral support. It was now 6.30pm, just an hour to go and I was panicking.

"Calm down," Camara soothed, handing me another slice of one of the pizzas Bailey had thoughtfully ordered for everyone from Pizza Hut. "It's gonna be fine."

"Stop worrying cuz." Dijon took a huge bite of his Meat Feast with extra pepperoni and chillies.

"Yeah cuz, it's gonna be big!" Kelloggs said, munching on his Chicken Supreme. "It's emotional," he mumbled.

Did he just call me cuz? Who was he calling cousin? Did Dijon tell him there was money involved or something? The way he was acting.

"But what if no one tunes in? What if we don't get any viewers?"

"Trust me," Kimar piped up. "We will get viewers, look at this." He beckoned us over to his computer, switching between Facebook and Twitter, explaining that he'd set up a Facebook page specifically for *The Sweetest Sound* weeks ago and already it was generating a huge debate about music and attraction, with over 10,000 people saying they were planning to tune in to watch.

"Oh my days!" I was elated. "Why didn't you tell me this before?" I asked, gushing.

"'Cos I didn't want it to make you even more nervous." He laughed.

The tweets ranged from how stupid the idea was, how there was no way we could prove music had anything to do with attraction, to people saying they'd always believed this theory and what we were doing was simply genius.

"Look, I've got these three phone lines set up as well for us to take all the calls after the show," Monique mentioned.

"Between that and the chat room I'll have up and running on here," Kimar added, "it's gonna be insane!" He laughed. "Oh how I love social media! We're about to go viral on the World Wide Web!" he sang, deep in Facebook. The exact kind of speech Money would have loved to hear. Shame he'd turned out to be such a psycho.

"Right, anything else we need to do or we good to go?" Marcus popped his head out from around the studio door. It was now 7.20 pm.

"Let's do it," I said smiling, as the whole team began to get cosy in the long sofa and various arm chairs dotted around the viewing room, in front of the 52 inch plasma.

We kicked back and glued our eyes to the screen.

Bling & Ting's phone lines were blowing up before we even came off the air. Callers were raving about everything from how amazing our idea was, to how badly they wanted to be on the show. Others were saying how impressed they were to see international artists expanding on the lyrics and the inspiration behind the music we'd featured. We were pleasantly surprised that the positive feedback far outweighed the negative.

All in all *The Sweetest Sound* was a massive success and I was in my element! After a quick debrief, which mostly consisted of Bailey praising the programme and Kimar sharing feedback, we all left the office and headed over to Marco Pierre White's Steakhouse at the Cube in The Mailbox, to celebrate. Bailey's treat.

Admiring the stunning view from the 25th floor of the glass fronted building, I marvelled at how pretty the streets looked lit up at night. Making my way out on to the rooftop terrace to enjoy a little fresh air, I sipped my Ciroc as I looked out across the city, taking a minute to revel in this moment. The cool breeze caressing my face was exhilarating. I felt on top of the world as I gazed in awe at the sweeping skyline. I'd done it! The response was incredible! This definitely called for a proper celebration, I thought, downing the rest of my drink and heading back inside to the bar for another.

The next morning I woke up with a banging headache. I must have drank way more than I'd realised last night. I could barely remember anything. I was mash up, so I went back to bed until midday, then took a quick shower, cleaned the house, slipped into my hot pink onesie and crashed out on the sofa. Bailey had given me the rest of the week off, thank God.

After snoozing and watching the last two episodes of Scandal, which I'd recorded on Sky Plus, I felt a lot better so decided to get up and cook. I slid Jaheim's 'Ghetto Love' album into the CD player, turning the volume up loud, before going into the kitchen for a good rummage around in the fridge.

The sight of food made my stomach rumble, in fact I was starving, so I chose to make a big Sunday dinner, despite it being the middle of the week.

Draining the water off some kidney beans that had been soaking overnight, I washed and put them in a pan of fresh water, adding a little salt and pepper, thyme, coconut cream, diced onions, garlic and margarine and placed the pot on the hob to boil.

I then cleaned and seasoned some chicken with paprika, onion, mixed herbs, garlic, curry powder, jerk seasoning, scotch bonnet and mixed peppers and left it in the fridge to marinate for a little while. I usually preferred to keep the chicken in there overnight for a fuller flavour, but this would have to do for now.

I peeled some Maris Piper potatoes as I sang along with Jaheim, threw them in a pan of hot water on the hob for about fifteen minutes until they were soft, then drained off the water and gave the pan a thorough shake until the spuds crumbled around the edges. I always did this so they would taste crisp and crunchy on the outside and soft and fluffy in the middle, just the way I liked them. I glazed the potatoes with virgin olive oil and put them in the oven, along with the chicken to roast.

Next, I chopped up some veg, threw half of it in the steamer and the other half in a bowl. Grabbing a jar of mayonnaise I placed it beside the bowl, with some sugar, salt, pepper, vinegar and mustard, in preparation to make coleslaw.

I checked on the kidney beans which had now softened and added some basmati rice along with more thyme and coconut cream to the pot, leaving the rice and peas to cook, whilst preparing sweet potato candy, macaroni cheese and Pineapple Punch, using the traditional Jamaican recipe, with the twist that my mum had shown me. The extra ingredient gave the beverage a smooth, creamier taste, making it easy to understand why the drink was also known as Sexy Juice, although I had no idea of the real reason it was called that.

Some people claimed it was because it's an aphrodisiac. Others had varying theories. Regardless it tasted delicious, so I treated myself to it once in a while. It always made me think of my mum, who I'd recently started to miss more than usual. I hadn't seen her for over two years now, so was definitely due a trip out to Jamaica. I'd ask Bailey for some time off and book that flight as soon as the furore around *The Sweetest Sound* died down a bit. Be good to see her. We didn't speak on the phone often, but whenever we did, she always said she was longing to see me, especially with her health being so poor.

I studied the small framed picture of her on the wall near the fridge. So beautiful, with her rich golden-brown skin, long, flowing hair and pretty features, but such sad, haunting eyes. I turned away, tending to the rice and peas, and then checked on the chicken and potatoes. Everything was coming along nicely. With most of it nearly done, I made a cup of tea, went back into the living room and sank down in the sofa, allowing the soothing, butter-soft tones of Jaheim's voice to relax me, until the meal was completely ready.

On cue, Dijon, who had a knack of turning up unannounced around dinnertime, rang the doorbell, just as I was about to sit down and eat. Joining me in the kitchen, he helped himself to a healthy slice of hard-dough bread whilst waiting for me to dish out his dinner.

Throughout our meal we talked about how well *The Sweetest Sound* had been received, with him mostly reminding me which bits of it were his idea and insisting that he should be making a profit from his contribution. Loved my cousin. Always on a hustle. We then moved on to discussing relationships, with Dijon once again reiterating that he didn't like the sound of Sadiq.

"Just be careful cuz," he warned, spooning food into his mouth so fast, that the food that was already in there, was falling out as he was putting more in. "This is delicious cuzzy," he complimented, whilst stuffing a whole roast potato into his mouth. I laughed, watching him. "I can't believe you made my favourite as well. Sexy Juice. Is that you though?" he teased, before guzzling a generous amount of Pineapple Punch from his glass. "It almost tastes as good as auntys," he enthused, referring to my mum's unique secret ingredient, that she'd had the whole neighbourhood popping round to ours on Sundays for, even if just for a sip, when we were little.

Stabbing at a huge portion of macaroni cheese smothered in mustard with his fork, Dijon picked it up, attempting to cram it into his mouth. Too big to fit, the pasta separated and dropped back into his plate, sending chunks of sweet potato, bits of chicken, kidney beans and grains of rice flying everywhere.

"I'm beginning to realise why you're single. Is this how you eat on your dates?" I snapped, bothered by the food all over my floor.

"Minor ting cuzzy, minor ting," he said, as we both knew with his good looks, fit body and endless charisma he was never short of one or two females hanging off his arms, regardless of how he ate.

I finally kicked him out at midnight as my head was starting to hurt again. Took me ages to fall asleep but no sooner than I did, I ended up having some crazy dream about riding white horses through huge crashing waves… with Sadiq!

So when the phone rang startling me out of my sleep, I was a bit disorientated.

"Hey, I was just dreaming about you," I mumbled, when I heard Sadiq's voice on the other end of the line. Wrong move… as his ego instantly inflated beyond all reasonable proportions.

Once I'd told him my dream, Sadiq interpreted it as me falling for him and fighting my feelings, represented by the waves in the ocean, with him strongly guiding me through on horseback. He said passion and obsession couldn't keep us apart and even wild horses couldn't drag us down, symbolised by the force with which we battled the huge waves. Didn't really see it that way myself and wondered what the dream was really about, but didn't give it too much thought as he moved on.

"I was just ringing to congratulate you again on how great your programme was."

"At six in the morning?" *Like Really?* I grumbled, as I squinted at the red LCD light boldly displaying the time on my digital alarm clock.

"The early bird catches the worm," he stated, then immediately began apologising for waking me up when I didn't respond. "Sorry, I woke up hours ago and couldn't get back to sleep. You were on my mind so I called. I was half expecting to be leaving a message on your voicemail."

"Ok, so can I go back to sleep now." I hated anyone interfering with my rest.

"I'll let you go, if you set a date with me."

Now that *The Sweetest Sound* had been broadcast, he was certain I should have more time on my hands, which was true. He had a project to finish off in London but said he could be in Birmingham by the end of next week, so I agreed to go to the cinema with him next Saturday, as I had no plans. He then apologised again for ringing me so early, at which point I glanced at the alarm clock again to see that it was now six thirty. Why *was* he calling at this ungodly hour? It wasn't the first time he'd rang this early either, but the last few times I'd missed the calls.

He spun me more of his yarn about how he couldn't sleep or stop thinking about me. Not sure why as we didn't really have it like that, but I guess each to their own and anyway, why was I even complaining about the attention, because after all, he *was* a sexy Tyrese look-alike CEO.

But it was when he started banging on again about the white horses in my dream that enough was enough, so I rushed him off the phone.

Chapter Twenty-Two

Monday morning and the office was abuzz. Everyone was still raving about *The Sweetest Sound*. The phone lines were blowing up with all sorts of diverse feedback, mostly positive. Our Facebook page crashed several times, I'm sure due to the sheer level of activity on it and we were all over Twitter.

Bailey couldn't stop singing my praises whilst trying to work out how we were gonna up the stakes in the programme. I spent most of the day just basking in the afterglow, didn't really do much work at all. The rest of the week was the opposite though, as Bailey had come up with a few fresh ideas that needed intense research.

By the weekend I was beat, so I rang Sadiq and postponed the date, which was cool with him as he still hadn't finished his project. We agreed we'd rearrange in a few more weeks. He tried to say we were now even, claiming that I was dissing him as I was cancelling, but it wasn't the same. I had to remind him that I'd given him at least a day's notice, unlike what he'd done to me.

All the same we said we'd meet up soon. Camara believed I was unnecessarily stalling and wasting valuable time and that I'd regret it if some other girl snatched Sadiq from under me. Dijon said it was a sign that we weren't supposed to meet up 'cos Sadiq seemed too shifty and the horse dream had been a warning, something about drowning.

Whilst I didn't particularly agree with either of them and actually liked Sadiq a lot, I did have a nagging feeling that something wasn't quite right. But maybe I was just being paranoid? Nevertheless, I was definitely interested in seeing him again. I'd grown used to our daily banter on the phone and enjoyed talking to him, so I wanted to actually spend some time in his company now, to see how I'd feel.

For the following weeks the excitement around *The Sweetest Sound* continued. We'd found more contestants and each week the ratings got higher. We'd filmed each of our couples from programme one on a date, to see if there were any sparks and those episodes were proving to be a huge success. The next move was to call them back into the studio soon to see how they were getting on as all their first dates had gone reasonably well. I spent most of my days between filming and the editing suite with Darren or Marcus and most of my evenings and weekends simply resting or catching up on stuff I'd fallen behind with.

Work was crazy as we were also busy doing a Bling & Ting Commonwealth Games 2014 Special. We'd gone big on the Olympics in 2012, revelling in the success of the fastest man on earth, Jamaican track star, Usain Bolt. Now we had further Jamaican athletes to brag about, Rasheed Dwyer and his team mates, so Glasgow, where it was all happening was the place to focus on. Plus I also had my Carnival Season strand to concentrate on, as every year we did a popular summer series on Caribbean Carnivals around the UK.

On top of that I'd also produced a one hour special celebrating the 52nd anniversary of Jamaican Independence Day. This year we'd gone all out, showcasing Jamaicans as world leaders in everything from music to style to food to creativity to athletics. We'd explored the phenomenon of how such a small island, a tiny dot on the map, came to have such universal influence, with all nations worldwide imitating and copying Jamaican culture, wanting to be a part of its very essence, from the dialect to the dancing, to the catchphrases to the island people's style, right down to the swagger, the distinctive walk. Bailey loved the show as soon as he saw the first edit, immediately abandoning the title I'd chosen, and aptly renaming it *'One Love? No Problem!'*

I even threw in a few lesser known treasures, for example the fact that Jamaica played a leading role in pioneering what people around the world now enjoyed as all-inclusive holiday resorts. It was a Jamaican entrepreneur who'd opened the island's first all-inclusive luxury resort back in the seventies. This small island was offering all-inclusive trips way before most countries world-wide had even thought about it, heard about it, or cottoned on that a concept like this could change the face of tourism and boost local economy, forever. I'd secured guests and contributors from all over the place to feature in this special and with everything else going on I was literally working myself to death, so it was a refreshing welcome break from work when the time finally rolled around for me to go on my date with Sadiq.

For the past week or so we hadn't spoken at all on the phone, just by text, but we'd agreed to go for a meal and then on to the cinema this evening. I'd just finished spritzing myself with 'Very Irresistible' by Givenchy and was pretty much ready to leave the house to go and meet him. I was probably a bit overdressed for this date in my little black DKNY babydoll cocktail dress with diamante accessories, but I'd made an effort as I'd become quite fond of Sadiq and it *was* Saturday night.

He'd gone above and beyond trying to make up for letting me down that first and last time. He'd sent me a couple of gifts in the post, including a very expensive, gorgeous Tiffany bracelet. The man kept a smile on my face, with his playful, fun-loving attitude. Today we'd been texting non-stop and he had me on a frisky vibe, so when a fresh text came through from him, saying how much he was looking forward to this evening, whilst I was applying my MAC lip gloss, I responded immediately.

"*Me too,*" I enthused, attaching the cheeky monkey emoji and the smiley-face one with the tongue poking out, as we were now on that warm friendly level, where I felt I could be honest and open with him, instead of hiding my true feelings and being hostile.

Spending the evening with my Tyrese look-alike CEO was well needed.

"*Just checking everything's running smoothly for our date… lol,*" he text back, upbeat.

"It is," I confirmed. *"I'm leaving now so I'll see you there in about half an hour?"*

"Cool, I'm looking forward to it," he reiterated.

Grabbing my Michael Kors bag and car keys, I left. I felt a little nervous about seeing him again, but nothing a shot of Grey Goose couldn't sort out. I'd be fine once I'd got that down me. About twenty minutes later I'd almost arrived at China Town, The Arcadian, where we'd planned to meet when my phone started vibrating. Picking it up from the dashboard I glanced at the screen to see another text message from Sadiq.

"Pull over, I'm behind you," it read, with a smiley-face attached.

Looking in my rear-view mirror, I glimpsed his pearl-white Lexus. Wasn't sure why we needed to stop here as we were almost at our destination, but noticing an empty parking bay I slowed down, parked up and wound down my window.

As I watched him park behind me and saw his car door opening, I quickly pulled down my sun visor to check my hair and makeup in the mirror.

Next thing I knew, a stunning female appeared at my car window. Decked out in Louis Vuitton from head to toe, the expensive scent of Coco Chanel wafted into my car as her Rolex gleamed, alongside a diamond bracelet. Her skin was flawless and her long hair was pulled back into a sleek ponytail. Stunned by her incredible beauty, I blinked a couple of times, trying to work out where this tall, Amazon, supermodel-looking woman had appeared from and why she was at my car window glaring down at me. Before I could say a word, she spoke coolly and clearly.

"You don't know me, but I know who you are. In fact, I know all about you."

Completely taken aback, astonished, I managed to speak. "I'm sorry but who are you and what are you talking about?"

"I'm someone who you really don't wanna play with," she snarled.

"Listen, I don't know who you are or what you're on about," I said, looking in my rear-view mirror. *Where was Sadiq?* "I think you've mixed me up with someone else," I told her.

"No, I think you'll find I haven't." Pure venom. Her pretty eyes became two narrow slits. "I've actually been talking to you all day… and reading your texts for quite some time now… been having quite a bit of fun responding to them actually. My favourite was the one you sent a short while ago about how much you're looking forward to this evening."

What the fuck?

Her tone was vicious. "Well I have news for you. There *is* no *this evening*. There never was."

I was lost for words.

"*Sadiq* has no idea I'm here," she carried on. "He thinks I'm in London, across the river, at my sisters, with the kids. But he's the one in London. At work. He didn't arrange to see you this evening. *I* did. It was oh, so easy, accessing his phone and using it as I pleased. The ridiculous photographs you sent him, along with the tedium of your life, made this little trip even easier… so when you drove past me at that last junction, you were instantly recognisable. Bottom line is, *Sadiq* will not be meeting you today or any other day for that matter. So step off. Do not contact him again."

"Hold on a minute!" I didn't take kindly to being threatened by anyone, including this beautiful statuesque stunner, raging in front of me. I didn't give a damn who she was. My blood began to boil. "I don't know who the fuck you think you are…" I began.

"Understand this," she cut me off. "Because I'm only going to say it once. I'm not one to be played with. Trust me, I will fuck you up!! So, I don't care how you do it, but know that it will not be a pretty picture if you don't. You have no idea what you're getting involved in or who you're dealing with, but if you value your life, stay the fuck away from my *husband!*"

Chapter Twenty-Three

After that experience I shut myself away. I didn't go anywhere or do anything. I didn't want to. That was it now. No more. I'd had enough. As angry as I was with Sadiq, sadness clouded me. My days felt empty without his constant attention. Didn't realise exactly how much presence he'd had, till he was gone. We'd had no contact. He hadn't tried to reach me and I hadn't tried to reach him.

I'd told Camara what had happened but I couldn't tell Dijon or he would have been hunting Sadiq down with a sawn-off shotgun. I'd had a feeling something wasn't quite right with Sadiq, but *married? A wife? Kids?* How did I not pick up on that? I guess it all made sense now, the early morning phone calls, the little 'situation' that had made him cancel our first date at the last minute and a few other things I'd noticed. It was all too much, so as usual, I was spending another evening alone at home brooding.

Curled up in the sofa, I stared absently at the TV, watching the drama unfold in an episode of EastEnders. *I should be selling my life story to them for storylines, could make a fortune* I mused, feeling sorry for myself. I sighed, irritated, as the sound of the doorbell penetrated my thoughts.

"I'm not having it," Camara announced, sweeping into my apartment like a fresh spring breeze with flowers in one hand and a Chinese takeaway in the other. "Come-on, it's time for you to stop wallowing in self-pity." She grimaced at me in my crumpled pyjamas. "Let's brighten this place up."

She practically skipped into the kitchen and came back minutes later with a beautiful arrangement of pink carnations, yellow, red and peach roses, white lilies, purple lilacs and other pretty flowers I couldn't recognise, in a tall clear vase and placed them in the centre of the coffee table, before plopping down beside me on the sofa.

"I'm not going to ask you how you are." She was firm. "Because I'm not giving you an opportunity to start dwelling on what's wrong. We are not doing that today. We are not getting on the emotional rollercoaster. We are going to remember the slogan we love, what is it?" She closed her eyes, looked up and inhaled deeply, exhaling slowly. "What is the saying Sahai?"

"Don't get mad, get moving," I solemnly repeated.

"Ok. So that's what we are going to do. Let me get this Chinese."

I stared at her as she strolled back into the kitchen and started clattering about. Is this what friends were for? To just take over your life and start calling the shots whenever it suited them? To begin making decisions for you on a whim? Clearly, as Camara was now shoving a plate of fried beef strips in black bean sauce with egg fried rice, mini spring rolls and prawn crackers under my nose, whilst she enjoyed chicken foo yung with garlic bok choy.

"This is what we're gonna do," she managed, through a mouthful. "We're gonna focus on what you want. What do you want Sahai?" She chomped away.

"Um, right now for you to kinda disappear, so I can carry on doing what I was doing before you arrived? Before you just breezed in here, taking over?" I offered.

She looked at me and smiled. "Silly question. My bad." She helped herself to a prawn cracker from my plate. "What I meant to say was, I've worked out what you need."

"What do I need Camara?" The food actually tasted delicious, so I was starting to feel thankful for her visit after all. I hadn't eaten all day.

"Well, three of my friends at work have met nice guys on the internet. I'm talking fine with a capital F. You need to start internet dating."

"Internet dating?" I was insulted. "I don't think so. Online dating is for people who are past it, who can't get a man. It's like a last resort thing."

"Nope. That's where you're wrong. Trust me," she assured me. "There's this new website. You need to join it. Everyone's talking about it. '*Getahotblackmantoday.*'"

"*Getahotblackmantoday?*" I burst out laughing, spitting out a mouthful of rice. "That's the name of the site?"

"Ugh." She moved away from me looking at the rice from my mouth that had landed on the coffee table. "Don't laugh. Don't knock it. There are some sexy brothas' on it. You wanna meet someone don't you?"

"Camara. I am not dating any of those crazy desperate people on the internet. You know I like to have that moment where you meet someone in person, feel a spark, electricity, have chemistry. You can't get that on the internet by looking at some dodgy picture or reading some fake-ass profile. Not feeling that."

"How do you know when you've never tried it?"

"How do you know when *you've* never tried it?" I shot back, *coming in here, taking over my house, telling me what to do.*

"Look, I know you feel like it's for the oldies, but trust me, there's nothing to be embarrassed about. It's 2014. It's the way forward. Everyone's doing it." Except her of course, as we could safely say she was practically Dantés wife, although you'd never believe it sometimes, with the amount of knowledge and authority she exercised, on what was best for single people.

"Camara." I sighed. "I appreciate your help, support or whatever you're calling your behaviour this evening, but honestly, I'm not ready for that. I'm done with men. I just wanna be single."

"You know that's not true," she said.

"Everyone I meet messes me about. They're all time-wasters so I'm serious. I'm gonna be by myself from now on," I maintained. "I'm not dating anymore. I'm taking time out."

"But that's not what you really want," she said softly. "Sahai, don't let your past ruin your future."

"Ok. Alright. I want to meet someone in person then who is gonna make me happy," I snapped.

"That's where you're going wrong," she piped up. "Happiness comes from within. You can't find someone to make you happy. That's the mistake a lot of us make going into relationships. You have to be responsible for your own happiness, that's something only you can do for yourself. Don't get me wrong, a man *can* and *should* try and make you happy, but you shouldn't *rely* on him for it."

"Can I go now?" I looked at her. "Or should I say, can you go now? Thanks for the love and the care and the pep talk and feeding me, but I'm really not in the mood today," I admitted.

"On one condition." She was stern.

"What Camara?" I sighed, wondering when this evening would end, as I put my empty plate down on the coffee table. She scooped up both our plates and stood up, poised to take them into the kitchen.

"That we log on and you let me create a profile for you on that site before I leave. It's free to join and the beauty of it is that you can even do instant chat for free as well as sending smiles and messages. There are beautiful guys on there from all over the world including right here in Birmingham. Your future husband might be on there."

Within five minutes Camara had fired up my laptop, logged on to the site and was well underway on a mission.

Scrolling through the pictures in my gallery, she seemed to be in a bit of a quandary. "This one or that one?" She hovered the mouse between two photographs of me, which were both nice if you ask me. One of them was of me looking hot in the club in my little white Dior dress the night I met Money and the other was of me chillin' in the sunshine in Miami, last year. "I'm gonna use both of them, but which one do you think would be best as your main profile picture?"

"I don't really care." I was honest.

"This one." She ignored me. "Because you look sexy, sophisticated, smart and demure all at the same time. We don't need too much flesh on display," she concluded, going for a totally random picture that had been taken of me at a Bling & Ting event earlier this year, wearing a black and white Karen Millen dress which complimented my curves. "We need to think about what kind of signals your sending out. The message you're conveying. What type of man you're trying to attract. What type of man are you trying to attract?" She looked at me squinting.

"Um, I don't know Camara, because at this moment in time, my life seems to have been hijacked by some frenzied zombie who is trying to control my mind and sabotage the rest of my day." I glared at her.

"Very funny." She was blasé. "Come-on this is serious. This is your future. In fact, I know what you need, so I'll just get on with it and you do what you're doing. I mean, if you wanna go take a shower or anything, go ahead," she said, scrunching up her face at my crinkled pyjamas.

"What are you trying to say?" I was annoyed. "I had a shower not long before you got here."

"All I'm saying is that if you're just gonna sit there and be miserable then you might as well go and do something else."

"Camara I was fine till you got here." I jumped on the defensive.

"Yeah? I bet you were. More like probably sat there reading all your old text messages from Sadiq."

The joke is, that is exactly what I'd been doing just before EastEnders started. She knew me so well. I'd been trying to work out which messages Sadiq had sent and which ones his wife had sent. I was analysing every single word to see if it sounded like him talking or maybe her? How embarrassing?

"In fact, pass me your phone," Camara demanded. "I need to delete all of them. Hanging on to the past will hold you back. Clearing out the clutter allows for new experiences to come into your life. You know what they say, as one door closes, another one opens."

At this point she was talking to herself as I was no longer listening, opting for a nice little snooze instead, whilst she did her thing. I curled up in my corner of the sofa and left her to it.

Twenty minutes later she was nudging me excitedly. "Look, look at this."

"What? What?" I stirred from my peaceful sleep.

"You've only been a member for five minutes and you've already got three smiles."

"Three smiles?" I was confused.

"Yeah, from guys who fancy you."

"Let me see them." I sat upright, suddenly interested.

"In a minute. Look at your profile first. Tell me if you like it."

"Black Diamond Deluxe? That's my profile name?" I was not impressed as I glared at the screen.

"Yeah, don't you like it?" She seemed surprised.

"Camara, I sound like some kind of exotic dancer."

"Don't be silly, no you don't. The guys will like that name. They'll go for it. Sounds... intriguing, mysterious."

"Like a stripper?"

"No... like a beautiful, exclusive gem, which you are."

"Fun-loving, playful, vibrant woman, seeks intelligent, laid back, cool guy to vibe with." I was now reading the text.

"Sounds good, doesn't it? Do you think I've described you properly and what you want? I said it like that 'cos I thought you don't want anyone too serious. Nothing heavy. Just someone to hang out with, you know do the whole friendship thing to start with?"

"Let's just see who has sent me these smiles first shall we?" I blocked her out.

"Ok." I watched her navigate the site like a pro and I hated to admit it, but she had done a really good job creating my page making me sound fun and interesting, using complimentary pictures of me. I'd fancy me, if you know what I mean. She hovered the mouse over the messages inbox and left it hovering there.

"May the best man win!" she cried, as she got up, scooping up her bag and jacket off the sofa.

"Where you going?" I asked.

"Home. I got an early start in the morning," she said, glancing at her watch.

"But I don't know how to do this," I complained, looking at my page.

"It's easy. You'll work it out. We had a deal right? You asked me to leave. I said on the condition that you allow me to create you a profile. The rest is up to you now."

"Yes, Miss Camara Boot Camp," I joked, as I got up and followed her to the door, hugging her before seeing her out.

Shit. This internet dating stuff was addictive!

It had been three hours since Camara had left and I was now chatting to *'Sexy-Candlelight'* on instant chat. We'd been engaged in conversation for about an hour after he'd requested we speak. It was like a virtual 'date'. He was the second guy I'd spoken to. The first one had been a bit boring with nothing really to say, but *'Sexy-Candlelight'* was keeping me thoroughly entertained, with his quick wit and cheeky sense of humour. He was 34, lived in Brooklyn, New York and was very cute, with the sexiest smile.

"So tell me, what do you want in a man, Miss Pretty Eyes?" He notched it up a level.

"Well, I used to have a long list of qualities." I added a smiley-face emoji. *"But then I realised that was a bit too ambitious... lol... so I narrowed it down to about three. I just want someone who is genuine, who I can vibe with, who treats me nice. What about you?"*

"You definitely sound like my kind of woman." He attached a wink. *"I'm looking for my ride or die! A chick who is down for me no matter what! I can't tell you all the qualities she'll possess, but I'll know her when we connect."*

Smooth. We spoke for about another fifteen minutes, before I knew I had to log off. It was now gone midnight and I had a busy day ahead at work tomorrow.

"Well it's been a pleasure," I told *Sexy-Candlelight*. *"Would love to stay and talk all night, but need to get some sleep."*

"Ok, Pretty Eyes. You do that... be nice to talk again some other time."

"Most definitely," I agreed, before we said our goodbyes and signed out of instant chat. I scrolled through all the emails, messages

and smiles I'd received whilst distracted talking to *Sexy-Candlelight*. I ignored a couple from guys I didn't fancy, sent a smile back to *'The One You Need,'* who looked a bit like Hollywood heart-throb Will Smith, who I was crazy about back in the day, and a wink to *'Your Deepest Desire,'* who was very good-looking. He'd mentioned something on his profile about earning a six-figure salary, which made me send him an extra smiley-face, before calling it a night.

Chapter Twenty-Four

"I'm sure it's this way," I said, pointing down a side road on the left as I sat in the passenger seat next to Darren who was driving.

"You reckon?" Kimar asked from the back seat. "The sat nav's saying to go straight ahead."

"I think Sahai's right you know," Monique said, sitting behind me, peering out of her window. "I remember us going this way last year."

"Follow the road ahead for 200 metres and take the next road on your right," the robotic, ice cold, monotonous female voice commanded with a sense of urgency.

"Turn that damn thing off, she's getting on my nerves," Darren snapped, frustrated, as I fiddled with the volume on the sat nav, trying to turn it down.

It was a Sunday afternoon, we'd been driving around lost for about thirty minutes and he'd had enough. In a sudden quick manoeuvre, he swung the jeep around towards the direction I had suggested and within a few minutes, there they were. Hundreds of revellers, dressed in bright colourful costumes and party clothes, blowing whistles and dancing along the streets to loud calypso music, all headed in one direction. Thank God, we'd finally reached Nottingham Carnival.

Kimar immediately hoisted his camera up on his shoulder, rolled the back window down and started filming out of the window as we cruised slowly in the traffic. I took this opportunity to straighten out my clothes and touch up my makeup in the mirror before turning around and looking directly into the camera which Kimar now had pointed at me.

"It's that time of the year again!" I smiled. "Carnival Season! Party time… and today it's all happening here in Nottingham. Let's get the inside scoop on the hottest DJs, best stalls, carnival queen, who's hot and who's not. It's all happening here at Bling & Ting, stay tuned in."

This year we were focusing on the history of the Caribbean carnival in the UK, looking at who pioneered it in each city, what set it apart from the others and so forth. Our series would culminate in a big special on two of the most significant carnivals, Leeds and Notting Hill during Bank Holiday Weekend at the end of August.

We'd already covered Preston, Reading, Luton, Huddersfield, Bristol, Derby, Manchester and Leicester Carnival. I'd enjoyed Bristol the most, my favourite by far, as it always seemed to have the most vibes, but I hadn't really got too involved with the others as I was keeping busy on *The Sweetest Sound*. Last year our big Carnival theme had been costumes, the year before cuisine, as part of our 'Nyaam Food' special and before that music, where we'd been able to include Birmingham's annual 'Simmer Down' Reggae Festival in Handsworth Park, as a bonus.

As Darren expertly parked the jeep in a tight space, we all got our various bits of gear together and took to the streets. Merging into the thick crowds, I immediately got into the party mood. The sun was beating down and for the first time in weeks, I actually felt in really high spirits.

We knew the procession would be coming through this area any time soon as it had already left Friar Lane, so we decided to get some general shots of the revellers before filming all the floats and the costumes when the Parade arrived. The plan was to stay here for a while, then hit the Forest Recreation Ground, where we could capture the big artists like reggae royalty Sir John Holt performing on the main stage. Afterwards we'd film activities at the fun fair, some of the various arts, crafts and food stalls, and sample some of the best African-Caribbean cuisine on offer.

This summer we seemed to be having the warmest weather we'd had in years, so the filming was going well.

We always did a big feature on the sound systems, exploring who was playing the best in dancehall, soca, reggae, R&B and hip hop. It was gonna be a long day, but I was used to it. I thanked God for Nike as I glanced down at my comfortable all-white Air Max trainers. *I should have worn my pink and black ones*, I thought, as no sooner had I looked down, someone pushed into me, trampling on them and leaving a brown smudge.

Cursing silently I scowled, as the teenager shrugged at me apologetically. I raised my Vuvuzela and blew hard straight into his face, startling him, before he danced off into the crowd. Yes I know that was a bit childish, but this loud horn instrument that I'd got from the South African musician, who'd appeared on our channel during the 2010 World Cup in South Africa, was the most annoying thing I'd ever owned, so I sometimes used it to vent my frustrations.

The musician had explained that the plastic trumpet was originally used to summon distant villagers to tribal gatherings in Africa. He said some claimed the traditional horn was linked to the Zulu tribe and had special healing powers. Either way, many of our viewers had rung in to complain that the sound of the instrument, which spectators had been blowing continuously throughout each game at the World Cup, was too intense and distracting. The musician's only response was that the instrument was a popular symbol of South African football, and no one seemed to have a problem with it in his country. Neither did I, so I blew it again.

"I need to take that thing off you if you're gonna be blowing it all day," Darren complained, trying to grab my Vuvuzela. "You're supposed to be representing Bling & Ting, not attacking kids with that. How immature?"

I held on to it firmly. I'd become quite attached to it. "I'm here to work *and* party," I corrected him, sashaying to the loud calypso beat and blowing into it again, embracing the party mood.

The crowd thickened as thousands of people lined the streets, enjoying the hot weather, lively vibes and fun atmosphere.

As the floats came through, I got swept along with the throng, marvelling at the creativity of some of the costumes and the flurry of colours fluttering, floating and dancing past me; teenage girls sashaying and shimmering in hot pink feathers, little girls skipping along in sunflower yellow, a dance squad in stunning turquoise and silver, led by a crew of guys in tornado blue and white, hollering, whistling and blowing horns.

"Make sure we get that on camera," I instructed Kimar, as they were so hype.

Apple-green fairies twirling and swirling and scarlet-red vixens shaking their booties, danced closely alongside us. Behind them, a group of women in a stunning array of tall peacock feathers, flocked together to create a riot of colour in a spectacular display, followed moments later by a further cluster, spray painted from head to toe in red, gold and green. Forming a unique archway, supported by wooden poles, the women allowed for a dance troupe in bright luminous orange to pass under, showing off the latest dances straight out of Jamaica. A fuss of golds, purples, oranges, crimson, and all shades of blue and magenta completed the impressive parade, as it trailed off into the distance.

"Rewind that bit of footage," I told Kimar, as he was about to switch his camera off. I wanted to make sure we'd captured clear shots of my favourite float, which featured an Empress, designed in the shape of a crown, sitting high on a throne. The entire creation was the same colours as the Jamaican flag. The spokes of the crown were formed out of her black, yellow and green hair extensions, moulded, shaped and sculpted together with hairspray and gel. Tiny gold trinkets decorating her hair twinkled like diamonds. Her skin, spray-painted black, yellow and green, camouflaged with the stiff fabric masking most of her petite frame. The material was starched, twisted and bent into the high rounded coronet shape. Her arms and legs akimbo, intertwined with the structure to finish off the creation. The whole thing was pretty amazing. You had to see it, to really appreciate how eye-catching it was.

By about 7pm I was satisfied that we'd filmed pretty much everything we needed. "Right, let's put this equipment back in the car and enjoy the rest of carnival," I announced, ready to party.

After we'd locked everything safely away, Darren and Kimar went in one direction, no doubt to check girls and Monique and I went in another, agreeing to meet back up at the car a little later.

"Let's go in here." Monique pointed towards a huge marquee with people spilling out. Throbbing bass vibrated through the thin canvas.

Before I had a chance to protest, she dragged me across to the tent, where the DJ was rinsing Ninjaman and Super Cat, like Killamanjaro sound system back in the day. Even though I'd been hoping to walk around for a bit and hear some hip hop, I soon began to enjoy the vibe once I realised it was a sound clash. Allowing the seductive dub plate to take over my body, I began swaying softly to the reggae. Within minutes I felt someone push up behind me.

"Gimme a dance nuh," a rough, gravelly voice commanded. An even rougher pair of hands attached themselves firmly to my hips.

I looked around to see a short old man trying to dance with *me!* He had a matted beard, pockmarked skin and was wearing a black woolly hat and a dusty red, gold and green tracksuit that looked like it had seen better days.

Horrified, I quickly side-stepped him. "No thanks." I was polite.

"Wha wrong wid yuh? Yuh tink seh yuh nice?" he immediately began cursing in patois, as he leaned into my face. His breath reeked of Dragon Stout and White Rum. It smelt rancid. I backed off a little before he continued. "Jus' gimme a one dance nuh? Yuh sweet nuh raas. Why yuh a gwarn so stush? Pretty gyal like yuh nuh fi stan up in ere pon yuh own," he insisted, with his frowsy breath, as he tried to grab my arm. "Yuh need a man fi hold yuh and squeeze yuh, nuh true?"

"She said she doesn't want to dance."

I looked up to see where that sexy deep voice was coming from and found myself staring into the most beautiful face. This guy looked like an Ethiopian warrior. He had a golden-bronze complexion with straight, sharp features, complimented by soft, full lips and he was towering above me and I mean towering. He must have been about 6ft 8 or 9. His black, almond shaped eyes, framed by long silky lashes, twinkled, flashing dangerously, as he looked down at the scruffy little old man who'd obviously decided he wanted to fight for me.

"A who yuh a bloodclart chat to?" The old man drunkenly shouted at Ethiopian warrior. "Yuh a try fi test big man?" he slurred, agitated, rising up to all 5ft 2 of himself, poking his chest out.

Ethiopian warrior simply stared him down like he was an irritant.

Uneasy, the old man staggered and tripped, as a stream of expletives came spewing from his mouth. "Move yuh bumbaclaat, raasclatt, pussyclaat..." the little man cursed.

Ethiopian warrior inched silently towards him, his menacing presence unnerving the old man. His eyes were dark, deadly. He looked crazy, lethal, like he was not to be messed with. The old drunkard clearly picked up on that signal and stumbled off into the tent cursing and mumbling under his breath.

"Thank you," I said, staring up into those same brown eyes, now soft and kind.

"My pleasure." He smiled warmly. "Are you alright?" His voice was full of sincerity.

"Yes, I'm fine, thanks to you."

"Good," he said, extending his hand. "I'm Malachi, but everyone calls me Kaden."

"Sahai," I said, shaking his hand.

"Cute name. Different." He stared at me.

"Yours too," I bounced back the compliment. "Where are you from? You got an unusual look."

"Yeah, I'm half Jamaican, half Ethiopian," he explained. "I was born in Jamaica, that's where I mostly grew up, but I live in Birmingham now," he said.

"Interesting. So do I. Whereabouts?"

"Great Barr," he stated. "You?"

"Edgbaston," I replied.

"Not too far from me," he said smiling. "Can I get you a drink?"

"That would be nice thanks. I'll come with you." I looked around to introduce him to Monique, but she was busy dancing with some sweet boy, to the bashy sounds of Alkaline, so I indicated I was going to the bar and left her to it.

I assessed Kaden as he strided tall in front of me to his destination. He was wearing dark green khaki combat trousers, a matching jacket and cap with red, gold and green stripes and some beige Timberlands. The outfit suited him, although it wasn't really my kind of style. Long, silky, slim dreadlocks flowed down his back. I admired them swishing from side to side as he swaggered through the crowd.

"So did you drive to Nottingham today?" he asked, as I enjoyed my Bacardi and Coke whilst he sipped his Guinness.

"No, my colleague drove, we've been here working."

"Working? You a performer, singer or something?" he asked with a serious face, seducing me with those bedroom eyes.

"Nah, nothing like that." I laughed. "I'm a television producer," I confirmed. "We were filming earlier."

"Sounds interesting." He had this intense way of looking at me. The more I looked at him, the more his eyes reminded me of the actor Al Pacino in 'The Godfather', just staring, that blank stare, with those brooding, captivating eyes. *Damn!*

"What about you?" I managed.

"I'm a musician and an artist," he stated. "I paint, generally on canvas and also play the drums, bongos, keyboard and guitar."

"I'm impressed," I said genuinely, as Buju Banton's rugged voice replaced Mavado's, with his hit, 'Destiny'. "I love this song," I murmured, swaying back and forth as the chorus kicked in. Kaden smoothly found his groove behind me and before long the two of us were wrapped around each other, locked in a tight embrace, where we remained smooching to lovers rock and enjoying light conversation until the bright lights came on in the tent, announcing that carnival was officially over.

"Let me walk you back to your car," he offered, as we stepped outside. Monique was busy exchanging numbers with the guy she'd met, so I waited patiently for her as I was not trying to lose her in these heaving crowds. People were everywhere, staggering around and pushing into us as they left the tent. Kaden wrapped himself around me like a shield, protecting me against all harm and glaring at anyone who dared push into us. I liked that. Protective. My bodyguard.

"I'm ready," Monique chirped, as she detached herself from her man and moved next to us. The multitude of people rushing in all directions was so thick, Kaden reached for my hand and held it firm but gently, guiding me safely through the masses. His hands felt warm and smooth. I liked his touch.

Darren and Kimar were already chillin' in the jeep when we got there, so after Monique jumped in, I quickly said goodbye to Kaden with a brief hug.

"Wait there?" He looked at me. "Don't I get a number? How can I contact you?"

I was about to begin my 'don't give out numbers' mantra, I mean, he didn't look like he had much to offer me, but then I remembered how he had saved me from the old drunkard and wondered if he might have some good contacts in the music industry who might be useful for Bling & Ting. With that, I whipped out one of my business cards, placed it in his hands, smiled sweetly and jumped in the jeep.

Chapter Twenty-Five

I was still vibing when I got in from Carnival. It was well after midnight as Darren had dropped the camera kit back to work first and then everyone else home before me. Even though it had been a long day, it had been fun. In fact the first fun day I'd had in a while.

Grabbing my iPad I flopped down in the sofa and logged on to check if I had any messages or smiles from anyone on *Getahotblackmantoday.* I was loving the whole experience of internet dating, being able to choose whoever I wanted. It was a bit like shopping in my favourite stores, selecting everything from my perfect colour, size and shape to all the qualities that I admired. It was a no-brainer.

As soon as the computer fired up, the message 'you're beautiful' popped up with a smile from the sexiest guy, *Hot Chocolate.* Damn! He was fine and from *Birmingham*? I could hardly contain myself. *Here? Living in the same city as me?* Happy days! I had to do a double take 'cos this was rare. Most of the fine guys on the site always seemed to be African-American. I quickly scanned his profile. He was 33 years old, single, no kids, a Capricorn, looking for someone to hang out and have fun with. Very good-looking, he reminded me of the actor Boris Kodjoe. Cute and ripped from head to toe, with a body built to last.

Whilst reminiscing about how good it had felt smooching with Kaden, I noticed that *Hot Chocolate* was online right now, so I quickly clicked on instant chat, inviting him to have a conversation. Hoping and waiting for him to respond, I opened my music folder and selected some slow jams to get me in a relaxed, flirtatious mood.

As Maxwell's smooth silky tones oozed softly from the speakers with his track 'Pretty Wings', I reflected on my day. Kaden was fine, but I could see that he was as poor as a church mouse, so I wasn't really trying to entertain him. *Hot Chocolate* on the other hand, who had just accepted my request to chat, claimed to earn a high salary, I noticed, as I quickly scanned his profile.

"Hey," I said, excited to be communicating with this sexy Adonis.

"How you doing?" He greeted me warmly with a smiley-face emoji.

"Great thanks. You?" I practically dribbled over his profile picture as I typed back.

"My day just got a lil' better," he flirted.

"Lol... thanks for the smile and the compliment... I like your profile," I told him.

"How did I get so lucky to get the attention of such a beautiful woman at this late hour tonight?" he asked.

I explained that I'd just got back from Nottingham carnival. He said he was up writing a report for work. I found out his name was Michael and he lived in Sutton Coldfield, which was about 30 minutes away from me.

"You are stunning," he complimented.

"Just trying to keep up with you," I shot back.

"Funny as well I see. Single?"

"Yup," I said a bit too quickly for my own liking, but *damn*, it's not every day you meet a Boris Kodjoe lookalike online who lives around the corner from you.

"Can't stop looking at your picture... you're gorgeous," he said.

"Takes one to know one," I flirted back as Maxwell's track, riddled with angst, reminded me of the heartache relationships could bring. Wasn't really doing anything for my mood, so I scrolled through my playlist and replaced Maxwell with Keith Sweat. Maxwell's voice was beautiful, but Keith Sweat was the man when it came to turning up the heat.

"Are you single?" I checked.

"Yeah, been single for about six months," he confirmed.

Lovely! I thought as I scanned his sexy picture again.

We enjoyed friendly, flirty banter for about another fifteen minutes, during which he explained he worked in banking at managerial level, but was currently struggling with his report. He'd gone over it so many times he wasn't sure if it was making sense.

"Just stay focused," I advised. *"You know you can do it, otherwise you wouldn't be in the position you are right now. Don't worry about a thing. You're gonna blow them away with that report."* I was confident.

"You're very inspirational." He sent me a smile.

"Thank you."

"You're golden... super sexy... love your positive attitude."

"Thanks," I said again, lovin' the way he was talking to me right now.

"Be good to talk to you a lot more. Are you on Facebook?" he queried.

Hell nah!

"No. It's not really my thing." I was honest. *"I know it has its benefits, especially from a business point of view, but on a personal level it's a bit too intrusive for me. You know, everyone in everyone else's business and all that. I'm quite a private person. I have got a Facebook account but I rarely use it."*

"Let me hear your voice then, put a sound to that pretty face. Can we talk on the phone?" He asked. *"What's your number?"*

I wasn't really trying to give out my number just like that, so I took his down and promised to call him in about twenty minutes. I logged off, had a quick shower, slipped into a t-shirt, jumped into bed, and then dialled his number, placing 141 in front of the digits to withhold my number. Definitely didn't want him to have any of my personal details until I knew him a bit better. He answered on the first ring.

"Wow. You've got a sexy voice," he said, as soon as I said hello.

"Thanks." Unfortunately I couldn't say the same. His voice sounded extremely high and super squeaky. Bit disappointing as I'd imagined it to be deep and seductive.

"So, what did you like about my profile?" he asked straightaway.

"I'll be honest." I nestled down, getting comfortable in bed. "I was attracted to your photo."

"Is that all? Just my image?" he grumbled, sounding offended.

"Well initially yes, but then when I read your profile, I liked what you had to say plus the fact that you're local."

"Be good to meet up," he said, wasting no time jumping on the benefits of our close proximity.

"Would be nice," I agreed, although I knew I wasn't trying to see him anytime soon. After Sadiq, I was keen to take things even slower with anyone else I met, even if he did look like Boris Kodjoe.

"So you really liked my photo huh?" He mentioned it again.

"Yes," I repeated. "I mean, you are really good-looking." I stroked his ego. *Well he did say he was a manager at a bank! Must be on good money!*

"Is that the *only* reason you invited me to chat? Because of my photo? Be honest."

Where was this going? "No," I said. "But looks are important."

"Why?" he asked.

"Because you have to be attracted to your partner." *Dimwit.*

"Yeah, but looks aren't everything. Looks can fade," he said.

"True."

"And you said earlier that the most important thing is a guy who makes you laugh," he stated. *Was he arguing with me? Didn't really have time for this* I thought, glancing at the clock on my bedside table to see that it was now well after one a.m. I had work in the morning. "I mean," he continued, "what if you met up with me and I didn't look how I looked in the picture? Would you still be interested in me?"

Strange. "Maybe… um Michael, what are you trying to say?"

"I'm just saying that what's really important between two people is that connection. You know, being able to communicate and vibe. It's a bit shallow to be all about image. It would be a shame if you only liked me because I look like that."

Hold on a minute? "Michael?" I was curious. "Is that you, in your profile picture?"

He answered my question with a deadly silence.

"It's not you is it?" I laughed, incredulous. His hesitancy confirmed my suspicion.

"No it's not," he finally confessed sheepishly.

"Why have you done that?" I blurted. "Why would you put up a picture that's not you, pretending it is?"

"Because the most important thing in life is sincerity... once you've learnt how to fake that, it's all good."

"What?"

"I did it so that I can get attention from pretty girls like you. I mean, you wouldn't have been interested in me if I didn't look like that? You wouldn't be talking to me right now, would you?"

Damn right! I sat up straight in my bed. "Michael, that's crazy. I mean, if you met up with me I'd soon know that it wasn't you anyway, so that ain't cool."

"But by then you would've gotten to know me a lot better, so my looks may not have bothered you," he argued.

Was this guy for real? Getting me all excited thinking I was speaking to *Hot Chocolate,* when actually, I was probably speaking to *Lumpy Porridge.* "Well, what *do* you look like?" I was intrigued.

"I'm good-looking," he mumbled.

"If that's the case why didn't you put your own picture up then?" I challenged.

"I'm average height, fair skinned, a little on the heavy side, but not overweight, hazel eyes, short hair."

"Ok." I didn't really know what else to say, as lying and deceit were two of my pet hates, unless of course I was the one doing the lying and deceiving, so I couldn't get past that. There was one thing I needed to know though. "So, if that isn't you, who is it in the picture then? Do you know him?" My mind was racing.

"I made it."

"Made it?" I was stunned.

"Yeah, made the picture. It's easy, just used some computer graphics to create an image."

Backside!!

What if this guy was some kind of serial killer, stalker, psycho? I mean, he was already using science and technology to attract, deceive and manipulate women online. *Should I just hang up now or ease out of this conversation gently?* Damn Camara, why did she get me into this internet dating stuff? I knew they would all eventually turn out to be weirdos.

"Anyway, it's late. I gotta go now." I opted for a peaceful exit.

"Oh that's convenient." His high voice got squeakier. "You're just like all the rest. A shallow, simple bitch..."

Oh shit. I glanced around like he was about to come crashing into my bedroom wielding a butcher's knife or something, before it occurred to me that he didn't know my real name or where I lived. I hadn't told him where I worked or even what I did for a living. He didn't have my telephone number. *Why was I entertaining this psycho?* Comforted by those thoughts, I hung up.

That's when I remembered I'd agreed to go for lunch with *'Your Deepest Desire'* tomorrow. *Shit!* We'd been speaking online steadily for the last few days. He lived in Oxford, but casually mentioned that he would be in Birmingham tomorrow at a work conference. Wasn't keen at first, but I figured, why waste time talking to someone online for months, only to meet up and find there's no chemistry. But now, I was having second thoughts after this creepy little experience with *Hot Chocolate*.

Chapter Twenty-Six

"You can't let that change your mind," Camara insisted, when I rang her up the next day to curse her for getting me involved in this internet dating stuff.

"Camara, I didn't sleep at all last night," I huffed. "I was half expecting that crazy lunatic to track me down and come to my apartment to kill me."

"Look, he obviously had issues, but not everyone you meet online is gonna be like that. My colleague recently got engaged to a guy she met on the internet two years ago. It's so romantic," she cooed.

"Great for her, but I'm not sure meeting up with this guy for lunch is a clever idea," I stressed, glancing at the wall clock in the edit suite as Darren shoved a magazine under my nose.

I studied the section he pin-pointed, till my eyes rested on an article he was showing me with a review about *The Sweetest Sound*. I silently began reading the short article. '*Bling & Ting are the one to keep watching this week with their innovative, fresh new concept. Interestingly, their controversial new dating series, which hails music as one of the undiscovered laws of attraction, has seen their ratings soar through the roof. Pulling in millions of viewers every episode, The Sweetest Sound has pundits worldwide twittering ...*'

Wow. I was impressed.

"So you're not gonna go then?" Camara's voice popped up from the telephone receiver cradled in the crook of my neck. I'd forgotten she was still there for a minute.

"Nah."

"Well have you cancelled?" She was beginning to sound like a school teacher.

"No," I admitted.

"You're standing him up then? Aren't you supposed to be meeting him in about an hour? You said you two really got on."

"We did." I rewound some of the Nottingham carnival footage, trying to pick out the best bits to use for a short trailer. "But what if it's all lies? Clearly people are just saying anything on these damn dating sites, making up any old shit to make themselves look good. I mean, let's look at it this way, if they were cool, then why would they have to start dating on the internet in the first place? Surely someone would have snapped them up in a club or a bar or at a wedding or some friggin' where? Surely someone would have locked them down?"

"Look, why don't you just go?" Camara urged, flustered. "People have all sorts of reasons for internet dating, you know like busy lifestyles or tired of meeting the same kind of people. He sounds like a decent guy. You've got nothing to lose. You're meeting him in the city centre at Starbucks! What can he possibly do to you there?"

"Drug me? Spike my latte?" I was taking no chances.

"You're being very dramatic now." She sighed. "He might be the one."

"But what if he's lied about his picture like that madman last night? What if there's no chemistry?"

"What if there is? He seems friendly enough. Nice personality and didn't you say he was a psychologist or something unusual like that?"

"He's a psychoanalyst," I remembered.

"You should definitely go meet him then. He might give you some new ideas for *The Sweetest Sound*. Psychoanalysts look at how the unconscious mind influences our conscious thoughts and behaviours don't they? He may have a fresh insight."

"Good point," I realised, thinking about Sigmund Freud's theory that there are mental processes that are not conscious. A few psychologists had actually contacted the station talking about the same thing, offering to come on our programme to give an expert analysis and assessment of our theory. But Freud had *invented* psychoanalysis, was famously known as the father of it, so no doubt must've had a major influence on *Your Deepest Desire,* who I'm sure would've had to study the man. Guess I *could* try it out first on him, I thought, as my mobile phone beeped letting me know I had a text message.

"When can I c u again?" It was Kaden. Talk about getting straight to the point. Not even a friendly 'hi'.

"Gotta go," I told Camara, hanging up the desk phone, before busying myself trying to quickly finish editing the trailer before I rushed out to meet *Your Deepest Desire*. Kaden could wait.

As I neared Starbucks I stopped rushing, slowed down and put on my best Naomi Campbell walk, just in case he was nearby watching me. You never know!

I was nervous and twitchy as hell, as I glanced in every direction to see if *Your Deepest Desire* had arrived. Ok, so he had looked hot in his pic. He was caramel coloured with slim features, nice eyes, a sexy smile and yes, good teeth. He'd probably be wearing a suit as he was at a conference. But no one and I mean no one within my radius fit that description. It was ten minutes past one now. We'd agreed to meet at one o' clock and I had to be back at work by two.

Maybe I'll just leave now, I thought, as I saw some movement to my right. The guy to my right was definitely clocking me. There was no one else waiting outside Starbucks but hell no, it couldn't be *Your Deepest Desire*. He'd said he was *tall,* not *short*. He'd said he was *slim,* not *fucking wide*. He'd said he was *muscular,* not *stocky and built like a damn pit bull terrier* and what the fuck were all those piercings all over his damn face? Just as I began retreating, backing up into Starbucks trying to be discreet and make myself invisible, he stepped right up to me and smiled.

"Black Diamond Deluxe?" he guessed, sounding a bit embarrassed, extending his hand.

"Excuse me?" I did my best to look offended. I was going down the lost and confused route.

"Sorry, I must have mistaken you for..."

"Yeah, I think you have," I said, disappearing into Starbucks and rushing into the queue. *Damn that Camara! Talking me into this shit!* A toffee nut latte would definitely calm me down, along with a steak and cheese melt, but as my favourite beverage was only available during the festive season, I ordered a strawberry and cream frappuccino instead to go with my melt and began rummaging in my bag for change. No sooner than I'd joined the short queue, waiting to collect my lunch, I felt someone tap me on my arm. Spinning around I was face to face with *Your Deepest Desire* again, who was now rapidly becoming '*My Worst Nightmare.' Why, oh why?*

"It is you," he said, holding up his iPhone, fully displaying my profile page on the internet, with a crystal clear picture of me smiling underneath the words 'Black Diamond Deluxe'. *Damn!* I was even wearing the same outfit today as the one in the picture. *Fucking Technology!* I attempted to give him a sort of half smile, but he quickly pulled me in close for an awkward hug. "Good to meet you," he added, gushing. "I know I look a little different from my picture. Obviously you didn't recognise me."

A *little* different? The guy was fucking deluded.

I really didn't know what to say, so I just didn't speak.

"I'll grab some food and join you," he insisted.

Mesmerised by the multiple piercings on his face, dumbstruck, I meekly nodded and dropped down into the nearest chair as he moved into the queue. I'd counted nine piercings so far, adorned with silver studs. He had one on both eyebrows, one in his temple, one under his lower lip and one on his upper lip that looked like a silver cold sore, one in his cheek where I think he may have had a dimple, one in his tongue that I'd noticed whilst he was speaking, one in his nose and one under his chin. *I was officially on a date with a fucking dartboard!* When did my life get to this?

Munching on my steak and cheese melt, I wondered if it was a good idea to be eating at all, 'cos surely I'd be throwing up in the next fifteen minutes or so, after engaging with this 'character' who'd now plopped down in front of me.

"You're even prettier in real life. Absolutely gorgeous," he said smiling, which was when I noticed a snake crawling up his neck through the collar of his biker jacket, ending just below his chin. He slipped out of his jacket, revealing more of that monstrous snake tattoo peeking out from beneath his extremely tight white T-shirt and *what the fuck? Were those man boobs? Moobs?* "I know I look a bit different. I've gained some weight since I took that photo. It was taken a couple of years ago."

He was obviously used to having one sided conversations, as I hadn't said a word since he'd hijacked me in the queue. I was speechless. All I could do was sit and stare at him, as he removed a glob of chewing gum from his mouth, wrapped it in a napkin, bit into his tuna melt and kept on talking.

"You probably expected to see me in a suit today, because of the conference, but it's a real casual informal affair, so I'm just doing me."

In the end I couldn't resist. "What's with all the piercings and the studs?" I asked. "You didn't have any in your photograph."

"Oh these?" He fingered the one in his temple." Original right? It's something I got into recently. I don't wear them all the time, just sometimes. I like to be unique," he boasted.

"Don't they... hurt?" I wondered.

"Sometimes... if I leave the studs out too long. I got a bad infection in these two once." He pointed to his nose, then his lower lip. "But other than that, no problems."

"Oh," was all I could muster, as I glanced around thinking about making a quick exit. "Yes, you do look very different from your picture," I added. Hideous, to be exact.

"Yeah, that photo was taken before I started getting in the gym, pumping up." He raised his right arm, displaying a colossal bicep bulging with thick, blue veins.

His arm looked like it was about to burst, like it was in the worst kind of pain. I actually thought I was gonna throw up, as he showed off, striking a range of poses, beaming. Couldn't believe he thought I was complimenting him. That's when my mobile phone started ringing. *Thank You God!* I said a silent prayer as right now this was the sweetest sound to my ears. I smiled inwardly as I saw Dijon's name flash up on the screen.

"Hello?" I answered, in an anxious, nervous voice.

"'Sup cuz?" Dijon asked, sounding relaxed.

"You what?" I screamed. "Oh my God, when?" I jumped up.

"Cuz?" Dijon was bewildered.

"Oh my life, I'm coming right now. I'll be there in five minutes. That's awful. I'm on my way." I hung up, scooping up my handbag. "Sorry. Gotta go," I told a confused looking *Your Deepest Desire*.

"Are you ok?" He genuinely seemed concerned.

"Family emergency. Sorry about this." I rushed off before he had a chance to say another word.

Chapter Twenty-Seven

I was officially done with internet dating! In fact any kind of dating. That's it now. I was staying single. And this time, I meant it. No amount of pep talks from Camara or anyone else was gonna change my mind.

Throwing myself into my work was the way forward and it was proving to be very fruitful.

"So why don't you think it worked?" I asked, holding the microphone up to Reuben's mouth, giving him a reassuring smile to relax him and encourage him to open up and be honest. I'd warned everyone to be careful not to use any obscenities during this live show, a follow-up to the first episode of *The Sweetest Sound*.

"Well, after those first couple of dates, she got a bit... clingy."

"Clingy?" Tia exclaimed, as she shifted away from him on the red love-heart shaped velvet couch. "I'm not clingy. You cheated on me!" An audible, collective gasp from the studio audience heightened the drama.

"Is that true Reuben?" I persisted. It had been a few months since that first show aired.

"Well it's not like you were my girl." He looked at her. "We were just dating."

"Just dating?" Tia was beginning to sound like a parrot, repeating everything Reuben said. "Um, excuse me, but after our third date, you asked me to be your girl and I agreed."

"That's because I liked the way we partied, you know in the club."

"So you're saying your mutual music tastes kept the attraction alive?" I jumped in, keen to keep the theory going. "The fact that you both love reggae?"

"Guess you could say so," Reuben commented.

"Why did you cheat then?" I pressed him.

"I *have* to cheat," he admitted, as the studio audience erupted in a wave of gasps and giggles.

"*Have* to?" I queried.

Tia was now visibly sulking with her bottom lip pushed out and arms folded tightly across her body.

"Yeah," he bragged. "Listen, girls nowadays, you can't trust them. They'll make out like you're the only one they're seeing, then two two's you find out they're dealing with some next man, so I ain't putting all my eggs in one basket. You get me?"

Claps, booing and raucous laughter came from the studio audience as I posed my next question, this time directed at Tia. "*Were* you seeing someone else Tia?" I was curious.

"No. I swear down." Sadness washed over her.

"How do you feel to hear that?" I asked Reuben.

"It's all good," he said, smiling. He turned to Tia, gently placing his hand on her forearm. "Those other girls, don't watch that. They don't really mean nu-un to me still," he confided, playing up to the cameras. "Yuh done know, me a de bun, you a de cheese. Maybe we can get through this?" he reasoned, with fake sincerity and puppy dog eyes. Dismayed, she turned away from him as I addressed the audience.

"What do you think? Can they?" I stared into the lens. "Join us after the break to find out. Seems like it's time to face the music! We'll also be hearing from the other couples who took part in Episode One and a psychologist who joins us all the way from the States to enlighten us a bit more! You wouldn't want to miss it. Bling & Ting, where it all begins, make sure you keep watching, stay tuned in." I smiled, as we went to a commercial break.

"How did you find out Reuben was cheating?" I quizzed Tia, after returning from the commercial break, during which the two of them had been engaged in a strained, heated argument.

"On waste book innit... I mean facety book." Tia rolled her eyes in his direction, rotating her neck.

"Facebook?" I clarified for our audience, as she clearly wasn't willing to use the correct name. She nodded.

"What?" Reuben looked confused.

"Don't act like you don't know I'm talking about Cassandra?" she spat at him.

"How do you know Cassandra?" Reuben looked mortified.

"Cassandra?" I glanced at the audience with an exaggerated bewildered expression.

"You're so dumb." Tia eyed him with contempt. "Always on Facebook, well guess what? So am I and yes, I have been logging into your account, pretending to be you."

"You gave her your password?" I asked Reuben, who sat quietly glaring at Tia.

"Of course he didn't." Tia was unstoppable. "He's so stupid. He can't even think of anything original, so it was easy for me to guess that his password would be his favourite artist, Alkaline," she hissed, now on a roll. "You're so obvious. I've read every single message between you and your little hood-rat friend Cassandra Johnson over the last few weeks. I know you took that ratchet bitch to see Nicki Minaj in concert, after you told me that you weren't going." Tia was on fire. "Yes, I saw the pictures of you two together in Cassandra's photo gallery and I know you've slept together."

At this point Reuben's face took on a deadly, dark, sinister appearance, but that didn't stop Tia who was clearly milking her moment.

"I've even been talking to *Cassandra* from your page," she confessed, "sending her sordid, seedy little messages from you."

Oh my days! How awful, I thought, recognising the similarities with what Sadiq's wife did to me. Texting me pretending to be him. Was everyone doing that these days? Was this what modern loving had come to?

"And if you must know," Tia continued, enjoying the spotlight, "Cassandra's been flirting right back, acting real freaky! Skanky bitch. Anyway she can have you 'cos your dick game was wack!"

Pandemonium broke out in the crowd, with the audience laughing, booing, clapping, stamping their feet, shouting and hurling comments towards the stage, whilst Reuben, sat dead still, eyeing Tia as though she'd just violated him in the worst possible way. His expression was chilling, the tension palpable. Teeth clenched, he looked like he wanted to kill her. The only thing saving her right now was live television.

Shit! "I guess it really is over between you two now then?" I interjected, looking around to see where the security guys were. I hadn't planned for any of this.

The crowd was becoming rowdier. People were getting wild, jumping up and congregating in the aisles. A few of them looked like they were about to kick off, I noticed, as I observed a small commotion brewing. I wondered if the dispute was between Reuben and Tia's friends in the audience, maybe even the elusive Cassandra's. Plus I was annoyed with Tia's last few comments. I'd warned the contestants, no obscene language. That's all we needed, for the programme to be pulled off air.

I watched as the security guards made their way through the ruckus towards the growing disturbance in the walkway, then Bailey off stage behind the curtain, giving me a signal to keep it moving, at which point Pharrell Williams' hit song 'Happy' rang out loud around the auditorium, drowning out the noise. The studio audience seemed to respond well to the music. The small gathering in the aisles dispersed, the racket died down and order was restored as people returned to their seats.

Taking that as my cue, I swung around to face the camera and put on my best Grammy award-winning smile. "Let's bring out our next couple. Josiah and Tasha, come on out!"

The two soulful house lovers appeared from backstage, holding hands, looking loved up, as Reuben and Tia continued to glower at each other. At least security were nearby.

"Looks like someone's found love," I observed. "What's the secret?"

"She's fun-loving, down to earth, real cool." Josiah beamed at Tasha, still holding her hand.

"He's caring, funny, always taking me out, we like to party hard." Tasha giggled.

"Well you know what they say. The couple who play together, stay together," I chirped.

This was more like it. I was pleased. They were confirming my theory. Tasha and Josiah, who loved that upbeat, breezy sound, were getting closer every day.

Within an hour, all six of the original couples who had taken part in the first episode of *The Sweetest Sound* had joined me on the sofa and to my delight, four of them had become an item and were still together. Javon and Dionne had started seeing each other but it hadn't lasted. According to Javon, "she was on some long ting, unwilling to free up the goods," but she'd put their split down to his love of commercial "money and bitches" hip hop, her words. Javon hadn't challenged her, so I was still winning. Music was the key influence!

I looked into the camera with a complete air of authority. "From what we are seeing, it's clear to say, that music and mating go hand in hand and we have a very special guest here today who's going to explain just why. Let's bring out psychologist Doctor Dewayne Devant, who has flown here all the way from Chicago, to join us. Please put your hands together and show some love for Doctor Dewayne Devant."

Wolf-whistles, screams, applause and cheers erupted from the audience as this thirty-something fine brotha' stepped out on to the stage. He was the whole package, tall, smooth, fit and handsome with a bald head, killer smile and wearing the hell out of his Armani suit.

Making his way towards me, he gave the couples a quick once-over. "We about to get real personal up in here," he warned, in a deep, smooth, liquid-gold voice, sending the excited, screaming women in the studio audience crazy, as he joined me on the sofa.

Chapter Twenty-Eight

"Welcome to the show Doctor Devant," I greeted him warmly.

"Thank you. It's my pleasure to be here," he drawled, flashing his million-dollar smile, sending the females in the audience into a frenzy again.

"I understand you've been conducting research into the theory that our taste in music can have an effect on our personalities and our subconscious minds, which in turn may influence how we see and treat our partners and how successful our relationships might be as a consequence of this," I said.

"Yeah, it's been an interest of mine for many years. You know, when I was younger I be goin' to the clubs." He purposefully slipped into street slang for added entertainment value. "I be seein' how we like to bump and grind and get down. I figured music was the appetiser… lovin' was the main course. You feel me?"

The studio audience laughed, already warming to him.

"In what sense?" I probed, purely for audience benefit as he and I were definitely singing from the same hymn book.

"It ain't no secret that most of us love music and most of us love to get intimate. Right? We get dressed, hit the club, hook a hottie, then hit the bedroom. In that order."

Raucous laughter and clapping came from the crowd as he carried on.

"It may not be on the same night, it may not even be in the same week, but trust me, it gon' happen! You gon' hit that bedroom! Fo' sho'." Squeals rose from the audience. They were loving him. "This goes for those of you who ain't on the club scene too," he said, waving his finger at a delighted audience. "Don't get it twisted, you included in this as well, you may be staying home but trust me, you know you behind closed doors getting your swerve on with the slow jams or whatever it is y'all be listening to, getting y'all heated. Can I get an amen?"

"Amen," the audience chorused, clapping and laughing, agreeing with him.

"What has your research highlighted?" I wanted to know.

"Well, I'm a break it down like this," he began in his sexy, deep voice. "This couple right here?" He pointed at Jasmine and Tyree practically snuggled up on the sofa. "Ain't they beautiful?" he asked the audience who immediately broke out clapping again. Gosh, Dewayne had the viewers under his full command. They were melting under his spell. He was proving to be a total hit. "You on a jazz tip right?" he confirmed with the happy couple who nodded in agreement. "When did you discover your love of jazz music?" he asked Jasmine.

"When I was about thirteen. My dad used to play it all the time. Some of the greats like Louis Armstrong and John Coltrane," she said.

"I was pretty much the same age," Tyree spoke up. "My mum loved Billie Holiday and Miles Davis. She was always playing their music," Tyree explained.

"So you see what we have here?" Dewayne piped up. "It was during your adolescence that jazz music became a big part of your identity."

"I guess it was," Jasmine reflected. "I've always been a free spirit, you know, live and let live. Jazz gives me that floaty feeling, makes me feel mellow, relaxed. It represents freedom for me, you know?"

"This is very interesting," I assessed. "This whole childhood association with sound and rhythm and how it connects to our wider understanding of life."

"Precisely," Dewayne agreed.

"At school I mainly hung out with the other two guys in our year who loved jazz," Tyree informed us. "The three of us were amongst a few who played instruments, so we became friends in music lessons. I was on the bass guitar, whilst they played the keyboard and saxophone," Tyree recalled.

"This is exactly what I'm talking about," Dewayne said enthusiastically. "You were drawn to others who shared your same musical passion," he articulated, before glancing back towards Jasmine. "You were both at an age where you were impressionable, looking for a sense of belonging. As teenagers we are all trying to figure out who we are and what we want, so we put together a set of symbols that allow us to express our identity to the world." He turned to face me. "Music functions as a badge we use to draw like-minded people towards us, those who we feel share similarities.

"This is why all around the world birds of a feather flock together," he explained. "We see hip hop crews, rock chicks with rockers, gospel groups. It's correct to say a shared preference in music undisputedly creates strong bonds between people," he professed. "We cannot deny that music is a powerful force, arguably *the* most powerful force and clearly, as we've seen here today," he drawled, squinting seductively into the camera, "music helps us figure out who we wanna roll with. It stands to reason then, how and why this key element would go on to become one of the major laws of attraction in adulthood. Music is more than music. It's a life-force, the air we breathe, a way of life, a lifestyle," he emphasized.

A low mutter rose from the audience who seemed to be now discussing the theory amongst themselves.

"Some may argue that's a bit of a sweeping statement," I said, playing Devil's advocate.

"Listen, they may argue all they want but it's crystal clear." Dewayne was adamant. "Music is the trigga' honey," he drawled in his thick dialect. "Take these two." He pointed at Omar and Cherelle. "Tell me about your relationship."

"He's awesome," Cherelle admitted, staring at Omar. "Propa. A real gentleman, he always opens doors for me, carries my bags, looks after me, and I like that because I'm a hopeless romantic."

"She's got class," Omar said, looking at her with pure adoration. "She's smart, ambitious, knows how to handle herself and likes to pamper me. She definitely keeps a smile on my face which is cool as I'm also a bit of a romantic."

"Right. There we have it," Dewayne clarified. "Your musical preference is R&B right?" They both nodded. He continued. "These two enjoy music that reflects their values of romance and togetherness. Love songs. This has manifested in their close connection, they are likeminded partners. Kindred spirits."

The studio audience were getting louder and louder so I decided to open it up to the floor.

"Let's take some questions from the audience," I said, as Kimar and Monique roamed the studio with their microphones.

Kimar approached a short, round woman with her hand up. She stood.

"To be fair, I think a lot of what you're saying is obvious. It's nothing really that ground-breaking. I mean, surely everyone can see the influence of music, how it affects our moods and behaviour. I know I can." She sat back down.

"Thank you for your comment," Dewayne responded. "But you may find you're in a minority lady, which is why I'm working hard to raise awareness of this. You can definitely judge a person by the music they listen to. And whether or not you like the same music as them, trust me, it will definitely have an influence on your relationship."

A sexy guy at the back with long hair in a bouncy afro, stuck his hand up and started speaking before Monique even reached him with the microphone.

"It's all a load of rubbish if you ask me. The women I date couldn't give a damn what music I listen to. They're more interested in what I've got in the bank and in my boxer shorts, from what I can see."

His frank comment sparked laughter and cheering. *He did have a point.* I knew I wasn't trying to date anyone with no cash, or the other.

"Young brotha' you are right," Dewayne said, keeping his audience on side. "A woman will always be interested in finances… and size." He chuckled. "But trust me, music is right up there too. Y'all just don't realise it yet."

A leggy attractive woman in the front row stood up. She turned around to see where Kimar was with the mic.

"Hey, I need to know what music *you* like," said Bouncy Afro. "That's my favourite too," he added cheekily to the woman.

The audience erupted in laughter. I had to chuckle myself. This was going better than I'd hoped.

"Now you're beginning to understand young brotha'," Dewayne said, joining in with the fun and laughter, as Kimar hot-footed it across to the lady. "What's your question please?" Dewayne asked, as Kimar gave her the microphone.

"I agree with the last speaker," she said. "I sort of get what you're saying about music and attraction," she analysed. "But to me it doesn't really make sense. Isn't this all just stereotyping? Surely this theory cannot apply to everyone?"

"Look at the evidence." Dewayne pointed to the couples on stage. "Four out of six of these couples have stayed glued to their compatible music partner. You heard some of them say, before I came out here, that previously they'd tried dating people with incompatible music tastes and it ended in tears," he reminded us. "And for the two remaining couples that didn't work out, it's clear to say, music even played a big hand in the breakdown of their relationship. Remember… this beautiful lady," he said, pointing at Dionne, "wasn't feelin' the mood he be creatin' with the commercial stuff," he clarified, pointing at Javon. "And this one," he drawled, indicating to Reuben, who was still simmering, "committed the ultimate offence, by taking *another* female to The Nicki Minaj Concert!"

I'm sure most of us would agree that Tia had done far worse to Reuben, but for now it was all about proving my theory, so I wasn't about to comment on that. Instead, I moved the debate on a little.

"With everything you're saying," I investigated, "can you back it up with any actual research?" I pushed.

"According to a recent study conducted back home in the States," Dewayne said confidently, "musical taste often indicates class status and values. Therefore," he elaborated, raising his index finger, "this gives us clues about a potential mate's worldview or ideology."

Puzzled glances were thrown around the studio as people shifted, restless in their seats.

"Stay with me, work with me folks," Dewayne added, scanning the room. "Various scholars," he continued, "have explored the definitive relationship between music preferences and lifestyle. They conclude that our taste in music tells people who we are and what we value, whether it's the high life, the fast lane or trying to change the world."

Dewayne paused for everyone to grasp what he was saying before continuing. "My own experience of growing up in Chicago showed me a lot. My folks, they were political activists, they marched for civil rights, fought for equality and boy, they loved them some Motown. Hell, they even bundled me and my siblings in the car a number of times, for the five hour drive from Chicago to Detroit to visit the old headquarters, Hitsville. Man, those were some good days. And look at the influence of Motown! It was a movement that changed America, hell, the world! You cannot deny the power of music. Believe me y'all, when it comes to lovin', music is the key! It's the D, N, freakin' A."

The audience laughed along with him, loving his light-hearted nature. I liked his way of illustrating serious points with humour.

"Bottom line," he concluded, his voice taking on a more serious tone, "and this goes for all of y'all… is that music… without a shadow of a doubt… predicts sexual attraction!" Dewayne resolved, to an explosion of cheering, laughter, clapping, stamping and general mayhem from the studio audience.

This was my cue. Our time was up. "You heard it here first on Bling & Ting, the station that keeps you staying in. Doctor Devant, thank you for sharing with us today." I turned to the audience and yelled. "Please put your hands together and give it up for Doctor Dewayne Devant."

The applause was so deafening as they gave him a standing ovation, that I could barely get my closing lines out. "That's goodbye from me, Sahai Martini at Bling & Ting, bringing you the latest big thing! Don't forget to join us next week for more from *The Sweetest Sound!* Too hot to handle, too cold to hold. Remember, you saw it here first!" I cried, as the credits began rolling.

Thirty minutes later… and the feedback was epic! Our phone lines were going crazy, ringing off the hook, everyone was tweeting, our Facebook page was being flooded with messages and once again we had captivated a huge audience.

"You smashed it," Bailey congratulated, as we scrolled through some of the messages on the internet.

"Thanks," I beamed. "And thanks for flying Doctor Dewayne Devant over. As soon as I saw him on that talk show in the States, I knew he was gold dust. I thought, if he's good enough for one of the hottest talk show hosts in America, he's good enough for Bling & Ting. He really brought that extra element to the show. He added value right?"

"He sure did. He was a hit. Look, everyone's talking about it," Bailey said proudly, as he scrolled between tweets of people completely agreeing with Devant's analysis to others totally rubbishing the idea, to viewers commenting on how refreshing it was to see such a fine, young, handsome expert on our station. A few went further, asking for Devant's personal details. "We've even got tweets here from people who are now trying out our theory for themselves, in their own personal lives, and claiming to have found love," Bailey exclaimed.

"Are you serious?" I peered at the screen. "I'll start keeping a file on them," I responded, "as I'm sure we can feature them down the line. This is amazing." I was elated.

"Incredible. Excellent," Bailey praised. "Let's record some more stuff with Dr Devant before he flies back to the States. Get his view on a range of related relationship issues that we can pull out the bag at a later date." He scribbled down some notes.

"Good idea," I agreed, as Bailey eased up to head back to his office.

Maybe I should be giving my theory a try my damn self. Take a leaf out of my own book, I thought. I not only needed to date a wealthy man, but one who liked the kind of music that I felt could enhance our relationship. That should be my next move I realised, as my mobile beeped indicating a text message had just come through.

"Loved your show." It was Kaden. He'd been texting me every day since we met asking to see me, but I hadn't met up with him. As I said, I was done with dating, not that he'd ever stood a chance in the first place. He'd begged to see me this evening, but I'd explained I was presenting the live show.

"Thanks," I text back.

"So what u up 2 now?" he wanted to know.

"Tired. Heading home." I was honest.

"So I can't see u tonight?" He was disappointed.

"Maybe another time," I suggested.

"How about 2mora evening? What time do u finish work?" he text back.

"6pm, but listen, I don't think I can make it tomorrow sorry."

"Why not? It's Friday night. Be a good start 2 your weekend. U can come round my yard and cotch? I'll cook u dinner. Anything u want. Oxtail, Stew Chicken, Curry goat, u name it."

I thought he was a Rastafarian. What happened to Ital food? Vegetarian dishes? Were there *any* genuine people left in the world?

"I'll let you know," I text back, with no plans to get back to him.

As striking as he was, I wasn't ready to be going to his house when I barely knew him. Anyway, hadn't he heard of dating, taking a girl out? Wining and dining her? What was all this business of going round his yard to crank? *Cheapskate!*

Chapter Twenty-Nine

The following morning Bailey called the whole team together for another debrief of last night's live show. Once we'd deliberated over how badly things could've gone if a fight had broken out, and what safeguarding measures to put in place for future shows, we moved on to the subject of Devant.

"He was definitely hot and you were right Sahai, the programme absolutely needed that element," Bailey said, leaning back in his plush black leather chair. He swivelled around as we gathered in his office. "The man had the audience eating out of his hands, hanging on to his every word," Bailey added, chuckling.

"Listen, like I said, if he's good enough for one of America's top talk show hosts, he's good enough for Bling & Ting," I repeated, remembering watching the talk show about dating in the 21st Century and drooling over Doctor Devant after he'd been brought on as a special guest.

"You got that right," Bailey agreed. "Now I want all of you to put a hundred percent effort into anything that's needed for *The Sweetest Sound* from now on. Last night's audience topped the three million mark, which is the highest number of viewers we've had for any of our shows in years. You should all be proud. I want to thank you for the hard work each and every one of you has put into making this show a success." He paused for a moment for us to take in what was a rare and welcome speech from Bailey. Praise and gratitude. "I think that wraps up this morning's meeting, so if all of you could get back to what you're doing, that would be great. Sahai can you stay behind for a minute please."

What for? I wondered as everyone began shuffling out of the room.

My thoughts quickly drifted back to last night's live show. Even though Bailey had indicated he was happy with the way it went, maybe deep down he was furious about the incident Tia had caused and somehow felt I was to blame, or what if he'd found some dirt on Doctor Devant? It had been easy enough to locate Dr Devant on the internet and after reading that he specialised in 'urban love', I knew he was the one.

"Urban love?" Camara had scoffed. "What the hell is that?" she'd quizzed, when I'd first mentioned Devant.

"Y'know, ghetto love," Dijon explained, whilst chewing on a chicken bone, drizzled in mustard, as we chilled in KFC.

"Ghetto love?" she asked, scowling at him. "Do you have to spit the bones out like that?" she snapped, glancing around uncomfortably.

"Relax Mara." Dijon chuckled. "We're in Kentucky Fried Chicken. Damn girl, it's not like we're at The Ritz in L.A!" He gnawed into a chicken ankle, chomping down hard.

"Urban love..." I began, before Dijon swiftly cut me off.

"Is girl meets boy," he stated. "Boy talks a good game, makes girl feel special, girl thinks she's found the one, begins to fall in love. He's funny, educated, handsome, intelligent, has a good job, affectionate, caring, loving, great to be around. Then appears baby mother number one, who girl had no idea existed, then baby mother number two, who traumatises girl, as baby mother number two thinks she's still boy's current girlfriend," Dijon said casually, pausing to pick some chicken skin out of his teeth, before carrying on.

"So girl confronts boy, who finally breaks down and confesses he's still living with baby mother number two, but of course he's only there for the kids. He's unhappy and their relationship has been over for a long time, he reckons, but the kids need him," Dijon explained, whilst spitting out a chicken bone and belching loudly before continuing. "Of course, this information only comes out after girl has literally begged for the truth.

"Girl is devastated. She'd really believed in him, thought he was the one, thought they had a future together. Naturally boy tells girl their relationship can still work and offers girl a role as his side chick, which of course she doesn't want. Now, crumpled in the corner at home, single, crying, alone, she realises that she is just another *statistic*. Another victim of 'ghetto love'," Dijon concluded, punctuating the last two words for dramatic effect, eyes staring wildly.

Stunned, Camara glared at Dijon in silence, and then burst out laughing. "Are you for real?" she finally managed.

I knew he'd been recounting the story of one of his best friends, Elijah, who was now living in a poky bedsit alone, after his woman had found out about his side chick and kicked him out. A similar thing had also happened to one of Monique's female cousins. Turning away from Camara, Dijon looked at me, as though expecting me to support and agree with what he'd said, but I had my own version.

"Urban Love," I began again, "as defined on Doctor Devant's website, is romantic love between a couple who face the specific challenges of economic and social disadvantage, which can often affect the natural healthy development of a positive relationship, and instead lead to dysfunction and destruction within that union," I corrected.

"Thank you." Dijon smiled. "That's exactly what I just said." He laughed.

"What you just said is bullshit Dijon," Camara quarrelled. "There are loads of decent men out there and plenty of healthy relationships, regardless of the environment people are in, so clearly as usual Dijon, you're stereotyping," she said, cutting her eyes at him.

"Call it what you want baby." He eyed her smugly. "You wanna count your blessings Mara and realise that you and your chocolate prince are in a minority. I'd say the opposite of urban love is what? Sub-urban love. Marriage, big house, white picket fence, cupla kids and a happily ever after. How many people do you personally know living that lifestyle?"

Camara glowered at him. Silent.

"I thought so," Dijon said triumphantly. "That's why people like Professor Divine or Doctor Deceit or whatever his name is, are making a killing 'cos they recognise that ghetto love is in *crisis*!" Dijon preached, slapping the table. "Trust me. That was just one scenario, but I could give you many more examples of love in the hood," he provoked, laughing, polishing off his sweetcorn.

"If you ask me," he continued, on a roll, "most of us are so busy being hostile to each other, hiding our true feelings, acting like we don't give a damn when we do, acting like we do give a damn when we don't, that we can't get this love thing right. Especially you women, more time you lot are so miserable and moody, then you wonder why you're single, why you ain't got no man. If we could be honest with ourselves and each other and flex on that level, maybe the shit could run smooth. Anyway gotta bounce." He hopped up, kissed us both on the cheek and exited KFC as quickly as he'd arrived fifteen minutes earlier.

"As I mentioned yesterday," Bailey said, breaking my thoughts, pulling me back into the moment, "we need to think carefully about what else we can get out of Devant before he flies back to Chicago. You say he's in the UK for a week right? We need to be strategic with this."

"Do you think urban love is different?" I quizzed Bailey.

"Urban love? Different to what?" He looked confused.

"Suburban love," I said, reflecting on Dijon's comments.

"Sahai, love is love. What the hell are you talking about?" He asked, getting up from his desk to open one of the windows.

"Oh, it's just something my cousin said, which ties in with Devant's work. I wonder if we can look at how social and economic dynamics affect dating and relationships in disadvantaged communities. I mean, after all, that is one of the areas Devant specialises in."

"Sahai," Bailey reminded me, as he sat back down. "In case you've forgotten, this is a music and entertainment channel, not politics and documentaries!"

"I guess," I said disappointed. "It was just a thought."

"Have you any idea how you sound right now?" Bailey asked, shaking his head, peering hard at me. "Urban love..." he muttered under his breath. "Whether couples are rich, poor, black, white, national or international, all relationships have problems, so I don't get where you're going with this. Maybe I'm overworking you?" he wondered out loud.

"Like I said, it was just a thought." I quickly brushed it off.

"Well if you're in a thinking mood, why don't you think about how you can spice up *The Sweetest Sound* a little more, with the help of Devant?" he advised, still shaking his head. "As well as the episodes we're planning to film with him over the next few days, we need to think about what else we can get out of him, what's gonna really add value," he reiterated. "Anyway, the real reason I asked you to stay behind is to let you know that I'm really impressed with your performance right now. I know I just mentioned it in the meeting, but come and look at these." He picked up some paperwork. "It's the actual exact figures that cover the last quarter. Look how well we're doing. Ratings have gone through the roof with your programme. As I've already said we're pulling in more viewers than we've ever had and that's all down to you." He shuffled some papers on his desk.

"Thanks," I said. "This is brilliant news." I gazed at the paperwork.

"Crazy to think that when you first told me the idea, I thought it was laughable. Now look at us. I'm glad I believed in you and took a chance. Well done."

"Thanks Bailey," I said again. "I had a good feeling about this from the start. I'm glad it's all worked out."

"Me too. I just wanted you to be clear of the extent to which I recognise your role in all of this, as the single driving force." He closed his folder. "Send Kimar in please. I need to see him," he requested, shifting around, letting me know it was the end of our meeting. "And make sure you get some good rest this weekend Sahai. Looks like you need it. I wanna see you in here with some fresh ideas Monday morning."

Thank God it was Friday. I was knackered. The last few weeks had drained me.

Back at my desk, I glanced at my watch to see that it was only 11.30 am. It was gonna be a long-ass day!

Couldn't have been more wrong. By the time I'd gone through the emails, tweets, Facebook messages and the long list of contestants applying to take part in season two of *The Sweetest Sound*, the rest of the day had flown by.

Happy to see it was now almost six pm, I grabbed my satchel and left the office.

Chapter Thirty

The first thing I noticed as soon as I walked outside was the gleaming chrome Kawasaki motorbike parked directly outside our office across the street. The biker, chilling astride it, was jacked up on double yellow lines, seemingly without a care in the world. Sexy black leather from head to toe, topped off with a shiny black and chrome helmet, concealed the stranger's identity. The bike was so hot I couldn't stop staring at it, as I'd always had a thing about motorbikes.

I was stunned when the rider peeled off his helmet, glancing in my direction and his flowing locks dropped to his waist.

"K... Kaden?" I stammered. "Wh... what are you doing here? I mean, where ... how...?" I managed, once I'd made it across the road to him.

He smiled at me with his sexy Colgate grin. His handsome Ethiopian features complimented his overall image, as he cocked himself at an angle on his bike in a gangsta' lean. He looked absolutely gorgeous in the daylight.

"This is where you said you worked right?" he confirmed, glancing up at the sign displaying 'Bling & Ting'. "And that you finish at six pm today," he added smiling.

I nodded feebly, admiring the chromed-out panels on the bike.

"Well you know what they say, if the mountain won't come to Jah Lion, then Jah Lion must go to the mountain." He'd obviously put his own spin on the famous saying. "I thought I'd surprise you Empress."

I smiled, but *what was it with men stalking me?* First Sadiq, now him? Despite this, I smiled at the sweet gesture, although

I'd ignored the two texts he'd sent me earlier that day. He wasn't an option for me. *Or was he?* I thought, as Kaden slid off his bike, all 6ft 8 or 9 of him towering over me, as he enveloped me in a warm hug.

"Nice bike." I ran my fingers across the chrome.

"Thanks," he said, strapping his helmet back on before sliding back into his seat, grabbing the handlebar and holding out a spare helmet to me. "Come, let's go for a ride. Get on." He glanced over his shoulder.

Hell yeah, I'll go for a ride I thought, as I moved closer to him reaching for the spare helmet. Then I came to my senses. What was I thinking? I hardly knew the man. "Thanks for the offer, but my car is parked around the corner," I explained.

"No problem," he insisted. "I can bring you back to your car after."

"No really, I shouldn't." I think I was pleading with myself more than him.

"What's wrong?" He eyed me. "Scared?"

"I never said that," I blurted out a bit too quickly for my own liking. Damn!

"Well come on then. It's a nice summer's evening. I'll just take you round the block if you're scared." Kaden threw me that seductive grin again.

"I'm not scared," I snapped. *I'm a hot girl! We don't do scared!* I wasn't having him thinking I was soft and for some bizarre reason, all of a sudden I cared what he thought. *A perfect stranger! What was happening to me?*

I stood there, stuck on stupid. Hypnotised by his mesmerising eyes penetrating into me, I slung my purple satchel across my body, strapped myself into his spare helmet and climbed on to the back of his ride. I had to admit that I was excited. Despite my love of bikes, I had never actually been on one and at a rough estimate, this baby had to be worth at least about what? Eighteen grand?

Maybe Kaden wasn't that poor, I thought, as pound signs started flashing in my mind's eye.

No sooner than I was secure in my seat, he took off at about 100 miles an hour, whipping through rush hour traffic and jumped straight on to the M6 heading towards London! *Shit!* I knew I shoulda kept my ass on the pavement. For all I know the man might have been kidnapping me and I was hardly in a position to protest, as the wind zipped through me as we sped past other vehicles. Clinging on to his back, I cursed silently, whilst secretly loving the thrill of holding on to this big strong sexy man as he took me for the ride of my life.

"You said around the block!" I barked, as we finally pulled up back outside my workplace about forty-five minutes later. I felt disorientated and breathless as I hopped off the bike.

"You know you loved it, so relax," he said. "You wouldn't have got the proper experience if we just went round the block. That's why I had to hit the motorway. We only did a few junctions before I came off. Wasn't that bad was it?"

"I need a drink." I was honest. I was feeling a little light-headed. A swift shot of Brandy would calm me down and bring me back down to earth.

"Good idea. I'd like that." He started dismounting his bike.

"It wasn't an offer, suggestion or even an invite," I told him. "I'll have a drink when I get home."

"Are you always this cold?" He eyeballed me.

"Not always," I said. "Only after I've been kidnapped against my will and taken for a daredevil ride that leaves my nerves frazzled."

"It wasn't even like that baby-love." He moved a wisp of hair out of my eye, as I removed my helmet and tried to smooth my hair down. "Come on, we're here now... let's make the most of it. We can go to that pub right there, on the corner."

He pointed to a rundown shabby-looking establishment that I'd never been in, even though I worked on the same street. It looked like the kind of place I wouldn't be seen dead in.

"One drink. That's all," he promised, swaggering off.

This guy had some serious persuasive power, totally supported by those beautiful eyes I realised, as I trotted dutifully behind him like a little lost puppy. Enchanted by his confident glide, I barely heard my mobile phone ringing until Kaden turned and looked at me. "Aren't you gonna answer that?" He had the nerve to look like *my* ring tone was annoying *him*, even though he was the one hijacking my evening.

Reaching into my pocket, the loud ring tone was replaced with Camara's high-pitched screaming as soon as I answered it. "Where the hell are you? What's taking you so long to get here?"

"To get there? Get where?"

"To my house!" she shouted. "Everyone's supposed to be here before seven!" she yelled. "I thought you were coming straight from work. I've been ringing you for the past hour. Why weren't you answering my calls? Danté's gonna be here in about ten minutes."

Shit! Danté's barbecue! His 30th surprise birthday party! *I completely forgot!* Hearing how stressed out Camara was, made me feel ten times worse.

"I'm sorry," I blurted. "I forgot." I was honest. I'd been so caught up in work, then Kaden, it totally slipped my mind.

"Forgot?" she screeched in disbelief. "Where are you?" she demanded to know. "And how soon can you get here?" she shrilled. "Sahai, I need you here before Danté gets here."

By now Kaden was at my side with a concerned expression on his face as he listened in on our conversation. "I'm still by my workplace. It's gonna take me at least about forty-five minutes to get there, with the traffic, you know how busy town is and Soho Road, on a Friday night." I was apologetic.

"*Forty-five minutes?*" Camara shrieked, loud enough for Kaden to hear.

"I'll take you," Kaden said smoothly. "Just tell me where it is."

"Handsworth Wood," I mouthed.

"We'll be there in five," Kaden said, leading me back to his bike.

"*Five minutes?* You sure?"

"Yeah man. Everyting' bless."

Reluctantly I joined him, not wanting to let Camara down any more than I already had. Didn't really wanna get back on the bike, but I was supposed to be the one stalling Danté outside on the front lawn for a few minutes when he arrived, until Camara gave the all clear for him to enter the house. Anyone else would look suspicious, as he was so used to seeing me there. *Great friend I was!*

"Alright. Alright. Calm down Camara," I said softly. "I'll be there in five and I'm bringing a friend." I hung up before she even had a chance to ask any more questions. The worst thing about me messing up was that she'd originally planned to have the barbecue tomorrow, as she felt a Saturday afternoon would be better, but I'd persuaded her to have it today as his actual birthday was today and with it being a Friday evening, everyone would have the whole weekend to recover. Danté thought she was taking him out for a meal.

"We have to get there before him," I instructed Kaden.

Ten minutes later, we pulled up on Cherry Orchard Road, outside Camara's house.

"Ooh la la. Who is *that*?" Camara asked, eyeing Kaden, before anxiously peering down the street, as she greeted me at her front door wearing blue jeans and a white vest. "He's gorgeous!" she said drooling, studying Kaden as all 6ft 8 or 9 of him dismounted his bike, like some magnificent lion, dreadlocks flowing everywhere. "Is he one of the guys off the internet? He's criss'! I knew I'd get you hooked up with a criss' man." She gawped, as Kaden glanced in our direction, whilst locking up his bike.

Before I had a chance to respond, she carried on rambling, whilst removing my satchel from across my body. "Can't believe you forgot it was tonight." She shook her head. "But I'm glad you made it. I'll put this in my bedroom, otherwise it's gonna look a bit weird, you standing outside with your bag. Now I need you to stay out here till Danté arrives and pretend to be talking on your phone," she spelled out. "Then as soon as you see him pulling up, ring or text me, so I can alert everyone and get them ready for the surprise." She paused to admire Kaden as he began walking in our direction. "Mmm... he's fit," she murmured. "Very nice indeed," she noted, observing Kaden's every move. "Hi." She beamed, as he approached us. "I'm Camara. Thanks for coming."

Kaden clearly had the hypnotic effect on every woman. He smiled, his easy, warm smile and extended his hand. "I'm Kaden. Nice to meet you."

I watched the exchange. I hadn't even had a chance to apologise to her for bringing a complete stranger to her house, which was a big no no for us, or even at least explain what had happened. But seeing her gush over Kaden showed me that on this occasion she was cool with it, as she held on to his hand like she was kneeling at Jesus's feet.

"Oh no, that sounds like Danté's car coming. Get inside," she practically screamed at Kaden who obeyed her command, disappearing into the house. "You stay here," she barked at me. "Where's your mobile? Keep him out here till I come back out." Once again, she'd turned into that frenzied zombie, the same one who had visited me the night she'd decided I should start internet dating. "What are you doing? Inside quick," she yelped at Dijon who'd just poked his head out from around the front door. Shoving him back, she quickly ran in behind him, slamming the door behind her.

Seconds later, Danté's gleaming black Range Rover came into full view, bass thumping, as The Notorious B.I.G. urged everyone to '*Get Money*.'

"Hey." He greeted me with a hug minutes later, looking fine as hell in a pearl-grey Ralph Lauren sweater and Armani jeans.

"Wow. You smell nice," I stated. "What aftershave is that?" I asked, making small talk, trying to stall him.

"Armani Diamonds." He glanced towards the front door. "Why are you outside?"

"Oh, I just had to make a quick call and you know Camara, she always has the music up loud." So much for me not looking suspicious.

"I can't hear any music." Danté looked like he suspected something was going on. He was about to step past me into the house, but I hadn't quite worked out a plan to deter him. *What the hell was taking her so long?*

As if reading my mind Camara suddenly stepped outside.

"Hi babes," she exclaimed. "I didn't hear you get here. I was just coming out to see if Sahai had finished on the phone yet. She's just popped round to quickly grab some DVD's before we go out."

Her acting was ridiculous, and the girl had the nerve to actually get changed, whilst I'd been out here going for an Oscar. She now stood before us stunning, in a black thigh-length, figure-hugging backless Chanel dress and diamante studded stilettos. I looked pretty plain next to her in my skinny jeans and T-shirt as I hadn't even had the chance to quickly go home, shower and get changed as originally planned. Thank God I had a pair of heels and a few accessories in my satchel. I always carried a spare pair of heels when I wore flats. You never knew when you might need them, today being a perfect example. Once I'd finished off my outfit with my oversized D&G shades, I'd be straight Hollywood!

"Baby, you look stunning." Danté couldn't take his eyes off her. "Beautiful. I can't wait to get you to the restaurant to show you off."

"I need to grab a couple of things from inside first, so you might as well come in," she said, and then flashed me a look, which I took as my cue to disappear, so I slipped inside and swiftly scooted towards the kitchen.

Chapter Thirty-One

As soon as I entered the kitchen, I made a slit in the blinds covering the patio doors with my fingers, to take a quick look outside. I saw at least about sixty people in the expansive back garden, surrounded by purple, silver and black party banners, balloons and a long table boasting a huge spread. I was impressed. The delicious aroma of juicy steak, burgers, ribs, onions and sausages sizzling on the barbecue, had my mouth watering.

Within a split second of stepping outside and hitching up beside Kaden, taking the place of some girl I didn't recognise, standing a bit too close to him for my liking, the patio door dramatically slid back. Danté stepped outside to a chorus of "Surprise," from everyone yelling at the top of their voice as instructed, followed by three loud renditions of 'Happy Birthday'. First the original, then Stevie Wonder's version, kick-started by Danté's parents, then Fifty Cent's hit, 'In Da Club' coming from the youngsters.

Danté was a picture. It was a true Kodak moment. He had no idea. He looked at Camara, then at us, then back at Camara, then swooped her off the ground in a warm embrace, giving her soft kisses on the lips, before laughing and pointing at individuals accusingly, who he knew had gone above and beyond to keep this event a secret from him.

Dijon, on the decks at the back of the garden, slammed on Jay Z's 'Encore'. The lyrics asked what the hell we were waiting for, hinting at everyone to get the party started right. Kelloggs, next to Dijon, bounced wildly to the heavy hip hop beat, whacking up the volume several levels, waving his arms around. The original hype man.

"Everyone, please help yourself to food and drinks," Camara shouted over the loud music, before Danté pulled her in close for another affectionate embrace. I actually felt a bit emotional. Considering they hadn't been dating that long, I could see how in love they were and I was happy for her. Prior to Danté, she hadn't been out with anyone for years, chatting some nonsense about saving herself for 'the one'. I couldn't see the logic myself when I thought about how much money, clothes and jewellery I had accumulated from men in the same space of time.

"Do you think he knew?" Camara asked, sidling up beside me, as excited as a butterfly in a spring meadow.

"Nah, he was genuinely surprised," I decided. "You could tell by the look on his face that he was not expecting this at all," I said, gesturing around. "You kept it from him well and he's lovin' it." I smiled, glancing across at Danté joking and mingling with guests.

"Thanks." She beamed across at him. "You know it's taken me ages to organise."

"You've done well. It looks wicked." I gave her a congratulatory hug.

"Sorry about earlier," she apologised to Kaden. "Rushing you into the house and everything. I was a bit flustered as you could see, but it's really nice to meet you properly." She extended her hand.

He took it with the charm of a President and warmly greeted her. "It's my pleasure," he said. "I hope I'm not imposing."

She physically quivered.

Kaden towered over Camara like some high priest, looking as regal as the late Ethiopian Emperor himself, Haile Selassie.

"Imposing? You? No, not at all," she said, gushing. "The more, the merrier. Can I get you a drink or anything? As for food, please, help yourself, there's plenty to go round." She indicated towards the spread, before directing her attention away from him and leaning in towards me lowering her voice. "I need to tell you something." She took on a serious, urgent, expression. "And before you say anything, I had no idea. You're not gonna believe who…" she began, as one of her cousins came and tugged at her arm.

"Where are the napkins? We're looking everywhere for them," her cousin fussed, dragging her away.

"She seems nice," Kaden said, as Camara excused herself.

"Yeah, Camara's lovely, we grew up together, that's my bona fide," I explained. *But what was she on about? Something to tell me?* "Thanks so much for getting me here on time," I added. "I would have never forgiven myself if I hadn't."

"That's cool," he said. "Especially as I was the one who delayed you in the first place. I'm happy just being able to finally spend some time with you Empress."

"Thanks," *sexy Ethiopian*, I almost added, admiring the way his smooth, golden-brown complexion glistened in the sunshine.

"Wha a gwarn cuzzy?" said Dijon, approaching me from behind, wrapping his arms around my shoulders in a tight hug. I giggled and squirmed out of his embrace.

"You alright Sweetie?" I replied, turning around to hug Dijon properly, as he scowled at Kaden. "This is my cousin Dijon," I explained, introducing them.

"Yes King. Bless up," Kaden greeted, touching fists with Dijon, who responded to the gesture without a word, but managed a slight menacing smirk, although he was looking up at Kaden, who easily towered over him by at least five inches.

"Anyway I'm gonna get back on the decks. Check you later," Dijon said, and slunk off into the gathering with an exaggerated limp.

"He's friendly," Kaden joked.

"Just overprotective," I corrected. "Listen, why don't you go and help yourself to some food. I need to nip to the bathroom and freshen up. Be right back."

"Cool," he said, as I made my way into the house.

Damn! Couldn't Camara have told me my hair was a mess? I thought, running my fingers through my long curls as I stared at my windswept reflection in the hallway mirror. *Was that lipstick smeared on my chin?* This was not a good look.

I made my way into her bedroom where I found my satchel placed neatly in a corner and retrieved my makeup bag. I applied a fresh coat of lip gloss and MAC Ambering Rose blusher, put on some mascara, brushed my hair, sprayed on a bit of Dior's sweet, powdery fragrance that I loved, Hypnotic, and smoothed down my clothes. That was better.

I admired my flawless skin and shapely curves as I spun around in the mirror, doing a 360. I was so thankful that Camara had paved over most of her back garden last year, as I was able to wear my 6 inch heels without worrying about them getting stuck in the grass. As usual, I knew I was the hottest chick at this barbecue, so anyone who thought they were gonna outshine me, especially that hoe who had her eye on Kaden, better step, I told myself, as I slipped on my shades and exited the room.

"Loving you... " Mary J. Blige's voice filled the air, with her remix of 'Love No Limit', as I stepped outside into the warm summer's night, feeling the vibe and finally beginning to take in my surroundings properly. Seems like a few more people had arrived, I noticed, as I grooved to the soulful hip hop beat, getting my party on.

Greeting a few of Camara's friends, I manoeuvred through the steadily growing crowd, to see who was here and what was what. I noticed there were a few handsome guys milling about. Probably some of Danté's friends or even clients. *Damn!* Why did I bring Kaden with me? I thought, conveniently forgetting that Kaden had actually brought *me* here and in fact, had he not, right now I'd be in deep trouble with Camara. Still, my reasoning had always been, why bring sand to the beach? Didn't want to miss out on any opportunities and these guys looked like they were working with something.

I leaned against an apple tree, admiring two particular brothas' standing nearby sipping Hennessy straight. One was sporting Armani from head to toe and the other was an advert for Gucci. *Very interesting.* I guess there was no harm in talking to them, I thought, preparing to make my way over. It wasn't like Kaden was my man or anything.

As I took a step I was halted in my tracks.

"Excuse me," I heard, and turned to see two young girls hovering. They looked like twins and couldn't have been more than about fourteen. They were giggling and nudging each other.

"It's her," one whispered to the other.

"Oh my days," they squealed in delight. "Can we have your autograph please?" they said in unison, holding out a napkin and a pen. "We love your show." They both grinned. "Since we started watching it, we try and find out what music guys listen to now, before we date them. We think it's working." They giggled. A right double act.

"Cool." I smiled, not really wanting to get into a debate with these chicks who didn't even look old enough to be dating, as I was trying to catch the eye of these two guys any second now, whilst Kaden was still out of sight.

With one eye on the men and the other on the napkin, I quickly scribbled my initials and shoved the napkin back at the girls.

"Ooh thanks," they cooed, walking off cradling the napkin, like they'd just met Beyoncé.

"So you're famous now? I see you still got the bangin' body and was wonderin' if I could interest you in this here hot dog?"

OH MY GOD! There was only one person who owned that familiar voice and those kind of corny-ass lyrics. I grimaced as I spun around to see him standing there live and direct, beautiful as ever, holding out a hot dog to me, with that sexy swagger. In trade mark white t-shirt and blue jeans, he was dripping in bling, his cute dimple in full effect as he wore the brightest smile.

Money!

"Wasn't expecting to see you here," I managed awkwardly.

"Yo, you know I wasn't gonna miss my lil' cousin's big birthday," he said, biting into the hot dog, munching hungrily. "I flew in from Miami this mornin'."

Lost for words, I stood and stared.

"So what's good with you baby girl?" he asked pleasantly, holding the hot dog above his mouth, as ketchup dripped from the sausage on to his juicy lips and he slowly licked it off. Damn. Why did he have to be so fine? "You still runnin' from me or we talkin' now?" he asked.

"Are you for real?" I snapped. "You got a cheek even trying to talk to me after what you did to me in Miami. That was real low."

"Like I said to you at the time, wasn't nothin' shady about it," he said casually. "I told you I had some business to take care of. I left my assistant to look after you. I don't know what bullshit she put in yo' head that made you take off like that 'cos everythin' we had was real."

"Please," I hissed. "You're about as real as Santa Claus, you fake-ass little shit!"

"*God damn!* You sexy as hell when you mad!"

"You were gone for *two* days Money... and as for your assistant? My ass. Your little girlfriend told me all about your three year relationship and parenthood plans."

"See, this is the shit I'm talkin' about. You girls be runnin' your mouth and the shit just ain't true. Ok, so she likes me, so she made up a few lies, you know how scandalous you bitc... I mean girls are already. You gon' choose to believe her over me? Trust me ma, she's my assistant, nothin' more, nothin' less. I told you about my businesses, so whatever she told you that made you skip out on me like that, she was lyin'."

"You really think I'm some kind of fool, don't you?" I said seething, as Camara and Danté appeared at our side.

"I see you two have been... reacquainted," Danté said chuckling, as Camara discreetly mouthed, 'sorry, I was trying to tell you.'

"Happy Birthday Danté," I congratulated, hugging him, refusing to let this little incident interfere with or spoil the occasion. I knew how much effort Camara had put into organising everything.

"Thanks." Danté hugged me back warmly, glancing between me and Money. "Listen, he surprised me too," he said, picking up on the tension. "I had no idea this fool was coming," he added playfully, punching Money's arm. "My family kept it from me... I roll up here tonight and see *this* punk acting like some damn chef over there." He indicated towards the grill. "Now he's gonna get me involved in all sorts of shit that I was trying to avoid this weekend like keeping me drunk and high," Danté joked, as he gripped Money in a headlock and steered him off.

"Fucking muppet!" I scowled, as Camara tried to calm me down. I was boiling. The man was pushing me to the brink. "He'll be lucky if I don't grab one of them pitchforks and stab him to death," I said fuming, as fresh memories of how badly he'd humiliated me in Miami came flooding back.

"Want me to do it for you?" Dijon suggested, edging up beside me, following my death stare, as my eyes bored into Money's back. "I noticed the little pussyhole when I first got here," Dijon confessed. "But I'm just waiting for you to give me the signal cuz."

"You two!" Camara huffed. "Hello? It's Danté's birthday party. We're supposed to be celebrating."

"I'm sorry Camara, but you know what he did. That was fucking out of order, fucking piece of shit, and now I have to be in the same place as him, acting like everything's cool?"

"Sahai, I had no idea he was coming. Danté's brothers invited him and kept it totally quiet until they all turned up a few minutes before you. I was trying to tell you."

Just then Kelloggs rushed past us. "I need the bathroom fam', hold it down for me," he said to Dijon.

"I told him to 'low the drinking. He can't handle shit, fucking lightweight," Dijon grumbled, laughing. "If you need me though cuz, holla, I'm right here. Man's ready to put in some work." He cracked his knuckles, glaring at Money.

"Listen, you ain't starting no shit tonight," Camara warned Dijon, before he took off back to play music.

Seeing the worry on her face, I reassured her. "Look, I'm alright. Obviously a bit shocked and super pissed off, but it's not your fault. I'm just upset 'cos you know I genuinely liked Money and he messed me about so badly but you're right, we had no idea he was gonna be here, so I'm not gonna let it ruin our night. Come on it's our song."

I dragged her towards an area where a group of her little cousins were shockin' out to Kiesza's track 'Hideaway'. The beat was bad!

We joined in with them, messing about doing old school dance routines, whilst they kept it up to the times, cutting shapes, which, to be honest, the more I watched, seemed to be pretty much the same as the shuffle, the dance that was killin' it back in the eighties and nineties on the hip hop scene. We even had footage at work to prove this. But you couldn't tell these youngsters nothing. According to them they created everything, every style, every fashion, every fad, every slang word, this dance and every other rehashed version of something original, from back in the day. They didn't have a clue. All they did was call it a new name and insist they invented and owned it. Maybe it was time to reclaim our history and culture? Maybe we should do a programme on that, I thought, making a mental note to bring the idea to Bailey as soon as I'd developed it a bit more.

I could start by telling him how I'd recently noticed that a traditional African-Caribbean greeting, known as a 'firms' or a 'touch', was being commercially reinvented and relabelled as a 'fist-bump'? People touching fists, with no idea of what it means, where the tradition originally comes from or the fact that it's been around for generations.

I knew Bailey was big on this kind of stuff, passionate about it. He always complained that we needed to do more to preserve our rich, cultural heritage, so he'd probably go for it. Plus he felt today's young people needed educating, described them as superficial, referred to them as the 'MTV Generation'. But right now, watching them trying to out-dance each other was hilarious. I couldn't stop chuckling, until Dijon mixed into Snoop Dog, commanding us to 'Drop It Like It's Hot' and that's exactly what Camara and I started doing, dipping down low, grinding back up, as I noticed Money from the corner of my eye, gazing at me. I'd show him exactly what he was missing.

Right in the middle of my heated performance, Kaden, coming from out of nowhere, suddenly moved up on me from behind, in sync with the beat. I leaned my body into his, turning up the heat a little more, as I eyed Money and enjoyed his jealous glare.

Kaden was proving to be a bit of a hit with his perfect timing and his Knight in Shining Armour routine. First, rescuing me from the drunk that night at carnival, then getting me to the barbecue on time. Now this. Might have to keep him on board. I smiled as I turned to face him and obeyed R.Kelly's orders to move my body like a snake, thrusting myself against Kaden as Dijon continued taking us back in time on the decks, playing everything from Tupac to Lauryn Hill. Maybe Danté's barbecue would be alright after all.

"So you just gon' keep ignorin' me all night shorty? It's like that huh?" Money asked, approaching me a few hours later as I sat alone on the garden wall, rocking to the loud bass line of will.i.am's 'Feelin' Myself,' whilst polishing off a plate of T-bone steak, spicy hot chicken wings, corn on the cob, spare ribs and hard-dough bread. Kaden had gone out to the front garden to smoke, so I was enjoying a quiet moment to tuck into some food.

"Why you trippin'? You know you still feelin' me," Money observed, as I continued to enjoy my meal.

"Go away." I didn't even look up from my plate.

"Ok. So you out here now tryin' to diss a brotha' wit' that fuckin' wild Amazon jungle lookin' punk, but it's cool, we got plenty of time, 'cos here's the thing, I ain't just back for tonight, I'm back for good."

Those words caught my attention. I looked up at him.

"That's right baby girl." He smirked. "I'm signed to a new team, the 'Birmingham Best Squad'. I'm here for the whole basketball season and me and you got unfinished business."

I sat there astonished, trying to take all the information in. I really thought I'd seen the last of him in Miami. I couldn't even muster up any kind of congratulations, so he carried on talking.

"I don't know what you doin' wit' that mothafuckin' predator lookin', jungle warrior, but that bitch-ass needs to step," he threatened. I ignored him. "That mothafucka needs to say somethin' to me. Punk ass bitch! And you need to stop trippin' Sahai! Dead that shit! You can't play a playa' baby," he continued. "I can see right through you. I know you're feelin' the kid and what Money wants, Money gets," he provoked, snickering. "You still want me as much as I want you."

"You're a fucking idiot, you know that, don't you," I stated matter of factly, eyeing him. "With your delusions of grandeur."

"Huh?" He was puzzled, thrown off for a second. "You tryin' a intimidate me with all that aristocrat talk... the Queen's English bullshit?"

"The word's aristocratic, if you must know, and I'm just saying you have delusions of grandeur. Get over yourself! Clearly you like to put yourself in high places but you really ain't all that. Trust me!"

"Baby girl you killin' me with that fragrance. What is it? Mmm... smellin' sweet... and sexy as hell," he said, switching from rage to romance in true psycho style, ignoring everything I'd just said, whilst leaning in closer, seductively biting down on his bottom lip.

I was glad I'd freshened up just before I'd sat down to eat, spritzing myself with Japanese Cherry Blossom from Camara's bathroom cabinet. His ego was incredible, but he was right. I was still attracted to him, despite everything, and I especially liked the fact that he was jealous of Kaden.

Why did I always like the wrong men?

"Keeping all the pretty ones to yourself as usual cuz." A random voice.

We both turned to see the two good-looking guys I'd spotted earlier dripping in Armani and Gucci, sidle up next to us.

"You know how it goes," Money drawled. "Just protectin' what's mine. Sahai," he said, indicating towards the two guys. "These are my cousins Andre and Diego. Danté's brothers."

I reached out and shook hands with both of them. This was one helluva fine family of men. Why couldn't I have met one of these two first? They were obviously local and loaded.

"Good to meet you," Diego said with a cheesy grin, holding on to my hand just a little longer than necessary.

"You're the presenter from, what's that station called again, Bling & Ting right?" Andre quizzed, studying me as he now shook my hand.

"Yes, I am." I blushed.

"Well I'm honoured to be meeting a celebrity." He raised my hand and stooped to gently kiss the back of it. "Been watching your programme. The shit's hot."

"Thanks," I said

"Hol' up, hol' up," Money hollered. "That's enough now. Anythin' more you need to know about her, you gon' have to go through me fellas," he said, like he was my damn agent. He must've noticed the chemistry flowing between me and Andre. "This ain't no freakin' free for all," he muttered, steering them towards the grill, keen to break up our little party. "I'll hit you back in a bit lil'mama," he said to me, as he strode off with them.

Fifteen minutes later, I was still rooted to the same spot, silently reminiscing about Money, recalling everything from the night we'd met to the time we'd gone to the Rihanna concert, our day trips, shopping sprees and then, Miami. Had he really forgotten how he'd spoken to me that day on the phone? Calling me a gold-digger and all kinds of other shit? Did he really have no comprehension of how bad it was that he'd left me in the penthouse with his girl? No remorse that he'd acted like it was my idea to go to Miami that weekend when it was clearly his?

I sipped my fruit punch, contemplating my next move. Did I just run up and karate kick him to the ground or set Dijon on him for a slow and painful death? I chuckled to myself fantasizing about hurting Money, before realising that Kaden was still missing. Felt like ages since he'd gone outside to smoke.

Easing up I made my way through the house and peered out the front door. About to step outside, I stopped dead in my tracks at the sight before me.

Engaged in animated, friendly conversation, Kaden and Money were smoking, joking and laughing like old friends, whilst Andre and Diego stood next to Kaden's bike, admiring the chrome finish.

Money had obviously befriended Kaden to get at me. And why was Money smoking anyway? Wasn't he supposed to be an athlete? *Asshole!*

This was just fucking great! I thought. *That piece of shit,* I cursed, as I watched Money climb on to the bike, switch on the ignition and start revving the engine as Andre and Diego stood back. Kaden pointed to something on the dashboard and they all laughed.

"There you are," Camara said, approaching me from behind. "I wondered where you were," she said, looking past me outside.

"Boys and their toys," I muttered.

"You gotta admit, it is a nice bike," she reasoned, as Money looked across and noticed us. *Was that a smirk on his face?* "Have you seen Danté? I can't find him anywhere," she asked.

"Nah, I haven't seen him," I told her, as Kaden, following Money's eyeline, glanced over at me. *Shit! Now what?*

I headed towards them with Camara in tow glaring at me with a 'don't start no drama' expression. Kaden slid his arm around my waist as I approached. I didn't appreciate the intimate, territorial gesture, but I didn't move away from him either.

Money smiled. "This your girl?" he asked Kaden, feigning ignorance, like we were strangers. "Damn! She's fine!"

"She is, ain't she?" Kaden agreed, smiling down at me.

"Hope you're lookin' after her. There's a lot of snakes out here, always wantin' what's yours, always ready to take your spot, believe that, especially with someone as beautiful as her." Money stared hard at me.

The comment easily washed over Kaden.

I noticed Andre and Diego exchanging confused glances, probably because Money had practically introduced me to them as *his* girl like what? Twenty minutes ago. *Great!*

Dismounting the bike, Money touched fists with Kaden. "It's been real. We gon' have to hook up some time. You know I wanna ride this baby," he said, staring directly at me, whilst tapping the seat of the bike.

"Whenever you're ready," Kaden replied, oblivious to Money's double meaning as Money swaggered back off into the house. I saw Camara visibly relax, relieved that we'd got through that little exchange drama free. Couldn't believe Money had the audacity to think he was just gonna waltz straight back into my life after the way he'd dealt with me in Miami! Hell no!

Chapter Thirty-Two

"So shouldn't you be applying it to your own personal life?" Camara asked me, as her hairstylist Angel, sewed in her weave, whilst my friend Brandy ran the tongs through my wild waves for a silky straight effect.

It was Saturday morning, a week after my 'altercation' with Money and we'd decided to enjoy a pampering session at the salon.

Since the barbecue, Money had bombarded me with text messages and phone calls apologising, asking for my forgiveness and a chance to make it up to me, so Camara was now trying to talk me into seeing him on a double date with her and Danté tonight. Shifting on my stool, I admired my glossy tresses in the mirror.

"Keep still Sahai," Brandy snapped. "I'm not trying to mess this up."

I smiled up at the reflection in the mirror of the 5ft 8 beauty, expertly doing my hair. Brandy was a stunner. Definitely Money's type, I thought. Very pretty, glamorous, with honey-hazel eyes, a creamy cappuccino coloured complexion and bronze curls, always clad in the latest designer gear from head to toe and hugely successful. We did a special on her at Bling & Ting when she threw a spectacular shindig, a massive hair and beauty extravaganza to mark the opening of this salon two years ago.

She'd worked hard to turn her dream of owning a business, into a reality. Decked out in hot pink and chrome, 'Brand New' boasted the best hairstylists and beauticians in town, expensive marble furnishing, personal booths for each customer complete with state of the art mini-entertainment sets, floor to ceiling mirrors, a relaxing chill-out zone, and all the latest products and equipment to keep me looking hot. Which was all I really cared about. As long as I was on top of my game, it was all good. But now Camara was trying to throw shade, doing her best to toss me off my throne. I glanced across at her on the stool next to mine.

"Did you hear me?" she repeated. "I said shouldn't you be applying your music, men and attraction theory to your own personal life?"

"Funnily enough, I've been thinking the same thing lately and considering giving it a try," I admitted. "But hello? With Money? I don't think so. Camara have you forgotten what he did to me?"

"No I haven't but everyone makes mistakes. We all deserve a second chance," Camara said, flicking a stray strand of hair from her face. "If you're so confident your theory works, then you should definitely come out with us tonight because Money is perfect for you. After all, you're both crazy about hip hop." She rolled her eyes.

"What's that got to do with anything?" Angel asked, feeding fresh thread through the eye of her weaving needle. Unlike Brandy, Angel was a quiet stylist, didn't really say much, just mainly got on with her work, observing and listening. I'd forgotten she was there.

"Long story," I mumbled, 'cos if she hadn't been watching *The Sweetest Sound*, like the rest of the world, I couldn't be bothered to bring her up to speed right now. "Look, why don't you invite Brandy tonight?" I suggested to Camara. "Money would love her." I glanced up at Brandy, busy smoothing my hair. "You'd be up for a date with a sexy African-American basketball player wouldn't you?" I asked her.

"Hell yeah! When?" Brandy blurted, as we all laughed.

"Brandy," Camara explained, "the guy's been chasing Sahai all week. Ok, so like most men he made one or two mistakes in the past but he did have his own reasons and he's apologised. He said he was in a bad place at the time. Don't you think Sahai should give him another chance?"

I'm sure Danté must've put Camara up to this, as I hadn't seen her fight so passionately for anything in years.

"This guy sounds alright to me. He's doing the most. What's stopping you?" Brandy reached for the oil sheen.

"Um, maybe the fact that he's a liar or how about a cheater or how about a psycho or perhaps the fact that he completely dissed me when I went to visit him in America?"

"Ouch!" Brandy flinched. "Maybe not then."

"Brandy," Camara interjected, "it didn't quite go like that. When we first met him, I tried to talk Sahai out of dating him myself, because I thought he was no good. But being around him now, I realise he's not that bad at all."

"Not that bad? Camara, the man's practically married," I reminded her, remembering the Hispanic beauty Carlita, weeping and wailing over him.

"No he's not. Don't be silly. He said that girl was lying, exaggerating, and I believe him."

"Well I don't," I snapped. "*You* didn't see her."

"He said it was a casual thing and anyway, I'm sure whatever it was it's over now. It's probably history," Camara assumed.

"Well I'm not interested," I replied bitterly, reflecting on my whole nightmare trip to Miami.

"Maybe you *could* give it another chance?" Brandy suggested. "I mean, the thing is, you gotta remember, *every* man's gonna have some kind of baggage, you just have to decide *which* bags *you're* prepared to carry and which bags you're not."

Both Camara and I glared up at her wondering when she'd become so philosophical.

She smiled, shrugged, like her remark was no big deal.

"I can't get past what he did to me in America." I was honest. "The man's deranged!"

"The thing in America? Seriously, I think that was a misunderstanding now that I've heard his side of the story," Camara insisted. "Look at how he treated you before you went there, taking you out, spoiling you, having fun. You two really got on. So you can see that he was just in a bad place when you went to see him."

"A bad place? Camara, the way he dealt with me was hardcore. He called me a fucking gold-digger. Said I was only after him for his money, remember?"

"Why shouldn't you be? He's a man, ain't he?" Brandy added her two cents.

"He didn't mean it," Camara said. "He was venting. Angry 'cos apparently he'd got back to the States to find out a couple of his businesses had folded, after he'd trusted people to look after them whilst he was here. He lost a lot of money."

"Still not a good enough reason to go off on me like that. He's a knob."

"Far from it. He's kinda cool actually, but then, well, he is Danté's cousin. Guess it runs in the family," she said beaming, eyes lighting up as she mentioned Danté.

Was she for real?

"Talking of family," I suddenly remembered, swivelling towards Camara, "Hello? Danté's brothers? How fine?"

"Keep your head still I said," Brandy nagged, rearranging me back into the seat properly.

"What are their names again?" I continued. "How comes you kept those two a secret from me?"

"You like Danté's brothers? Diego and Andre?" Camara smirked, one eyebrow raised.

"Um yeah... so why haven't I been introduced to them before?"

"Maybe because you've been dating Danté's *cousin*, so there was no reason to introduce you to his *brothers* and secondly I'm sure they're both in relationships. At least I know Diego definitely is. His girlfriend was at the barbecue."

"And the other one Andre? He was nicer with those sexy eyes. There was definitely a spark between us," I said gushing. "Can't believe you didn't tell me about them Camara... hating and blocking," I mumbled.

"I think Andre's seeing someone," she said. "Not sure how serious it is though, because he's never around us. Danté doesn't speak to him, cut him off years ago, says he's fucked up, bad-minded and wotless, doesn't trust him at all. He was pissed off that Andre even rocked up at the barbecue, but couldn't really do anything about it as Diego had dragged him along. But surely he's off limits to you anyway Sahai as you've dealt with *Money*?" She eyed me with what I could only describe as repulsion.

"Would you really go there?" Brandy asked me, overcome with excitement at the potential drama unfolding. "I mean, you're not trying to date *cousins* are you?"

"If the price is right, I don't see why not?" I chuckled.

"That's what I'm talking about!" Brandy agreed.

"Lord have mercy," Camara said, shaking her head. "There has to be a limit to this madness."

"It's called self-preservation. Simple." Brandy winked.

"Is that how you see it?" Camara said. "You may think the grass is greener on the other side, but if you took the time to water your own grass, it might be just as green."

"Why would I need to be watering my own grass when my man pays the help to do that?" Brandy joked dumbly.

"Oh forget it, whatever, enough of that anyway, just come out tonight Sahai?" Camara whined.

"Has Danté threatened to dump you or something if you don't manage to persuade me? Is that it?"

"Very funny." She moved more hair out of her eyes. "We're planning to go to Marc Ryder's party. You know his parties are always on point. Roadblock! You need to come. Remember how much joke we caught the last time us four went out," she said, referring to a mad day we'd had at Alton Towers, followed by a night of pure vibes at Marc's club night R&G.

"Look," I tried to reason. "All jokes aside, to tell the truth, you know I'm off men at the moment. It's all about taking time out to find myself."

"Bullshit," Brandy disputed, kissing her teeth. "Everyone needs a man. I know I do."

I glanced up to catch her greedily lick her lips.

"All this stuff about independent women is crap," Brandy carried on. "Yeah we can all be successful in our own right. Look at me, look at all I've achieved." She waved her arms around the salon. "But I still want some lovin' at the end of the night and someone to share my success with. We all need a man."

"Amen to that," shouted a curvaceous customer, sitting opposite at one of the basins having her hair washed. We all laughed.

"It's debatable," I said. At one point I would have agreed, but after all I'd been through with men in the past few months, I was beginning to wonder.

"Your hair looks bad!" Camara complimented, as Brandy put her final touches to it, patting down my tresses.

"Thanks. Yours too," I said, glancing across to see that Angel had hooked her up with a criss' 18 inch Remi Goddess weave.

"Selfie!" Camara demanded, as she reached into her bag for her mobile phone.

When I didn't budge, she scooted across and leaned into me, holding her phone out at arm's length, whilst pouting into the camera. Watching her posing, like Britain's next top model, I struck a few poses of my own as she clicked away, taking multiple photographs of the two of us. "We look hot girl," she said, scrolling through the images, pleased with the results. "So let's do this! Let's go out tonight. Just one date Sahai. See how you feel. It can't do any harm."

"That's what you think," I disagreed, as Brandy escorted me over to the nail bar for a manicure. I could see Brandy was determined to definitely send me away looking brand new, offering me the works, as well as draining me of every penny. I'd already had a pedicure and facial, so you'd think she'd give me a discount, considering we'd been friends since school, but no, Brandy was the consummate professional. The ultimate businesswoman.

"Let's get these nails sorted and then that's everything." Brandy directed me to a bubble-gum pink massage chair. "What are you wearing out on your date tonight? I can do your nails to match," she teased laughing, looking across at Camara as the both of them winked.

"You two leave me alone. I will not be bullied into this."

"Sahai? Bullied? It's more like the other way around isn't it?" Brandy said, referring to when I'd done the Bling & Ting filming for the special on her salon and kept insisting we do it my way. She'd been amused by my bossy nature.

"That's different. That was work," I said, defending myself.

"Work," Brandy expressed, "is trying to hook, catch and keep a man. Everything else is just play," she chimed loudly, high fiving a random stylist walking past laughing at her comment.

Camara, ignoring her, plopped down in the huge pink and chrome leather throne next to me, opposite a swirling hot tub surrounded by pink frosted glass.

"Anyway I can't go tonight," I reminded Camara. "Because I've promised Kaden I'd go to his music and art exhibition remember?"

"Kaden? Mmm... nice name," Brandy murmured.

"But you're not even interested in Kaden, as fine as he is, so what's the big fuss?" Camara nagged, wincing as her nail technician filed down her nails.

"You've got two criss' men fighting over you Sahai and I'm here on my lonesome. Bit greedy don't you think?" Brandy complained. "Just saying."

"Listen, I don't want any of them. You can have 'em," I told her. "The first one, Money, is a first class idiot and the second one Kaden, is skint, he can't help me."

Based on the conversations I'd been having with Kaden, I was now under the impression that his motorbike seemed to be the sum total of his riches.

"I hear that," Brandy said. "I ain't wasting time with no man who can't pay my bills if I need him to." She kissed her teeth. "This place ain't paying for itself and I've got other things to spend my money on, like clothes, exotic holidays, my new Porsche that I'm working my way towards, so every little bit helps. Who wants to be with Mr Average Joe living pay cheque to pay cheque when you can be dating Mr Bank? I tell all my men upfront, 'pay as you go!'"

"Um, maybe that's why you're still single?" Camara considered.

"Not for long though," Brandy joked. "If Sahai hooks me up with this Money character I'm nice. So what if he's a bit of an idiot? He sounds sexy enough and his name says it all." Brandy chuckled.

"I think Money's got his heart set on Sahai," Camara reinforced.

"He ain't got a heart," I snapped. "He's a joke."

"Well how about you introduce me to one of his cousins instead then? That Andre one sounds interesting."

"Girl bye!" Camara retorted. "From what Danté's said, I don't think you're ready for Andre Brandy and I don't think Andre's ready for all of your drama either, no matter what issues he has." Camara laughed.

"You calling me a drama queen?" Brandy batted her eyelids as the three of us laughed with the full knowledge that Brandy loved chaos. She thrived on it.

"I still think you're a hypocrite, wasting time hanging around Kaden who you're not even interested in, instead of putting your money where your mouth is," Camara griped at me.

"Camara what are you talking about?" Brandy asked, buffing my nails.

"Don't tell me you've not been watching Sahai's programme either? What are you and Angel doing in here? Making hair from scratch?" Camara asked surprised. "You never usually miss anything Brandy. The dating show about men and music? We left flyers in here for you to hand out months ago?"

"Oh that. Obviously I know about it, but I haven't had a chance to watch it yet."

"Well it's old news now, but the bottom line is, Sahai's insisting you can tell a lot about a man by the music he listens to, so I'm saying rather than just talking about it and telling other people what to do, she should date Money again, as he loves the same music as her. She should be an ambassador of her own concept."

"Oh I see," Brandy said. "Yeah, I heard about that simple bitch Tia, from over Nechells, on the programme making a fool of herself with that guy Reuben, going through his Facebook page and shit,"

Brandy squealed, happy to own a salon that was the hub of all local gossip, breaking news and follow-up stories.

"So don't you think Sahai should practice what she preaches?" Camara reiterated.

"I guess Camara's got a point," Brandy reasoned, applying acrylic to my nails.

"According to her theory they should get on like a house on fire," Camara predicted, admiring her freshly painted blood-red diamante-tipped nails.

"I can't forget everything he's done Camara. He totally played me and I don't get played! I play men," I asserted. Or at least I used to, I thought, troubled by my recent spate of bad experiences.

"Maybe it's time to play him back then. Payback!" Brandy smirked.

"What's wrong with you two?" Camara sighed, exasperated. "If that's how you're dealing with people, how can you expect anything good to come out of it?"

"Listen, if the guy messed her about and wants her back then why not give him a taste of his own medicine?" Brandy rationalised.

"Oh I give up, we're going round in circles," Camara moaned. "Revenge is a waste of energy if you ask me. You're better off spending the time doing something positive for yourself that's gonna benefit your life, rather than plotting and scheming against others. It's negative and can only prevent you from moving forward in your own life. You need to change the focus."

"I disagree," Brandy objected. "There's nothing sweeter than the taste of revenge. Trust me," she said with glee.

"If you wanna spend your life dwelling on others Brandy, good luck," Camara cautioned. "And as for you Sahai, you may as well start dating Kaden. He loves reggae, which is *not* your favourite music, so you can carry on living in your own little hypocritical world!"

"Calm down Camara." Brandy tutted. "Sahai, I say take Money for everything he's got." She laughed wickedly and soon I joined her, whilst Camara looked at me, simply shaking her head.

"You know what Sahai? You need to realise that all that glitters is not gold," Camara warned gravely.

But I wasn't trying to hear that. I was too busy thinking about Brandy's last comment. Maybe she had a point. I could really come out on top, if I played my cards right I started to realise.

"What colour do you want?" Brandy inquired, moving across to the rotating hot pink and chrome shelves, displaying every shade of nail varnish under the sun.

"I'll go with the jade green," I told her, as Brandy fumbled with various jars. "If you airbrush it like last time, with a hint of turquoise, that should blend nicely with the top I'm wearing this evening. Nah, actually, the deep purple," I said, eyeing a new range of polish that I'd never tried, as it spun into view. "That colour looks hot." I had the perfect outfit to match in mind.

"Good choice." Brandy was impressed. "It has a special ingredient that protects your nails. The finish will last longer."

I noticed Camara was now listening to her iPod, sulking. I know she only wanted the best for me, but both her and Brandy had made good points. Perhaps it was time to start dating someone who was my musical equal, and if it *was* Money, then there was no harm in me helping him deplete his finances? After all the shit I'd been through with men in the past few months, anything was worth trying.

Maybe if I'd met someone decent since dating Money, I wouldn't even be entertaining the idea, but everyone who I'd dated since him had been a big let-down. So what did I have to lose? I was still single, he wanted me back, so why not give it a try?

But he would have to wait. Tonight was all about supporting Kaden. It was my way of saying thank you for the scrapes he'd got me out of lately. Plus the evening might throw up something interesting for our station, I thought. I was actually quite looking forward to his event.

Chapter Thirty-Three

The first thing that struck me as soon as I walked into the arts centre was the impressive artwork sprawled across four vast white walls. A colossal painting of a majestic lion rearing back on its hind feet, dominated the gallery. The glittering jewels in the red, gold and green crown adorning the lion's head captured my attention immediately. They were dazzling, sparkling... so... life-like.

Dim lights and soft drumming in the background created a relaxing atmosphere as I moved closer to the picture to take a good look. The lion's eyes were boring through me, its smooth golden mane giving the work magical warmth. Long blades of green grass with a velvety sheen, merged softly with the bluest sky. I couldn't tear myself away from the painting. It looked so real, was mesmerising. As I lost myself in it, a friendly voice filtered through the silence.

"Like it?" he said. I turned around to see Kaden towering behind me. "It's my bestseller."

"What? Y... you did this?" I choked.

"Thanks for coming tonight." That warm, easy smile again. "I appreciate it."

"No. No. It's my pleasure," I said. "This picture is incredible. Awesome."

"Thank you."

"So when, how, I mean, where did you do this? It must have taken you ages."

"I did that one earlier this year. It was commissioned by a local art dealer after he saw some of my work."

"It's amazing," I murmured, unable to draw my eyes away.

"The Conquering Lion of the Tribe of Judah, King of Kings, Lord of Lords," he explained. "Come on, have a look at this one."

He took me by my hand and led me to an abstract painting. Blue and purple.

"A man right?" I pointed to what looked like a lean, elongated, male physique, wrapped around a petite slender figure, in silhouette. "Lovers?" I asked.

"You got it," he said. "What about this one?" He steered me towards an oil painting.

"Wow," was all I could manage, silenced by the brilliance of a glorious sunset beaming down on me.

"Africa," he confirmed.

"Sorry?"

"The Gambia last year. I sat on the beach one evening, meditating. Captured the image as the sun went down."

Speechless, I stared at him. All this time he'd had me believing he was a struggling, penniless musician, an unknown artist and here he was, one of the most talented people I'd ever met. His work was exceptional. A halo practically appeared over his head as I stared up at his gorgeous face. Sexy, gifted and possibly *filthy rich!* I was beside myself with this new revelation.

"Yes, me Lion!" boomed a short scrawny dread, with locks flowing below his waist as he bopped past us, hailing Kaden. "Forward," he instructed, without breaking his stride as he bobbed along.

"I gotta go. Looks like we're on in a minute, order yourself a drink." Kaden pressed a ten pound note into my hand whilst nodding towards the bar. "Then grab a seat over there." He indicated towards a row of seats in front of a small makeshift stage where a drum kit, two keyboards, a couple of guitars, some bongos and a few other random unidentifiable instruments resided.

"Thanks." I took the money.

"And by the way, you look stunning tonight Empress." He gave me a quick once-over before practically gliding away, graceful in his movement, towards his position on the stage.

There was no queue at the bar thankfully, so I quickly ordered an orange and passion fruit J20 and made my way over to one of the seats.

It was an intimate setting, a crowd of about sixty to seventy people, most of whom looked rootsy and earthy to me, wearing colourful robes, not quite as loud as Joseph's in the Technicolor dream coat, but going in that direction, if you know what I mean.

Quite a few of the women looked angelic in their long flowing white skirts, head wraps and sandals. *Maybe that's how Kaden would expect me to start dressing, if I was his girl*, I thought, glancing down at my flimsy, sheer, DKNY, purple top, with purple killer heels to match and super skinny jeans, which all of a sudden seemed far too tight.

I felt a little uncomfortable as I adjusted myself next to a large woman, practically draped in brown sackcloth. *Did she just shift away from me like I'm some kind of heathen or something?* I smiled brightly at her. She responded by casting her eyes over me, turning her nose up as though she'd smelt a bad smell and looking in the other direction.

All of a sudden I felt better about myself. *I am Sahai Martini. No religious nut is gonna try and make me feel like shit. Trust!* She might be here in all her royal splendour but I was quite confident I could hold my own, so I pursed my lips, applied a little more of my purple Afrobella MAC lip gloss and crossed my legs, nestling down into my seat, as the low hum of a drum roll began rising to a startling crescendo.

I looked up to see Kaden positioned behind one of the keyboards as a tall, bulky male guitarist with long dreadlocks leaned into the microphone and yelled, "trample and paralyse all enemies of Jah!" His deep rugged voice reverberated amidst a chorus of "Jah… Rastafari," and "Selassie," from the audience.

A petite female singer took to the microphone crooning, "Jah Jah love a de sweetest love," as I tapped my foot to the pleasant reggae beat. This might not be such a bad evening after all.

"What did you think Princess?" Kaden asked about an hour later, approaching me at the bar, after they'd finished their set.

"It was cool. You were great on the keys. I enjoyed it, especially the drumming at the end."

"The Nyabinghi drumming."

"Nya what?"

"It's part of my culture. My parents are Nyabinghi so I've been raised in this way." I must have looked confused 'cos he started pointing. "You see those three drums over there?" He indicated towards the stage. "They're called The Thunder, The Funde and The Repeater. They are normally played at special events and ceremonies. The drumming identifies the different mansions of Rastafari. For example you have the Twelve Tribes of Israel, the Bobo Shantis and then there's us, the Nyabinghi Order."

It was all sounding a bit heavy to me. A bit deep, so I quickly changed the subject. "Maybe Bling & Ting could do a feature on you?" I suggested.

"For real?" He smiled, genuinely touched by my idea. "A dat me a seh!"

"Yeah... between your artwork and the music and the nybeen..."

"Nyabinghi." He laughed. "Just say Binghi. Everyone will know what you mean."

"Yeah, well with all those ingredients I think it could be quite a lively, colourful exposure into some of the meanings and traditions behind what you do. What do you think?"

"I'd have to speak to the idrens and see wha dem a seh, but I'd definitely like to."

"Greetings sista'." An elegant, softly spoken, dark-skinned woman, in a gorgeous golden gown, approached us.

"Hi," I said, extending my hand. She shook it, then practically curtsied and bowed in Kaden's direction, eye's averted. He responded with a gentle nod. I was taken aback by the level of humility in their exchange. The sheer respect.

"Sorry to interrupt you." She peered into my face. "But I recognised you from the television." She studied me as if she was still trying to decide whether or not it was even me. "I think your programme is very um, err, different, but I wondered if I could interest you in a shop I've recently opened around the corner. We sell all natural beauty products, cosmetics imported from the Caribbean and Africa for women of colour." She handed me a leaflet with a picture of a serene looking woman, resplendent in a white head wrap and robe, kneeling gracefully in a field of white lilies with the word 'Naturalites' above her head. "Maybe you can pop in sometime, see what we do? We offer ital... natural treatments."

"I'd love to." I was humbled by her warmth and spirit, although I had no intention of letting anyone other than Brandy ever touch me. Brandy was the only person in the world I trusted enough to take care of my beauty routine, but this strange woman had a certain quality, a charm and grace that made me warm to her.

"Thank you," she said. "It would be my honour to host your visit, if you were gracious enough to come to our establishment, even though you probably don't need our treatments."

"Sorry?" I was confused.

"You are a queen. A blessed woman. You possess extraordinary natural beauty." She gazed into my face. "This colour," she spoke, indicating towards my top, "compliments your skin tone, your hair and your smile superbly. You do realise that purple is a royal colour, don't you?"

What the hell was she talking about?

I glanced up at Kaden, towering over me, looking as majestic as ever. If we weren't at a Nybeen event, I would be a bit suspicious of this woman.

"Purple..." she murmured, closing her eyes, tilting her head upwards, as though connecting with an unseen sacred force "...is a colour associated with royalty and nobility." She opened her eyes and stared at me. "No eyes have seen, no ears have heard, no hands have touched and no mouths have spoken of the blessings Jah has in store for you. Your beauty is your power. Use it wisely. Recognise, magnify and never abuse your power. May Jah guide and bless you. Please come and visit us sometime sista'." With that she did another kind of nod, curtsey thing at Kaden and then sort of floated away.

I felt like I'd been visited by an angel. I looked down at the pamphlet in my hand to make sure it was real. Looking at it filled me with a weird kind of peace and tranquillity.

"That was Sista' Imani Ashanti," Kaden said. "Inspirational, isn't she? You should pop into her shop sometime," he suggested.

Clearly he didn't realise that I wasn't here to join the peace and love troops. Although in fairness, Sista Imani Ashanti's calm and peaceful aura had left me feeling quite mellow.

"So what was with that greeting? The way she curtsied at you?" I wanted to know.

"The idrens." He placed his hand over his heart. "And the sistrens," he explained, gesturing towards the women, "always deal with each other with the highest level of respect. A man is supposed to respect a woman and vice-versa, not like the disrespect you see going on between men and women in society around us. We try to follow and uphold the teachings of Jah… Rastafari! The morals and values by which He asked us to live. If we live our lives according to the will of The Almighty, we can only enjoy multiple blessings. Seen?"

Yeah right! I thought. He needed to come out of the dark ages. No one was really following all that anymore. I know I certainly wasn't. It was all about getting paid.

"What would you like to do for the rest of the evening?" he asked. "We can go somewhere else." He stooped down and wrapped his arms around my waist. Awkwardly I stepped out of his embrace as Sack Cloth brushed past us, scowling in our direction.

"I don't think some of your… um… sistrens are too impressed with me," I mentioned, staring around.

"Nuh worry bout dem," he said chuckling. "Me nuh know bout dem, but me nuh judge, criticise or condemn others. I man only practice Jah love! Yuh see me?" *Did he just discreetly squeeze my bum with that cheeky grin?*

"I guess the night is young," I said, picking up on how relaxed he was in his own environment. From the way he was talking, to his mannerisms, he was so… different, completely at ease. Or maybe he was just being himself as he felt more comfortable with me. Either way, I was seeing another side of him and I liked it. I was having a nice time and in no hurry to leave. "How about we stay here for a bit more, so I can look at the rest of your paintings?" I suggested, as we noticed a few more of his sistrens shuffling past, eyeing me with contempt. They seemed jealous that he was talking to me.

"Don't watch dem. Dem jus' a watch me 'cah me a de star bwoy!!" he said, laughing at his own humour. "De special guest! De gyal dem sugar pan!" he continued joking. *Ok. No confidence issues here.* "But me a tek time," he added, holding me still, staring me dead in the eye. "Me a call pon Jah fi bless I an' I with a special woman, a queen, a good wife fi give I an' I some strong yout' dem."

Awkward!

I quickly stepped away, pulling him towards the gallery area. A haunting painting of an old black man in a wicker rocking chair, with greying dreadlocks, reading a worn bible, caught my attention immediately.

"My grandad. He died last year." Kaden's eyes glazed over.

"Sorry to hear that," I said.

"Thanks. He was the one who inspired me to start drawing. When I was little he used to brag to his friends that I was the next Michelangelo in the making, after seeing a couple of my scribbles."

"That's lovely," I said, moving on to a small oil painting of a mother cradling her newborn. "So how much would you sell this one for? I mean, what's your rate?"

"I sold this one last week for fifteen grand."

"Fifteen grand?" I coughed. The painting was no bigger than the little mirror over my bathroom sink. I quickly did the maths. So if this one was fifteen grand, how much was the lion one? And all the ones in between? I linked arms with Kaden. This could turn out to be quite a lucrative situation.

"You hungry?" he asked. "Let's go and grab something to eat." Kaden tugged my arm towards the direction of the exit.

"To be honest, I'd quite like to stay here for a while longer and see the rest of your collection." I wanted to try and calculate just exactly how much he was probably worth.

"Nuh worry yuh self baby-love, this exhibition is gonna be up for a few months and right now me belly a hot me. Come, let's get something to eat."

Something to eat turned out to be ackee and saltfish from a nearby Caribbean food shop. Delicious as it was, this wasn't quite my idea of 'eating out' as we sat in his fifteen year old, dusty, beat up Ford Fiesta, parked up outside the shop. Said he didn't fancy a restaurant, wanted traditional West Indian home cooking. Worse still I'd offered to pay for our order as a kind gesture, so he wouldn't think I was just after his dosh. Considering it was our first proper date surely he should've refused and paid for it himself, especially with the money he was raking in. But he didn't. He let me pay. *The cheek.* I was only being polite when I'd offered. I didn't actually mean it. That was my last tenner as well after blowing over two hundred pounds at the salon earlier.

For a moment I lost myself in the sexy, sleek, silver Mercedes gliding by, fantasizing about being a passenger in *that* car, until Kaden's voice broke my trance.

Grudgingly, I ate my food as he prattled on about something or the other. *Guess I better show an interest*, I thought, tuning into his conversation, as I remembered his lion picture. That piece of work alone could probably fund my lifestyle for at least six months.

He seemed to be in the middle of some kind of speech, so I nodded like I was engaged and listened.

"Yeah, I give all the proceeds from my paintings to a charity back home in Ethiopia." I choked on a fried dumpling, as I actually clocked what he said. "You know, to help starving children," he carried on, radiating an aura of peace as he said this, whilst pressing play on the car stereo.

Within seconds the sounds of reggae royalty Dennis Brown flooded the car, with his track, 'The Promised Land'. The lyrics seemed to fuel Kaden as he continued talking. "I wanna see an end to poverty in Africa. I've bought land out there and I'm building a school. Education is what our people need. To elevate ourselves. Overstand?"

Was this guy for real? What about me? The poverty stricken woman in his car right now?

"Just exactly how much do you spend on... err... Africa?" I tried to sound casual.

"Pretty much everything I make," he said. "Over a hundred thousand a year."

"A hundred thousand?" I blurted. That sum could keep me ticking over nicely.

"I'm a humble guy." He shrugged. "You know, just following in the footsteps of man like John the Baptist."

What the hell? "John the Baptist?"

"You don't read your bible?" he questioned, sipping his Ital juice. "You need to read your scriptures, learn about him. I man a try fi live a righteous life like de Prophet. Me a try fi trod in a de steps of de Messiah! Support the teachings of His Imperial Majesty. Soon you'll see me in my priestly robes, trodding with my rod and my staff on Lozells road, living on a diet of locusts and rice," he joked.

I couldn't see the funny side of it myself. Right now I was more intrigued in his bank account. "If you're giving away, I mean, donating all the proceeds from your paintings to Africa, how do you um, support yourself over here?"

"I make a little money from the music ting, so that's enough to keep a roof over my head and provide the basics," he explained, as he finished his box juice. "My bike was a rare gift to myself after I sold my first painting, my only expensive purchase. I wanted to give thanks, but me nuh inna all dis material stuff weh de western world a promote. No sah! The whole heap a designer clothes, jewellery, luxury cars and ting," he said frowning, crushing his drink carton in his hand. "Me nuh like dem ting deh!"

I gathered that by the beat up car we were rolling in. It sounded like it was about to conk out any minute. I'd left mine at home so I could drink, but I would have gladly driven if I'd have known Kaden was driving such a battered piece of metal, I thought, as he reached into his carrier bag and replaced his empty drink carton with a full bottle of Baba Roots, shaking it vigorously. After taking a long swig of the potion, he continued preaching. "Rastaman nuh run down riches! Ongle levity and itativity I man a deal with."

He nodded along to the heavy bass, as the reggae artist Pablo Gad, now chanted about hard times, providing the perfect soundtrack to his monologue. I half expected Kaden to step out of the vehicle and start skanking, as his nodding became more and more frenetic. "I never squander my blessings, yuh see me?"

"Right," was all I could muster, as I sat there quietly, sipping my nutrament. I stared out of the window as rain began to fall, watching all hopes of cashing in on Kaden's talent drizzling, along with the raindrops, down the gutter.

I should've gone out with Camara after all. I'm sure I would've been having a much better time, I thought. I began thinking of excuses to try and make a quick getaway. If I left soon I'd still have time to meet up with Camara and make it to the party.

Chapter Thirty-Four

"What's with the sudden change of mind? I thought you didn't like the geezer?" Dijon grumbled a few weeks later, as I sat with him behind the counter in his record shop watching him build a playlist on the computer for me.

"I didn't, but he kept pestering me and in the end I gave in," I explained, as Dijon converted the music video on YouTube into audio using an online converter.

"You gave in? Sahai, as I said before, the guy invited you over four thousand miles across the world to the States and fucked you over! How do you come back from that?"

"I know, I know, but let's just say we had a good talk and patched things up," I said beaming, thinking about how much fun I'd been having with Money for the last few weeks. After that night with Kaden I realised that it was time for me to stop stalling and start enjoying all the blessings Money was willing to shower me with. Best decision I'd made in a long time 'cos I was having the time of my life. Once again we were inseparable.

I'd insisted Dijon compile a mix-tape of all the hottest hip hop tracks coming out of New York this month, so I could impress Money, who'd been bragging that the best hip hop came from the Dirty South. As a die hard fan of East Coast hip hop, I had to prove my point. Naturally I hadn't told Dijon the CD was for Money.

"Sahai, you're a joker!" Dijon shook his head. "I thought you were dating the ras' who was at the barbecue?" he asked, rummaging through a draw for a blank disc.

"Nah, we're just friends," I said, feeling a tad bit guilty as I'd been ignoring all Kaden's calls, texts and messages since going to his event. I had no idea how he was.

"He was a cool cat. Seemed like a decent brotha'. He hailed me up and we ended up reasoning at the barbecue. He was safe."

"Yeah he is cool, but you know, we didn't really have anything in common."

Since that night with Kaden I'd had a good think about Doctor Devant's analysis and following his logic, Camara's challenge to practice what I preach and Brandy's two cents, I was finally putting my own theory to the test. The fact that Money and I both loved hip hop seemed to be enhancing our dates tremendously. We liked going to the same nightclubs, discussing similar issues, and we enjoyed a lavish lifestyle, spending, splurging and flossin' without having to excuse, apologise or justify our excessive behaviour to anyone else. His money, of course.

"You must have had something in common with the Rasta cuz or you wouldn't have brought him to the barbecue." Dijon inserted the blank CD into the computer and pressed '*start burn.*'

"Not really. I mean, he only ended up coming by accident. Plus he's really into reggae and you know I love hip hop."

"Are you for real?" Dijon looked at me.

"Meaning?"

"Your programme! You following all that now? Is that how caught up you are in your own hype? Only dating men with the same music taste as you?"

"Well you know there's some truth in it Dijon. You saw it yourself," I said, as I watched each track successfully copying on to the disc.

"Sahai, I see a lot of things in life, but I ain't about to start dating some fucking *eedyiat* who treats me like shit 'cos we both get down to the same beats!"

"Money doesn't treat me like shit," I blurted, defending him. "We really get on." What had started as payback for what Money put me through in Miami had fastly evolved into a genuine relationship. Given the chance, I actually got to see how sincere, kind and loving Money truly was. He was still funny as hell and cocky with it, but also very attentive and caring. He made me feel warm and fuzzy inside.

"Well I ain't feelin' him at all star." Dijon ejected my CD from the computer and began writing on it with a black marker. "There's something shady about that geezer."

"You say that about everyone I like Dijon."

"Nah seriously, the way he was flexing at the barbecue, acting like he owned the world."

"That's how he is. Confident," I said, admiring the diamond bracelet glistening on my wrist that Money had bought me yesterday, along with a bunch of other jewellery, designer clothes and shoes. He'd been taking me out on a regular basis, cinema, casino, restaurants, any and everywhere. He couldn't stop spending money on me. He was driving his cute cousin Andre's white Audi A5, and in the process of sorting out a penthouse to rent whilst in Birmingham.

"Can't you date someone local cuz? Someone down to earth, from the endz? Like Kelloggs?" Dijon handed me the CD in a case.

"Kelloggs? Your bredrin?" I spluttered.

"You know he likes you. He always has."

"You're kidding me right?" I burst out laughing. "Dijon, he's a roadman. You know I'm not on that… and he's broke!"

"Here we go again! Sahai, I'm broke too and yes, like you I wanna make a raise, but we can come up with our own hustle. Why have you always gotta deal with men for their money? It's not a good look cuzzy."

"Easy enough for you to say, but you saw what mum went through when we were younger. I ain't going out like that."

"Yeah, aunty worked three jobs, and I rate her for it. At least she wasn't just going from one dodgy man to the next."

"She hated men," I snapped, aggravated. "What exactly are you trying to say Dijon?" I could feel my temperature rising.

"I'm saying that this obsession with wealthy men needs to stop cuz. 'Low dat. You need to fix up. I mean, all that stuff with that footballer McKenzie, and then that fake-ass Sadiq guy, yeah they had money, but where did that get you? The way you're going on is ridicks cuz."

"It may be ridiculous to you, but it makes perfect sense to me," I huffed.

"Kelloggs might be broke, but I've known him all my life. He's good people, a decent guy and he ain't really on road like that again. He's on his ting, just finished a course and he starts a new job next week. He's been single for a while and he likes you. Trust me, I wouldn't even be mentioning him if I didn't think he was good enough for you. I wanna see you settled and happy, instead of getting with all these... strangers, who come into your life, mess you about, then dip. Come better than that. You're making your own money, good money too, so what's the fucking problem?"

"The problem is," I said fuming, "that I don't know why you're going off on me. If it wasn't for you I would have never met Sadiq in the first place, as it was your idea for me to start looking for contributors in places where I'd find a wealthier clientele, remember?"

"Yeah, candidates for the programme Sahai. Not rich victims for you to personally prey on. I was thinking about how *we* could try and make some money from your idea, but I didn't realise you were the predator."

I couldn't believe Dijon was attacking me like this. "Dijon, what's this really about? You're forever in and out of this girl and that girl's bed, trying to see what you can get out of everyone, talking about keeping your options open, so how comes all of a sudden you're now on some high horse?"

"I'm a man Sahai. It's different for men. It's a man ting and yeah maybe I *was* like that, but recently I've realised it's not about that. I would like to be in a serious relationship for the right reasons."

"So would I. What? You think I don't want more out of life? I wanna settle down and have kids, like everyone else."

"Which man is gonna wanna wife you, the way you're going on? Trust me, no decent man wants a woman who's been smashed out, bashed out and trashed out! Standard!"

"Fuck you Dijon!" Tears of anger stung my eyes.

A few customers in the record shop glanced our way.

"Keep it down Sahai," Dijon cautioned. "You know I got mad love for you. All I'm saying is that you need to check yourself. Watching you running around with that *eedyiat* burns me when yuh done know you wouldn't even be dealing with him in the first place if it wasn't for the money he loves flashing about."

"Maybe so," I retaliated. "But I like him now... and you're right. Mum didn't have relationships with dodgy men, in fact she didn't have any relationships at all, but that was her choice, she was bitter and as a result of that she had nothing. Nothing!" I could hear my mum's voice in my head loud and clear right now. *Men only want you for one thing so make sure you're getting something out of it!* "I want more for myself Dijon and if Money wants to look after me, then can't you be happy for me for once?"

"You just don't get it do you?" He shook his head sadly. "He's a wasteman. He's mix up. I can sense it. He means you no good. Rolling with him you're playing a dangerous game cuz. He's bad news. I hear what you're saying about music and attraction and *The Sweetest Sound* and everything, but remember what my mum always warned us about when we were younger, 'what sweet you now is gonna sour you later.' Sometimes the sweetest things are the most deadly. It's about being careful. How can you trust him after what happened in Miami? How do you know he ain't using you?"

"Give it a rest Dijon," I snapped, fully pissed off with this unexpected lecture.

"True seh you don't know how much I wanna hurt dat yout'," Dijon admitted, vexed. "I wanna dark him up." He clenched his fist. "I still don't see what the problem was with the Rasta," he continued, like he was now an expert on the best man for me.

"Look, I don't tell you who to like, so don't tell me who to like." I folded my arms across my chest thinking about how lovely Kaden was, in fact far nicer than Money in many ways. He was humble, kind, caring and it was admirable that he donated so much money to Africa, that he wanted to build schools out there and help stamp out poverty, but he couldn't do jack for me with his 'giving all his money to charity' self.

"You know what?" Dijon responded, breaking my thoughts. "I was wrong when I told Camara that what she's got with Danté is rare," he confessed. "She was right when she said there are a lot of good men out there. But I can guarantee you, Money is not one of them." Clear to say Dijon had successfully wrecked my mood.

"Oi! Easy, easy."

I looked up to see Kelloggs at the counter.

"What's going on blud? I could hear you as soon as I walked into the shop fam," Kelloggs said, tearing into a curry patty.

"Safe," Dijon mumbled, as he firmsed Kelloggs.

I gave him a quick once-over. Fully kitted out in Adidas from head to toe, with a fresh fade and trim Kelloggs looked alright. Quite nice actually. He was a good-looking dude. But as my man? Hell no! What could he do for me? Dijon must be crazy trying to put us two together. Thinking we could make a good pair. Me? Hot girl? With him? Some luke-warm geezer? *Hell to the no!* I thought, as I fumbled with my bag.

"I better be getting back to work. Thanks for the CD." I eased up out of the chair.

"Whoa. Was it something I said? Or maybe something I did?" Kelloggs gave me a cheesy grin that seemed to be hiding much more, like disappointment. Funny how I'd never noticed before that he was attracted to me, but it was crystal clear now. No wonder he was always hanging about.

"It's not you," I reassured him. "My lunch break is up."

"That's a relief," he joked. "Thought I was losing my touch," he added playfully, plopping down in the chair I'd just gotten up from. "Cheer up," he told me, noticing my sullen demeanour. "It's Friday."

"Thank God," I replied, fully looking forward to a relaxing weekend.

"If you need any more help with your programme, you know where to come. You know I got that unique, extra special flavour that Bling & Ting needs… the ting can turn up… holla at ya boy," Kelloggs called after me, as I made my way out of the shop.

Dijon didn't say a word.

"Seeya later cuz," I said, glancing back at Dijon, who ignored me as I headed out into the street.

Chapter Thirty-Five

Back at work I couldn't concentrate. I felt troubled. It was rare for Dijon to get so personal, emotional and mad with me. We *never* argued. Yeah, I knew he didn't necessarily approve of my lifestyle and only wanted the best for me, but something about the way he came across today left me feeling totally unsettled. He'd never had such a strong reaction against anyone I'd dated, not even Jerome back in the day, whom he'd despised. Distracted, I sat at my desk, absently playing Candy Crush on my phone, until that familiar smooth baritone voice interrupted my idleness.

"Sahai. A word please?"

I looked up to see Bailey leaning around the door of his office. Walking into his room, I sank down into one of his luxury leathers.

"What's wrong?" he asked, glancing up from the paperwork he was sifting through.

"Nothing. I'm ok," I lied.

"I can see that you're not ok Sahai and I'm not liking it at all. I can't have my star employee upset."

Star employee! That comment got my attention, so I looked up, admiring his muscular physique as he stood up to brew coffee using the filter machine behind his desk.

"So, what's the problem?" He handed me a steaming mug.

I quickly took a sip, enjoying the sensation of the sweet hot liquid trickling down the back of my throat. I watched as he sat back down, confident, like the king of the castle on his throne. I wasn't about to bore him with my troubles.

"There's no problem. Honestly," I said, sipping more of the coffee. "But you seem in a good mood though."

He looked up and grinned. "Might have something to do with this," he said, holding up some paperwork, an excel spreadsheet. "I've just had the latest figures in." He waved the document around before putting it back on his desk, staring directly at me. "We've done it Sahai. We've done it."

"Done what?" I asked blankly.

"Our ratings have gone off the Richter scale Sahai. It's all thanks to you."

"That's fantastic." I found myself livening up as he transferred some of his positive energy across the desk to me.

"We're doing better than most of our competitors. For the first time in years, looks like everyone's watching us again thanks to *The Sweetest Sound.*"

"Really? That's great Bailey."

"You know what this means?" he questioned, realising that I wasn't getting the full magnitude of it all. "It means that Bling & Ting can now afford to keep broadcasting for a good few more years. I've had fresh interest from advertisers. They wanna invest in us. We're no longer facing closure. *Everyone* wants a part of us."

"Wow," was all I could manage.

"Sahai, they're jumping all over your idea like it's a revolution. The second coming! The interest is epic! We're getting attention from everywhere, Sweden, Indonesia, Colombia, Peru, Brazil, Argentina, Bulgaria, Ecuador, Slovakia, Mauritius, Croatia, you name it," he cited, scrolling through a long list on his desk. "It's absolute madness."

"That's incredible, astonishing," I said. I knew we'd had a lot of interest from the United States, the Caribbean and Africa, but I had no idea of the buzz we were creating in other parts of the world.

"I think the celebrity input we had from artists and the episodes we did with the psychologist catapulted our ratings into a whole new stratosphere. Our viewers want him back over here. They wanna see him with his own show," Bailey informed me.

"That's crazy."

"Exactly. We did it Sahai and as a consequence you know what this means for you?" he said smiling brightly, giving me the whole Colgate experience.

I shook my head dumbly.

"It means… I'm giving you a promotion."

A promotion? More money?

"Your new salary will reflect your new role."

"New role?" I repeated, anticipating his next words.

"You are no longer a producer. You, my dear, are now my Assistant Editor."

"Shut the front door!" I screamed, shocked. "Editor?"

"Yes," Bailey said, laughing at my reaction. "You've made the best editorial decision anyone has made at this station for years, so I'd say you've earned yourself that position, wouldn't you?"

"Oh my gosh. Thank you," I blurted, finally registering what he was saying.

"You deserve it. You had a unique, original idea, believed in yourself, convinced me to take a risk and worked so hard on making it a total success. It was a bold and dynamic move."

"Thanks. I knew I was on to something."

"That is true and it was definitely a risk worth taking. When I began building this empire, this is exactly what I dreamed of. Visualised. Prayed for… and now here we are. So here's what I'm offering you." He held up a document. It looked like a fresh contract. I stood there, staring at him, then stood there some more, still staring. "Well come and take it then. Have a look at my offer. If you agree to the terms and conditions, sign and return it to me within a week and it's official."

I was frozen. I'd never had a pay rise in all the time I'd been there and was pretty shocked to say the least.

"Um, thanks Bailey," I said, stepping forward to take the document. "I really appreciate this."

I was touched. Even though I knew it was well deserved and earned, the reality of it was still surreal. A new title would mean more perks, exclusive benefits. I couldn't wait to read the contract properly. In the meantime, two key words were leaping off the page, 'Assistant Editor', until my gaze dropped to the line below. *Ten grand! A ten grand pay rise?* I looked up at him.

"Are you serious?" I questioned. I couldn't believe it.

"That's how big this thing is Sahai. You did it. *You* did it."

Jumping out of my shock, I ran around his desk and threw my arms around him.

Hugging me back he steadied me. "So you can leave now. Finish early. Take the rest of the day off. Celebrate," he said smiling.

I glanced up at the big chrome wall clock behind him. It was four pm. No doubt I'd be celebrating all weekend. I couldn't wait to get out of there to tell Camara and Dijon. This was unreal. Unbelievable. Yes, I knew I was on to something when I had the idea, but all this?

A ten grand pay rise! A promotion! EDITOR!!

"Thank you Bailey. Thank you so much."

"Naturally it's gonna mean bigger responsibilities, more series of *The Sweetest Sound*. I'm gonna need to advertise for your old post. Get someone new in."

This was all so surreal. I felt like I was floating on a cloud. Since I'd been there, I hadn't really experienced much staff progression. As a small business in such a competitive market, it was a daily struggle just to get people tuning in. We'd had our ups and downs, but nothing this significant ever.

"And I've got another idea I haven't even told you about yet," I disclosed, suddenly remembering. "It's to do with young people nowadays reckoning they've invented stuff that's been around for yonks, like dance crazes, slang words etc, not realising that they ain't the creators… or carrying no latest swag! The swag's carrying them! We show them the true origins, introduce them to some of the original founders, give credit where it's due, that kind of thing. As it's about people trying to steal our history and culture, I was thinking of calling it *Culture Bandits!*" I garbled.

"I'm liking it." Bailey smiled. "It's commissioned."

Amazed, I gaped at him. "But I haven't even sold you the idea properly yet."

Bailey never commissioned anything without seeing it first on paper, then giving it a thorough work through.

"Listen, after what you've done with *The Sweetest Sound*, I have every bit of confidence that it's gonna be a hit. It's the same thing that me and the man dem are always talking about. Our roots are just getting more and more watered down. Practically eradicated, dying out with our parents. People are stealing our culture and identity, hijacking it, claiming they invented things *we* invented and then trying to tell *us* how to do it! *Culture Bandits* is the perfect title, trust me. Cha!" He kissed his teeth. "It's a sad situation, all these youts' coming up with no idea of their true African-Caribbean heritage, when all these other youts' who ain't even *of* Jamaican descent are speaking the lingo, trying to talk patois, using our practices and street slang like they *own it!* Picking it up and putting it down as it suits. You don't see this happening in any other culture. Everyone else? They claim their shit! They make sure the world knows exactly what's theirs, what's *intrinsic* star, and it gets passed down from generation to generation. With pride! Make no mistake!" He shook his head. "It's time to take back what's ours!" he stipulated, sounding like he was about to take to the streets and start a riot. "We can go through the idea in more detail on Monday."

Overwhelmed, I couldn't move. I'd only heard half of what he'd just said. I was stuck on a ten grand pay rise!!

"So what are you waiting for, *Miss Assistant Editor?* You're free to go now," Bailey said laughing at me, as I stood there paralysed, in a daze.

"Yeah course." I took one step back, wondering if I was dreaming.

"And uh, I'd appreciate it if you didn't mention this conversation or your promotion to anyone in the office on your way out. I'll announce it first thing Monday morning. Need to decide how we're gonna celebrate as a team, as this whole project really was an outstanding team effort."

"Definitely," I said gushing. "I couldn't have done it without your support and all the work from the rest of the team and my cousin Dijon. Thanks for letting me bring him in. The music he selected and played at that first shoot kept the vibe flowing nice and really illustrated what I was trying to achieve."

"You're right. I think we can afford to pay him something now. Tell him to raise an invoice and I'll pay him for the filming. Probably be able to stretch as far as his friend, that character who's always hovering around him." Bailey snapped his fingers in the air trying to recall the name.

"You mean Kelloggs?"

"Yes that's him. I noticed he kept the contestants really hyped up on the shoot, although why anyone would choose to be named after a cereal brand beats me!" Bailey said, chuckling.

"Apparently he was addicted to Kellogg's Rice Crispies and Cornflakes when he was younger and the name just stuck," I explained.

"Dijon? Kelloggs? What's it all about? What? You need to be repping a supermarket known brand to be a member of their set?"

"Nothing like that," I said laughing. "But thanks for paying them something. I'll tell them."

"Ok. You do that and have a good weekend."

As soon as I rushed out into the street I couldn't think who to ring first, Camara or Dijon. I dialled Dijon's number. After all, he had just said he was broke. I couldn't wait to tell him that he was about to get paid. Knowing how generous Bailey could be, I knew it would be a decent sum too.

Dijon's mobile rang straight through to voicemail. *Shit.* I remembered how pissed off with me he'd been when I was leaving the record shop earlier, but there was no need for him to ignore my call. I'd have to keep trying him, I thought, as I dialled Camara. Her phone went straight to voicemail as well. Disappointed, I pushed my phone into my pocket and started making my way to my car.

Chapter Thirty-Six

"You the *sheeiitt* baby girl!" Money hollered. He was the only person I'd managed to reach on the end of a phone line after failing to locate Dijon or Camara.

"Thanks," I replied.

"So we gon' celebrate tonight right?"

"Hell yeah," I said laughing. "But I'm trying to get hold of Camara and Dijon. Be good to all do something together," I suggested, parking up outside my apartment.

"Fo' sho', but I was thinkin' me and you could do somethin' a lil' extra special."

"Yeah?"

"Well I've finally got the keys to the penthouse, so how about you come over and I cook you somethin'."

"You? Cook?"

"I can throw down in the kitchen with the best of 'em shorty, you just ain't had the pleasure yet. But you can sample it tonight."

"I'd like that, but as I said, I was thinking more of a group celebration this evening. Maybe go out for drinks or something?" I reiterated, pushing my key into my front door lock and making my way straight to the kitchen.

"I feel ya, but ya girl ain't even here. Danté's taken her away this weekend remember? To that Highlands place. Scotnan? They left about an hour ago."

"You mean Scotland," I corrected him, laughing, remembering the romantic weekend that Camara had told me Danté had planned

270

for her in Edinburgh, but I'm sure she'd said they were leaving in the morning.

"Yeah, that's the place. He's confided in me that he gon' propose to her."

Propose!! "Wow! She's gonna be beside herself!"

"Yeah, he's crazy about her! Bought her the biggest rock he could find! You wanna see the diamonds in that mothafucka'!" he relayed, chuckling. "I'm gonna invite them round next week to celebrate."

"Yes sorry, congratulations... on getting the penthouse. Must feel nice, finally having your own place, your own privacy now." I thought about all the fun we were probably gonna have there.

" Fo' sho'. So tonight we gon' do our thang. Just the two of us. Lil' housewarming private party and all that good stuff." I liked Money's commanding nature.

Dijon was still ignoring my calls so he probably wouldn't be up for anything anyway.

"Yeah, that can work," I finally said, opening the fridge door.

"That's what's up!" Money yelled. "A lil' candle-light, some Dom Pérignon, strawberries and cream! We gon' have fun," he promised, sounding gleeful that he'd have me all to himself. "Be ready for about 7pm then and I'll come scoop you up a'ight?"

"Sounds all good to me," I chirped, hanging up and reaching for a large bottle of Moët that had been cooling in the fridge for months. I'd been saving it for a special occasion and couldn't think of a better time to open it than right now. I was excited about Money cooking as we always usually went out. Maybe he was *The One*. I could certainly get used to this lifestyle. The attention, affection, the gifts. I was on top of the world. *Camara! Marriage?*

Popping open the champers, I reached for a glass, poured until the bubbly spilled over the edge and took a large gulp of the sweet liquid. *Ten grand!* I couldn't stop thinking about what I could do with the extra cash.

Dialling Dijon's number again I was frustrated to get no answer. Camara rarely used her phone whilst travelling, which now explained why I couldn't get hold of her either. *Danté proposing? Camara... getting married?* Oh well, I'd just have to share my news with them when I could. For now I was concentrating on becoming the future Mrs Jabari Anderson as I headed upstairs to hop into the shower. Maybe Camara and I could have a double wedding?

No sooner than I'd walked out of the kitchen, the loud ring of my mobile phone, which I'd left on the kitchen counter, lured me right back. Racing towards it I snatched it up, quickly answering before voicemail kicked in, without checking the caller id, happy that either Dijon or Camara was finally returning my call.

"I got a promotion!" I yelped, swigging more champagne from my glass.

"Congratulations Empress." Kaden. *Shit.* He sounded genuinely pleased. "Why haven't you returned any of my calls Princess?" he asked softly.

"Oh I've just been really busy," I blurted.

"I can see that," he acknowledged. "That's great news about your promotion. You deserve it."

"Thanks," I said, instantly feeling bad about ignoring his calls and text messages.

"I've been thinking about you... a lot. I really enjoyed that evening we spent together."

"Me too. It was nice." I guess parts of it had been, so I wasn't completely lying.

"I'd like to take you out tonight to celebrate, that's if, you're not already busy." He was so sweet, he wasn't even giving me a hard time for ignoring him which made me feel even worse.

"I've already got plans, sorry." I was honest.

"Of course, you must have. I guess you're celebrating with your family? Friends?" he pried. "Maybe we can all do something together?" he suggested, totally on my wavelength. That would've been my idea of the perfect evening, if I'd have managed to get hold of anyone.

"Nah. Camara's out of town so I'm doing something else."

"Sahai," he said seriously. "I know we haven't known each other for very long but I just feel something special in you y'know. When can I see you again?"

"To be honest Kaden," I said, thinking about his financial situation, "I don't think that's a good idea."

"Why not?" He sounded hurt.

"Because I'm seeing someone."

"Oh," was all he managed.

"Probably best if you don't call me again actually," I said, grabbing the bottle of Moët and heading upstairs. I knew that was harsh, but like Camara said, no point in leading him on.

"Surely we can still be friends?"

"I don't think my man would appreciate that," I told him. What was the point of being friends with a man who wasn't intending to pay any of my bills, buy me any clothes or jewellery, take me anywhere extravagant, or spend substantial amounts of money on me at all 'cos he was giving *all* of it away to some *charity!!* "Look I gotta go," I said, walking into the bedroom and switching on the stereo.

"Well please know that I care for you and I'm here for you if ever you need me."

"I think it's best if we don't stay in touch," I mumbled, as I grabbed a towel, made my way to the bathroom and switched on the shower.

"If that's your desire Empress, then I will respect your wishes."

"Cool," I said, before hanging up, selecting a CD, turning up the stereo and stepping into the shower. What could I possibly need him for?

As the steaming jets of hot water caressed my body, I moved seductively to the silky tones of Trey Songz, crooning about pleasure, pain and passion. Reaching for my Victoria's Secret 'Love Spell' body wash, I lathered myself from head to toe and basked under the stream of water for a good twenty minutes, until I felt a hundred percent refreshed and invigorated.

Whilst moisturising myself in the bedroom, I glanced at my alarm clock and saw that it was 6.00 pm so I had an hour before Money would be picking me up. I took another huge gulp straight from the bottle of Moët.

What was I gonna wear? Money cooking for me? I chuckled happily. What kind of an outfit did that warrant? *This slinky red dress?* I thought, agonising over the perfect look, as I pulled one of my favourite Donna Karan numbers out of the wardrobe. *Nah, too sexy,* I reasoned, putting it back in the closet. A bit over the top with that plunging neckline. I didn't want to look like I was trying too hard. Just wanted to be casual but still hot.

What about this black jumpsuit? I thought, reaching for an exact replica of the one I'd seen Kim Kardashian rocking on the red carpet at one of her celebrity events. I could accessorise it with some silver bling or leopard print. My mind was made up as I slid into it, feeling glamorous as the slinky satin material hugged my curves. Admiring myself in the mirror, I quickly slipped out of it and laid it neatly across the bed.

Grabbing my brush, comb and make up bag from my dresser, I swigged more champagne from the bottle and headed back into the bathroom. Time to transform myself.

Wow… was all I could think as I sized up my reflection thirty minutes later in the bedroom mirror. Maybe I *should* suggest we go out? I looked far too gorgeous to be hidden away behind some dining table indoors. As I pondered this issue, the sound of my phone ringing interrupted my silent reverie. Money's name flashed up on the caller id, so I answered it, purring into the phone.

"Hey babe," I said softly.

"What's good sexy?" he asked.

"Just ready and waiting for my knight in shining armour to come and pick me up," I revealed, as seductively as I could.

"Yo, that's what I'm ringin' to talk about," he said. "Listen, something's come up. My cousin needs the car tonight, so I ain't gon' be able to come scoop you up."

"Okay," I said, not sure where this was leading. I hoped he wasn't about to cancel on me.

"So you cool to make your way over here? It's not that far from where you are."

"Where is it?" I asked, disappointed that I was no longer able to enjoy the excitement, mystery and surprise of being whisked away and escorted to his.

"It's the new apartments near the city centre, just at the back of town."

"I think I know where that is," I said, picturing the luxury penthouses I admired every time I drove past. I'd watched them being built over the last 12 months. "Text me the postcode," I told him, just in case I was thinking of the wrong ones.

"Cool. I'll do that right now."

"Ok, see you in a bit," I said listlessly, barely hiding my disappointment that I wasn't being picked up. Still on a high about my promotion, I wanted to be fussed over and pampered.

"A'ight baby girl. Hope you wearin' somethin' sexy for the kid?"

"You'll have to wait and see," I teased, as I felt myself slightly melting under his charm.

"So what, fifteen minutes?" he asked.

"Yeah should be there in about that time babe," I confirmed.

"That's what's up. A'ight. One," he said, and hung up.

Maybe I should take a taxi? I thought, feeling slightly tipsy, but then quickly changed my mind. A taxi would take ages to come as it was a Friday evening, and I hadn't had *that* much champagne, I should be alright to drive. It's not like I had far to go.

As I pottered about, doing last minute things, popping my lip gloss, mascara and a pack of soft mints into my oversized Louis Vuitton purse, my mobile phone rang again.

"Hello?" I let the word roll smoothly off my tongue as I realised it was Money once more.

"You left yet?" he asked.

"Nah. Just about to," I told him.

"Shorty, could you do me a favour on your way here?"

"Sure no problem," I lied, irritated that my evening of indulgence was turning into me running around for him.

"I've left some things in my cousin's car. When he came by to pick up the Audi he was in such a rush I forgot to take my stuff out the boot. I've only just realised."

"Right." *So now I was Money's lackey?*

"So could you please pick them up for me baby girl?" he asked nicely. I hesitated, irritated. This was not how I'd seen my evening panning out at all. He could go get his own things in the morning. "Some of it is stuff that I need tonight," he said, as though reading my mind, instantly squashing my idea about him collecting it tomorrow. "Including a lil' special somethin' I picked up earlier for you, a congratulations gift for your promotion, to let you know you da bomb."

Well that definitely put a whole new spin on it. I felt myself weakening, imagining a sparkling diamond bracelet or a Birkin bag or some flashy earrings.

"It's not out of your way at all. I'll tell Andre you're comin'," he continued confidently.

Andre. My mood began to lighten even more at the sound of Andre's name as I remembered how sexy the man was. I pictured his seductive eyes the day Money had introduced us at the barbecue, reflected on how soft his lips were when he'd kissed the back of my hand. Plus he'd been dripping in Gucci from head to toe and did own the latest Audi A5. I supposed maybe I *could* pick it up.

"Well, if it's on the way I guess," I said. Money was only here for the season, but maybe Andre was someone I could seriously get with. After all he had definitely been smitten with me at the barbecue. The chemistry between us was insane.

"So, you're cool to grab it then?" Money pressed.

"Fine," I muttered, reaching for my car keys.

"That's what's up shorty, good lookin' out! I'll text you the address. See, this is why you so cute. Always got a brotha's back."

"Yeah whatever," I mumbled.

Chapter Thirty-Seven

Strapping myself into my car minutes later, I sighed. For some reason I no longer felt the same sense of elation that I'd experienced earlier when Money had first invited me round for dinner. In all fairness, I really wanted to be celebrating with my cousin and Camara. They were the main two people who knew just exactly how much this promotion meant to me, after the way Bling & Ting had been going downhill for the past year. Dijon, in particular needed to be sharing in tonight's celebration, after how much he'd helped with the music and stuff for *The Sweetest Sound*.

It was only when I was almost at Andre's house that I began to feel excited again. I guess this little extra-curriculum activity made the whole evening worthwhile, I thought sneakily, as I pressed his doorbell a few minutes later. Smoothing my hair and running my tongue over my glossy lips, I felt anxious waiting for him to answer. *I should have double checked my reflection in the mirror*, I thought, as my nerves began to kick in when I heard footsteps approaching on the other side of the door.

Oh my God! No he hasn't got the nerve to be answering the door topless!! I shuddered, taking in all 6ft 2 of his strapping physique as he appeared in nothing but a pair of True Religion jeans. Ripped with a six pack, broad shoulders and the silkiest skin I'd ever seen, he stood in the frame of the door, with one arm stretched high above his head against the wall, accentuating his biceps as he kind of leaned back. Flashing me a million-dollar smile, his sexy eyes twinkled as he gave me the once-over.

"Damn. You look good. Come in," he said, smiling.

Oh shit! Come in? Not sure I was ready for this, I thought, filling the empty space where he had just been standing as I followed him into his contemporary, stylish lounge. White plush leather sofas, glass and chrome furniture and modern artwork screamed opulence, as I hardly knew where to look.

"Um, hi," I said stupidly, as he headed towards what looked like a small bar in the corner and began pouring two glasses of Brandy. "I'm not stopping," I quickly spluttered, suddenly losing all my confidence.

"Just one quick drink," he said, eyeing me mischievously. "To say thank you for your troubles," he insisted, as he added Coca Cola to the Brandy.

"Troubles?" I was now competing for 'Stupid of the Year' award.

"Yeah, coming to pick up Money's stuff. I'm sure that wasn't part of your plan this evening. Sorry, you've caught me in the middle of getting ready myself," he said. "I'm just rushing out in a minute," he explained, walking towards me with the two glasses in his hand. The heat alone coming from his body made me feel like I was gonna pass out. Couldn't help noticing how his muscles rippled as he moved.

"Thanks, but I really shouldn't," I said, taking the glass out of his hand. "I'm driving."

"A small glass of Brandy won't do any harm. Come on, sit down," he invited, tantalising me with every step as he made his way over to the sofa, looking across at me expectantly. "You joining me or am I gonna have to come and physically make you sit down?" Clearly, the arrogance ran in the family.

"Well, just a quick one then," I said, moving towards him, sitting down in front of the 52 inch plasma screen on the wall, displaying a raunchy music video with the volume turned down low.

"What I wanna know," he said, sipping his drink, studying me, "is where a beautiful woman like you has been hiding all these years? My cuz rolls into town and snaps you up, just like that, yet we're practically neighbours," he said flirting, as I drank.

"I could ask you the same question," I mumbled, feeling a warm pleasurable sensation, as the sweet liquid trickled through me.

"I mean damn, you are fine, with that hair and those killer eyes and that *body*." He moved an inch closer and I could feel tingles rising up my neck as I scooted away slightly.

"You don't have to be afraid of me." He let out a low chuckle.

"Look, I really should go. I only came by to quickly pick up the things," I reminded him, feeling way out of my depth.

"I hear you." He considered my words for a second. "How about this though? When you have a little more time we hook up and have some fun?" he suggested, placing his hand on my thigh. His brazenness was a turn off I realised, coming back to my senses. There was something very menacing about him that suddenly made me feel totally uneasy. His clear disloyalty to Money was ugly. Yeah, I know I was no angel, but at least I was loyal to my family, my loved ones. He had no remorse whatsoever. His sleazy behaviour repulsed me.

"That can work," I lied, not wanting to show him that I was uncomfortable. "But I really do need to get going now." I stood up, swigging the remainder of my drink. Nerves.

"Me too, I'm late," he said, glancing across at the wall clock. "But I'll be looking forward to our lil' rendezvous. Maybe we can make a weekend of it." He guzzled down the rest of his drink, then stood up to escort me out.

"Maybe." I went along with him.

"Shit, almost forgot, one sec." He disappeared down the hallway, returning minutes later with a rucksack.

"Oh yeah, thanks," I said, quickly grabbing it and letting myself out.

Once back in the safety of my car, I placed the rucksack on the passenger seat and took a moment to analyse what had just happened. Crazy to think that the only reason I'd agreed to pick up the stuff was for another chance to see Andre. If Money had asked me to pick it up from anyone else I would have said no, only to realise that Andre was pretty much a total snake. No wonder Danté couldn't stand him. I guess Camara had lucked up with Danté. So far, he seemed to be the only decent man in that family, 'cos although I'd enjoyed hanging out with Money these last few weeks, I can't lie, I still wasn't a hundred percent sure if he was genuine or fake.

My hairdresser Brandy's words came back to me. *'Listen if the guy messed you about and wants you back then why not give him a taste of his own medicine? Payback.'* Was that what I was doing or did I really like him? Did he really like me or was he still playing me? I thought, feeling a little confused and light-headed as I started the car engine and pulled away from Andre's house. As I'd told Dijon, the original plan was to get back at Money and to take him for everything he had, but we'd been having a good time and he was growing on me. Still, I couldn't get Dijon's words out of my head either. *'There's something shady about that geezer.'*

Turning into the main road, I was eager to get to his penthouse. A good meal would probably sort me out. That's most likely what I needed, I reasoned, feeling hunger pangs as I realised that with all the excitement I'd barely eaten anything all day, and the champagne hadn't helped at all. I felt a bit giddy. Weak even.

I couldn't wait for Bailey to make the announcement at work on Monday morning and tell the rest of them about my promotion. I had worked so hard for it. I was looking forward to all the challenges and rewards this new position would bring. Finally my opportunity to shine, to start making my mark and move up in both my professional and personal life. I could think about getting a new place, start building a show reel with the possibility of moving to a mainstream channel at some point, so much to consider.

My thoughts turned back to Money. It was nice of him to cook for me this evening to celebrate. He really didn't have to go to all that effort, but would be good to see what he'd rustled up, I thought, eyeing the rucksack, tempted to take a peek at what he'd bought for me. Dinner *and* a gift? Regardless of my initial motives for being involved with Money, I couldn't grumble. The man was spending top dollar on me, whilst my bank account was steadily maturing. Here I was, enjoying the good life, although I'd barely touched my salary in weeks. I don't know why I kept doubting him. Maybe I was just being paranoid.

Stopping at a red traffic light, I loosened the string holding the neck of the rucksack together, hoping for a glimpse of my gift. I saw a parcel poking out, but didn't get any further, as the car behind impatiently beeped to let me know the traffic light had changed to green. As I pulled off, my mobile phone began to ring. Didn't normally like to answer it whilst driving, but when I saw Money's name flash up on the screen I decided to quickly take the call, as I knew he could only be ringing to see what was taking me so long.

"Hey babe," I answered cheerily, with my handset clamped to my ear, feeling a little guilty about the way things had gone down with Andre.

"Where are you?" he asked, as I sped up, attempting to beat the next set of traffic lights before they turned red.

"Literally two minutes away," I explained.

"What's taken you so long? Did you pick up my stuff?"

"Yeah, it's right here," I told him, speeding up a little faster.

"Thanks for that," Money said, as the lights turned red just before I accelerated and drove right through them. It was then that I heard the siren and saw the blue light flashing behind me, in my rear-view mirror.

"Shit!" I yelled into the receiver.

"Whassup?" Money asked, concerned.

"The police are flashing me. They're pulling me over. I just ran a red light. Shit. I've been drinking. I'm not supposed to be on my phone. I need to hang up," I shrieked.

"The Feds? Fuck!" was the last thing I heard Money say, before I threw my phone down beside the rucksack in the passenger seat and pulled over.

Chapter Thirty-Eight

As soon as I parked, I switched off the engine and sat patiently. *Shit!*

I could see in my rear-view mirror that one of the policemen had now got out of his vehicle and was approaching my car. The other cop remained in the passenger seat. I rolled down my window as sweat gathered under my armpits. I rested my hands on top of the steering wheel as the policeman appeared at my window. Bulky, with a mean face, the officer glared at me with contempt. *Damn!* Why couldn't I get good cop?

"Evening," he said with a hard stare, his eyes roaming past me to the passenger seat.

"Good evening," I answered back.

"Miss, would you mind stepping out of the vehicle on to the kerb please?"

Shit! What if I stumbled or something? He might notice I'd been drinking.

"Step out of the vehicle on to the kerb please?" he repeated firmly.

I opened the door and reluctantly got out of the car, joining him on the pavement.

"Do you know why I stopped you?" he asked.

"No," I said quietly.

"Are you aware that you just ran a red light?" He simultaneously beckoned the other officer to come and join us.

"Sorry… um officer," I stammered. "It changed just as I was going through it," I replied nervously, hoping he couldn't smell the alcohol on my breath. *If I got disqualified from driving, would I lose my job?* Why all of this now? Just when things were looking up?

Glaring at me like I was dumb, his eyes scanned the interior of the car.

"Do you know how fast you were going?"

"No," I lied.

"Are you aware of the speed limit on this road?"

"Yes, I believe it's thirty miles an hour," I answered meekly, as the other officer started walking around the car, scanning the exterior and peering inside, flashing a torchlight.

"The reason why we stopped you is because you were doing fifty miles per hour in a thirty mile per hour zone, you were talking on your mobile phone and you ran a red light."

Great! A criminal record for dangerous driving! That's all I need.

"I'm really sorry officer. I've got an emergency. I didn't realise."

"Are you aware that it's an offence to be talking on your mobile telephone whilst driving?" he asked, his eyes boring into me.

"Yes," I mumbled, as his colleague who had been snooping around the car approached us and said something quietly to him. His body visibly stiffened and his voice took on a new sense of urgency.

"Is this your vehicle?" he interrogated.

"Yes." Anxiety swept over me.

"What's your name?"

"Sahai Martini."

"Miss Martini, we're going to have to search the vehicle under Section 23."

"Search my car? Section 23? What are you talking about?" I asked, beginning to feel scared. I'd never been stopped by the police before. I'd been expecting maybe a breathalyser test and was praying that I'd be under the alcohol limit, but *search my car*? Where was Dijon when I most needed him? He would know exactly how to handle this. "Don't you need a warrant to search my car? There's nothing in it. Why are you searching it?"

The officer looked at me with what I could only describe as pure hatred in his eyes and repeated himself like an angry robot. "We are searching the vehicle under Section 23."

"What's Section 23?" I could feel a lump forming in my throat, heart palpitations.

The policemen exchanged awkward looks before angry robot spoke again.

"Section 23 is the Misuse of Drugs Act," he divulged. "We have reason to believe there may be drugs in your car."

"Drugs? In *my* car?" I laughed nervously. "I'm sorry officer. I think you've made a mistake." *Why weren't they just doing a breathalyser test?* Alcohol I could admit to, however painful, but *drugs*? I didn't even *smoke*!

"We have reason to believe there are drugs in that package," he informed me, pointing to the parcel poking out of the top of Money's rucksack on the passenger seat.

What the fuck? "That's not drugs," I said, embarrassed. "That's a gift! I got a promotion today and it's a gift from my boyfriend." Fuming and humiliated at being treated like a common criminal, I glanced around at pedestrians and drivers peering at us.

The other officer flashed his police badge at me with authority. "We are searching the vehicle under Section 23 Miss, if you wouldn't mind stepping to one side," he asserted.

"I'm an upstanding citizen!" I cried. "Why are you doing this to me?" I pleaded, as the snooping officer headed back around the car to the passenger side and opened the door. "You can't do this," I protested. "This is a violation." The words tumbled from my mouth, scattered at my feet.

"Miss, please, we need your co-operation," the policeman standing next to me said, as we waited at the roadside. I felt the sweat trickling down the back of my neck. *Shit, what was going on? Was this really happening to me?*

The other cop picked up the rucksack from the passenger seat and began walking back round to us. I needed to call someone. Camara, Dijon, my lawyer, anyone. I just didn't wanna be going through this on my own. Angry robot watched me intently, as his colleague seemed to be taking forever to join us. I felt like he was walking slowly on purpose to increase my suffering and humiliation.

By now, pedestrians were beginning to gather in a little huddle watching us. With it being a Friday evening, the streets were teeming with people making the most of their weekend. I began to feel even more self-conscious in my glamorous black jump suit with leopard print accessories, including five inch heels. I guess I didn't look like the usual kind of suspect people would expect to see getting harassed by the police. I could see a teenager filming us on his mobile phone. *Fucking great!* This was all I needed, to be up on the internet within the next few minutes. Bailey was gonna go nuts. 'A high profile position requires a certain standard of behaviour when in public', he always told us. Understandably he didn't want his company associated with anyone or anything negative.

"Is this really necessary?" I snapped at the cop.

"Please calm down Miss," he said.

"That bag isn't even mine," I tried to explain. His colleague had now finally reached our side of the car. He loosened the top of the rucksack even further to reveal more of the parcel poking out.

This is not happening to me. The cops began to retrieve the package from Money's rucksack, whilst glaring in my direction.

"You say this rucksack is not yours? Who does it belong to?" one of them asked.

"Um... just a... friend."

"Can you reveal your *friend's* identity?" he probed, sounding like a document.

"Um, just someone I know." *Shit!* I panicked, not knowing what to say. I couldn't think straight. I couldn't even remember Money's actual proper name, his 'government name' as he liked to call it. I didn't know which penthouse he'd moved into, as he'd only given me the postcode for the road and told me to ring when I got there. I didn't fucking know anything about the man!

"We need to inform you that we have to treat this item as yours as it is currently in your possession, in your vehicle," the policeman said.

My whole body was now trembling as Dijon's words from earlier flashed across my mind. *'He means you no good. Rolling with him you're playing a dangerous game. How can you trust him after what happened in Miami? How do you know he ain't using you?"*

Fuck! Why didn't I listen to Dijon?

All sorts of images and thoughts started break-dancing in my head.

My mum's voice, *'use men for whatever you can get out of them.'*

Sister Imani Ashanti's words, *'your beauty is your power ... use it wisely... never abuse your power.'*

Camara, that day in the salon, *'all that glitters is not gold.'*

An image of Kaden... kind, warm and humble... replaced by Doctor Devant, flashing his million-dollar smile, winking and talking extremely fast in street slang.

Now Bailey, behind his desk, gushing about how brilliant I was. A *ten grand pay rise* was the fantasy that shattered, as the policeman's authoritative tone penetrated my thoughts.

"Miss Martini," he said, examining what looked like a clear food bag. Full to the brim, it was practically bursting at the seams with *flour? What the fuck?* The substance in it, a fine white powder, wasn't fucking *flour.*

"There's more of it in the rucksack," the cop informed his colleague. "Loads more."

Frozen with fear, I felt like I was having an out of body experience, as it became crystal clear to me what that substance was. I'd recognise it anywhere. I'd made programmes on it.

For the first time I noticed the lights everywhere around me. Street lamps, neon-lit signs hanging from shop windows, traffic lights, car lights. Dazzling, blinding lights, everywhere, burning through my skin. Intense heat. It seemed as if every light was beaming in my direction, highlighting my shame, my degradation, my downfall, as the crowd thickened.

My throat constricted as water fell from my eyes. I couldn't hold back the tears. They were flowing. Uncontrollably.

"I swear, that's not mine," I managed, but the police weren't listening. They exchanged a tired glance as if to indicate they had been in this situation many times before, as one of them reached for his handcuffs whilst the other one spoke up.

"Sahai Martini, you are under arrest on suspicion of possession with intent to supply a Class A drug. You do not have to say anything, but it may harm your defence if you do not mention when questioned something which you later rely on in court. Anything you do say may be given in evidence."

Through teary eyes I caught the expressions on some of the onlooker's faces. They were shaking their heads, looking at me like I was scum. *A drug dealer! Lowlife!* The lowest of the low. And could I blame them? They'd witnessed the police finding cocaine. In *my* car.

The hostility was unbearable.

I abhorred drug dealers. I couldn't respect anyone who distributed poison.

My heart was racing, sweat trickling down my back, tingles throughout my body. This was it. Everything. Ruined. My career. My livelihood. My future. My freedom. My life. Gone. I was going to jail and I had no idea for how long.

Money hadn't even rang back once. To check if I was ok, find out where I was, see if I needed any help. He knew I'd been pulled over and he'd just left me to it and now I knew why. Somehow, deep down I knew I wouldn't be hearing from him or seeing him again. He was probably already on the next flight back to Miami.

The cop grabbed my arm roughly, pushing and shoving me, as he frog marched me to the police car and bundled me into the back. As the vehicle merged slowly into the traffic, I glanced out of the back window to see the dazzling, glittering lights fading, dimming, disappearing, until there was nothing.